By Eileen Charbonneau
from Tom Doherty Associates

Waltzing in Ragtime
The Randolph Legacy
Rachel LeMoyne

For young adults

The Woods Family Saga
The Ghosts of Stony Clove
In the Time of the Wolves
Honor to the Hills

Waltzing

— in —

Ragtime

Eileen Charbonneau

TOR®

A TOM DOHERTY ASSOCIATES BOOK
NEW YORK

This is a work of fiction. All the characters and events portrayed in this book are either products of the author's imagination or are used fictitiously.

WALTZING IN RAGTIME

Copyright © 1996 by Eileen Charbonneau

Jacket art by Albert Bierstadt, *Valley of the Yosemite*.
Gift of Mrs. Maxim Karolik for the M. and M. Karolik
Collection of American Paintings, 1815–1865.
Courtesy of the Museum of Fine Arts, Boston.

A Tor Book
Published by Tom Doherty Associates, Inc.
175 Fifth Avenue
New York, NY 10010

Tor® is a registered trademark of Tom Doherty Associates, Inc.

ISBN: 0-812-54468-4
Library of Congress Card Catalog Number: 96-3148

First edition: August 1996
First mass market edition: June 1997

Printed in the United States of America

0 9 8 7 6 5 4 3 2 1

For Susannah
my teacher in things courageous

acknowledgments

This book was born during an unseasonably severe spring snowstorm in Sequoia National Park. I'll always be thankful to the ranger who not only kept my snowbound kids delightfully informed and entertained with his passion for preserving our American wilderness, but became the inspiration for Matthew Hart.

My thanks to my family, especially my sister Patricia and brother Dave, and dear friend John Kelly for transplanting themselves to California and giving me an excuse to come out to visit and find another piece of this book there each time.

To lovely Eileen Nauman, my friend and mentor and spirit guide, thanks for encouraging me to become an ever-changing woman, and to have Matthew sing himself out of the black. Mitakuye Oyasin yourself, kiddo!

Many readers, editors, and fellow writers have helped the story come alive, among them I thank: Juilene Osborne McKnight, Jim Green, Patricia Rogers, Susan Shackelford, Kathleen Dehler, Dolores Oiler, Margie Rhoadhouse, Alex deBritain, Barbara Ward Lazarsky, Jean Gold, Florence Kaye, Rose Eichhorn, Charlie Rinehimer, Holli Rovitti, Carol Lambert, Vicki McKechnie, Barbara Scalia.

With special appreciation to my agent, Sue Yuen, who took this impossible book on, not because she thought she could help sell it, but because she loved it, and to my editor at Tor, Natalia Aponte, for her patience, keen eye, and skill at helping me make it the best telling of the story I can manage.

The beauty of the world, which is soon to perish,
has two edges, one of laughter, one of anguish, cutting
the heart asunder.

—Virginia Woolf

prologue

It was the first time in Matthew Hart's life that Joe Fish looked old to him. Full-blooded too, his coppery leather skin drawn tight over high cheekbones. His steps were unsteady, his once-keen eyes squinting, lost and afraid as he stepped from the train. Matthew smiled, pulling his wide-brimmed Stetson from his head.

"Hello, Grandfather."

As the train roared off from the Fresno station, they embraced for only a little shorter time than if their women were about. Then they took in each other at close reach—the spare, stooped mixed-blood Cherokee and the rangy, blond Anglo towering over him. Their eyes were their only kinship link, both clear and blue as the distant mountain sky.

"You want to sit?" Matthew asked.

"Without moving? Yes."

Matthew Hart took his elder's arm and led him to a wooden bench in the shade. Joseph Fish had taught him to stare down vipers, stalk the elk and the grizzly. It was still hard for Matthew to understand his grandfather's aversion to trains. But he respected it. One of the two horses waiting nudged the old man's back. He stood, rubbed each behind the ears.

"Yours?"

"No. They belong to Thomas Parker, the man who hired me. He's chief forester, the trailmaster."

"He trusts you with fine animals."

"He heard who our visitor is to be," Matthew contended. "That you went to school at New Echota and learned the written language from Sequoyah himself. He's honored."

"In your letter—why did you spell this tree given Sequoyah's name without the *y*?"

"There are no *y*'s in Latin."

"Latin?"

"Yes. The naming of the trees? The botanical tradition is to make them look Latin."

He watched his grandfather measure the explanation, hooding his eyes so Matthew could read neither acceptance nor anger from them. He'd seen that look many times before.

Matthew Hart leaned his long arms against his knees and ran the worn rim of his hat between his fingers. "Mr. Parker will ask you many questions. You might regret the honor of his invitation."

The etched face eased into a smile. "If so, I'll complain of my ancient bones and retreat. It's the privilege of the old."

Matthew reached into his saddlebag for the canteen and offered it. "From the stream running through the grove of giants," he said. His companion swallowed a long draft.

"Good, clear," he approved, then pointed with his chin at the distant ridge. "I wish to travel the road you're making, see these trees named for my teacher. But your grandmother remains jealous of her rivals. She sends this, so you remember. Foolish woman."

He pulled out a brown folder from the canvas bag at his side and placed it in Matthew's hands. Matthew opened it slowly, then lifted the cloudy paper to stare at the image of the woman and child the photographer had captured in sepia tones. The child's tiny, placid face was surrounded by a white lace cap. Her gown drifted past the woman's knees. He almost didn't recognize the woman. The sharp despair that had marked her features for many years was gone. She looked soft. Her face was content, glowing, happy. Or was it the photographer's trick?

"Beautiful," he whispered.

"The one has made the other so."

Matthew Hart turned to the afternoon sky. His grandfather's attention remained on the photograph. "I wish the child were not asleep," Joe Fish said. "I wish you could see her long limbs, her probing eyes. But the photographer said the image would not be clear unless she slept."

"She's so small."

"But strong, Matthew."

Matthew felt the raw wound open. No more. Please. He replaced the tissue paper and closed the folder, tucking it into his vest. He pulled his hat low over his eyes and took up the horses' reins.

"The trail's hard," he told his grandfather.

The old man smiled. "As long as it is not along iron rails."

As the elevation drew them over narrowing roads, then trails, Matthew avoided the sound of the workmen's shovels. They wound around the wider trailblazing. He did not want to meet any of his fellow workers, not even Mr. Parker. He would share this moment in the giants' grove only with his grandfather.

It was dusk when they arrived. The mist was settling around the manzanita shrubs, swirling the fragrance of the western azalea blossoms throughout the forest. The July air became cooler, heavy. The haze grew so nebulous Matthew lost his bearing. He dismounted. Joseph Fish followed. Then the silvery leaves of the Chinquapin brushed his face. The guardian of the giants' grove told him they had arrived.

He still felt like a blind man, leading his grandfather to the center of the stand without seeing anything but the soft glow of red bark around them. Then a whisper sounded from high in the towering branches of the sequoias. It swept out the dense mist in a single, steady breeze, leaving diamond webs of dew in its wake. Both men dropped their horses' reins. Neither spoke for a long time. Finally, Joseph Fish turned a slow, complete circle.

"I promised your grandmother I would draw this place. But I think I will return home and wait for a vision," he said.

Matthew watched his grandfather step toward the ancient trunk of a burned tree. His arm disappeared in the depth of the trunk's scar.

"This one. It heals itself," he marveled.

"Yes." Matthew smiled. "High above, it's sprouted green."

"Stay among them," the old man counseled, his fingers glancing the incongruent shock of silver in his young grandson's unruly mane. "They will tell you their secrets."

From just beyond the grove of giants, voices welled, Farrell's above the rest. "Now, wasn't I telling you Matty'd get them in before dark—by the smell of the place if he had to?"

Matthew tried not to resent the roadworkers' invasion. The trail-master Mr. Parker presented himself to Joseph Fish, pumping his hand as the other men gathered around.

"Matty, you missed the hauling of Teddy's tub," Farrell chided.

"What?"

Mr. Parker stepped between Matthew and the Irishman. "Rumor has it Vice President Roosevelt might be making a visit, so the powers that be think the big cabin should be outfitted better."

Farrell grinned. "Government has to show him that this hallowed wilderness we're protecting has all the new century's amenities."

"So we have to break our backs hauling a bathtub when we're behind schedule with the road!" The worker punctuated his comment by spitting tobacco juice through his teeth.

"Hey, Mr. Parker, leastways we can offer the presidential suite to Matt and his grandpa here for a try out!"

The trailmaster smiled at the roadworker's suggestion. "That does seem entirely appropriate. I hope you'll accept the accommodation, sir."

Matthew Hart sighed, scraping the ground with his boot heel. He'd trusted his learned boss not to do this. Now Joseph Fish was to be put on display, a cigar store Indian. To his surprise, his grandfather smiled.

"My kin and I accept with thanks," he said.

Joseph Fish ran his fingers over the waist high, claw-footed bathtub with, what was it? Longing? Matthew tried to hide the displeasure in his voice.

"You want me to fetch water?"

His grandfather looked up and smiled, brushing off the dust from his clothes. "No. Of course not. I've been living with women too long. They wash all the time."

Matthew had planned to camp tentless in the grove, beneath the giants. He was restless as his grandfather slept peacefully in the feather bed. He rose before dawn and hiked away from the camp, away from the log cabins they were building for the tourists who would someday come in ever-increasing numbers to view his trees. He shifted his rifle from the crook of his arm to his shoulder and plowed through the dense underbrush. He would find a place for himself, deep in the back country, come winter. Away from them all.

He struggled to understand his own anger. The crew had treated his grandfather respectfully. Many had been railroaders and lumbermen, and often spoke with casual disdain for the Indians, Mexicans, and Chinese they'd worked beside. But the night before they'd listened as Mr. Parker asked his grandfather about the Georgia hills and the Eastern Cherokee, of the linguist Sequoyah. Of the nation greed had destroyed. His grandfather told of his journey west to the gold fields, the wild land speculation. Joe Fish and his grandmother had lived through it all.

A rustle in the open meadow made Matthew pause. He crept closer. At the base of a lone sugar pine stood a five-pointed elk, head up, alert. Slowly, wishing his grandfather was beside him, Matthew took his rifle from his shoulder. He aimed, held his breath, and felled the buck with one shot.

The animal was still by the time Matthew reached its side. He cut out the heart carefully and wrapped it in his deerskin pouch. He'd share it with the teacher who had shown him how to thank an animal's spirit for the gift of its life. He disemboweled the elk quickly, leaving the innards to the scavengers as a share in his good fortune. Then he hoisted the carcass over his shoulders and made his way toward the camp. The roadworkers would breakfast on fresh meat. In this way he'd thank them for honoring his grandfather.

Sweat formed on his brow from the effort of carrying his burden. Matthew stopped, released the carcass, then pushed his hat until it hung from its ties against his back. He was wiping the sweat with his sleeve when the sound came. A rip, a buckling. A mad sound. Matthew was knocked off his feet by the shaking ground.

He scrambled to his knees. Earthquake. Matthew had trusted these mountains to keep the ground steady under his feet. He should have known better. He stuffed his fist into his mouth and bit hard. Then he heard his name being called from the camp. He got to his feet, and ran.

A sea of arms, hands, relieved faces stopped him. The trailmaster took his shoulder.

"Matt! Thank all that's holy you're an early riser!"

"Earthquake—"

"No, not an earthquake, son! A limb fell from one of these beauties, fell from a good two hundred feet! Wait until you see what it did to—where's your grandfather?"

"I left him sleeping." Matthew watched the jubilant faces around him change. He twisted out of Mr. Parker's grip and rushed toward the cabin. The limb of the sequoia had smashed through the roof east to west. Some of his co-workers wandered aimlessly about. Others stared at the giant red limb embedded six feet in the mossy ground.

"Help me," he demanded. "Help me find my grandfather."

But there was nothing in what remained of the cabin, only fragments, splintered and thrown up like debris after a flood. Matthew narrowed his eyes and listened.

"He's under there."

Mr. Parker's hand took his shoulder. "Then we'll take care of him, son. You'd best go to my quarters and—"

"No, we have to hurry."

"There's no need for that now, Matty," came Farrell's voice as the Irishman removed his hat, reached for him.

Matthew shoved the wild, abandoned scream down his throat. "My grandfather's alive," he said quietly. "Not crushed. His air's all gone and now he's . . . drowning." He was confused by the words even as they left his lips.

The trailmaster turned to his team. "Let's get this limb up, boys, double quick," he commanded.

Something was depressed in the ground, even farther than the sequioa's limb.

"I'm damned," the burly mule driver declared. "Teddy's tub."

Matthew leapt into the trench, reached into the tub's still water, water Joseph Fish had hauled himself for his bath that morning. He hauled his kinsman over the side, pounded his back. Matthew felt the power of his grandmother's healing hands ride through his fingers.

Finally, he yelled. "Don't you die on me, old man! Not here, not now! Go die at home in my grandmother's arms where you belong!"

Joseph Fish heaved, then vomited. Matthew wiped his mouth, laughing through the tears flowing freely down his face. Farrell threw them a blanket. Joseph Fish rested against his kinsman's chest.

"Matthew?" he whispered.

"Yes, Grandfather?"

"Living with women may not be such a bad thing."

BOOK ONE

one

Sequoia National Park, California
1903

"This is an evening to quote John Muir: 'The forests we so admired in summer seem still more beautiful and sublime in this mellow autumn light. Lovely starry night, the tall spring tree tops relieved in jet black against the sky. I linger by the fire, loath to go to bed.' And don't we all have those thoughts tonight, ladies and gentlemen? Was not the glory around us worth our trek up the new road and into the forest of the giants?"

Olana Whittaker's face feigned intense interest, one of the few useful accomplishments of her finishing school education. It amused her to practice the skill, not on those her mother would have favored—dull but wealthy marriage prospects—but on this assortment of soldiers, road crew, tourists, Sierra Club zealots, and locals. Would any of them guess that the wilderness of the new national parkland bored Olana to the same degree it enchanted Thomas Parker and his audience? She thought not.

The road had turned her green serge coat the same dusty gray as their poor homespun. The lavender gauze of her hat netting was ruined. This was the sort of event a journalist had to write about? How could she have insisted on coming here, enduring these conditions? Because Sidney Lunt, new editor of the Gold Coast Chronicle, San Francisco's fourth largest newspaper, was her best friend. And after losing Hettie to her stuffy count and Belinda to an ancient Marquis, she wasn't going to lose Sidney to his newspaper. Thomas Parker's words arrested her wandering attention.

". . . And so let us join John Muir, Frederick Olmsted, and President Roosevelt himself in the noble endeavor to keep crass commercial interests out and reserve this spacious beauty for future generations."

This was beyond the pale. Olana tapped her ivory walking stick on the rough hewn bench, and stood. "You speak of commercial interests, Mr. Parker, as if they were not the foundation on which our country was built."

Heads turned. Olana felt her cheeks color. Why had her elocution lessons promoted only a high-toned, birdlike softness? "Her greatness and her shame, Miss Whittaker," the sad-eyed man replied.

Olana drew a deep breath. "If a tree were struck down in one of Mr. Olmsted's eastern city parklands, it would be an occasion of considerable grief, I'm sure. But our western wealth is endless."

She raised her chin, glad she'd gone to the trouble to have the heels of her riding boots elevated. A man in the audience stood slowly, removed his hat, and faced her.

He was dressed like a roadworker—homespun shirt and neckerchief, brown wool trousers, suspenders. Only the lack of patches, and the material itself—more dense, finely woven, set him apart.

"I'm a Westerner who does not share your opinion, miss," he said quietly.

Farrell, the crew's cook and her self-appointed chaperone, pulled Olana down on the bench. "Now you'll get a good story, Miss Whittaker!" He whistled, delighted, through the gap in his front teeth. "You went and got Matthew Hart riled enough to talk up for his trees!"

Matthew Hart? The man Sidney insisted she interview? Olana had expected the park's head ranger to be much more military. This man had the untrimmed beard, the easy stance of the roadworkers around him. She resented beards, and men's ability to hide so much behind them.

"He doesn't sound the least bit riled," she contended.

"He opened his mouth, Miss. He's riled."

Even the ranger's age was difficult to surmise. Farrell had hinted at a colorful enough past to make him sixty. But Olana guessed half that, even with the streaks of silver invading his unfashionably long hair. Matthew Hart looked only at her as everyone in the audience gave him attention. "Perhaps you would feel differently if you'd seen the casualties I have. These trees were held sacred for millennia by the natural world. They've overcome pestilence, even fire, only to be felled by intruders ignorant of the uselessness of their enterprise."

"Uselessness? My father's fortune was built on—"

"The northern coastal redwoods, Miss Whittaker, whose properties are much different from these giants."

Did they all know of her father? Did they all wonder, as she did, if he and Sidney had conspired to make her assignment impossible?

Matthew Hart continued, his voice a learned contrast to his rough appearance, though the slight drawl marked him as a Southerner and therefore unacceptable company at her parents' table. "*Sequoia gigantea*'s wood has been proven to be of no commercial value for anything but cigar boxes. Do you think our children should be deprived of this beauty for the sake of cigar boxes?" he asked her.

Olana's fingers felt cold. Thomas Parker put his hand on the ranger's shoulder. "Whatever our differences, may I speak for us all when I say we admire our visiting correspondent for the fortitude, grace, and beauty she's brought?"

The ranger's face pinched with, what was it, regret? His friends shouted, "hear, hear!" and clapped the evening's formal festivities to a close. Olana stepped into the aisle. Her heel caught on a protruding root. She felt a steadying grip at her elbow.

"Your gallantry matches your eloquence, Mr. Hart," she managed for their audience.

The ranger only frowned, swept his wide-brimmed hat to his head, and took a stronger hold. "Come with me," he almost growled.

Olana had to hoist her skirts to keep up with his long strides through the rising twilight mist. She looked back for Farrell, but couldn't find him. Matthew Hart seemed oblivious to her distress as he darted them along an overgrown trail of his own making.

Just before she was going to demand he slow his pace, he released abruptly. Olana stood, locked between him and the soft red bark of one of his trees. She could see little else, between the growing twilight and the mist. It was colder, something she sensed captured his attention too, for he seemed absorbed by the tiny diamond patterns of mist captured in her hat's netting. She forced her breathing back to normal. The scents of the forest mixed with those of the nearby camp fire, its soups and stews.

Olana felt her raised boot heels sinking into the damp moss. Now she barely reached the head ranger's shoulders. When she moved, he held her waist as not even the most daring of her suitors ever did. As she sputtered her outrage, his fingers drummed along her side, casually. "Listen," he demanded. "That part Mr. Parker said—about grace and beauty—I should have said something like that. First."

He was apologizing. Casually. "I was not offended, Mr. Hart."

He smiled, showing good teeth. "Sure you were. I was rude."

Olana twisted out of his hold, even though the action pressed her closer against the sequoia's bark. "I am a journalist, Mr. Hart. You've done nothing to provoke emotion of any kind, I assure you."

"I see." The smile disappeared. "The park's got your contempt, then?"

"Not contempt, exactly. But I find the notion of protecting nature ludicrous. My father says the West was opened up only a generation ago for civilization's use. There is infinitely more beauty in a fine chair than in the tree that provided the raw material. Beauty for civilized people comes in reshaping the environment, not in the environment itself."

Why hadn't he interrupted? His head was bent at a curious angle. She must have some power in her argument. Heartened, she thumped on the sequoia's gigantic bulk. "If our purpose were to dreamily admire this tree, the great cathedrals of Europe would never have been built! Why, we'd pave the way for godless anarchists around the world to rise up, catch us in our slumber and . . . Why are you laughing?" she demanded.

"That's a mighty burden for one tree. Even one of these giants," he drawled, slouching against the giant in question.

"It's not the tree! It's what the tree represents! My father says—"

"Do you let your father do all your thinking?"

"Of course not! Why, he was furious that I came among you . . . you . . ."

"Godless anarchists?"

He didn't spend all his time among trees. He also read the fourth largest newspaper in San Francisco. Olana swallowed. " 'Czar Parker and his Cossack Rangers?' " Matthew Hart pressed.

"I didn't write that."

"Your newspaper did."

"My editor enjoys a cleverly turned phrase."

"Which you'll be happy to provide, at the forests' expense! Miss Whittaker, that ain't—" He looked sharply up into the heights of the sequoia. Olana had the peculiar sensation that the tree was chastising him. He passed his hand over his unkempt beard, then spoke.

"Aw, look around," he began, curving his arm in a wide, graceful arc. The evening mist had lifted from the open grove of *Sequoia gigantea*. Lacy ferns adorned trunks of astonishing girth. This was off the road, the official trail. It seldom had visitors, Olana surmised. Matthew Hart kept it to himself. The color, texture, vibrancy tore at Olana's very breath. Far above their heads, the canopy of green admitted starlight. "This is a cathedral, Miss Whittaker," Matthew Hart said quietly. "More ancient, more holy than any manmade religion. What right do we have except to wonder at it?"

Wind raced through the stand of trees and among her skirts. Concern replaced the shining marvel in his light eyes.

"Are you cold?"

"No," she lied.

He began folding her wide collar closed. His rough hands worked on her clasp and buttons like an impatient nursemaid's. Olana smelled pine resin and leather. Long fingers lingered at the last silk covered button. Before she found her outraged voice, he was glancing up at the clouding sky. "I told them not to bring greenhorn—not to bring guests up here so late in the season, even if the road's finished."

Olana yanked herself free of him. "Perhaps you'd prefer the government to have created the park for your solitary enjoyment?"

A languid smile. "Then you do like it here, a little," he said, taking her arm to lead her from his cathedral.

* * *

Farrell welcomed them back to the camp of open fires and conversations. Everything about these people was so casual, Olana decided. Well, what did she expect? To be treated as she'd been treated all her life? As a timber princess? Isn't that what she was trying to get away from, people who fawned over her because of her father's wealth? Farrell held out her ivory baton.

"Left your fancy stick, Miss Whittaker. I didn't let a body else touch it. Matty, Mr. Parker was asking for you."

The ranger grunted, touched the rim of his hat, and left them.

The cook's grin widened as he offered Olana a chipped bowl of pea soup. She let it warm her hands. "Are you not hungry?" Farrell asked.

Olana brought the soup past her lips and swallowed quickly. Cloves and the savory taste of smoked ham made her disregard the questionable origins of the other elements. She even managed a thin smile of appreciation. The laugh lines sprouting from her chaperone's eyes glinted in the firelight, forcing her own smile to become more generous.

"Cook's the highest paid member of the outfit, did you know that, Miss Whittaker?"

"Indeed? I did not," she answered politely.

"Been doing the cooking since my mining camp days. Don't have to anymore. Do you know I've got more money than I'll ever need, and a few investments besides? Ah, but the glory that is this road through the wilderness, that's why I'm here! I collect stories. From the rangers, the loggers, the ranchers down to Three Rivers. They tell me things and I weave them back, do you know? Into tales."

"Tall tales?"

The Irishman smiled. "Maybe so. But when you're as old as I am, seen what I have, you may come to my conclusion, Miss Whittaker. That life's got to be whittled down into stories. There's a secret to the gathering of them. Be invisible. Hard for you, pretty as you are. But if you're drawing attention, it'll put them on their guard, spoil all your fun."

Matthew Hart sat, cross-legged, at Thomas Parker's feet. Olana tried to put the cook's words into practice. She couldn't hear a word of their conversation, but the admiration of the ranger for his elder was strikingly apparent, though, as she also sensed rather than saw, they were arguing.

"I'm thinking your newspaper did right sending you," Farrell said.

Olana felt herself blushing. Sidney Lunt should have sent her to a charity ball, a flower show, the opera; somewhere within her own milieu. Certainly not to Sequoia National Park. She was a fraud. She didn't even know the difference between her father's trees and Matthew Hart's. But she would learn. She would do anything rather than be swallowed by the money-hungry titled families of the European continent. Swallowed, like Hettie and Belinda, who used to be such fun, and were now as pale and lifeless as the marbled tombs on their estates.

Olana Sarah Whittaker would not find herself a titled husband, so her mother could gloat to her friends and her father could be bled dry. She was an American. That was one thing the year abroad had taught her. And it felt so good to be home. Even here, in the vast wilderness without amenities.

"Best turn in now, miss," Farrell advised. "We're all heading back to Three Rivers tomorrow, back to Mrs. Goddard's place."

"But we've only arrived!"

"Matty says it's on account of the winter's coming in early. He doesn't want us caught up here at this altitude."

"And since when did Mr. Hart add the title of barometric prognosticator to his accomplishments?"

Farrell scratched his head. "Must admit, the skies look Indian Summer fine to me. To Mr. Parker too. But I'll wager when their argument's done, he'll trust Matthew Hart."

Olana hadn't taken down a note. "Write pieces vivid with description, sport," Sidney had commanded. She thought of Matthew Hart's remark about her greenness. For all his engaging her in political debate as if she were his equal, the ranger was like the others—her parents, her editor, her refinement schooling. Determined she'd fail.

two

"I think these are the last of them, Mrs. Goddard!"

Olana strode through the back door with an armful of wild-flowers as the older woman poured ground coffee into the pot. It was Olana's favorite part of the morning, just before the men stumbled down to their breakfasts.

"The rangers, they were right cheery with you here with us, miss."

Olana tried on her most modest smile. "Why, who wouldn't be in your house and company, Mrs. Goddard?"

The stout woman squeezed her hand gently. When was the last time Olana's mother had done that? Years. Stupid thought. She'd better not stay too much longer or she'd come home acting as sentimental as these country people. She began setting Matthew Hart's place at the table.

"Oh, Matt's gone now, dear girl!"

"Gone?"

"Up in the mountains."

"But Mr. Farrell said the rangers hire themselves out to neighboring ranches when the park closes."

"All but Matt. He's the winter guardian, didn't you know? He's come down only to fetch supplies. I told him to bid you a proper good-bye, left him outside your door this morning. Land, that boy is skittish!"

Olana slammed the cupboard door. It caught her thumb. Her screech of indignation was not discreet. The woman ran to her side. "Let me see. Oh, that'll be a nasty bruise, beneath the nail, too."

"I should like to walk a bit."

"Of course. Go on, I'll manage."

Mrs. Goddard's hand rested on her shoulder. Olana had enough of these people and their uncalled for touching. Didn't they know their place?

As she wrapped three biscuits in a napkin, Olana heard the matron outside her bedroom door, walking down the corridor, ringing the men out of their beds with her schoolmarm's bell. How far had Matthew Hart gotten, especially loaded down with a winter's worth of supplies? She didn't have to know where his camp was, precisely, she reasoned. She'd find him long before he reached his destination, and get the interview Sidney demanded. Farrell's bay mare would do for her excursion.

Olana eagerly slipped off her simple day gown. She stared, dismayed, into the wardrobe's mirror. Was there a trace of freckles on her face? And her shoulders rose up a little thinner out of the ample bosom nature and her corset still provided. Not at all fashionable, showing bone. How she would love to get out of this place and back to steaming baths and French wine sauces at home. She frowned. Perhaps that's the reason Sidney and her father had allowed her to come. Were they hoping she'd be discouraged by physical hardships? Didn't they know that fears of her mother's neurasthenia were stronger than any hardship she could imagine? Due to her illness, Dora Whittaker languished in darkened rooms with headaches for days at a time. Olana buttoned her russet riding ensemble and spread out the elegant French lace of her blouse. She was not her mother. And she would not become a hothouse countess like her friends, either. Sidney was her model, she would be as devil-may-care as a man of independent means. She would show off her horsemanship to that tight-lipped ranger. Meeting him on the trail with her picnic lunch, her daring would either cool his anger or fan it hotter. Either prospect had its charms.

By noon Olana spotted a steep, overgrown trail splitting off from the main road. She was doing so well, why not? How lost could she get, with the crucial direction being up into higher elevations? And wouldn't it be delicious, skimming ahead, meeting Matthew Hart triumphant? She slapped her quirt against the mare's flanks.

Hours later her hands began to hurt inside the soft kid leather gloves. Cooler. And dark. It couldn't be getting dark this early. Olana pulled her gold watch from its place pinned to her blouse and stared at its Roman numerals. Three-fifteen. What had happened to the sky? It was gray, getting grayer. Olana stared just past her mouth. Her breath was fogging. Thunder sounded in the distance. No fear, she reminded herself, don't let a horse smell it. But the air itself was charged. "Easy," she soothed, reaching for the mare's mane. But with the streak of lightning and thunderclap, the animal turned and bolted. Her shoulder hit the ground first, taking the brunt of the fall.

She rose to her knees. "Damn you for a weak-livered pole cat!" she railed, shaking her fists, realizing she'd repeated language she'd been surrounded by at the boarding house. Olana didn't even know what such a feline looked like. A giggle bubbled up her throat and burst into the cold, damp air.

What did Farrell call the mare, she wondered, rambling through the dense underbrush. Something sentimental, keening, like the Irish. Rosaleen. Olana called out the name, then listened. Nothing. She called again when the drops pelted her hat netting.

Soon the rain had soaked through every layer of her clothing. Olana had thought the mare would seek a level area, a meadow, to slow her frightened charge. If the beast could find such a place. She stumbled on in the undergrowth, the twisted roots. Her teeth chattered involuntarily. She'd never felt this cold. But the rain was stopping, the sky getting lighter. Wasn't it? She stared up at the clouds. The squinting smile that stretched across her face froze in horror. It was snowing.

Matthew Hart dreamed of being in the Klondike. Lottie was alive again, and shaking him awake.

"Get up Fandango Man, work to be done."

He was ecstatic, but careful not to show her. If there was one thing Lottie couldn't abide, it was sentiment. So he rolled onto his side and reached his arms around her waist. He pulled the ties of her dressing gown and nuzzled between her breasts. Some mornings, if it was early enough, if his touch was gentle, he could get her to come back to her brass bed, even let him love her once more.

Other times she'd whack him between his shoulders with her hairbrush before her girls discovered she'd let any man stay longer than hourly.

It was a hairbrush morning he figured, from the angling glide of her hips. Still, he raised himself on one elbow to admire her weathered grandeur before she chased him out. To his surprise, she took his face in her hands, let him see her eyes fill with tears the way she only had when she was dying.

"Work to do," she said again. "Don't let the fear stop you. Use your gran's good sense now."

"Work?"

"Yes, work!"

He opened his eyes. Wind howled at the window. And snow. When he rolled over, a pain cracked between his shoulders. "Damn it, Lottie, I'm going," he surrendered, on his feet, straddling two worlds.

He tried to hold onto the dream as he put the pine log on the fire. The scream of the bay mare brought him fully to his senses.

Outside, the sudden drop in temperature further alerted him to the vagaries of October in the Sierras. He pulled up the collar of his buckskin coat. The snow was already drifting up the base of the giant red trees that sheltered his home. He approached the horse who was wandering, sniffing at the smoke from his chimney. He spoke softly, holding out his hand. Matthew stroked her neck until she was content to be led into the small stable with his animals.

It was Farrell's mount, Rosaleen, but the stirrups were set too high for any of the men. A growing fear crept up to the roots of Matthew's hair as he removed the saddlebag's contents. There was a napkin from Mrs. Goddard's and a mahogany box. A writing box. He yanked it open. Gold-plated fountain pens, ink, fine bond paper, and initials carved in a brass plate above the inkwell. *O. S. W.*

"Shit," he whispered, letting the box drop from his hands.

Olana stared up at the towering trees, their height swallowed by the blowing snow. What did they care? They lived thousands of years, didn't he tell her that? And they mended themselves of every disease, pestilence, even fire. Everything but the likes of her and her father, scheming for their wood. This was the trees' revenge. They wouldn't tell her where the horse was, they wouldn't shelter her from the cold, the wind. They even directed the fury about her.

The cold was white now. White, blistering, and as unforgiving as these mountains. A picnic, that was all she wanted. Wasn't it? A picnic, to make his sad eyes laugh. Then let him kiss her, let him just try and kiss her. Olana's hair blew out before her face. She'd lost her hat long ago. She could still raise her arms, but couldn't move her fingers to make a proper job of clearing her hair from her face. Well, don't come, her giddy mind flittered again, as I am no longer properly attired or coiffured to be a source of attraction to any man. Even you, Matthew Hart.

Her wild, fragmentary thoughts settled on the ranger's large, gentle hands. Once, during her few days at Mrs. Goddard's, those hands had guided hers as she lifted the apron full of chicken feed. She'd looked over her shoulder then, and her breath had caught in her throat because his eyes were so beautiful.

"Matthew!" she screamed up through the ever-descending sky. "Matthew Hart!"

She listened. Beneath her feet a stream of water flowed. Below the ice. She forced the blocks that were her feet to follow it.

A cave's opening loomed before her. It contained the source of the stream, and another wind, a warmer one, coming from deep inside. Shelter. She entered. The relentless wind still rang in her ears.

She leaned her back against the wall just inside the cave's mouth, and tried to fold over the flaps of her riding suit. She couldn't even raise her arms. It didn't matter, her collar was frozen open. Where were Matthew Hart's fingers now, his gentle hands spreading warmth?

She felt herself sliding down, and knew she wouldn't be able to get up again. But she couldn't stop. It didn't matter, suddenly. Nothing at all mattered. It became an effort to keep her eyes open. In that effort Olana Whittaker was still stubborn, determined to last a little longer. To see what happened next. But what was all the fuss about, she thought vaguely. It wasn't so difficult to die.

Matthew Hart's eyes seared across the whiteness. "Damned woman," he said, believing that if he continued to curse her, she'd be alive. His head still told him she couldn't have gotten as high as seven thousand feet. Once he found her hat in the birch tree, he stopped listening to his head. He let his eyes scan the horizon until he felt a direction. Come on, you're one of my kind, send out a signal. There. He felt a cold that rattled his teeth. To the northwest. He urged his horse on. Around the next bend he saw the mouth of the cave.

He stood over her, her bright hat dangling from its netting in his hand. It was there, on her hat that her eyes finally focused, then up at his face.

Her voice was a thin grate. "Don't hold it like that," it demanded, "you'll rip it worse."

He came closer. "Damned woman," he said, but softly now, like an endearment.

Her mouth twitched, her eyes closed.

He wrapped her in his coat and lifted her into his arms, then onto the saddle.

three

Her muscles were rigid, her breathing shallow. Matthew's fingers eased her eyelids open. Dilated, no reaction to the lamp. He picked up his long-blade knife, cut away her clothes quickly, precisely, as if he were skinning an animal. The hooks of her corset tried his patience. He growled low and tore open the last of them, then pitched the contraption into the fire, cursing the fashion that decreed her breasts be so vulnerable to the storm.

Direct contact. It had worked with Klondike miners whose skin had taken on the same waxy sheen. It had worked for some of them, at least. A sickening fear made Matthew shiver as he slipped off his clothes and lay beside her, drawing the soft flannel sheet, then the red wool blanket, then the deer and elk skins over them both.

The woman moaned softly, pressed closer against his chest. He tried to concentrate on counting her heartbeats, but found himself thinking of the others—of Lottie's teaching fingers guiding his awkward ones, of Seal Woman's ebony braids glistening in the moonlight. It had been so long since he'd decided to make himself content with his trees, that his rushing, powerful physical reaction to her was a surprise. He winced, then sighed into her hair. "Well, my proper Miss Whittaker . . . *I'm* alive," he told her.

His care had not kept his women beside him. Why had this one come, with her proud eyes masking the part of her that attracted him, that troubled innocence behind her airs? Was it his desire alone now? Was that all it took to kill? Cold. He was suddenly, unbearably cold.

He pulled himself out of the bed and stumbled to the hearth. There he took up the pile of her cut clothing and added it to the flames. The lace of her blouse caught first. It spread the fire through the burnished orange silk of her skirt, her coat. But the steel stays of her corset were glowing coals beneath it all. Mocking him, defying burning.

When he turned back she was shivering, her body working on its own to warm itself. Matthew dressed, and allowed himself a measure of hope.

But the woman's fingers, feet, and breasts remained ashen and swollen. Matthew wrapped them in gauze. How bad were they? He knew they mustn't turn black. He stared at the blade of his skinning knife, wondering if he could cut off a piece of her. He saw the reflection of her terrified eyes trapped in the knife's steel.

Olana's first memory was so dim, she wasn't sure it was real. The sound of the wind, incessant, tinged blue. The smell of pine, leather, breaking through, holding her, taking on the blue. Then crackling flames, a hearthfire, a man standing naked before it, his hands opened out, absorbing the radiant heat. Under the mound of animal skins, Olana realized she was naked, too.

Was it real? It couldn't have been, for the next instant he was clothed and sitting in a chair by her side, staring at a silver blade. He put it down, spoke softly. "I'll look after you. Sleep." Olana was a little girl again, turning away from her brother, stamping her foot the way he hated most. "You couldn't even take care of yourself," she told him. "A sore throat, you told me. When I came back, you'd be better, you'd have a surprise for me. But you were gone, the house draped in black crepe and after that I could never do anything right!"

She forced herself to turn around, because seeing him angry would be better than not seeing him at all. Weary, red-rimmed eyes, the startling color of robin's eggs. Leland's were brown, like hers.

"Mr. Hart?"

"Yes."

"My hands hurt."

He smiled as if she'd told him the next dance was his. Irritating man. "They have to heal," he said. "It will take time."

Time meant nothing to her. She was so confused. What was this dark place of red wood, stone hearth, spare furniture? A white glare came from the one high window. But the noise she thought would forever lash at her ears had stopped.

"The storm—"

"It's over. You're at my quarters. Safe."

It began to come back. "A cave."

"Yes, that's right. That's where I found you." His drawn face was relieved by a smile again. "You've made a new discovery. Accessible and deep, from what I could see, too. Come spring I'll chart it and—"

"I'm suffering and you're charting caves!"

His eyes turned fierce. "A more constructive activity than your attempt to come up here."

"I had no intention of coming up here. I was on a morning ride. I'm an experienced horsewoman. If it weren't for that unruly nag—"

"That unruly nag had the sense to get out of a storm. She and the cave you found helped save your life." He heaved a sigh and poured a large spoonful of amber liquid. He held her head and put it to her lips. "Swallow."

It was honey mixed with something else, something that dulled the edges of her pain. He set up bandages and tinctures on the small table beside the bed.

Olana looked down at herself. "Whose clothes are these?"

"Mine."

Then he had undressed her. She'd been naked. Was the rest of it real? How long had she been here? What else had he done? "I should like mine returned."

"I burned them."

"Why?"

"Had to cut them off you. And I'm no seamstress."

"But I could have—"

"They didn't protect you the way they should have!" His sudden anger startled her. He looked away again.

"Mr. Hart, I shall have to ask you to take me home."

"Home?"

"At your earliest convenience."

He shook his head and laughed without humor. "At the moment, it's no way in hell convenient."

No man had ever blasphemed in her presence. It frightened her, but as when most things frightened her, she became even more imperious.

"My father will absorb any expense for your time and trouble."

"Oh, will he? And from where do you think you're asking to be returned? A formal cotillion?"

"Mr. Hart, I insist—"

"Insist all you want, but look out there, woman!" He motioned to the room's one window. The snow had drifted past the middle of its pane. "That was a full-scale October blizzard, Miss Whittaker, and you are currently at over eight thousand feet of altitude in one of the most remote regions of the Sierra Nevada range. A few days ago your heart had slowed down to—"

"Days? I've been here days?"

"Three. No, four," he corrected himself. Good heavens, the man couldn't even count. "And you've got frostbite of the hands, feet, and breasts of a severity I've yet to determine."

Breasts? That accounted for her absence of feeling there. But how could he even mention them? He reached for the buttons of the worn woolen shirt. Yes. She remembered. He'd done this before, invaded the privacy of her bosom. Before. But not while she'd had her wits about her.

"Avert your eyes, sir!"

"Avert—"

"I forbid you to look."

"Now, how am I going to care for you without looking?"

Olana planted her gaze on his shoulder. "My mother's physician had such respect that he didn't even . . . look . . . when I was born."

"Only thing that idiot had respect for was his inflated fee. Birthing doctors!" came out of him, a sigh of contempt.

"Oh? And I suppose you possess a vastly superior education to be so cognizant of their deficiencies?"

"I have eyes." He slipped the nightshirt off her shoulders, leaving her bare but for the swaddling gauze wrap. He took up a pair of bent but gleaming clean scissors. "Which I intend to use in determining—" He stopped cutting through the thick gauze and took in a deep, even, breath. His voice became the comforting one of her dreams. "Can you feel there yet?"

So. He knew of her disembodied sensibility. Olana concentrated harder on looking at his shoulder. "No, for which I am quite thankful. My hands and feet are painful enough."

Olana's thoughts scattered as she finally followed his gaze to her breasts. Blisters—large, horrible, drove even modesty away. It took all the control she had to keep from screaming.

"Break them," she whispered.

"That wouldn't be wise."

A wail escaped her throat.

"Listen to me," he called. "Look at me, damnit!" She found him through the blur of her tears. "They'll go down on their own," he said softly. "They'll help heal you."

Olana surrendered, exhausted as he cut, wrapped, issued his curt, gruff commands.

"Will I feel there again?" Olana whispered when he was finished.

His hands stopped, then resumed dressing her, all in silence. A sob erupted, unwanted, from her throat. When he touched her shoulder, the nightshirt was on again, covering the monster she now was—half woman, half biblical plague.

He took up her hand. A sharp spasm of pain made her wince. He glanced toward the amber bottle. "Are you sure you don't want—"

"Yes. Go away."

"I can't do that. I need to treat—"

"I hate you! I hate this place!" she shouted.

"Tell me about some place you like then," he said, lifting his scissors. "Tell me about your home."

"It's not like here. It's bright. Mr. Hart! That hurts!"

"I know. I'm sorry. Breathe deeply. Talk to me. What makes your place bright?"

"Glass. European glass. Glass etched in the windows, the doors, the chandeliers. And we have electric light—all through the house. That was my father's idea." A throbbing pain rode up her arm, but she made herself see her house on the hill in San Francisco. "It's a different sort of light, electric."

"How's that?"

"Have you never seen—even a demonstration?"

"No."

"Well, it's white, instead of yellow like gas or oil. The servants love it because it leaves no dust. My mother swears it's brighter than daylight. I wish I could tell you how it works. Men like to know how things work, don't they?"

He pressed the cool cloth to her forehead. She'd endured it. He'd wrapped her hands again. But it wasn't over, she could tell from his face. "Feet now?" she whispered.

"Yes. The last. Promise."

She concentrated on the wild, partless, spiraling crown of his light hair as he positioned himself at her feet. He began to cut. More blisters. Terrible pain. She closed her eyes and thought of herself dancing in a new gown, a Worth gown, from Paris. "Oh, Mr. Hart, even you would like—" Purple spots burst behind her eyelids.

"What would I like?" his calm voice brought her back.

"All the wood in our house. The floors are a different parquet in each room—mahogany, walnut, cedar, ash. My father loves trees, too, you see? And the ballroom! Polished wood and mirrors. Skylights too, so it never overheats no matter how many guests are danc—" Her right leg jerked involuntarily. She covered her mouth with her forearm and allowed the tears to ease down her cheeks. ". . . are dancing," she breathed out. No more cries, no more complaints, she chided herself; he was doing his best.

"Over," he called softly. "All finished now, hear?"

She opened her eyes to see his. Exhausted. And pained. His left cheek, above his beard, was swelling. "Mr. Hart. Did I kick you?"

"I believe you were dancing. And I was busy studying your ballroom floor. Served me right."

"I'm very sorry."

"No matter." He smiled. Even that seemed an effort, she realized. The man was dead tired. His hand cradled the back of her head. The other took her arm down gently, held the glass to her lips. "It's water. Promise," he assured her.

She swallowed. "Mr. Hart, why didn't I feel . . . the area of the first bandaging at all? Why did my hands and feet hurt so much?"

"It's a good sign, the hurting. Means you're healing." He drew the covers up to her waist again. Then what did the numbness signify? Why didn't he tell her that? Well, at least his hands were clean, even under the fingernails.

"I didn't mean to be so difficult."

"You did fine. I'm not one to talk, after the carrying on I did."

"When?"

"Klondike. Winter of '98."

He pulled his gold hair back and she saw that the tops of his ears were missing, the sides misshapen, scarred over. That's why he wore his hair long. "Hollered a bloody blue streak, my partner said."

He smiled, and she returned it. "I wish I'd have heard that."

His grin broadened. "I'm sure you do." He reminded her of Sidney and his teasing, just then.

"Mr. Hart—I've not yet expressed my gratitude."

Another frown. "You don't need to be grateful. You need to get well."

What a strange man he was. He stood. He was going to leave her side; she had to ask now. She touched his sleeve with her swaddled hand. He turned.

"Will—" she began, stopped. No tears, she told herself. Steady voice. But she had to know. And she had the impression that this man, for all his faults, wouldn't lie. "Mr. Hart, do you think I'll ever leave this place?"

His eyes grew warm, though his voice got even more gruff. "What's your given name?" he asked.

"Olana," she whispered.

"Olana, listen." He stretched her name a little longer than she had. "It ain't time to worry yet," he told her.

She bit her lip and nodded quickly.

He yanked the covers up to her chin. "Now rest. I've got my own work to do. Ain't running a winter resort."

Her mouth formed an involuntary smile. "Mr. Hart?"

"Yes?"

"You should rest yourself. You look terrible."

Damn the woman. Matthew kicked his chair back against the stone hearth and opened his grandmother's book. He doubted he'd find anything about the discreet care of a spoiled socialite. Still, he pulled on his spectacles, and found his way through her compilation of remedies for generations of his family.

Did Olana Whittaker have to combine her fussing, her infuriating, misplaced modesty with the courage it took to look at her injuries, to ask calmly about the possibility of her own death? She'd sensed his fear, he was sure. He had to work harder to rid himself of it. She was young, strong. She would survive. Still, his eyes scanned the words he'd read many times before:

Gangrene: affected parts will turn blue-gray, remain swollen and paralyzed, with no sensation. When areas turn black, they are dead and putrefying. Amputate.

She couldn't feel her breasts. What if they blackened? Matthew drew a long, even breath and thought of the words his grandmother used so often—"Ain't time to worry yet."

He watched his patient sleep. The first days, she'd cry out loud. It had kept him awake to her needs. Now her sleep was deeper, and her face was letting go of its suffering. Once again it became the face against the red wood's glow, the face that made him forget who she was and want her. Brainless. Dangerous. But did she have to tell him to rest? He closed his eyes.

He was a child again in his dream, walking at the tall woman's heels. No, not a child exactly, it was after the massacre at Conner's Ridge, the court martial, but before his uncles turned on him. What was he, twelve? His father had so mixed him up about his age he had trouble figuring it. No matter, the dream soothed. Watch. They stood behind the grayed clapboard house, he and this new woman, his grandmother. The warm Pacific breeze chased her wondrous silver hair from its bonds. She turned on him sharply.

"What are you looking at?" she scolded.

"Your hair. It's resplendent."

She tilted her head, frowned. "Can you spell that word?"

"I think so."

"Don't think." She handed him a stick. "Write."

He began his marks slowly in the sandy soil, suddenly nervous. Would she send him away if he couldn't spell *resplendent*?

"If you can't spell it, you can't say it, that's what I tell my boys," she was saying. "You can't be any different. 'Course, now they only growl at me, so I wonder about my injunction. But you can't be any different."

She opened her hand when he was finished, and took the stick. "Had any schoolin', Matthew Hart?"

"No, ma'am."

"Well, it looks all right to me. Who taught you your letters?"

"Mama."

There. He'd said something right. A pleased look made her even more beautiful. "Well, I'm glad she was good for something."

"And, Gran?"

More pleasure. Because he used the name he'd longed to but hadn't dared call her?

"Hmmn?"

"Mama had the same injunction."

"Can you spell—"

"Yes'm!"

"Well, so can I. Watch!"

She finished the letters with a sweeping arc in the sand, then leapt off her feet in delight. She leapt like a girl, and he imagined her the girl she once was, leaping into the air when finding gold in her claim along the American River. No, not imagined. Saw it. Saw her at the river, its banks piled high with diggings.

That had been the first of his visions of his grandmother in her youth. The force, the reality of it made him shake all over. Annie Smithers held him once it was over, made him tell it, tell the other times like it. Then she'd called him gifted, not peculiar, which was what he'd been in his father's world. Annie began remaking him as the hero of his own life that day. Then she'd pushed him toward the barnyard.

"Pick out a fat one, so's I can get some meat on your bones."

A fat one. Chicken. Strength. That was the dream's message, Matthew realized as he woke feeling whole and refreshed. Olana Whittaker needed strength. One of his hens would have to go before her time. Matthew righted his chair, rolled up his sleeves, and reached for the ax in the corner. Women. Always women pushing him, he thought in a mixture of annoyance and amusement, as he slipped out the door.

Later, the woman in his bed moved, moaning softly while he dropped the spoonfuls of batter into the pot and replaced the lid. Olana. What kind of a name was that? It had a smooth, exotic sound. He stood over her, wiping his hands on the floury cloth.

"Hmmm . . . Marcel," she called out with a lover's intimacy, "that smells wonderful! What is it?"

"I ain't Marcel," he said. "But that's chicken and dumplings on the hearth."

He fixed the bandages on her fingers so she could fist the spoon, lock it with her thumb. She ate with a relish that made him wish he could cook anything else from scratch. Then she put down the spoon defiantly.

"You keep telling me there's plenty. But I shall not touch another morsel until you begin, Mr. Hart."

"Begin?"

"Eating!"

He loaded his plate absently and joined her. The pleasure she took in the food delighted him. He felt a weight lifting from his chest as he answered her questions about how he'd prepared the chicken, put together the batter. It was marvelous, she proclaimed. It was as simple as cooking gets, he insisted, hearing his grandmother's tone in his voice.

Her injuries faded from prominence. Without her fashionable guises, Olana Whittaker's animated innocence sparkled. She seemed younger than he'd first assumed. Was she yet twenty? He watched the way her wild, tangled hair framed her face and was framed again by the pillow. What in hell are you looking at her hair for, he chastised himself; she's trying to scratch her palms with the spoon's handle.

"Stop that!" he yelled.

"The itching, Mr. Hart! I must! It's maddening!"

Her cheeks bloomed crimson. She turned away, pressing one side of her face into the pillow. He couldn't stop looking at her struggle to maintain her dignity.

"It's a good sign, the itching," he tried.

She would not look at him.

He left, returning from his back room with a tin of sheep grease. "Hands," he ordered. He massaged the grease into her open palms.

"That smells horrid. It's spoiled my appetite."

He took the almost emptied plate from her lap. It looked more like hearty eating had spoiled her appetite. He felt only barely polite enough not to voice his thought out loud. "Your palms itching any more?" he demanded instead.

"No," she admitted.

He dropped the tin on the table beside her bed and went about his cleaning up.

Her fragile voice returned, beaming out soft and warm like the yellow light of the oil lamp. "Might I try and walk soon, Mr. Hart?"

"After the blisters go down."

"When will that be?"

"I don't know!" She started, bit her lip. Shit. He didn't mean to yell. She faced the window, buried herself deeper in the covers. Farrell was right. He wasn't decent company after the first snow. He approached the bed, flinging the dishrag over his shoulder. Even that made her wince. Good Lord, was she afraid of him?

"You want to come outside? See where you are?"

She turned. It was the last thing she wanted, he surmised from the panic in her eyes. "Yes, all right," she whispered.

He brought her another layer of his clothes, letting her swollen fingers help with the largest buttons. He wound her head and neck in scarfs and put a deerskin robe around her shoulders. The heft of her was still light, lighter than that day he'd found her in the storm. But she had the strength to circle his neck with her arms.

It was a day of crystal clarity. He couldn't think about how high the drifts were, about how long it would take him to dig out. He could only stare at the fractured prisms of color beaming through the sequoias. She stared too. Matthew felt her cling tighter suddenly as a wood mouse scampered by his boots, grass stems in its tiny mouth.

"What's that?"

"Pika. He's in a hurry to dry his winter food. Looks like you weren't the only one caught off guard by the storm."

Her attention was diverted skyward.

"Clark's nutcracker," he told her as she shielded her eyes to watch the black and white bird. It tilted its head, stared down at her before continuing to peck at the pinecone's seeds. Her head tilted in response. The bird flew to a lower branch and started pecking at another pinecone, then tilted his head again.

"I've kept you out long enough."

When he turned back to his dwelling, her arms dropped from his neck. It was just as he wanted her to see it, snow shining in the afternoon sun, smoke curling from the stone chimney in warm contrast. So much snow, would she recognize . . . ?

"Mr. Hart. You live in a tree," she whispered.

"Yep." He walked closer to the downed giant, caught in some upheaval perhaps hundreds of years before. He'd worked a summer through, carving it out, building the stone chimney and hearth, the pine board front. He was proud of the place. How did she see it? She only stared. Well, what did he expect? And what did it matter, what she thought? Damned woman. He held her close and ducked through the low doorway.

When he slipped her back into his bed she cried out. A burst, mixing pain and joy.

"What is it?" he demanded.

She colored up pink, even as her gauzed fingers stretched out, gripping the front of his shirt. "I . . . feel them, Mr. Hart."

"What?"

She colored deeper. "You know, my . . . bosom. Warm. Like when my hands, then my feet first came back. Yes. Warm pain." Tears traveled down her cheeks. But she was smiling.

"Both?"

"Yes."

"Well. Well, good."

No gangrene. No more wondering if she could survive his knife. If he could even cut her. The flush of relief that coursed through his system left him lightheaded, without speech. He tried to escape her eyes, glistening now. Their dark luminance called him closer. Didn't they? The tips of his fingers brushed against her wild hair, grateful. He was grateful to it for saving her face. He just wanted to touch it that way, grateful. Soft. Christ. Women were so soft.

Her eyes did not narrow in indignation, but got wider, curious, childlike. And she was still holding his shirt. Let go. Let go of me, now, he wanted to tell her, but had not yet found his voice. He lowered his head, felt her wet lashes against his cheek. It hurt, his cheek, where she'd kicked him. He smiled. She was strong, would get stronger. Lower. His lips touched hers. His hands crushed her cascading hair, finding, cushioning her neck as he delved deeper into the recesses of her mouth. She tasted of the chicken, the biscuits, forgotten springs.

Her eyes went wild, she didn't know enough to breathe. What was he doing? He broke away, pulled himself back. She stared at him, her ripe mouth still open, her face flushed.

"I—I'm sorry."

What in hell. Didn't she know how damned beautiful she was, he thought suddenly, angrily. She sensed it, her shining eyes got even wider. He backed away from the bed, yanked his coat so hard from the nail that it ripped, and went out among his trees.

The prisms of light were gone. The sky was clear, but there was no sign of a thaw. The sequoias' warm red bark stood silent in the dying light. Their everlasting presence, once a comfort, now taunted him. Beside them human life was so fragile. She was so fragile. Stop it. She could feel again. She would recover, be gone.

"Well and gone," he whispered fiercely at the ground that had taken the others.

four

Olana pushed her plate against the saltshaker. "I shall not eat another egg as long as I live!"

"They're good for you. Build up your strength."

"If only they were in a custard, a flan—"

Matthew's eyes grew hopeful. "Can you make custard?"

"No."

"Well, neither can I. So you'll just have to suffer them boiled until you get home."

He stood, reached for his coat. "If you can manage to get me home before my parents die of grief!" she challenged his back.

He turned slowly, his eyes cold. "I'm doing the best I can. Your blasted feet aren't helping."

"How dare you decry my infirmity?"

"How dare you ignore my instructions to keep them raised?"

"I cannot lie still for hours in this dreary place!"

Olana knew that fierce look in his eyes. He'd lost his patience, was beyond speaking. He pushed away the table and lifted her from the chair, almost in a single motion. He deposited her on the bed, yanking the pillows from behind her head, stuffing them under her swollen feet. He took out his remaining anger on the door as he left.

Olana still felt Matthew Hart's strong arms across her back, under her knees. He was never rough enough to hurt her, but she was always made aware of his strength, and that threatened her enough to hate him for it. He left every day, now that she could get along without his constant ministrations. Where did he go?

"Digging out. You'll be all right," he'd demanded rather than assured her, as if she had no right to cause him yet more trouble.

Sometimes she heard him talking to his small brood of animals as he banged around in the barn. But sometimes he went away altogether and the place grew horribly silent.

Olana thought of when he'd put his mouth to hers. Was it a kiss? It was nothing like when suitors brushed their quick, cold lips across hers. She'd felt Matthew Hart's strength ride through her. A delicious sensation made her long to open . . . open what? He knew. He knew what he'd done, how he'd made her feel. Was that why he was so distant now?

Olana sat up, reached for her traveling desk, her pen, and writing papers. She forced her peeling, tender fingers to write.

I start to wonder if I've not been here forever. This tree, angered by my intrusion, is alive again, its rings of age, its roots, growing in again—catching, crushing me . . .

Olana stared at the words she'd written. She started again.

Mr. H. brought me my writing desk, which was trampled into shambles on his barn's floor. With a patience he has yet to demonstrate to my physical person, he thawed the ink, reshaped the paper in stacks. It all smells of unsavory odors, but I'm happy to have it.

I struggled with the knots and brambles in my hair until yesterday morning. It was then there appeared a mirror and comb on my bedside table. They are coarsely made, but carved with almost delicate primroses. They are not his. I don't believe Mr. H. would groom himself properly were the King to call. Still, he's clean, as are his clothes. I managed, with my mysterious gifts, to plait my hair into a single braid. That evening he granted me one of his rare smiles, but said nothing.

She frowned. This was not what she wanted either. But she couldn't stop, as if she didn't know what she herself was thinking, feeling, unless she wrote it down.

> We have been living on the most awful assortment of dried, smoked, and canned foods. Mr. H. does not ask my opinion, only frowns when I leave so much of my share un-eaten. Happily, I am free of the bandages, though not of the shrinking blisters and the itching. Mr. H. made Indian-style moccasins to cushion my feet, and I wear them as I take my necessary few paces a day. I can do almost everything for myself now, and the joy I take in my independence rivals, I feel sure, the glee a child feels at increasing mobility from crawling, through standing upright and walking. Only my stubbornly swollen feet cause both my benefactor and me continued worry.

There. A start. And, miraculously, Olana felt better, less hemmed in by the spare, dark dwelling. Benefactor. Is that what Matthew Hart was? Now she must date the entry. What was the date? Was it still October? Olana's eyes focused on the place where she'd hit her finger in Mrs. Goddard's cupboard. The purple bruise had worked its way to the middle of her nail. A clue. At Mrs. Goddard's, it had been the second week of October. That last morning, the cramp in her side told her that she was halfway through her monthly cycle. But it had been weeks since then, it must have been. A creeping re-alization set in. Late. She was late, and she'd never been late since her monthly cycles began. What was wrong with her? How could she find out?

The book. The large, worn book he'd been so engrossed in when he kept his vigil, that might help her. It was in his curtained-off room. It was Matthew Hart's refuge, she knew, from the way he yanked the loosely woven material across its rod when he'd enter. He wouldn't want her in there. Still, he'd never actually forbidden her entry, she reasoned, as she eased her feet off their perch, slipped them into her moccasins, and walked across the wooden floor, a blanket in tow. She had to know if she was ill. Where had the blood gone? Was it festering inside her?

The room beyond the blue-striped curtain was smaller than she'd imagined. Olana could scarcely stand up straight. The ceiling got even lower, meeting the dirt floor in the dark recesses of the sequoia's hollowed bark. He slept here nightly, this animal's den but for the shelves of glass bottles containing liquids, powders, leathery shavings. Those reminded Olana of peeking into a Chinese chemist's shop as a child, before her nurse pulled her away.

There were trunks, all closed. Intriguing her. What was inside? She fought a delicious terror, imagining herself the last of Bluebeard's wives. Silly. Leave the man some privacy, Olana. Then she saw the book, on top of one of the trunks, in plain sight. Well, it couldn't be so confidential, she reasoned, if he left it out so carelessly. Olana sat on the trunk, pulling up her feet inside the blanket's warmth, and took the massive book on her lap.

Matthew Hart discovered her, hours later, shivering from more than the cold. He yanked the curtain back farther. "You have no business in here. Or with that."

Olana clutched the book against her. "Get away from me!" she almost screamed.

His eyes began to thaw. "What's the matter?" he asked softly.

"Stay back!" she warned.

But he picked her up anyway—book, blanket, and all. First he nested her in his bed. Then he built up the fire she'd let go down to embers. Then he returned to her side.

"Now. What in hell ails you, woman?"

He squinted at the opened book, its pages crammed into her bosom. Then his eyes seemed to read something in hers. He stepped back, straddled the chair beside the bed, sat. He rested his forehead in its pressed-wood back. When he looked up again his voice was the gentle one he'd used when she first was ill.

"Is it your flow? Don't fret on it. You'll need clean rags, won't you? I'll fetch you some. Cramping? I'll make up hot packs if you want, how would that be?"

Flow. Olana had never heard anyone call it that. It sounded so normal. "It's not . . . that," she whispered. "It hasn't come. I've never been late. And I wanted to know why it hasn't come."

His eyes stayed on hers. "What are you saying?"

"You know what I'm saying, Mr. Hart! It explains in the book why I could be late. I was at your mercy after the storm. Benefactor. I thought you were my—" No tears. Head high, eyes on his. "I demand to know if, in my helpless state, y-you—" He was still staring. She would have to finish, he would not even spare her this humiliation. "If you took your pleasure with me."

When he stood, she thought he might strike her. "What do you think I am?"

"I—I don't know what you are. The way you kissed me—"

"I said I was sorry, damn it!"

"And, before that, I remember, or think I remember—"

"What?"

"You. Lying next to me, with no . . . neither of us had on any—" Her steaming face collapsed into her arms and she sobbed. She heard him place his chair closer to the bed, sit properly, wait. When he spoke there was no anger in his voice.

"I didn't think you remembered any of that. Didn't want to upset you further when you're already so damned sensitive about—" He pulled in a pained breath. "I'm sorry. That's not for me to judge. Aw, 'Lana, look at me, will you?"

She took in a breath and lifted her head. What had he called her?

"I didn't hurt you, take advantage. I was trying to keep you alive. You needed my warmth to bring you back. Learned it up north. Cold winters up north, you know? In the Klondike? Olana. It doesn't seem proper, but I had to. Do you understand what I'm saying?"

She nodded slowly.

"Do you believe me?"

She stared at him.

"All right. That's all right, you don't have to, yet." He looked up at the single window. Though it was dusk, the light appeared to make his eyes smart. "You've been under my roof, wondering all this time if I—" He looked back at her. "Lord, I'm sorry."

Olana hadn't been wondering any such thing until she realized her monthly visitation was late, but she was enjoying the look of remorse on his face too much to say so.

"Things have to change around here," he declared, suddenly

earnest and animated. "We have to talk more, you think?"

Olana remained silent.

"All right, I'll talk more."

He drew his wire spectacles from their case in his pocket, put them on, then reached for the book in her lap. She held it fast. "Please," he sighed. She surrendered it, then watched him carefully straighten the crushed paper.

"Wrong part," he told her gently as he turned from the "With Child" section to the pages headed "Female Ailments." Olana felt herself grow calmer watching him scan the small, imperfect lettering. Who had written it?

He lifted his head. "Amenorrhea. That's a mouthful, ain't it?"

"What does it mean?"

"The absence of menstruation when it should occur." He read further. Then he sighed hard, sounding almost like his horse. "Appears I haven't been taking good enough care of you, Miss Whittaker."

She was Miss Whittaker again. "It says that?"

He smiled. "The cause might be the exposure, part of the toll it took on you. But I ain't—haven't been—attentive enough, that's clear. You've lost weight, even I can see that. Your body's reacting to the trauma and my rude care. I'll fix up the remedies set down here, then we'll talk on the rest. All right?"

When she didn't respond this time he gifted her with one of his lopsided grins. "Come on, have mercy. I'm going hoarse in my efforts, dar . . . miss."

Olana felt herself coloring. "All right," she agreed.

Another smile. He was much less fearsome when he smiled. He backed away into his curtained enclave, but returned with one jar containing dried sheets of something green, the other, a dull-colored powder. He pulled out a piece of the green substance first.

"I don't suppose you'd want to chew on this?"

Olana inspected. It smelled briny, tasted worse. "Ugh," she said.

"Have to have it stand between you and starvation on a desert island, maybe."

"It's seaweed!"

He grinned. "Dried kelp, yes. The other's smartweed. I'll

grind them together, try to make it palatable."

He shaved the kelp into a stone mortar, added the powder, crushed them both with the pestle. And, miraculously, kept talking. Olana didn't think he had so many words in him.

"I thought you were just fussy. About the eggs, the food. See, I'm so used to being alone, and don't need much—I'm not excusing myself, you understand. Can't slaughter another chicken, but I'll try to find a deer tomorrow so you can have some fresh meat. If the ice ain't too thick on the creek, I can get a few fish after that."

"But you'll be gone so long—"

The ranger looked up from his task. "Do you get lonesome?"

"I . . . no, of course not!"

He ventured closer. "You like Dickens? Mr. Twain?"

Olana could feel her face brighten with remembrance. "I was reading *A Connecticut Yankee in King Arthur's Court* at home. Mama wouldn't let me take it along. She says Mr. Twain is coarse, and has dangerous ideas."

"Got it!" He disappeared into his refuge and returned with a stack of books packed under his chin. "Top," he directed. Her fingers righted his cocked spectacles instinctively. Their eyes met, and he smiled at the contact she'd initiated. Olana took the new edition of the book from the stack. "Order came in to Mrs. Goddard's day before I left," he explained. "You read it first."

"Perhaps we could read it aloud—to each other."

"Sure. We could do that."

He reached into his back pocket for a soft cloth and began dusting his older, well-used books. "Brought out more Twain, a Poe collection, Hawthorne. Got Dickens' *A Tale of Two Cities. David*—

"These will keep me company for awhile!" Olana took the cloth from his hand and resumed his dusting. "You are a scholar, Mr. Hart."

His face widened again, this time into a grin that was boyish, despite the beard. "No, I ain't. Just like a ripping good story."

Olana continued dusting, then became entranced with the soft cloth. "Even your rags are beautifully woven, like your shirts."

"You want more?"

"More?"

"Of the cloth, I mean."

He disappeared again, rummaging through another of his trunks. Cloth and books. Bluebeard, indeed, Olana almost laughed to herself. He returned and set bright, deep-colored fabric before her. Cards of needles, too, and spools of thread, a pair of scissors. Olana felt like a child at Christmas.

He cocked his head. "You can sew?"

"I am somewhat useful, Mr. Hart." She couldn't maintain the irritation in her tone, when he looked so roundly chastised. "May I use . . . choose from all this?"

"Sure."

For the first time, the way he pronounced sure like "shore," made her smile. He pulled off his spectacles and searched her face.

"Give it time. It will come back," he promised.

Two days. Two days was all it took. Olana was mortified. She fixed her gaze on the venison he was cutting for her.

"I—will now be able to use the clean rags you mentioned."

No anger. No flaming vindication. Only a warm smile. "It's come. Good."

He rose from the table and brought a bottle of dark wine from the recesses of his curtained room. As Olana watched him fill her cup, she dared to think that his new attentiveness might not stop, even now. Still, she must apologize. For assuming the worst from a man who'd kept her alive, who was doing his best to return her home. But how? How could she find the words for such private, forbidden things?

He touched the rim of her cup with his. "To your continued recovery," he offered a shy toast.

"And to the discontinuation of wretched tasting sea kelp!"

He laughed. She joined him, hardly recognizing the deeper tones her voice was making in its mirth. She stopped suddenly, realizing they were celebrating what every woman she knew kept as her own dark monthly secret.

"Mr. Hart, you are the strangest man I've ever encountered!" No, that was not what she meant to say at all.

But he only laughed again. "And you are hardly the first indelicate enough to make that observation, Miss Whittaker," he assured her.

five

The air was crisp, clear, not as cold as it had been. Was it the beginnings of a thaw? Matthew had been tricked before, in the Klondike. The mistakes he'd made there kept him cautious. If he were just sure her feet could take the cold in case they got caught somewhere on the way down to Three Rivers.

He scanned the wide, white horizon, enjoying the stillness. He was used to his winters alone. Even if he had no duties, no charts to make, no wildlife to observe, he would need time daily, alone. That was part of his nature. Would her eyes ever cease their pull, give lie to her nod, her "Until later then" when he left?

Still, he had to keep reminding himself who she was, that he was responsible for her until he could get her back to her own people. Then his life would return to its constants—his books, his fire, his trees. Why did the anticipation of that no longer give him peace?

Out here was beauty surpassing the glowing descriptions of her father's house, the life she led in San Francisco. He'd only been in San Francisco long enough to get himself shanghaied on a Pacific freighter, then to get Lottie's girls launched. He saw the youth that city had stolen from him in Olana Whittaker's eyes. They were too bright, her cheeks too glowing.

She'd transformed the cloth he'd heaped upon her into clothing that fit her shape a sight better than his. Though he'd had little trouble treating her frostbite, it was now hard to bid her goodnight when her arms were bare, shimmering in the fire's light. When the ties of her dressing gown were loosely drawn he'd caught himself staring, remembering the delicate pink blush that spread from her breasts to the roots of her hair when he used to change her bandages. Staring, when she'd forgiven the kiss, when she trusted him like a brother.

The ranger's eyes narrowed at something moving in the distance. A thin trickle of gray smoke. He mounted his horse.

The freshly abandoned camp had all the earmarks of the Carson brothers—whiskey bottles, food, smoking fire. How did they get up this high, this early? He'd been ejecting them from the park for two years now, confiscating the equipment of their latest scheme, first shepherding, then prospecting. Matthew had driven them to the park's western boundary twice. Sent them on their way, the last time with revenge in their eyes. There was nothing stronger he could do, considering the California legislature and federal government were still dancing around each other over protection of natural resources.

Mr. Parker had warned him that the Carsons were heating up a personal grudge. Warned him of what he'd already known from too many men like them—the brothers were in full possession of a lethal combination of meanness and greedy intentions. He'd tracked them down twice. They'd come back when it was just him on patrol, Mr. Parker had predicted. Here they were, though the road and trails were blocked in drifts. Damnation. Where was their passage?

Matthew kicked the half-empty can of beans. A low sound. He listened. An echo of the skittering can? His own growling thoughts? He had a few, along the lines of Olana Whittaker was problem enough. Couldn't the Carsons leave him some peace until he'd returned her?

Olana. Alone. The tingling intensified. Fear crept up Matthew's spine as his eyes followed the men's tracks. Due west. Toward his tree. Could he overtake them before they reached her? He was so absorbed in figuring how long it would take that the animal's breath, hot on his neck, was a surprise. As were the claws lashing through the coat on his back before he'd even turned around.

* * *

Halfway through with the laundry, Olana peeled off his blue woolen shirt and tied the sleeves around her waist. The steamy hot water had moistened her self-fashioned camisole as well. She sat, exhausted, before the fire and smiled at the clothesline he'd helped her string up that morning, at the great potful of snow she'd brought in to melt.

Matthew had grumbled that he never did a wash until Christmas. But she'd teased him about it until he brought forth the tub, fetched her the line in one of those bottomless trunks of his. They laughed more than they argued now. And he never left her angry.

But still he left. Every day. He was the park's only ranger in winter, she reminded herself. It was not so bad. While he was gone she had his generous supply of worn books, so different from the pristine volumes in her father's library. But the worlds inside were the same—colonial New England, revolutionary Paris, and the place they shared nightly, Mr. Twain's version of life at King Arthur's court. His fine-timbred voice read well, and with a child's enthusiastic anticipation over what would happen next. She'd forgotten how to read like that, she'd been so busy playacting at being bored in recent years.

Matthew Hart always returned with the darkness. He'd pull off his boots and sit, talk with her by the fire before supper. She needed him to do that, to break the silence that the day without him had imposed on her. She showed her appreciation by helping him prepare their meal, trying to assist him afterward, if he didn't chase her back to bed with her feet raised.

Then he'd pull on his rimless spectacles and return to his chapbooks full of charts, sketches, figures. He would talk about where he'd been, about the creatures and sights he labored to represent on paper. The only thing that tried his patience as much as she had was his own sketchings. Olana was even finding his grumbles over his artistic limitations endearing.

The warm fire had already dried her six-paneled skirt. She slipped it on. It had shrunk, and fit her hips better now. Olana turned and let its lovely deep colors swirl around her ankles. How she missed dancing. Could Matthew dance? She laced her camisole tighter and cleared a curling strand of hair from her forehead, before setting herself back to work in the steaming water.

Tramping feet, outside. Already? At an hour before sunset? She smiled, turning. But her smile was erased by the cold blast of wind, the faces of strangers. The door slammed shut behind them.

"Well, the ranger went and got himself a woman to do his squaw work this year!"

Olana's hands gripped the side of the tin washtub behind her. The fur-clad men were as tall as Matthew Hart. One was twice his girth. Their faces, compressed by the cold, were monstrous duplicates of each other. One stepped forward, yanking off his hat, shucking his coat into the arms of his bigger twin. His face was sharp, gaunt, pockmarked above the beard.

"Can you talk, woman?"

Olana's voice emitted a low growl.

"Ain't the welcoming type, is she?" the other man proclaimed, circling. Olana's mind raced. Scissors. Needles. Could she get to them? Was anything long enough to pierce their heavy clothing, their skin? They were both circling her now. The larger man took hold of her braid and yanked her head back. Olana felt his massive hand paw her thigh. Her eyes appealed to the other.

"Why don't you break a few things, brother mine," he suggested.

"Aw, Cal," the brother complained with a high whine. But like a well-trained dog, he released her and headed for the back room, where Matthew Hart's jars were soon shattering.

Olana edged toward the sewing supplies. She found scissors, but couldn't raise them before the one called Cal caught her wrist, twisting it hard. The scissors clattered on the floor. She gasped out her pain.

"Skittish, like a fawn." He grinned. "And a little dangerous. Charming." His breath reeked of whiskey. Olana saw rotting teeth in the stale confines of his mouth. He twisted her wrist while his free hand scraped the sleeve of her camisole off her shoulder, baring a breast. Her breasts were not monstrous anymore, but tender, new skinned, vulnerable. Olana felt the hot tear glide down her face.

"Please," she whispered.

"Ah, but surely you're not so shy for him. And we men of the forest share even our most prized possessions. Didn't he tell you?"

"Cal—" the whining voice of the brother returned along with

his bulk, crowding the small room. "Let me have a quick run through her first, will you?"

They were all distracted by the door's slam. Matthew Hart yanked back the cartridge of his rifle. He took aim. All the anger the ranger had shown toward her paled in comparison to what Olana saw in his eyes now. "Step away from my wife, Carson," he said quietly.

"Wife? She didn't say—"

"She didn't say anything at all!" his brother insisted.

Cal Carson lowered his voice. "Except 'please.' Your wife was asking for it, Hart. Begging us."

Olana took advantage of the man's lightened hold to twist away. But her feet felt frozen again and she stumbled, falling against Matthew's side. She saw a flash of relief invade his hard eyes.

"You want me to take them outside, not make a mess?" he asked her.

That incongruous whine burst from the mammoth brother. "Christ, man, she's only a fucking woman!"

"Your woman, of course," Cal Carson amended.

The small eyes of the bigger man next appealed to Olana. "If we could just go, Ma'am. We'd never bother neither of you nor his woods again. Wouldn't we never, Cal?"

Cal looked perplexed, as if he'd written off his life already and was not prepared for this second chance. He was the brighter one, the one to watch, Olana knew, and something was dawning on him. She looked up at the ranger's set face, saw the sweat lining his forehead. And his rifle shook. Slightly. Perhaps only she was close enough to see. Yes. Something was wrong. She replaced the camisole to her shoulder and lowered her eyes demurely.

"They hadn't yet touched me, Matthew," she said.

He shifted his weight to one side. "Take off your boots," he commanded the men.

"What?"

"Off!"

They obeyed.

"Now get out."

The ranger backed out of the two men's paths. Olana saw the smile creep over the clever brother's face. Her sharp intake of breath was warning enough. Matthew Hart kicked the Bowie knife Cal drew from his hand. It slammed into the washtub. The larger man grabbed his brother's shoulder. They ran into the gathering dusk.

The cold ran up Olana's arms as she bolted the door. She wound them in the sleeves of the blue shirt still tied at her waist. Matthew Hart lowered his rifle. He was breathing hard.

"There's a pistol. A Colt Peacemaker. In the back room, 'Lana. Middle trunk. You think you might fetch it?"

She returned to find him in the same position.

"There. Good. Hammer's down and on an empty. But it's got five loaded cartridges. Aim at the head or heart, hear? They don't stop, you keep firing. 'Lana?"

"Yes?"

"You all right?"

Her wrist burned, her scalp ached. But she managed a quivering smile as she nodded yes and put the firearm in her apron pocket.

"Good," he breathed, finally easing his stance. To Olana's astonishment, the rifle came apart in his hands.

"Damned grizzly," he muttered softly.

"Grizzly?"

"Broke it across his snout. I'd of killed them both where they stood if I'd had the means, 'Lana, I swear it."

His grammar was slipping, his accent leaning on its soft Southern intonation. He put the parts of his rifle on the table. Sweat ran into his eyes now, making him blink.

Olana touched his sleeve. "Take off your coat, Matthew," she reminded him.

He looked up at her sharply. "You're all right?"

"Yes."

He tried to stroke her cheek with the back of his hand. But it went through the air, inches away. He dropped to his knees with a soft blasphemy. Olana finally saw the blood-stained slashes in his back. She covered her mouth to choke back her cry.

"Ain't as bad as it looks—"

"You can't see it!"

"Well. That's true." His head dropped between her breasts. "You smell wonderful," he whispered.

"That's lye soap."

He managed a thin laugh. She took his face in her cold hands. "Matthew!"

His eyes struggled to focus on her. "Yes, darlin'?"

"I don't know how to help you!"

"You did real well, Mis' Hart."

She took his arm, pulled. "Come," she pleaded, "a few steps, just to the bed."

"Bed?"

"Please."

"No." He frowned. "Trouble. Gran didn't raise a fool," he mumbled, but took her arm.

Olana stripped his coat, then eased his shoulders down so she could peel his shirt and his one piece to his waist. His energies were not focused on any shame or embarrassment, the way hers had been. His back was broad and straight and still had traces of deep summer coloring. The bleeding wounds were incongruous, torn through its knotted strength. He was quiet, too quiet. What would she do if he passed out? He must not pass out. She offered him a crockery cup of the ruby-colored wine. It brought a flush of color to his cheeks.

"Better?"

"Yes. You'd best have a long one yourself," he advised, before she took up the snow left in her basin to pack into the slashes. She didn't argue. She lifted the bottle to her lips. She'd never seen so much blood. Would he die? No. People who were dying didn't chat her fears away.

"Once my gun went to pieces, he sort of stared at me, you know, 'Lana?"

"The bear? The bear stared at you?"

"Yep. Trying to figure if this blame fool who broke a good rifle rather than fire it would give him indigestion, I wouldn't wonder."

"Why didn't you shoot, Matthew?"

"Don't know. Except that he was so close. And the pain hadn't started in my back yet so I wasn't mad, just damned surprised and . . . 'Lana, he was so beautiful."

"Beautiful?"

"Yep. So I growled."

"Growled?"

"To confirm his indigestion thinking, in case it was running along those lines."

She giggled. It felt good, knowing she could still make that silly, girlish sound. And it seemed to please him enormously.

"I was scared spitless, surprised any sound at all came out of me," he said. "But it was a sound, a big sound. Well, he turned tail, 'Lana. He turned tail and ran."

Her hot tears didn't start until then, until that quiet wonder entered his voice.

"What's the matter? Your hands hurting?"

She shook her head. "Stop being so—decent!"

"What?" His shoulders started to shake.

"It's not remotely amusing!"

"Sure it is," he insisted, turning, breathing life back into her trembling hands, then pulling her in against his chest.

"I was so frightened," she whispered into its pine-scented warmth.

"I've got you. I'll be all right and I've got you now, hear?"

Even Matthew Hart's burning anger began to subside as he held her. He felt her hand spread out against his chest. Her chin steadied itself into a pout.

"I'm terribly envious," she said.

"Of what?"

"Of how comfortable, free you are in your own skin."

"I been wearing it longer." He smiled. "But you've got more cause to be proud. You're a beautiful woman."

"As beautiful as your bear?"

"Oh, by half."

She giggled. When was the last time he'd made a woman laugh? Seal Woman seldom laughed, even with the baby. Olana stroked the wet hair back from his temple, then pressed lovely, delicate kisses there. He took her hand. " 'Lana," he warned gently, "we're both a little drunk."

Her brows lowered, but in something closer to intrigue than anger. "Is that the only way you could call me beautiful?"

"Out loud, yes."

There was still no anger in her eyes. He searched for ways to make her stop tracing his hairline, ways to provoke her fine, hot anger. It had been easy enough when he wasn't trying.

"Matthew," she whispered. "Please kiss me again."

He had to take control. He was older. Responsible for her. And their worlds were so different. There was no chance in hell it would ever come to any good. As he covered her mouth with his, he heard McGee's words, a faint echo ". . . the problem with you, Matt, is that you love women the way women love men." He tasted deep in eager, sweet recesses. How had he lived so long without this? Wait. Something was wrong. " 'Lana," he called, bringing her upright. "Breathe."

She took great gulps of air, all the while saying "Yes, of course, how silly of me," politely. He smothered his relieved laughter in her shoulder as he caressed her waist through the worn wool of the shirt tied around her.

"Olana, listen, if we go on like this—"

"Now you want to make speeches, you strange man?" She laughed. He drew her into his lap, took up her hand. Yes, speech. Not this need. He had to find a way to tell her, explain. That he wasn't free. Then he saw the bruise around her wrist. The Carsons. They'd hurt her, of course they'd hurt her. Now she was giving him what they would steal. He brought the wrist to his face, gently kissed around the purple mark. Her fingers opened up in his beard.

"Soft," she whispered, a tickle of surprise in her voice. "Of course. Even where you look rough. You're a complete fraud, Matthew Hart."

He shifted. "Not, ah . . . complete."

He found the remnant of cloth that held her thick plaited hair, pulled gently, and watched it swirl around her arms, shoulders, face. He wove his hands through it, finding her scalp. He massaged it until her head went back and she moaned her pleasure. God, she was beautiful.

He loosened the yanked taut strings of her camisole, kissed the rising fullness of her new-skinned, beautiful breasts. Her eyes grew large with delight, and a touch of fear. Fear. Of course. She was a virgin. He steadied his hand at the knot in his shirtsleeves at her waist.

"I won't hurt you," he whispered gruffly.

"I know."

She leaned back in the pillows. He lifted her feet to his lap. Her breathing, soft and skittish at first, guided him as he massaged her still swollen feet, her ankles, calves. He felt her trust grow as her breathing deepened. When he reached her thighs she opened with a tantalizing sweetness under his touch. The fire made a light and shadow play of the rich colors in her skirt. She called his name over and over as he touched, stroked, eased her out of the swirling colors. He didn't know he was so fond of his own name.

He kissed her eyelids gently after her first peak. She sighed, then locked his mouth on hers, fiercely starting over. He laughed, marveling again at how diverse and lasting a woman's pleasures were.

The night shrouded them in a darkening mantle, sparked by the glints of red in her hair, the glowing beauty of her skin. Matthew's reluctance, fears, even his pain dissolved in the growing power of their lovemaking. But he made himself content to stay outside her. He did not lead her curious hand down to his aching hardness, did not even shuck off his trousers and one piece until he thought he would die inside them.

When they were at last all skin to skin under the sheets, feeling her shy explorations of him was enough for awhile, that and helping her rise to her own delights. He lost himself in the wild music she made at her peaks. When he could hold back no longer he turned away, released without effort or thought, like a kid in a wet dream.

Matthew felt her reach through the flannel, carefully avoiding the bear's marks he was only now beginning to feel again. She touched his shoulder tentatively.

"Matthew?"

"Hmmn?"

"Are you well?"

He turned back to her and propped himself on his elbow. "Very well, sweet girl."

"It wasn't supposed to end that way, was it?"

"It can end different ways."

"But you could have——I wanted you to. I love you."

"No." He sighed, drawing her close. "No, you don't, darlin'." He kissed her hands, breathing in the harsh lye soap and knowing he'd never think the scent mundane again.

six

Olana awoke one sense at a time, the utter winter stillness of the outside broken by the hum of the warm, well-banked fire, the steady rhythm of Matthew Hart's breathing. He'd done that——banked the fire, set the pillow under her feet. When?

The smell of the Carsons' crude force, of Matthew's blood, of her own fear was cleansed, like the items of clothing strung, stiff and dry, on the clothesline. She felt the light hold of the ranger's arm across her waist, still protecting, though the rest of him seemed lost in the bed's depths, where he slept in childlike abandon. The dawning sun warmed her face and illuminated his. Olana no longer cared what he looked like underneath his beard, what life and the Klondike had done to his face. He stirred, nestled her closer.

She had never, she realized suddenly, ever seen him asleep. It hadn't occurred to her until now that he might miss the bed he had given up to her. She wished she'd offered it back sooner. As long as she could stay, too. Olana giggled at the audacity of the thought, not able to work up a shadow of real shame. She felt too alive.

She slipped on her new homemade camisole and petticoat, then left the bed without disturbing him. She found her clothes nesting happily with his, warm on the stones of the hearth.

The covers slipped off his back. Olana winced at the raw red slashes, at the swelling around them, at the remembrance of the blood. She kissed the hard, muscled knot of his shoulder before rebundling him in flannel and furs. He needed his sleep. Then coffee. She had watched him make coffee. She was sure she could do it.

She'd set the pot on a hearth stone when the animals grew so insistent she was sure they'd wake him. She could go out a few steps to the barn, feed them. But the thought of it kept her rooted to the wooden floor. She wanted to cry out her fear of the cold world beyond the treehouse, of the Carson brothers. Matthew would take her into his arms then, soothe her like a child. But she was not a child. Hadn't he treated her as a woman last night? The animals' cacophony rose higher. She slipped her moccasined feet into his boots, lifted his wide-brimmed hat from its nail, and headed out into the cold.

The barn was as neat and spare as his treehouse. His animals gave her welcome squawks until she removed the hat, freeing her hair and showing a face different from their master's. Farrell's horse backed into the stall she shared with Matthew Hart's speckled mare. The gray goose hissed at her heels.

Olana had more luck with the chickens, once she found their grain and held it in the apron already heavy with his firearm. She sprinkled it as he and Mrs. Goddard had shown her, then checked the nests for eggs. Four, a good morning. "I'm going to learn how to make custard," she told the hens.

"Will it be as good as your coffee?" Matthew Hart spoke softly from the doorway, two enameled cups in his hands. She approached, inhaling the steaming warmth.

" 'Lana—"

She laughed her skittish laugh, avoiding his eyes. "I'll have you know my name is—"

"Likely to get tangled in a man's throat," he groused.

"Call me anything you like then," she said softly.

He stepped back. "You didn't have to tend them."

"Yes, I did. You needed to sleep. Because of your back, I mean," she amended, feeling herself blush. "Shall we feed the horses?"

He led her to the grain bins, then showed her how to scoop out a bucketful and cast it into the horses' troughs. The two mares hesitated, then began chomping.

Matthew covered the barrel's bin, then lifted her on top so her legs dangled like a schoolgirl's and her eyes were level with his. His face was pale, his eyes ringed in shadow. He must eat, Olana decided. His hands took hers and rested in her lap.

" 'Lana. Last night. The things I did—I had no right."

"I gave you the right."

"Yes. But I'm older and I'm supposed—"

"Was I too young to please you? Is that why you turned away?"

"No. Oh love, you pleased me."

"I could learn to do better. I want to make you feel as glorious as I did, over and over."

He half smiled. "It doesn't work that way for me. The over and over part, I mean."

"Why?"

"Because I'm a man."

"How does it work?"

He kissed into her palm. " 'Lana, I—"

"Don't." Her fingers danced nervously against his mouth. "I'm so happy. You don't have to love me back. But don't say you regret it."

The goose honked madly as Matthew Hart lifted her off her perch and kissed her as if he were hungry for more than the warm eggs in her skirts.

He carried her to a pile of fresh hay, found their coffee, and joined her. They drank, she sipping, he in his long gulps as they watched a swallow's flight among the rafters. Olana leaned back. The silence between them was still charged, but now with a kind of peace that allowed her to enjoy the soft weave of his sleeve brushing her cheek, of the way the thin lines of steam from their coffee found each other, mingled.

She felt his chin nudge the hair off her forehead. The simple gesture was making her breasts tingle. Did he know? The chin was suddenly gone, as was his arm from her shoulder. Even his scent of coffee and pine and leather seemed to be drifting away, though he hadn't moved from her side. She couldn't bear it. Olana took up his hands. She turned them over, traced along the long, powerful fingers, calloused, but gentle, warm, and now—quivering?

"Matthew, the other women, before me. Which taught you how to be . . . so loving?"

His eyes shot back to the barn swallow. "Don't ask me that."

"Why not?"

"Ain't . . . proper."

She laughed. "I thought *I* was too concerned with propriety!"

He shrugged.

"However did you know all those places . . ." She touched between her breasts where he'd settled his feathery kisses the night before. "How to make me feel so—"

"It's not me," he insisted. "I can't make you feel anything. It's you do the feeling."

She touched his chin, trying to discover the outline of his face. "You don't have to tell me everything. I don't think I could bear everything. One. A teacher. A name."

"Lottie," he surrendered.

"Lottie."

"I dreamed of her," he ventured further. "The day of the storm. She sent me out to get you."

"Matthew."

He put his head back in the straw, winced. "Listen to what I'm telling you. And I ain't even drunk."

"I think it's wonderful."

"So do I," he admitted.

"When did you know her?"

"Years back. In the Klondike."

"But, there weren't any women in the Klondike, at least none except—" Olana's mind raced, searching for explanations besides the blatant one. She found none. "Matthew, you didn't consort with a—"

"She ain't a whore now, she's dead. You satisfied?"

He stood, yanked a pail through a bin of oats, brought it to the horses. Olana followed him.

"You loved her?" she whispered.

"What if I did?" he demanded.

"If you did, I would understand better. Oh, Matthew, do be patient with me!"

He turned, stood over her. "Come," he said quietly. He took her hand and led her behind the grain bins. The small area was scattered with sawdust and shavings. He uncovered a length of tar-

paulin from a sleigh. She stared. This is what the weeks of bang-
ing had been about. The sleigh was a curious, mixed design—long,
like the husky-pulled ones she'd seen in lithographs of the Alaska
gold rush. It had room for only her, with a running board across
the back for him to stand on. But it was set higher to take on the
Sierra drifts. She touched the curved side to steady her hands and
thought it graceful in its own way.

"It's finished," he said behind her. "I can take you back."

"When?"

"Today. We can start out today."

"But—the snow."

"This will get us through."

"Those men."

"They'll be busy tending their feet for a few days. I want you safe
before they take any notion to come back."

"What about you?"

"Me?"

"What's going to keep you safe if they return?"

"I have another rifle. And the Colt. And Cal Carson's Bowie knife
besides."

"What about your back? You can't reach to tend it yourself. And
your medicines are all shattered, ruined."

He raked his hand through his hair. "I don't understand. I
thought you wanted to go home."

"I do!" She turned away abruptly. "I'll gather my things."

" 'Lana?" he called her back. "I didn't burn everything." He
pulled her green velvet hat from the sleigh's seat and offered it to
her like a truant boy.

She stared at the remnant of a former life, at the few clumsy
stitches he'd made in his effort to repair it. Then she took the hat
from his hands.

"It's best, 'Lana."

She nodded. He wound his arm around her waist, and led her
inside his tree.

For him she had broken her promise to her brother, that she
would never let anyone else call her by a pet name. 'Lana. It sounded
like another of his whores.

* * *

The first part of their journey was as quiet as the woods around them. Neither spoke, except for Matthew's quiet urging of the horses. Even the woodland animals were silent. They traveled the steep, long path he had dug to the high meadow. Once there, the horses paved the way, their hooves crunching through the light-powdered snow into the ice layer beneath. The colors of the blue sky, red bark of the giant sequoias, and glistening white snow were so intense Olana had to rest her eyes with a glance at her lap. What kind of a journalist was she, Olana wondered. No kind. Just a spoiled heiress playing at writer, as everyone already knew. How else could she be only discovering this beauty only now that she was leaving?

She remembered no landmarks from her blinding journey there until she sighted the cave where Matthew had found her. She saw him again through her slowed, freezing senses, a great swaddled giant with eyes full of hope and her hat in his hands. Why didn't she know enough to love him then?

He drew the sleigh to a stop, came to her side. "We'll rest a while," he broke their silence. The worry, exhaustion on his face shocked Olana out of her own self-pity.

"Shall I—"

"No. Stay put till I get you."

He built a fire inside the cave's mouth before he allowed her out from beneath a mound of furs. He carried her to his camp. There he set her down, offered her a portion of hard tack, smoked venison, and a mug of the coffee she had made that morning. She ate, but he only swallowed his coffee, his hat low over his eyes.

Olana watched as the fire illuminated glimpses of the endless reaches of the cave. And she listened.

"There's a stream under the ice," he answered the question she hadn't voiced. "Listen." Olana held her breath, smiled slowly. Matthew took out his knife, dug. She leaned over the spot. The white stone veined in black shone up through the running water.

"The bed's marble," he said. Her hands slipped out of the muff he'd fashioned of rabbit fur, but he caught them before they reached the ice.

"No," he warned gently. "We worked too hard on those hands."

He pressed her fingers against his beard and breathed, spreading warmth almost to her troublesome feet. Then he slipped her hands back into their covering. He sat closer, yet his deep voice was almost shy.

"Olana? I hope you'll come back and see it, the cave, once the ice and snow are gone." She leaned her head on his shoulder as he bent a twig in his hands until it snapped. He laughed bitterly. " 'Course, why should you want to come back, after—everything? Here I am still touting my wilderness over your city when just yesterday, you very nearly, you could have been—" He shivered, making Olana remember the swelling redness around his wounds, and wonder if he'd worried too much about her to dress himself properly. She touched his arm the way she had when she'd played his wife.

"The actions of men, not your wilderness, Matthew."

"I want you safe," he whispered fiercely.

At the beginnings of the steep road that clung to the mountainside a twenty-foot avalanche of snow blocked their way. Olana watched Matthew approach, stare his Goliath down, then return to her side.

"I can dig for a while, test how solid, how deep it is. But if I can't get through . . . Olana, I'm sorry, I'll have to take you back."

"Back?"

"I'm sorry."

She raised the netting of her hat. He lowered his lips to hers. Their passion sparked through the layers of clothing and furs. She had demanded he take her home for so long. Now it was the thought of returning to his tree making her giddy with happiness.

She touched his face. "Do you spend Christmas at home in your tree, Mr. Hart?"

"What?"

"I want you all to myself that day at least! You'll take me with you if you go out? And I'll make us a lovely dinner. And presents."

"I haven't celebrated Christmas in years."

His voice. A boy's. A reader's. Wondering what would happen next. They heard faint scratching, sounds of human voices coming from the embankment. He uttered a soft blasphemy. She clung to his coat. The sounds grew louder. He reached behind her in the sleigh and put the long pistol in her hands.

"At a distance, heart. Close up, head. Remember?"

She nodded.

"Don't think about anything else."

Like the sight of him, dead, his blood splattering the snow, which would be the only way the Carsons could get to her, they both knew. Their eyes steadied on each other before he scrambled up the embankment with his rifle.

The snow dislodged about eight feet up. A foot booted its way through. Matthew Hart dug around the hole and watched.

"Matty! Bless my soul, it's Matty, boys!" Farrell shouted behind him. "You all right?"

"Sure."

"Want to be pointing your Winchester out of my snoot, then?"

"Oh. Sure."

Farrell's voice went mournful. "You ain't seen that fancy newspaperwoman Miss Whittaker anywhere in your travels, have you?"

"I have at that."

"What? Alive?"

"See for yourself," the ranger offered, pulling Farrell through the ever-enlarging passage.

The wiry camp's cook looked at Olana in amazement, then at his horse with wondrous love. "The devil take me for giving up on you and my Rosaleen both, Miss!" he shouted, waving wildly.

Olana threw back her head and laughed. She watched men climb through the passage after Farrell—rangers, men from the road crew, their faces beaming. Why? Because they'd given her up for dead.

Then Sidney Lunt, editor of the Gold Coast Chronicle appeared. Dear Sidney, looking out of place in his trademark latest fashioned, black-and-white creased trousers and flaring dustcoat, his black hair with a wave of dashing silver, his waxed mustache. He too was grinning like a child on Christmas morning. Dear, dear Sidney.

The last man through stumbled. Matthew Hart caught his arm, steadied him. The man's squared, pugnacious, familiar form looked short next to Matthew Hart's height. But his worn and grieving face made hers glow with pride. She bounded up from beneath the animal skins.

"Papa!"

Matthew Hart, usually as still as his woods, was pacing. This wasn't a good beginning, Thomas Parker reasoned. Best to tell him straight out. That stopped the ranger stone still.

"No."

"Don't you know the social circles the Whittakers travel in, man?"

"No, I don't, Mr. Parker. Don't care either. But I got my own work to do."

"It can wait."

"But I was just starting to chart—"

"I'm your superior and I say it can wait!"

Matthew Hart bristled visibly at the military tone in Thomas Parker's voice. Parker exhaled, started again. "Matthew. Your work healing Miss Whittaker is not finished."

"Due only to the fact that she won't pay my advice any mind."

"But she'd have to if you were in the paid employment of her father, brought to their home in San Francisco for the expressed purpose of overseeing her recovery."

"I hate San Francisco."

Thomas Parker transferred his look of dismay to the papers scattered on his desk. "I understand, Matthew. Didn't we share the glorious work it was to build that road? Don't I envy you, ranging those hills, now that the arthritis eating my knees has me stuck here writing petition after worthless petition?"

Matthew Hart looked into the eyes of the only man besides his grandfather he'd ever trusted. "Are you taking the concoction—"

"Yes, I'm fighting down that slippery witch's brew of yours. And it helps, with the pain. But my legs are going, we both know that."

The ranger thought about how hearty the frail figure before him had been three years ago, when he'd signed on the road crew. It was himself a liability then, broken with his loss. Only Mr. Parker was willing to give him a chance. No pity, Matthew reminded himself. He's still man enough to send you through the floorboards. He listened.

"The point is, I'm stuck here fighting on paper. Fighting the lumber companies and sheepmen, the land speculators who want to jack the price so high that the government will never purchase the remaining acres we need. Don't you see the value you'd be to us among the Whittakers, the people they know? If we could get their support—"

"I'm no politician."

"You can speak eloquently enough when roused—I saw that when Miss Olana Whittaker first came among us."

"Damn the woman!"

"Bless the woman, Matthew. Between her pen and her social ties she might help you save these splendid trees from further destruction."

Defeated before he even smelled it coming. Parker knew it, and was smiling. "Tell me, is it just Olana Whittaker or women in general that are the objects of your wrath?"

"Wrath?"

The older man laughed. "She's charming, intelligent enough to have a man's job, and more beautiful now than when she was plump and gussied up in her finery. You must have behaved yourself or she'd be hollering bloody blue murder. Wait. That's it, isn't it?"

Matthew Hart shifted his weight to both feet. "What?"

"This 'damned woman' business is nothing but a sham. You're fond of the woman."

"Never met a one I didn't grow fond of, sir. But that doesn't make them any less maddening."

Parker stood. "I'm seeing a new dimension to you tonight, Matthew! You're not the confirmed bachelor you'd like us to believe."

Bachelor? Christ, he had too many women. Why was it so warm in Mr. Parker's office? He shouldn't mention it. Not polite.

Thomas Parker circled his desk and put his hand on the ranger's shoulder. It hurt. "Did Mrs. Goddard dress your wounds?"

"Yes, sir."

"Good, good. But your eyes are heavy. Are you all right, Matt?"

"Sure."

"It won't be as bad as you imagine," he promised. "Just until Christmas. A month, Matthew. And shave."

"Don't shave until spring."

"It will feel like spring in San Francisco. Shave."

As his hand touched the door's latch, the ranger stopped, turned back. "I've got one last chance," he said.

"What's that?"

"I'll speak Mr. Whittaker's language. I'll ask a price so high he doesn't want me."

"Oh, Matthew." His superior sighed. "There isn't one."

BOOK TWO

seven

He was fifteen again, and in the smoke-filled gambling parlor on the Barbary coast. His uncles were raising their glasses to him, smiling, accepting him into their company at last. He tried to look into their eyes this time—was there pre-meditated treachery there, or just the desperation their gambling debts had caused? But the prisms thrown from the glass were catching the dusty light, breaking it into rainbows. Then the glass was dropping from his hand. No. He willed the dream to stop.

But the colors only blackened until the hull of the freighter, the stench of liquor, urine, and open, rotting mouths. The light shone again down the steep stairs.

"Get up, choir boy. You're too pretty for such common company. You're the captain's catch."

Matthew sprang up from the pillows, his arms tense. He was sweating, dizzy. Had he shouted? He listened for any echoes of his voice. The hull of the freighter was fading, the mahogany panels of the bedroom becoming real.

It was a mistake to come here. Mr. Parker didn't know what he was asking.

There was a faint light in the room. And movement—mechanical, whirring, clacking. Matthew stumbled out of the huge four-poster bed to find a child—a boy of seven or eight, watching a toy train on a track as it glided through a tunnel, past a miniature town, and countryside. The boy lifted his head, revealing an intense face, sparked with curiosity.

"Hello."

Matthew smiled. "Hello yourself."

"Did my train wake you?"

"No, not your train."

The child lifted his small, square chin higher, reminding the ranger of the same gesture in Olana. "I shouldn't think so. I keep the cars very well oiled."

Matthew watched for permission, which the boy granted with an elegant nod of his tousled head, then squatted down beside him. He marveled at the locomotive's tiny silver bell, the detailed pine and spruce trees.

"I went on a train like that once. With my grandmother. Went clear across the country, to Georgia."

"You liked that," the boy said, as he wound the locomotive, "You were happy then."

"Yes."

"You ought to think of that more."

"More?"

"Than what gives you nightmares."

He had shouted, he must have shouted, frightened the boy. The room went slightly out of focus, but he blinked and it came back. The child began grouping a pine forest on either side of the tracks.

"Where does your train go?"

"Constantinople."

"As far as that?"

The child shrugged his slight shoulders. "It may as well. It always comes back, always a circle. Who was in Georgia?"

"Gran's friends. From when she was a girl. They thought I was someone else."

"They will here, too."

"Will they? Who?"

"Me."

The ranger's smile disappeared. "But—you're a little boy."

The child went back to his rearrangement of the countryside. "I miss Laney. Did you bring her back?"

"Who?"

" 'Lana. That's your name for her, isn't it?"

He'd been so careful not to call her that, not to use any but her last name with the Miss attached, in front of her pale mother, the others. Hadn't he? Who had told this child?

"I have a present for her," the boy informed him. I'll show you."

"Why don't you give it to her yourself?"

Ignoring his question, the child stopped the train as it pulled in beside their knees. "It's in this car—remember. A comfortable car, one Laney would like." He opened the pullman car's door and took out a tiny doll in deep blue traveling clothes. She had chestnut hair touched with red flame, crowned by a resplendent hat.

"It's her," Matthew marveled.

"Is it?"

"Sure."

The child sighed. "Mother and Father, they say only pastels are proper for her. But she favors dark, jewel colors. Why shouldn't she have them? So, I ordered her the doll. But I never gave it to her."

"Why?"

"They took her away to Aunt Winnie's so she wouldn't get my sore throat, you see?"

Matthew nodded, though he didn't see at all. "She's home now," was all he could think to say.

"Find the doll, will you? Tell her it's from me."

"But—"

"Don't forget."

"I won't."

The boy smiled for the first time. A dazzling smile, a gift. "I like having you here," he said.

"This has been quite a welcome."

Matthew Hart stood, swayed as he felt a sudden rush of blood at his temples. The boy took his elbow and steadied him with a firm grip, though he barely reached Matthew's chest. A wistful look captured his small face.

"I'll never grow as tall as you."

Matthew smiled. "You never can tell."

The elegant shoulders shrugged again. Small fingers traced the carved bedpost. He glanced twice at the door, shuffling his feet.

"Would you like to stay?" Matthew asked.

"Might I?"

"Sure." He nodded toward the bed. "Which acre of this thing you want?"

The boy smiled. "Formidable, isn't it?"

"Whole place is."

"After you. I'll stand watch awhile over your dreams."

Matthew Hart returned to the bed's comfort. He was barely conscious as he felt the small back curl up against his chest. Cold. He pulled the boy closer, draped his arm across the sharp shoulders.

"Who are you, child?"

Did he say it, or think it? He had little time to ponder as a deep, dreamless sleep overtook him.

The sound of the great forest-green drapery being pulled back from the windows awakened him, not the faint predawn light that escaped through. A woman—stout, starched, and annoyed was pulling. Matthew sat up as she opened the French doors that led to the third-floor balcony. A foggy breeze blew in through the lace curtains. She remained by the windows in her severe black dress piped in green, white cap atop her black spun-with-silver hair.

"It will be a close day," she announced. "I'm Cook."

Matthew scratched his phantom beard, now morning stubble. He never shaved until he went home every spring, but Mr. Parker had insisted he do so before leaving Three Rivers for San Francisco. Olana had blushed at the first sight of him beardless saying, "It's nice to see you." What in hell did that mean? The stout woman was tapping her foot. Say something. "Cook. Is that your name, ma'am? Cook?"

"No, sir. It's Cole. Mrs. Cole. But I'm the cook, chief cook. Not chef of course, but cook. Marcel went over to the St. Francis Hotel. The Frenchies, they don't stay here. No matter how many parties for them to show off their fancifications, they're off to the hotels sooner or later. Loyalty, that's all they get from me—twenty-five years of service!" She tilted her head. "Where are your people from, Mr. Hart?"

"Here, ma'am. California."

She looked annoyed. "I mean before that?"

"Oh. Georgia."

"And before they were Americans?" she persisted.

He searched back through the tales of his grandmother and the healing women of generations. Why was this woman asking him such hard questions before he was even awake? "Uh . . . Scotland, I think."

"Across the water. We're neighbors!" she proclaimed.

"Oh?"

"Yes, good, Celtic blood we share. You are no savage, sprung from those dreadful big trees, you are kin!" she proclaimed. "Now, don't bother to align yourself with any Henri or Pierre, when we get one. No, sir. It's I know where everything is downstairs, no here today gone tomorrow Frenchie ever learns my kitchen! I know the butcher's wife likes lavender bath salts at Christmas, and how a jar of strawberry preserves for his little ones will get the iceman to leave me his best cut. I am, in a word, a force. A force not to be trifled with, Mr. Hart, by any member of or employed by this household, whichever it is you are, and notwithstanding our blood kinship."

Matthew grinned, enjoying the stream of images her words produced in his head. She frowned.

"I must see to breakfast. I've come early to treat you, by special request of Miss Olana, who says you could benefit from my healing salve."

"Thank you, ma'am. Did Miss Whittaker sleep well?"

"Better than you, I think." She cast her glance on the damp, twisted sheets. "Suffered a fever did you?"

"I . . . don't know."

"Don't know if you're sick or not? And you hired to look after Miss Olana?"

He smiled at her pursed lips. "Not much by way of recommendation, is it?"

She felt his forehead with the heel of her hand. "Gone now, by the grace of God. Wash up, there's a good gentleman, and I'll have a look at the back."

She had a light touch, so that he only winced at her own gasps as she lined each slash with her salve. "It must be a fearful place you come from, Mr. Hart!"

"No, ma'am. It's a beautiful place. Only it pays to stay alert. Which as you've seen, I'm not, always."

She laughed. He liked her softening voice, the healing scents that clung to the full white apron she'd donned, the way her strong arms moved in curving arcs as she worked. He judged it safe to mention the child without getting him into trouble.

"Mrs. Cole, who is the little boy?"

"Little boy?"

"He was here last night, with his train."

Silence.

"Dark hair—cut like a bowl was put around his ears. In need of plumping, but wonderfully bright-minded?" he tried, turning in time to see Mrs. Cole finish crossing herself. He laughed uneasily. "I don't mean to get him scolded, he was good company."

Her voice went toneless. "Why did you want to stay in these rooms?" it demanded.

"I was put here."

"Against Mrs. Whittaker's wishes. It's the Mister insisted."

Matthew thought of the meeting with Olana's mother, how she looked at him when her husband mentioned his quarters. "Did I put the little boy out? Is that what Mrs. Whittaker was angry about? No wonder he didn't want to leave."

The cook's voice became a hesitant whisper, as if she were asking him questions against her own will. "What did you do? When he didn't want to leave?"

"Why, I took him to bed with me."

"Saints Michael, Patrick, and Bridget, protect and defend me," she whispered. "And where is he now?"

"That's what I'm asking you, Mrs. Cole."

"Stop it!"

"Ma'am?"

"There is no little boy, Mr. Hart."

"But . . ." He rose from the bed, walked to the place where he'd first discovered the child. He got on his knees, scanned the Persian carpet's weave with his hands. "There. The imprint of the track—see?"

"Get up." Her voice was softer. "It may be in your fever, you thought you saw . . . something. Please. Get up, Mr. Hart."

He ignored her offered hand and crawled to the edge of the carpet. "There." He reached under, uncovered the source of the lump.

A pine tree, left in the child's retreat. He held it up to her. "See? Part of the mountains between here and Constantinople."

She took the tree, pressed it against her cheek. She was weeping.

"What did I say? What have I done?" he whispered.

She turned away, gathering her salve, her kit of bandages. Her no nonsense voice was back. "Get dressed now. The valet will be in to help you."

"I don't need help, I need—"

"Mr. Hart." She took his face in her hand, gently, firmly. "There's a legion of doctors coming this morning, brought in by Mr. Darius Moore."

"Moore?"

"You met him last night. Mrs. Whittaker was on his arm?"

The scowling man, he remembered. "Yes, but why—"

"Laying in wait for her, like some jackal, with his doctors, Moore is. Hold your own among them, Mr. Hart, with your good sense, your . . . your welcome from the child. I'll have Patsy look out for you when your work's done. Then we'll talk, yes?"

"Sure, but—all right, ma'am."

"Of course you lanced the other areas, Mr. Hart?"

"No."

Doctor Gaston let his assistant snort out his own disgust before he continued. "You left Miss Whittaker in unrelenting pain while—"

"I never left her."

Why had Dora insisted on these doctors, James Whittaker wondered, their words not clear to him, perhaps even meant to baffle him further on the state of his daughter's health? He turned to that odd duck, her ranger. At least the man spoke English. He had been so calm, so blessedly encouraging in Three Rivers. Now he looked ready to wring Moore's and his doctors' necks. Where was Sidney, damn him, he'd backed Hart's opinions, had even joined Olana in convincing him to hire the fellow to come home with them. Dora was having a bad morning, and had left everything to Darius Moore. As fond as he professed to be of Olana, why did he keep nodding gravely now? These men wanted to cut up his daughter!

True, she did not look well. Her eyes struggled to follow the abrupt movements around her bed. She'd looked healthier in the mountains, James thought. He must not lose her. It would kill them all, this time.

"The pain was not'unbearable," a pale version of Olana's voice spoke up from the pillows. "The worst part was the blisters. Papa. Mr. Hart said they would go down on their own, and they did." Another snort and the Olana he knew surfaced in her ire. "Kindly tell your colleague to use his handkerchief, sir!"

Doctor Gaston froze, then pointed to his associate's breast pocket, and then to the door. The man excused himself.

Hysterical. Was Olana being hysterical? Or just bad-mannered? She'd been an unruly child all her life, didn't they understand? No laudanum. Don't start his lively daughter on his wife's habit. James Whittaker sighed. "Gentlemen. Might you unite in the purpose of my daughter's recovery?"

Matthew Hart's eyes met Moore's. The ranger and Darius Moore had taken a mutual dislike to each other on sight last night, James could see it. Another time it would have intrigued him. Now, complicating the matter of restoring Olana, it was irritating.

Doctor Gaston moved in closer, yanked the covers back from Olana's raised, swollen feet. She started, her eyes frightened. The ranger's lips whitened.

"Doctor," Olana whispered, "the rest of my injuries healed."

Gaston nodded mournfully, like an undertaker. "On the contrary, they have congregated in your feet—where all the poisons will strengthen, before they rise up and paralyze, perhaps kill, unless—"

"That's plain nonsense!" Matthew Hart exclaimed.

Gaston turned to James. "Mr. Whittaker, you rescued your daughter from the wilderness, brought us to her at the last possible moment. If we make incisions here—" The physician pressed his ivory handled stick into Olana's feet. "And here—" She winced. Matthew Hart knocked the instrument from Gaston's hand. It struck the bedroom door.

"Get away from her. She's not cattle to be prodded."

The physician glared. "We can't make our prognosis if we're to be assaulted by this—barbarian, sir!"

The ranger made his argument to James directly, too. "There are no poisons, Mr. Whittaker. Freezing's a serious, but a simple ailment, and Miss Whittaker's been healing herself of it. Time, rest, gentle care, and her feet will finish their own work."

"How convenient," Moore's sardonic voice entered the fray, "a cure that requires nothing of the physician."

Matthew Hart moved closer to Olana's side and straightened his stance like a steadfast soldier on guard. "If you let them take a knife to her now, you're leaving her open to troubles she may not overcome. A whole new burden of healing, scarring, disfigurement."

James Whittaker looked around the circle. Were they all in league to torment him? The prodding doctor laid a hand on his shoulder. His colleagues closed in.

"We're trying to save your child's life, sir."

"She's not a child," Matthew Hart contended. "And she's bested the lot of us—she's saved her own life. Her heart was down to five beats a minute when first I brought her out of the cold."

Moore swung around to face him. "That's patently impossible!" he proclaimed. "The man's a fool and a liar both, sir!"

Matthew's jaw tightened, exactly like Leland's used to, when insulted. But just as quickly, his mouth went slack, and his words betrayed what Dora had called 'a Secessionist's drawl.'

"This lady's healing ought not get undone."

"What?" Gaston demanded.

Matthew kept his eyes on James Whittaker. "By folks who never felt the kind of cold she survived, sir," he finished.

Gaston spun him around. The ranger's smile broadened as he recovered, stood his ground. Go on, the smile invited. Hit me. Let's see which of us is the barbarian. An interesting tactic, James Whittaker noted, even in the midst of his own distress. And he noted Olana's fingers gripping the ranger's sleeve.

"Mr. Hart's approach has benefits—" James began.

"If you prefer to leave your daughter in the care of an unschooled country shaman, we will not be held responsible for the consequences!" Gaston shouted.

"Gentlemen, gentlemen." Darius Moore held up his hands. At last, Dora's Indian fighter to his rescue, James thought. "We share a joint purpose," he began. "Dr. Gaston and his associates have learning; Mr. Hart, experience. Let us leave it to the loving parents to choose, shall we?"

James nodded curtly. The man was bloodless, but quite correct. And at least he'd get some breathing room. "Thank you, Darius."

The black-suited men followed Moore out. James Whittaker motioned for Matthew to follow. Olana's fingers released his sleeve as her maid appeared from the shadows.

"Please open a window," he instructed before he left. His only instruction since he'd arrived to oversee Olana's care, and here he was risking her to the cold winter air.

Matthew waited for James Whittaker in a cavernous, two-storied room filled with books. James watched Olana's baffling, surly avenging angel as he breathed in the fresh bindings. He read over the titles on the leather-bound spines, then removed one from the section that held Whittier, Thoreau, Joaquin Miller. There. Unschooled shaman, indeed. The man was not as ignorant as Dora insisted. James Whittaker entered. He went to his desk, pulled out a wooden box filled with Havana cigars as Matthew Hart returned the volume. When he offered one, the ranger shook his head. What kind of a man would refuse a fine cigar?

"Sit down, Mr. Hart."

"I apologize. My patience wasn't what it should have been."

"Sit down."

Matthew took the wing chair he was offered, but sat leaning forward. Odd. James Whittaker busied himself preparing his smoke, lit, and tugged out the first ashes. "I love my daughter, Mr. Hart," he said, finally. "She is my future. It's important for me to know who you are. You'd feel the same in my place."

"Yes," he conceded, "I would."

James frowned. Go on, he told himself. Go after his pride first. "Do you consider those men colleagues?"

"No, sir."

"Good. I paid them half your month's fee for one visit wherein they frightened my daughter into anemia. The price of her complete confidence in you might prove disastrous to my holdings." The surprised merriment in the ranger's eyes quickly stilled. "I hope to God it's warranted confidence, Hart. If my daughter recovers you can name your price."

"I don't want more money, sir."

James knew that. The fact was, he didn't want any money. He didn't want to be here, that's why he'd tried to circumvent Mr. Parker's order to take the job by naming the most outlandish fee he could think of. Except it wasn't outlandish at all. He didn't know much about money. Or the power it provided. James felt sorry for him in that. He suspected the boy had already been bruised by his ignorance. James even felt protective of this fierce, direct stranger, who had saved his daughter's life, who had even praised her as 'a fine woman, with great courage.' Odd. Why did he say that? Women didn't need courage, did they?

"What do you want, Hart?"

" 'Lana's health. My leave."

"Permission to return to your trees?"

"Yes, sir."

Mr. Whittaker walked toward the leaded glass windows, his hands clenched behind his back. His legs were slightly bowed from being in the saddle so much, visiting his timber mills. He turned until Matthew Hart could see only a quarter of his face, and the smoking cigar. Because he needed to be stern, and he found the honesty of the young man's face too compelling, too refreshing. Buck up, James. Do it. The man didn't want to be here. He upset Dora, and the valet was ready to quit over him. He had dangerous politics. And Olana's affection.

"I thought that allowing my daughter's journey to the National Park's opening would solidify some notions about the proper use of timber and her own place in society. I wasn't counting on you to disrupt both."

"You're not exactly my idea of a lumber baron yourself, sir."

The older man turned. "Is that a compliment?"

"Wholehearted."

James Whittaker's face broke into a grin. " ' 'Lana,' eh?"

"It slipped out."

"I like it. But her mother won't. And Mrs. Whittaker doesn't care for you, I'm afraid. You're at odds with the doctors. That fool Gaston and his assistants treat her neurasthenia."

"Neuras—"

"Their expensive name for her bouts of debilitating weakness, headaches. She's suffered them since . . . for a long time."

"I'm sorry, sir."

"Yes, well. It's . . . it's only fair to tell you that my wife and Darius Moore are pulling me toward her physicians' advice." There. Let's see some anger. Quit, so I'm not faced with firing you. But the ranger only spoke softly.

"Who is Moore, sir?"

"He manages several of my businesses. And serves as a bookkeeper for my wife in her philanthropic pursuits. I'm so flat-footed he serves as her dance partner as well at their charity soirees. He cuts a fine figure, and she is so sad, has so few pleasures . . ." God, why was he telling him that? "Olana's heart was down to five beats a minute, you say?"

"Uh . . . yes, sir."

A sudden laugh erupted from James Whittaker, as it often did when he'd made a decision. "Yes, by God, you scoundrel! Turn my household upside down if you must! But we'll try your way first!"

James Whittaker knew the place in the room where he could watch, unobserved. He arrived well before Matthew reached Olana's side. He shouldn't have, but he had to see her reaction to his choice, and he had to see them alone.

Matthew Hart ignored the chair Patsy put out and sat on the bed. Olana was lost in the lace, the damask, the pillows, much like her mother had been now, for twenty years. Was Dora's condition going to be passed on? Olana's voice was just above a whisper.

"Are they gone?"

"They're gone."

"And you're still here."

"Your father's a patient man."

Her mouth quivered. "Come closer, Matthew." She frowned at his tie, pulled out the pin and had it realigned in seconds. "There," she approved. "You look very handsome. How is your back?"

"Healing."

His back. Of course. That's why he didn't lean into the chair.

"You've won over Cook," Olana told him, her voice sounding stronger. "But you frightened Papa's valet to death!"

Matthew winced. "I can dress myself."

"Well, I'm not going to send my Patsy to make sure everything's on you properly. She's too pretty." She looked him over once more, how? Boldly? Olana, who was bored by men of all stripes? Then she sighed. "Perhaps I'd best loan you my three-way mirror, though."

They laughed quietly together, until she was overcome by a dry cough. The ranger reached the bedside table, poured her a glass of water from a pitcher there, then held it to her lips. Her fingers twined with his until she finished. He laid her head gently back in the pillows. There were tears in her eyes.

"I'll be good. Don't let them cut me, Matthew," she whispered.

"I won't. You don't even have to be good."

She gave herself into his arms, reaching past the starched shirt to his suspenders. She held them as he rocked her and made quiet, humming sounds at the back of his throat. It was achingly familiar to James, seeing them like that. "There," Matthew whispered, stroking her hair. "You were wonderful. You didn't need me at all."

"But I do! Can you understand why I asked Papa to have you come home with us and oversee my recovery?"

"No. But maybe there's a place for me here. For a little while."

My God, James Whittaker thought from the shadows, she's in love with this man he'd almost sent packing moments ago. So that's what she needed to be admired for then, her courage? Strange girl. Well, onward, he determined his course. A little while, hell, Matthew Hart. You're going to father my grandchildren, Cossack or not.

Patsy was indeed pretty, doe-eyed, and waiting to lead Matthew down the impossible maze of curving back stairs and hallways to the kitchen. The kitchen was twice the size of his tree house.

Mrs. Cole looked up. "One moment, sir. I can't leave this to get warm now." He sat on a stool across from the marble slab where she was rolling out the floury dough.

"They ran you through the gauntlet, did they?"

"I won't let them hurt her."

"No, I daresay you won't, if you're already stabbing them with their own instruments!"

"But I didn't—" Two kitchen maids giggled together at a corner sink.

"Alice! Beatrice! Put the kettle on and fetch the tea things!" Mrs. Cole bellowed as she fluted her meat pie. Then she lowered her voice. "There now, Mr. Hart, give them their stories, it's a dreary life down here."

She shoved the last of her pies into the oven and motioned him into the spacious, low-ceiling parlor. This was, Matthew Hart realized, another home, with another family. And Mrs. Cole was unquestionably its matriarch. She pointed him into a chair plumped with two down pillows. He leaned into their softness gratefully. She'd remembered his inflamed back. With the appearance of the serving girls in the doorway, he tried to stand, only to be halted by her raised finger.

"Give them leave, they'll be putting on airs the day long, sir," she admonished. "Forgive me, but it's easy to see you're no gentleman."

"Is it?"

"Aye. You don't know how to be ignoring your inferiors."

"But no one's my—"

"Not in your woods, maybe."

Matthew sighed, steepling his fingers under his chin. He closed his eyes until all the sounds—the servants' giggles, the tea being poured, set out before him, stilled.

"Who is the child?" he asked.

The cook pulled in a nervous breath. "The little tree, I don't know how you found it. Every trace of him was taken from the nursery."

The ranger opened his eyes. "His name, Mrs. Cole."

"Leland. Miss Olana's brother."

He smiled slowly. "She never said she had a little brother."

"She doesn't sir. Leland was her elder by four years."

"Was."

"He died almost twenty years ago, sir."

The ranger felt the cold thin frame against his chest again. "Sore throat," he whispered.

"Yes, it started that way, then turned into diphtheria. Blessed Lord, Mr. Hart, what visited you last night?"

"A boy, with a train, telling me to look after his sister."

"Miss Olana."

" 'Laney."

The cook crossed herself. Then she put the cup of steaming tea into his hands. "Sip it slow, bound to revive you a touch," she advised gently. Matthew swallowed around the stubborn lump of grief in his throat as the woman spoke.

"They were a spry little pair, Olana and her brother, barely a cross word between them, as different as their temperaments were. He understood her even then, I'm thinking. Didn't he speak up when the parents tried to make a lacy little thing of her? How she searched for him, after, and how her calling cries pierced my heart. But soon she covered herself in that same cocoon the parents did. To this day they never speak of him, display no remembrances, not the smallest photograph. The rooms you're in upstairs sir—they haven't been opened in all these years. I don't know what Mr. Whittaker was thinking of to be so insistent—it's driven Miss Olana's poor mother to her bed for the day at least."

"But Olana, she needs her mother now."

Mrs. Cole's eyes turned sad and weary.

"Where's the train?" he asked, remembering his promise to the child.

"I don't know. It was so long ago. Everything was moved out. You won't find it in this house, I'm thinking."

"But I have to find it."

"Well, I know better than to discourage you after this day, Mr. . . . what is your Christian name, Mr. Hart?"

"Matthew."

She smiled with both sides of her face. "A good, holy, scripture writer's name! There. Your color's coming back. Eat now, the scones are good—akin to your biscuits at home, I would think."

"How did you know—"

"That you're used to biscuits? Only from your honey-coated speech, don't fret—this house isn't full of ghosts and mind readers both!"

He laughed with her, happy to be back in the realm of the

parlor, its steamy tea, the taste of raisins and butter and orange peel.

"Can you make custard?" he asked.

"Why I wouldn't have gone beyond kitchen maid if that were beneath my capabilities!"

"Would you teach me?"

"You, sir?"

"Olana craved it back in the woods; if I could learn, I'd be able to do something besides fight doctors and distress her family and make myself a troublesome pest to you."

The cook laughed. "Ah, it's going to be a Yuletide of some spice upstairs and below this year, I'll wager!"

eight

Sidney Lunt watched as Olana searched beyond the lace curtains, over the wrought-iron balcony, and down to where Matthew Hart walked through the solarium. She was smitten. Badly. Had they even been lovers in his tree house? Olana was not good at hiding her affections, the way so many other women of her class were. It was one of the things Sidney liked best about her. And why shouldn't she prefer her rough-hewn ranger to the colorless royalty of England and the continent? Sidney was more than a little taken with Matthew Hart himself.

The sequoias and this man had changed her, too. Despite the lingering pain in her feet, he'd never seen her more uncomplaining, joyful, enthusiastic. And he'd known her, loved her, all his life. Love? Is that what it was? That devastation when he thought that, were she frozen under one of those Sierra drifts, his own life would be diminished into its own white pallor? Well, was that so impossible? She'd become his touchstone, as infuriating as she could be. He trusted her with everything. Almost everything.

He loved her. Why else had he trumped up three excuses to cross paths with her while she was abroad? His parents had given him a newspaper when he came of age. On the same occasion she had gotten the husband-hunting trip to the Continent and a reminder from her mother that her eligible years were now numbered. Why was that the way of things?

"I can't get anything but grunts from him," he said aloud.

Olana turned, looking disdainfully at the stack of the Gold Coast Chronicles he'd brought. "Are you surprised?" she asked, "after calling him a Cossack?"

"When did I—"

"Your editorial, 'Trees or Timber?'"

"Oh. 'Czar Parker and his Cossack Rangers'?"

"Exactly." ·

He thumped the stack of past editions with his palm. "It was a nice phrase, sport. And it got letters! Now that your Cossack's out of his wilderness, get his story. He may make an appealing hero for your readers."

Olana looked startled. "My readers?"

"We've featured your plight daily—the many complications, setbacks in our search. It's made marvelous reading! Why, we concluded our running novel *Blood on the Orchids,* then did not replace it, without one letter of complaint! And we're creeping up on the *Sentinel* circulation—I may get the rag out of red ink next year after all! You've inspired a devoted following. A true life adventure!"

"Sidney, I can't."

"Can't?"

"I mean I could . . . I have pages of my thoughts, written while Matthew was out charting and patrolling and it was so quiet. But I promised him—"

"Promised what?"

"Not to write of him."

"What? I thought you said that was how Thomas Parker convinced him to oversee your recovery in San Francisco. So that he might convince people of the worth of the park project?"

"Yes, but Matthew is a very private person. And I believe he thinks certain . . . things might jeopardize the government buying more land the park needs."

"What things? Things that make the land of interest to private investors? What did he find up there, Olana?"

"Sidney, stop that!"

"What are you hiding for him?"

"You're insufferable with your questions!"

"That's what's going to help me succeed in the newspaper business, sport! Now, are you in my employ, or are you going to let Matthew Hart do all your thinking for you?"

"The both of you are such bullies!"

Olana looked over the railing again. The man she'd made her promise to was gone. "Couldn't I write about something else?"

Sidney took her hand. "Olana, be reasonable! How would it be if I give you an unrelated assignment—ignore the fact that yours has been the most dramatic story of this year?"

Matthew Hart came through the doors then, coatless, his shirtsleeves rolled up, a basket of greens under his arm.

" 'Lana, your father has a sassafras tree out there! And the most amazing selection of—oh, I'm sorry."

She stopped his retreat with a hold of his sleeve. "Nonsense, Matthew, come in."

His face sobered as he shook Sidney Lunt's hand.

"Looks like California laurel to me," Sidney observed. Casually he thought, though Matthew Hart's presence did what it had done to him every time since the ranger pulled him through that hole in the snow, it accelerated his heart.

The ranger's eyes lost a little of their suspicion. "Same family," he explained. "But the sassafras is deciduous, where the laurel's evergreen. I'm going to boil up both roots, see which makes the stronger tonic."

Olana sighed. "Now who's sick?"

"Patsy," he told her. "Needs strengthening. Sassafras will do it. 'Thickens the blood,' my gran always—" Something closed inside him, Sidney could almost hear it. "Thickens the blood."

Leave it be, Olana sent him the thought with her quick glance. Sidney pretended he'd missed the warning.

"May I ask if this remarkable woman is still alive?"

The ranger frowned. "No."

"A pity."

"Didn't say she was dead, said you may not ask."

"Well." Sidney smiled tolerantly. "Well, you've done her proud—isn't that how you people express it? For you've restored this lady in a remarkable—"

"No I haven't. It's her finally doing what she's told."

"Told by you."

"By her own body."

"Yes, of course."

Jesus, the man had the power to render him speechless, Sidney thought. Even Olana looked like she felt sorry for him. The ranger turned toward the glass doors. No. He would not be defeated. Not yet. "City life seems to be agreeing with you as well," he tried.

"I can forget where I am sometimes," Matthew muttered, his eyes fixed on the trees in the solarium below.

"How I wish I had such a luxury. But I breathe newsprint and deadlines. Mr. Hart, our readers wish to hear from their silent correspondent. Perhaps in your official capacity, you could put in a word with her father?"

"Word?"

"Recommendation. That she is now well enough to begin a career that her first assignment's circumstances cut so brief?"

"First assignment?"

"Sidney!" Olana looked ready to strangle him.

"Have I spoken out of turn? Surely Mr. Hart also wishes you to begin the profession so dramatically nipped by a real life adventure?" Sidney picked up his hat and gloves from the chair. He'd done it this time. She was furious. And he'd known Olana Whittaker in her fury. Let her handsome lover handle her now. He'd started it, with his unreasonable demands. "Well, I'm off! Glad to see you both!"

They watched Sidney Lunt's heels snap down the hallway before Olana returned to the sitting room. She spoke to the ghostly reflection of Matthew Hart she saw in the glass doors. She couldn't bear to look at him directly.

"Sidney's all right, really, and doesn't mean to pry. He's so used to his questions."

The ranger's head bowed, an uncharacteristic gesture for him. "I didn't realize how much I was asking of you."

"Well, now you know."

" 'Lana. Write about yourself, getting lost in the woods. You could do that, leaving me out of it, couldn't you?"

"Leaving—"

"The tree house could have been abandoned. I sometimes camp out for weeks at a time."

"But you didn't."

"No."

"Without you, I'd be writing a novel."

"Hey, maybe you should write a good, rip-roaring novel!"

"Matthew!"

He ran his hand through his hair.

"Don't trouble yourself so. Go ahead, gloat," Olana invited. "Your first impression of me was quite correct. I'm a sham journalist, Sidney is a childhood friend, who took pity on me. The essays on the park were my first assignment. Maybe he had no intention of even printing them, just of getting me out of his way for awhile. It almost worked, imagine that? It almost worked forever."

Matthew touched her shoulder gently. "You've got your chance now. To prove me wrong."

"Chance?"

"He's got you on the payroll now, doesn't he? Bring him a story."

"What story?"

"I don't know! It's your city."

"I've never done anything so brazen—"

"Brazen? You work for the man, 'Lana!"

"But—I've only ever seen him socially. At dinner parties, balls, and here. It's all Papa will allow."

"Miss Whittaker, you've braved a Sierra mountain storm. You've stood up to the worst human animals nature ever wasted life on. And you can't walk into a newspaper office without your father's permission?"

Olana turned away sharply, stood between him and the steamy world of her father's neat, hemmed-in garden solarium. "Of course I can." He rested his hand lightly on her shoulder. "Matthew, when I'm ready, will you come with me?"

"Sure." He backed away from their proximity. "Now you come." He held out his hand.

"Where?"

"Downstairs. It's time for your feet to be up for an hour. I can keep an eye on you while I boil these roots."

"I'd rather we read."

"Patsy's hurting, 'Lana."

"Going into the servants' quarters isn't as simple for me as it is for you. And they are as uncomfortable as I am down there, Matthew."

"Why?"

"It's just not done. They deserve some privacy, don't they?"

"They deserve warmer sleeping quarters."

"I've already presented that to mother."

He raised an eyebrow. "How?"

"In a way I thought she'd understand." His silence, his sharp, unforgiving scrutiny, spoke volumes. "I can't possibly discuss coal allowances with my father!"

"Why not?"

"He'll—he'll know you're behind it."

"So?"

"It's not your place to criticize."

"But it is yours, isn't it?"

"Matthew Hart, you are impossible, ungrateful and—"

"Suffering stiff-necked clothing and stiffer callers who come to stare at me like I'm some stuffed and mounted species."

"You're unfair! Sidney's quite fond of you despite your open hostility!"

He exhaled most of his anger as he opened the doorway to the back stairs. "I wasn't talking about your Mr. Lunt. At least he's got some purpose."

"Why, Matthew Hart," Olana exclaimed as she followed his long strides. "Wait until I tell him he's risen above your contempt."

He turned, his eyes became suddenly contrite. "Contempt? Is that what you think it is?"

"Isn't it?"

"No." His fingers grazed the rim of the basket in his arms. " 'Lana, you're almost well now. And I feel, sometimes . . ."

"Without purpose?"

"Yes."

"What about your secret mission from Mr. Parker?"

He smiled. "Which is?"

"To convince my father that he and his associates are not max-
imizing the efficient development of the West, but are responsible
for the devastation of California's natural resources. To convince
us that we are vandals destroying your sacred temples. To seek new
forest reserves and so leave us and all our employees impover-
ished."

"Now, would I be doing that before I've collected my fee?"

She frowned. "Why are you so intent on disarming my anger?"

"I'm not intent on any such thing. You have a fine anger, 'Lana.
I admire it." A cool breeze swept up the landing and among her
skirts. She moved closer to his heat. There. She had his eyes. They
were darker, here, in the shadows. How she wished he'd kiss her.
"Daniel would hardly talk that way in the lion's den." He said the
words softly, a touch distracted, Olana thought.

"Well, you haven't been . . . praying."

"Prayers!" he exclaimed with a laugh. "That's exactly what I've
offered up, prayers!" He spun away, intent on his crusade again.
Don't. Matthew. There's no one around, she felt like screaming to
him. Hold me again. "Prayers. For the responsible management of
the extractive industries. I helped build that road so folks could be
touched, as I was. We need these trees, 'Lana. We need them to keep
us in our place on the earth."

"Which is?"

"Part of it, not its lord."

"You sound like Mr. Muir. All religious fervor, no logic, practi-
cality, or reason."

"Thank you."

"You're welcome."

He gave her his arm. "You're a damn sight more fun to argue
with than your father's associates."

She frowned. "Casual blasphemy is not the language of a Bible
reading gentleman."

He swept her in close to his side and lowered his head until his
cheek glanced her temple. "Mrs. Cole says I'm no gentleman," he

confided, before easing away from her again, and swinging open the door to the downstairs world. Olana followed.

"Matthew, she adores you, she can't have said—"

"I think it was a compliment." He set his burden on the cook's massive cutting board, then set Olana in a plain armchair with a cushioned stool under her feet.

"Gives you wrinkles, frowning like that, Miss Olana," Mrs. Cole informed her as she joined them from the parlor.

"What's wrong with Patsy, anyway?" Olana asked, peeved.

The ranger cast a quick look to the cook before looking back at his opened book of remedies. Keep looking there, not at her. She was so sharp, she'd surmise it from the look of him. His eyeglasses steamed over from the boiling water. "It's digestion related."

"It's related to her broken heart, if you ask me."

He lowered his head further into the book he couldn't read for the steam. "Possible," he conceded.

Mrs. Cole unceremoniously lifted Olana's feet from the stool. "Look! Wrinkles in your gown now, too! Miss Olana, go up and change your clothes before we're all catching fury for making you late for tea with your parents."

"But Matthew's not finished!"

"He is also not the dutiful child of Mr. and Mrs. James Whittaker, determined to be more obedient toward her parents' wishes!"

"You are an old bore, Coldheart!" Olana stuck out her tongue before turning to the stairs.

The cook sighed. "Why, she hasn't called me that since . . ."

Matthew lifted his head from his work, safe at last. "When?"

"Since her brother made up the name."

"She's right."

"I beg your—"

"About Patsy's footman, I mean."

"Ah, Matthew. It's no use. I've gone to the heartless man. He would not so much as let me through the door. And after I'm nursing him through the croup for two winters straight."

"Where does he live?"

* * *

Olana stopped in the front hall. Her mother's raised voice rooted her outside the sitting room door.

"Do stop making light of that man's influence! Why, she complained to me of her maid's cold hands on her hair in the morning."

Her father sighed. "That doesn't sound like Matt's influence, it sounds like our Olana."

"That's because you're ignorant of their wiles! She was trying to get the servants' coal allowance raised."

"What? Since when has she concerned herself with—"

"Since that man stepped across our threshold!"

"Matt's put her up to it? Well, the weather has been awfully damp of late. Perhaps I should consider—"

"You'll do nothing of the sort! Give him another inch and he'll have us waiting on the servants!"

"Darling," James Whittaker tried to sooth his wife, "think of him as an eccentric young count come courting from your European sojourn—"

"He is nothing of the sort! Our Darius's first impression was quite right. He is a boorish, unschooled, backwater shaman. I have never so wished for the end of the Christmas season as this year!"

"You don't mean that, Dora."

"And you! Spoiling Olana with this Christmas Eve Ball. I must accept half of San Francisco here to celebrate your daughter's foolishness?"

"Not her foolishness. Her return to us."

Olana heard hurt in her father's voice. Even her mother became less shrill. "Don't you think I suffered too when she was gone? We've lost one child, I told myself—will we lose another to our neglect?"

"Neglect?"

"Indulgence, then. Indulgence in dangerous whims, like this newspaper fancy of hers. Sidney Lunt left an ugly contraption of a typewriter in her room as if she were some sort of . . . working person! This is all too much! Olana wouldn't have gone to that dreadful place if we hadn't allowed it. And now she clacks away at a typewriter and brings home this man who lives among bears!"

"And who was instrumental in restoring her health, here, in civilization."

"You are blind to all criticism of him, James!"

"Matt is our guest."

"But also in our employ. He's more comfortable with the servants. Why can't you treat him in his household station?"

"Because he came between our daughter and death, madame. For that there are few favors I would deny Matthew Hart."

"That's an achievement he himself denies. He does seem to know his proper place, despite his ill-bred familiarities."

"Don't you like it, Dora?"

"To what are you referring?"

"His familiarity—' 'Lana'—it suits her now, doesn't it?"

"She is twenty-three. Much too old for pet names. But you and that tree person continue to keep her a child. She won't ever want to marry, and so occupy her energies in setting up her own household, worrying over her own children. We must cultivate the introductions she made in Europe! Why, Florence Breckinridge has already been sent to England in preparation for her marriage to the Baronet Fermor-Hesketh."

"There's time. You make it sound so dutiful."

"It is her duty. To us. As the surviving child."

"Dora—"

James Whittaker reached out to his wife. She waved him away. "You've seen it too, haven't you?" he asked her quietly.

"Seen?"

"How the two of them talk, laugh, read, even scheme against us together. Doesn't the boy remind you—Dora, isn't it like having Leland back?"

Olana listened to the hushed silence.

"There is no resemblance," Dora Whittaker finally whispered.

"I don't mean in looks! I mean the pleasure they take in each other's company. Even when Olana's being . . . Olana, he's tolerant, patient, amused, even. And she—"

"None, I said! No resemblance!"

Olana walked slowly into the room, no longer caring about how she looked, about what pleased her parents. She fixed a smile on her face. Her mother's matched her own exactly.

"Has anyone rung for tea yet?" Olana asked brightly. "I'm terribly thirsty."

Sidney Lunt pulled his collar up against the dampness and joined his workers teeming out of the *Chronicle* building, smiling, bidding each other good night. Though dressed in the dark suit of formal clothes he'd been fitted for when still on the train out of Fresno, there was no mistaking Matthew Hart. He leaned against the lamppost across the street, his eyes scanning the crowd like a cunning bird of prey. And he looked as if his feet hurt. The editor's eyes lit with delight. "Matt!" he called, waving, then rushing forward in the swirl of humanity.

He took Matthew's shoulder. The sharp eyes hooded, went fierce in self-protection. Easy. Too close. He danced back, giving out a little laugh. "What are you doing here?"

Matthew offered up a scrap of butcher paper. "I'm lost. See, I got there all right, but following it all backwards, I started talking to the brakeman on the trolley, missed the stop. I walked and walked but things got less familiar. And then I saw your building and figured I'd stay put until you were off work."

"How long have you been standing here?"

"I don't know. Not long."

"Matt," he sighed. "Next time come in."

"I'm hoping there won't be a next time. I don't plan to get lost again."

Sidney Lunt laughed. "Right you are! And that requires some education. But first, you look destroyed with the hunger, as Mrs. Cole would say. Some supper?"

The ranger looked at his scuffed boots. "I only have four cents," he admitted.

"Matt, I'm asking you to supper. As my guest."

"Oh. All right, then."

The food was good and hearty and warming at Gus's place, as always. Sidney lost interest in spying on the other newspaper people out from putting their evening editions to bed. Gus's was alive with talk of art, politics, rolling presses. He could listen to that any night. Tonight Sidney Lunt listened intently to Matthew Hart's disjointed story.

"The footman took the marriage gift money Mr. Whittaker gave him to buy into the partnership of the automobile garage, see?"

"I follow."

"But that was only to impress upon this parson his responsible nature so as to get the daughter and dowry—the rest of the money he needed for his—what do you call them?"

"Garage."

"That's right, garage. If he'd been at home when I called, I'd have knocked him into the middle of next week for doing that to Patsy," the ranger declared.

"He wasn't there?"

"No. I put it all together from what Norma told me."

"Norma?"

"His wife. That was the worst of it, Sidney. Here I am watching her shining eyes. She has no idea and I couldn't do a damn thing except be the means of breaking both her and Patsy's hearts."

"So you didn't tell her what a scoundrel she married?"

"Figured she'll find out soon enough. Sidney, Patsy's pregnant. What will happen to her?"

He was Sidney now, not Mr. Lunt, here, away from Olana's house. Sidney Lunt paused, leaning back in his chair. "The Whittakers are good people. They might take her back, after."

"And the baby?"

"She'd have to give up the baby, of course."

"Why? Why is she the one who is punished, when all she did was trust that scheming bastard?"

"Damn. I never thought of it that way."

"Do you suppose Olana could——"

"No. Coal allowances are one thing, my friend. This is another entirely."

"I suppose. Olana told you about the coal?"

"We're friends, Matt."

"Yes. I'm glad. I'm glad you're friends."

"Well, I'm glad you got lost. Come on, let me show you this city, so that it doesn't happen again."

The stars were just appearing when the two men stood at the crest of Telegraph Hill. Matthew Hart stared down the lit piers of the waterfront. The panic that seized him subsided when he sensed a cool, green, ancient darkness. North. He knew there were still stands of sempervivens there, giant redwoods. He held on to the serenity of the giant guardians while tracing the tracks of city lights.

"Market Street, the opera house, the Palace, U.S. Mint, Nob Hill, Chinatown, Russian Hill—see, it's quite simple from here."

"It doesn't make any sense, Sidney."

"What?"

"San Francisco."

"What are you talking about? It's as gridded out as purposefully as New York—"

"But it's not built on flatland or granite. It's all steep hills, fog canyons, unstable ground. People don't belong here at all."

His companion laughed. "We know that, Matt! That's why we enjoy each moment spared from cataclysm! It's a city founded on the gold at Sutter's Fort, the silver of the Comstock Lode, the railroad, the timber. It's the gateway to the Orient. Look at the pattern of lamplights—jewels in the night! Can't you forget your politics and enjoy the man-made wonder of it?"

Matthew frowned. "I'm suspicious of anything man-made."

"I've noticed. Give me time to change your mind."

"Time?"

"Yes. Hovering over Olana now that she's nearly well isn't doing either of you any good. Neither is fretting about the belowstairs and all the injustices you can't change. You've outgrown that solarium, Matt, with weeks to go yet until Christmas. And if those trolley brakes fascinated you, wait until you see a moving picture, wait until you hear the syncopations of ragtime!"

Matthew Hart smiled slowly. "Why, Sidney, you trying to corrupt this country boy?"

Sidney Lunt looked down at him from the top step. "Matt, stop being ridiculous," he called quietly. "I always use this door!"

"But you ain't the hired hand."

"And you're hardly—"

The door in question opened and the sharp-eyed valet turned

footman stared down at them, flanked by James and Dora Whit-taker.

"Good evening, Sidney!" James Whittaker called. "Is that Matt?"

"Yes, sir. We chanced upon each other. Had ourselves a tour."

"Well, that's grand. Come inside and have a nightcap, will you?"

Dora Whittaker spoke before he could answer. "Mr. Hart. You did not join us for supper. Or inform us of this intention."

"No, ma'am. I apologize."

Her husband frowned. "Just so. This evening made me realize that you haven't had much time to yourself since you came. We ought to discuss a regular day off. Say, Thursdays?" Sidney's hand thumped Matthew's back. "Come into the study," James Whittaker invited them. "Tell me what you think of our city, Matt."

"I'd best check on Olana, sir." He nodded toward her mother. "If that's all right with you, ma'am."

"Has anyone paid you to consider my thoughts, Mr. Hart?" she demanded, before walking off.

"One of her headaches tonight," her husband said softly.

"You do try," Olana whispered. "With Mother, I mean."

Matthew was startled by her voice, her position huddled on the stairs. She looked very young. He squatted beside her.

"Hey. You waiting up for me?"

"Mrs. Cole said not to worry. That heaven would protect you."

He smiled. "Is that right?"

"I had a brother, Matthew."

"I know, darlin'."

"My parents do think about him. They do say his name."

"You say it."

"Leland. He would carry me sometimes. I used to hold onto him. Here." She reached through his open vest, found his suspenders, held them just below his collarbone. He lowered his head, kissed the knuckles of her right hand. "We could have had great fun, the three of us," she said softly.

"Remember your brother's train?"

"Train?"

"I'll show you where it was."

He seemed baffled once he'd peered down the long passage that led to his third-floor rooms. Olana took his hand.

"Matthew, what's the matter?"

He braved a look at her. "I usually go up the back stairs."

"And—"

"And . . . I'm lost."

She giggled.

"Second time today." He growled. "How is it anybody needs this much room?"

She giggled again.

"Ain't funny!"

"Sure it is," she mimicked his accent, saying "sure" like "shore." A smile made its way across his face. "There, that's better," she pronounced. "I thought I was the humorless one."

"This is the right hallway?" he asked.

"Not hallway. This is a home Matthew, not a—" She caught herself before she said brothel. "Yes. This is the one." She led him to the third door past the curve, then placed his hand under the smooth brass of the knob.

"Feel the circle scratched in?"

"Yes."

"Our nurse carved it there. I used to have the same problem when this was our nursery—don't tell!"

"If you won't on me."

"My lips are—" He never interrupted, not when he wasn't angry. So it surprised her when his mouth descended, quickly, sweetly, over hers, spiced with a sprig of mint. ". . . kissed," she finished with the breath she had left.

He took her hand, pulling her into the room, then knelt down on the carpet. "Here, see the imprint?"

"Yes. A circle, no—an oval?"

"Exactly! Train tracks. Your brother Leland's train."

"I don't remember."

"Sure you do," he insisted. "Touch where the tracks ran. Clear to Constantinople and back." He put her fingers to the carpet. "Quiet, well oiled. A silver bell on the locomotive. Hear it? And passenger cars, a fancy one, just for you, and you're inside, in a peacock blue coat, a hat that's your little girl dream of a—"

"Matthew, stop!"

"I—I'm not doing this right. I don't know where the train is. How can I find you?"

"What are you talking about?"

"Your brother left you a gift. I have to find it. I promised."

"Promised who?"

"It wasn't the fever!"

"Are you ill?"

"Damnation, 'Lana, I thought you'd understand!"

"Don't shout at me!"

"Mr. Hart, what is the meaning of this?"

Her mother stood in the doorway. Olana got to her feet. "Matthew asked me about the carpet, how it's worn in an oval. I didn't remember why. Do you remember, Mother?"

"You will kindly address Mr. Hart properly, and leave him the privacy of his rooms!"

"They're my rooms, mine and Leland's!" She did not take her eyes from her mother's face. "There," she said softly. "I said my brother's name. I will not forget him, Mother, not even for you."

Her father joined his wife in the doorway. Olana stepped toward him. "Where is the train now? I want it, Papa."

Dora Whittaker's face took on a gray look before she turned and left. James entered the nursery, his feet tracing the track's remains. "So, there are still echoes of the Orient Express. Winnie's got the train, darling," he told his daughter. "She was his godmother, remember? Perhaps we should take a drive out to her."

"Oh, Papa, could we? Aunt Winnie is such fun! And she lives on the ocean. Matthew, do you like the ocean?"

"What about your mother?"

"Oh, she never goes with us to Aunt Winnie's."

The ranger frowned. " 'Lana. Your mother's hurting."

"Oh, she'll write a letter to her African missionary. Or start a new committee. That will comfort her, won't it, Papa?"

"I'm afraid we're rather heartless in Matt's eyes, Olana."

Dora Whittaker was on her couch with her feet up, a cold compress across her eyes. Matthew carried the tray he'd intercepted from her maid. It gave him purpose, made it easier to enter the dark room.

"There," she said tonelessly, pointing to the small table beside her couch. Matthew approached. "Let me help you," he offered.

She hardly blanched. Nerves of her daughter, the ranger thought.

"Mr. Hart. I have not hired your services."

"It's your head, isn't it?"

"How did you find my rooms?"

"Don't punish anyone else for my transgression, ma'am."

"Why not? You are immune from any punishment."

"The tightness here," he pointed to the line beside her mouth, then hovered a circling finger at her cheekbone. "And here? It's muscular. You don't need nightly laudanum, Mrs. Whittaker."

"You surprise me," she said, a heavy weariness in her tone. "Why don't you have the opinion of the others, all except Mr. Moore— that it's all the product of my nervous mind?"

"Try loosening your hairpins."

"What?"

He smiled. "You sound like . . . I mean, Olana sounds like you. Just a few," he coaxed. "Go on."

She did, as if her hands were acting on their own.

"Good," he said. "Now, if you'd kindly allow me access?"

"Access?"

"To your neck, ma'am."

Her eyes never blinked, so close was her scrutiny, even through her pain. But she made no protest, so Matthew worked free the tiny buttons of her high black lace collar, then gently touched his fingertips to the back of her neck. He'd never felt such knotting. But it didn't keep her tongue still as he started to massage.

"Are you a phrenologist now as well, Mr. Hart?"

As well as what, he wanted to ask her, but exhaled instead. "No, Ma'am. It's not your head, it's your muscle I'm looking to ease. Here, packed up against your spine. I don't know the words that will make it sound important, but I know where I am. I know what I'm doing. You're safe with me, Mrs. Whittaker. Breathe easy, that's the way."

When she closed her eyes, he added his other hand's fingers. "Better?" he asked softly.

"Yes," she admitted.

"You can do it yourself. "Here, try." He led her hand over where he'd massaged.

He felt suddenly awkward and useless here in her black and rose-colored room, where the pillars of white marble intersected wallpaper swirled with flowers, gilt. He backed into her desk, and a stack of correspondence scattered to the floor, catching her attention. Her hands left her massage.

"I've been working three days on those letters!"

"I'm sorry."

"Leave them. Get out."

He turned, faced three doors, forgot which one he'd entered by, and panicked into inertia. He finally forced himself to try one, then heard her voice, softened by amusement as he took the handle.

"Not that one."

He tried another. It led to a closet.

"However did you get in here?"

He raked his hand through his hair. He wanted to tell her about a little boy with eyes as fierce as her own who'd made him come. But he only shrugged, cocking his head to one side, showing her, like a wolf challenged by a stronger one, how harmless he was.

He heard a gasp, then a stark, stricken whisper. "You are nothing like him," she said.

He took the handle of the last door, turned and stared, amazed by how her room and its extravagances almost swallowed her completely.

"Ain't hungering to be anybody else. And I got family of my own. Be going home to them soon," he promised.

nine

The long teakwood bench was in the center of a spiral of rocks of Eastern design. The sun had made a rare appearance. The children sat there. Even from her place in the tower, Winifred could tell Olana was complaining. About what? Her feet. The boy leaned over them, concerned. Why had she brought him here? Because her mother would not follow. Because her father liked the boy who'd hauled her in out of the snow so much he encouraged their intimacy.

But he should know more about women's wiles, this one. He unlaced the shoes carefully, removed them. Olana leaned back as he began his massage. Through her thin cotton stockings he stroked, his palms against her heels, his fingers exploring her instep, toes, until even Winifred, at her age, felt a flush at her cheeks. Silly woman. Finally, he teased one long finger along the pad and, yes, Olana giggled softly. She shifted, nesting one foot into the deeper hollow of the other. Winnie saw the imprint of Olana's toes, lined up in prim, aristocratic size order. Her niece sighed, kicked a little deeper into the, my, yes, increasing warmth of his thighs, before she drifted off to sleep. Poor boy. She'd left him in quite a state.

"Shit, 'Lana, I ain't made of iron," exploded from him softly, before he drew up the train of her apricot silk dress, swaddled those feet in it, shoved them toward his knees. He leaned back, stretched an arm over the length of the bench's back. There. Good boy, calm yourself. Now. If you will allow my dear Mr. Trap inside you? My. It was easy, with this one. Winifred suspected he was touched himself. She saw images of other women's feet. Strong, purposeful, as expressive as hands. Roaming a shoreline bare, free. Beautiful women, she could tell from their feet. His thoughts of them were not contenting him. He was lost here and his heart held a raw ache. It was overwhelming even Mr. Trap.

The boy forced his breathing to lengthen. Good. Control. Where had he learned that? Winifred caught the scent of ceremonial tobacco. Indians. Around him. His brass buttoned army shirt bloodied with their taunting efforts to break him. Changing now, turning toward respect. Wait. He was sensing Mr. Trap's presence. Impossible. Yes. He blocked it, turned toward her. Impudent boy. Strange? How dare he think her house strange! But there were his thoughts, as clear as a bell's peal. *All beginnings, half-done middles, and not an end in sight. So strange. Details—beautiful, intricate details, but no larger picture, no structure. Why? Gables everywhere. Even here, on the outside, can't count them all. Away. Shoreline. Face the shoreline, take comfort in its simplicity.*

And he was doing exactly that, that was the worst of Winifred's humiliation.

The two of them, there on the bench. Lovers. Male, female. Olana's peaceful sleep, the boy's mind lost in the essence of the sand and waves lent the garden a symmetry, a wholeness. Complete. No. Not complete. Complete meant over, and over meant death.

Winifred raced down the spiral steps of the tower, holding the scream of panic inside. She approached them. He sensed her presence, being a tracker. Another gift. From another woman. Poor Olana. This man was full of women.

"You're thinking my niece has a mad streak in her family, Mr. Hart?"

Matthew turned. The woman was pugnacious in stance, like her brother, but with hair as white as gossamer, where James Whittaker's was steely gray. Small but hearty, vibrant, smelling of the salt-sea air, like Matthew's grandmother. And trying to pick a fight like her, too.

"No, ma'am."

"No? But my house makes you dizzy."

"It does that," he admitted.

"I will die when the house is complete. A clairvoyant told me."

He faced the structure again. "Appears to me you'll outlive us all then."

Her chin jutted forward, even as her eyes avoided his. He'd offended her. "I like the window with the roses," he tried.

"In the front hall? A French artist created that—he knew the ancient methods, he knew how to get a blue close to that in the cathedral at Chartres!"

Matthew glanced at the clear sky, adjusted Olana's umbrella so it would continue to protect her face from the slanting afternoon sun. When he looked up at her aunt, the small woman's eyelids were flickering strangely, though her voice remained calm.

"Mr. Trap is getting an image. Gunfire. Much gunfire. But death later. From a single wound, a few drops of blood—here." She touched his chest lightly. But he felt the touch through his clothes, skin, muscles, ribs. To his heart.

"Mr. Trap's got me mixed up with my grandfather, ma'am, the one who died before my mother was born."

"Oh? I beg your pardon. That sometimes happens in visions. With close relatives."

"That's all right. I'm used to it."

"It . . . it was a very peaceful death. Perhaps you should tell your grandmother that."

"I expect she knows, ma'am. She was there."

"I see."

He grinned, delighting in the fact that he'd amazed her, for once.

"How is he connected to you, this grandfather?"

Matthew shrugged. "I favor him, so I'm always in his shadow."

"The shadow of death. Yes. Were you afraid—did you see death when the bear had you?"

"He never had me, Miss Whittaker. If he had, I wouldn't be here talking with you, but chatting with that grandfather."

Persistent woman. Was it true, that feeling he'd had that she was invading his thoughts? She wasn't going to stop until she got what she wanted. What did she want?

"What were you thinking of, child?"

He blinked. "Thinking, ma'am? When?"

"When you faced the bear!"

He was about to say he didn't remember when it came back, whole, almost as if he were living the moment again. "I was thinking about 'Lan . . . Olana, laughing at me. On account of I was always holding my wilderness up—as perfect, you know? And here I was about to be devoured by my own perfection. The notion of that was funny . . . but I wouldn't be able to laugh with her, if he killed me. That seemed a shame."

"No fear?"

"Oh, there was plenty of that too."

She approached. Her hands trembled as she patted his shoulder. "Do you love my niece, Mr. Hart?"

Matthew thought of the boy Leland and his questions. Ran in this family, questions. He looked toward the sea. Were there any seals out there? "It doesn't matter."

"Nothing will come of it?" The woman spoke his own thought. Then laughed. "Do you really think nothing further is destined after all you two have been up to already?"

Her words were like nettles in his skin. He was grateful when Olana stirred, opened her eyes.

"Yes, do wake up, you silly girl," her aunt commanded. "Keep a firm hold on this one. He lavishes more affection on your feet than most men do on any three mistresses! Now. To work. Leland's train. It started out in Olana's guest room. But her mother found it there once and was in bed three days over it. I moved it to the attic, where it was damaged in the spring rains of '91. So I sought to restore it under the healing power of the pyramid turret . . . before it was replaced by the octagon tower. Oh, bother, that still only takes us to '96."

"Aunt Winnie likes you, Matthew," Olana told him as they walked through the garden in the swirling twilight mist.

He shrugged.

"Don't make light of it, she's—"

He stopped, took her elbow. "I want you to listen to me, now. I'm a ranger, at the park."

"I know that, Matthew."

"What I mean is, it's the only thing I've ever been any good at. I'm descended from the poorest people of the Georgia hill country. I never even held on to much of the gold I dug out of our claim in the Klondike. Never went to school, except at my mother's knee.

I'm not ashamed of any of this, but your aunt's got me mixed up with my mother's daddy, your parents are battling over me taking Leland's place. 'Lana, I'm not your brother come back, you understand?"

"Yes," she whispered.

"And I don't have any place here. You're well now. Better than well. Vibrant. Thriving—"

What was he saying? Her breasts rose in response. It was so easy to imagine them in his hands, nipples responding to the pull of his tongue. He turned away. " 'Lana," he summoned quietly. "My place is with the trees. They need me. They need my protection."

"Yes," she agreed again. "And you're not angry with Aunt Winnie, or Papa, or even Mother because you didn't say 'ain't' once. But you are working for your trees here, Matthew, when you suffer Papa's cigar smoke and friends, and tell them about the park, about the land it needs added to stay in balance."

"Have you been listening at the keyholes?"

"And at the dinners, and parties. And in the solarium, with Sidney. Who will never call you a Cossack again."

"I'm that tiresome?"

"Purposeful. Let me straighten your collar. They'll be calling us in to supper soon."

Matthew suffered her hands on him again. If only he could have his trees, his family, and this suffering, all. He looked down into her dark, intelligent eyes, smiled, wishing he could work up some anger to replace his longing to feel the luminous skin that shone through the web of soft ivory lace placket of her bodice.

She patted his collarbone. "Done, Mr. Hart," she pronounced.

"Thank you."

"Oh, Matthew, be patient," she said, a little of her aunt's annoyance in her tone. "No one will hold you after Christmas."

He faced the sea again. She was right. He was being a damned nuisance about a job he'd agreed to. He was being paid double his year's wages at the park besides—enough to fix up the place by the sea come spring, maybe even buy a doll for Possum.

Again. That feeling that his thoughts were being invaded. Shit. Get out of my head. " 'Lana? Who is this Mr. Trap?"

"Mr. Trap? Aunt Winnie didn't introduce you to Mr. Trap already, did she? Matthew, you are in her good graces! He's imaginary. Something like Aunt Winnie's male half."

"Her—"

"He does all the things she can't—reads minds, travels through time and place—down the Nile and up Mount Kilimanjaro. Oh Matthew, don't look so grim . . . he's a harmless diversion for the dear old thing. Mr. Trap will tell her where Leland's train is, wait and see!"

Matthew stared up at the conflicting lines of the slate and tile roof, of the slow moving workmen packing up the tools of their never-ending labor for the day.

ten

Matthew Hart stared into the three-way mirror. Black, white, formal. He wished it was Thursday so he could go to Golden Gate Park and look at the lions, then meet Sidney Lunt for the latest show at the Orpheum. Then walk the streets to hear music pouring out the windows, homemade music from guitars, mandolins, accordions.

All this dressing up and scurrying about, room to overstuffed room, was just to eat. Courses upon courses, late into the night. No wonder these city people suffered so many ailments.

He knew the men were already talking of nothing but money, the women of he hadn't a clue what in their separate parlors. Olana was well, why couldn't they let him go home? Visiting her eccentric aunt was one thing, but now her father brought him on excursions to his logging camps, his deafening mills. Why? Why did her mother eye him with suspicion? He hadn't kissed Olana, hardly. He'd barely touched her, though there was motive, opportunity, and permission to do the wildest conjurings of his too fertile imagination. That steel-backed woman couldn't dictate that, his imaginings of Olana free of them, free of San Francisco social circles, free of her corsets. Water. Cold water. He'd stand under another shower of it tonight in the fancy bathroom within his quarters. His skin was going to fall off, while he was behaving better than any of them had a right to expect.

Damnation, he couldn't get everything looking straight if he had a six-way mirror. Perhaps he could find Patsy—she'd help him if she was finished with Olana's hair.

"This is impossible! I look quite lopsided!"

"Beg pardon, miss—"

"Start again, and do hurry, or Mother will be—ow!"

He entered the room as Olana whirled, snatched the brush from Patsy's hands, and struck her hard across the knuckles.

He came between them, yanking the brush from her grip. "Go on downstairs," his gentle voice directed the maid. "Rest a little while."

"What—" Olana began.

"Go on," he urged again. The maid made a confused curtsy to them both, and hurried out the door.

His stance starched. "You know she's been sick," he said.

"Sick? Only lovesick, because the footman left us. Her first duty is to me! She pulled my hair, Matthew," she said, a soft pout forming in her voice and under her lip.

"Damnation," he muttered, staring at the pearl handled brush.

"You are not to blaspheme!"

He threw her weapon on the dressing table. "Go on, stick that pole up your back now! But you know better than to—"

"That clumsy girl is lucky she's not let go."

"She's already been let go by that bastard."

"Matthew!"

He took her arm, lifting her from her chair. "Her feelings matter, 'Lana! She's part of your household, even if she ain't in your damned social circle!"

What was he doing, putting fear in her eyes again? He let go of her, realizing for the first time that her arms were bare, that she had very few clothes on at all. He'd done something wrong, even being there. He hadn't knocked when he'd heard Patsy's cry. Then he'd used language he swore himself off while he was in her father's house. He looked at her arm. Soft, white, glowing in the electric light. No marks. At least he wasn't a hypocrite, he hadn't hurt her in his rage over her treatment of her maid. But he'd put the fear back in her eyes. Mr. Parker had asked too much of him.

Matthew turned and walked from her rooms, kept walking as she called out, fiercely demanding his return. He'd gotten down the stairs, but had not found a door to get him outside before her father had his arm, was leading him into the men's parlor.

"I've taken to bringing Matthew up to the camps now that Olana is doing so splendidly," he announced to the familiar circle.

Sidney Lunt, lounging in his white pique waistcoat and formal black, grinned. "Capital idea, sir! Our ranger was growing pale as a hothouse flower away from his wilderness. How do our redwoods compare to your sequoias, Matt?"

"They have a similar, mammoth beauty—"

Darius Moore laughed, too loudly for this early in the evening. "Have a care, Mr. Whittaker, or another servant will be lost!"

"Matt's not a servant, and do not compare him to my footman in any case! He has not taken a marriage gift to set himself up in an automobile venture and then jilted his bride!"

"You must admire the man's ingenuity, sir! They say his little shop is the stable of the future—"

James Whittaker frowned. "Matt's got some interesting ideas about the timber business and its future as well!"

"I wouldn't wonder if they were revolutionary." Darius Moore raised his glass in Matthew's direction, pointing. But it was not liquor that had those black eyes looking pupiless, had sent his rigid manners slightly careless. Darius Moore smiled, an unnatural act for him, so unnatural it appeared . . . what? Crazed? "I do hope he's not convinced you to create a parkland of the new mill site. The Japanese market is quite taken with the possibilities of expanded trade."

"You were able to discuss our trading venture today?" James Whittaker turned to Moore as his hand finally left the ranger's shoulder.

"Better still, Mrs. Whittaker and I took the liberty of inviting him here this evening."

This was his chance to slip away. But Matthew's eyes lingered on the perfectly dressed man. His sense of danger heightened, like it did sometimes in the woods. What was wrong with him? Get out, now, while the conversation shifted to business. Only Sidney Lunt still appeared interested in his presence. Damnation, what wasn't on straight? He didn't care anymore. He slipped through the doorway as the new guest arrived on Mrs. Whittaker's arm—a small, Asian man with a red diplomatic sash and white gloves. Matthew Hart went through the dining room doorway and on into the night.

"Olana!" her father summoned. "Surely he's out in the solarium?"

"No, Papa."

"Well, ladies and gentlemen, if my daughter can't find our ranger, he is not in the house. I'm afraid we're left bereft of lively debate!"

"Nonsense. I shall be Mr. Hart's proxy."

She swept her skirts aside and sat, tugging at her choker of lace and garnets as if it were a stiff collar, drawing a muted guffaw from Sidney. Encouraged, she lowered the pitch of her voice dramatically.

"Now, Mr. Whittaker, are you aware that your company routinely destroys half to seven-eighths of each tree it cuts through wasteful lumbering?"

"Olana!"

"Hart, sir," she lowered her voice further. "The name is Hart."

The air was damp, heavy. Was it ever different in this blasted city? Matthew kept walking. James Whittaker's guests admired the jilting footman's enterprise. Mrs. Whittaker labored tirelessly for poor people a continent away, yet at best would demand Patsy give up her child. Even Olana was whacking knuckles. What kind of people were they? He wanted no more of them tonight.

He knew where he was, thanks to Sidney. And he liked the long distance sight of the city's lights. He'd trudge up the summit of

Russian Hill, then climb Nob and Telegraph Hills. That should wear his anger away.

But Matthew realized the streetlights were fewer, more of them broken on the eastern slope of Nob Hill. And the night fog almost obscured the buildings. He'd left the exclusive mansions, gardens, lawns. That scent—exotic, spiced, dangerous. The only white men on the streets were the ones stumbling in an opium haze. He was in Chinatown. So close to the place that called, mocking him, since that first night. Daring him to return to that other side of this guilded city. He turned northeast, toward the waterfront. Could he find the place? Was it still there?

Yes. It appeared, as it had that night a lifetime ago, out of the fog, the briny scent of the sea. The clapboard was the same worn gray, the swinging sign still creaked on rusted hinges. But where once a three-breasted mermaid beckoned, a clipper ship sailed over freshly painted waves. Men in tattered wool coats brushed past him, entered. There was new leaded glass in the transom over the doors. Don't. He had no business here. What did he think he was doing? He stopped thinking. He entered.

It was so silent, out of the salt wind. Matthew's eyes stung from the smoke, the oil lamps. The place was half full. He scanned the faces that regarded him, but avoided the tables, the same tables, now more deeply carved by sailors who couldn't stop whittling, even when ashore. He approached the bar.

"Looking for someone?" the proprietor asked.

Yes, he realized. Himself. "Whiskey," he said. The man looked somehow relieved at the word. He put down the glass he was wiping, filled it. He left the bottle. Matthew Hart stared at it. His empty stomach heaved.

"You going to drink that?" the bartender demanded.

Matthew raised the glass, sent the whiskey down his throat.

The proprietor smiled. "Well, you're not one of them rug biting temperance preachers then, are you?" he said, loud enough for his table patrons to ease their lovers' grips on their drinks. He poured Matthew's glass full again. The men went back to their conversations.

Damnation, taken for a temperance preacher, about to break up the place. Was he getting that single minded? He'd have to tell

Annie when he got home, to make her laugh. A smile played around his mouth, before he caught a glance of a sealskin coat. It was inhabited by a man talking to a dull-eyed boy. Christ. That voice. McPeal.

"We'll clear your debts first, tomorrow morning. Then you'll be free, lad, free for the adventure of your life!"

"The crossing to New York were no adventure, sir." The boy's head bobbed as the man refilled his glass.

"Steerage? Packed with immigrants? Not this ship. Wait until you see her outfitted for the Pacific—the balmy Pacific of exotic paradise. You like women?"

"Aye."

"The island girls, they give it away for free. And the things they know, and the way they serve!"

A faint smile slouched its way across the boy's mouth, even as his eyes were closing. The man's hand emerged from the too long sealskin sleeves. It slipped the document under the boy's chin, the pen into his hand. "There, make your mark."

McPeal's victim found the pen on his second cast for it, but his signature went askew with the pressure of Matthew Hart's hand. The boy looked up, smiled a greeting before his eyes went back into his head, which in turn fell into his arms.

"Still using laudanum and lies on your prey?" Matthew asked the spike-toothed man quietly.

McPeal's eyes squinted into pinpricks. "You'll regret that, brother." He kicked back the chair. A knife appeared, as in a magician's trick, down his overlong sleeve, into his left hand. His first cut sliced open Matthew's linen shirt, freeing the smell of starch but not blood. His second stabbed the air. The third changed direction to lateral. Matthew raised his forearm to protect his heart. He felt one sharp cut, then another. Stop. Matthew grabbed his wrist, twisted, shook. The knife fell to the floor.

The man staggered back. A hand emerged from his remaining sleeve. No. Not a hand. Blunt, cold iron. Something new in his arsenal. A blow from it glanced Matthew's head. The second struck his middle, sending him into the wall, driving the breath from his lungs, the strength from his legs. He heard distorted voices as the pounding continued, but listened only to the frightened fifteen-year-old one inside him pleading, "don't fall."

He thought of the bear, whose face was benevolent compared with McPeal's. Then he laughed. McPeal stopped his iron assault. He stared, his eyes steady, remembering. With his good hand, the ranger clenched the hand that blood was invading. Together they cut under the chin, then across his attacker's jaw.

McPeal staggered. Then he fell to the floorboards.

A giant with the bald head and face of a baby took his place. "Catch him, Serif," someone urged, "before Mr. Hart hits the skids atop his vanquished." The room dimmed around Sidney Lunt, resplendent in his red silk lined opera cape. Safety. The boy inside Matthew Hart finally gave him permission to fall.

Matthew sat, slouched, in the hard-back chair, eyes closed. But he sensed Sidney Lunt at his elbow, and the drugged boy sleeping in the bunk against the wall.

The proprietor came in with his lamp. Matthew stared into its light. "My pupils. Did they get smaller?" he asked softly.

"Easy to see, in eyes light as yours—yes, sir."

"Is that good, Matt?" Sidney Lunt asked.

"Yes."

"No concussion," the proprietor explained.

Matthew closed his eyes again, the pain behind them lessening with the news. "Could I have a drink?" he asked.

"Bottle's at your elbow, sir. Along with clean bandages. I threw McPeal out for his pack to fetch and carry. I don't allow such dealings in here, not since I took over. Bricked up the passage to the tunnel, too."

Matthew remembered being dragged through a network of tunnels before they reached the *Madeline*. He'd thought them nightmares. "Oh? Good," he said.

"What are you two talking about?" Sidney asked.

"Old times," Matthew told him.

The proprietor put out his hand. Sidney Lunt took it. "Ben Morris, at your service, gentlemen. That is, if you're not police sent by City Hall dealers, or looking to open a French Restaurant."

"Now I'm lost," Matthew muttered.

"Bribery or prostitution. Neither," Sidney answered for them.

"All right, then. The boy's got my protection for the night. I appreciate the help in getting the message to McPeal and his kind, even if you fellows are of the cloth."

The door closed quietly behind him. "Of the—"

"It's the black," Matthew said.

"Well, I'm damned!" Sidney Lunt laughed as he poured Matthew's glass full. "Why didn't you tell me your plans before you absconded from that deadly dinner, Matt? The Barbary Coast's not a place to go alone, not even for you."

Matthew swallowed past his pain. A long way past, he realized, coughing. He squinted at the bottle in the editor's hand. "Christ almighty, what is that?"

Sidney brought the bottle closer. That only blurred the label further. "It's St. Croix rum. The best, one hundred fifty proof. You must have done our Mr. Morris a favor all right." He refilled the glass. "There, it's helping already, isn't it?"

"Yes." Matthew wasn't sure if he felt less, or just cared about it less. He looked past the editor, to the sleeping boy. He cared about the boy. "Sidney, what was happening to him, is that something you and Olana could write up? In your newspaper? Would that help stop it?"

"If we can get him to talk to us."

"Olana could. There's a story for her. Isn't it?"

"I'll leave word to have the boy come around in the morning."

"To 'Lana's place. Her story."

"Hers! On my honor! Can we take your damned coat off now?"

"What? Oh . . ." Matthew looked down at his bloody hand. Then he squinted up at Sidney Lunt, who was now two-headed. No. The giant was back. "Who are you?" he whispered.

"Serif the Magnificent."

"I know. But who are you?"

Sidney laughed. "That *is* his name, Matt. He used to wrestle Nile crocodiles for Mr. Barnum's circus. I bought off his contract when I went into the newspaper business," he continued, as they worked Matthew out of his coat. "He's the perfect companion for the Barbary Coast. Wish I could bring him into boardrooms. Matt, your arm's still bleeding."

Olana's editor's face was tinged green. Following his glance,

Matthew inspected the wounds. "Almost stopped. Pour a little rum on it, will you, Sidney?"

"Rum?"

"You said it was good."

"To drink!"

"Have one first, then." He smiled, remembering when he told Olana the same thing.

Her editor laughed. "You're a good drunk, Matt."

"Ain't nowhere near drunk! Pour that damned rum, will you, before I bleed to death?"

The color had now drained completely from Lunt's face, but he did as he was told.

"It's not bad," the ranger tried to reassure him, as he cleaned the slashes with the gauze Ben Morris had left. "See? Two wounds, both superf—supflufic—"

"Superficial?"

"I can say that!" he insisted. Too loud. The tingling in his fingers warned him before the room went black. When it came into focus again Sidney was pressing the gauze to the worst slash, and Matthew was lying like a child in the giant's arms.

"You pay him well?" he heard himself whisper.

"Much better than the circus."

"Good."

Sidney lifted the patch of white and red. Clotted. Serif wound the gauze around his arm. Sidney poured another drink. Matthew swallowed it down. "Next time out, the three of us—yes, Serif? The three musket . . . mouseket . . . Shit, I *am* drunk. Can you get me home, Sidney? 'Lana's going to want my head on a platter."

Olana tried to sleep, but once she heard the gentle tinkling of three chimes from her bedroom's silver clock, she was sure that Matthew had caught a late train back to his trees. She thought of her father, grateful for the entertaining diversion she had been at dinner. But she hadn't felt deserving of his gratitude, for it was her temper at Patsy that had driven Matthew away.

Once the house was quiet Olana rose from her bed, and went to the solarium, where she almost tripped over Matthew, crumpled beneath the sassafras tree. She went to her knees. When she tried to remove the rum bottle cradled in his arms, his eyes shot open.

"Here, goddamn it, I want to stay here! Oh . . ." A wide, slow grin replaced his scowl. "Morning, 'Lana. You smell like lilies this morning."

"And you smell like—"

He spit into the carefully manicured ground. "Didn't bother me none, even when you smelled like death, woman! Always liked you fine just the same!"

Olana saw blood stains. "Matthew," she whispered, "you're hurt."

He only looked annoyed. "Don't fret none on my account." When he put his head back against the tree, she winced at the purple bruise above his eye. "I like it here. I'm staying here," he insisted. "I can see the stars, up through the roof, can you?"

"Yes," she said, probing his side with cold fingers. He smiled at her touch. How could he smile?

"I went back, 'Lana."

"Back where?"

"The place where they left me, when I was a boy. Left me to be preyed upon. They were my kin! What had I ever done to them?"

"Nothing, darling," Olana found herself saying, though she wanted to run away from his sudden, helpless shuddering, from the tears streaking down his face. He buried his head at her waist, fisting the folds of her gown with one hand. Olana stroked around the bruise until his breathing became regular again.

"Gran, when I could finally tell her, she made me into Joseph of old, being sold into slavery by brothers . . . making me the hero of my own life. Again."

"You are, Matthew."

"No. But I had to go back. And there was another boy there, sure enough, and I couldn't let it happen again. Shit," he raised his head, looked around, perplexed. "What did I do with that boy?"

"Boy?"

"Wait. I remember. Mr. Morris's got him. Till tomorrow. What happens then? What am I supposed to do with him? I can't even look after myself."

"I'll look after you tonight," she offered quietly. Olana put his good arm around her shoulder. He stumbled to his feet and she led him unsteadily from the solarium.

He seemed blissfully unaware of the strain he was on her, but she couldn't even work up an ounce of anger about that. "Say 'Lana, you ever meet that crocodile man?" he asked.

"Let's try another set of steps now."

"He works for Sidney—"

"Sidney Lunt?"

"Sure Sidney Lunt! Hey, who's drunk here, you or me?"

"Matthew Hart!"

She stopped, eased her hold on him to push the hair out of her eyes. He slipped out of her grasp. "Matthew!"

He drifted precariously over the landing before she caught him again. She wanted to cry out her relief, but rested her head against his chest instead. He tucked his precious bottle under his arm then stroked the sweat from her brow.

"It's been so hard to keep my hands off you, 'Lana. I got to take on the waterfront lately."

His knees began to buckle. "Oh, Matthew," she pleaded, "Not yet—we're almost there."

"Where?"

"Your rooms."

"Circle. Under the doorknob," he mumbled.

"Yes, I know." She pushed open the door.

She heaved him onto the bed, took his shoes off.

" 'Lana, what are you—don't do that," he pleaded. "I won't be able to look at you come tomorrow."

"Oh hush, you great baby," she admonished. "And you'd better look at me come morning, Matthew Hart, and be prepared to tell me of this crocodile man when you're fully sober!"

His eyelids flickered. "Yes'm," he promised.

Once she'd unbuttoned the braces, his trousers came off easily. Olana only allowed herself a brief glance at those long legs and hard muscled thighs. She felt her cheeks flame, and quickly covered him.

She found his nightshirt and gently replaced the bloodied remains of slashed coat and shirt with its soft comfort. It was easy, he was so supple and barely conscious. Only his iron grip on the rum bottle remained firm. She leaned him back into the pillows, easing the bottle from his arms. A tiny amount of its amber liquid had survived. She smiled, placing it on the bedside table, then kissed his mouth while it still had life.

"Damnation," he muttered.

"Good night, Matthew."

"Good night, 'Laney."

She closed in on his face again. "What did you say? Matthew, what did you call me? Who told you that name? Mrs. Cole? Was it Mrs. Cole?"

"Cold?" he murmured, then winced as he tried to lift the covers with his injured arm.

"No, darling, I'm not cold," she said, but slid in beside him anyway, silently thanking whoever dressed his wounds. She nested herself in the crook of his undamaged arm, listening to the strong, steady beat of his heart. Then she thought she heard another, faint heartbeat. She sat up, looked into the parts of the room in darkness. What was that? The clack of steel wheels? She thought of her brother, his trains, his love. And of Matthew Hart, his relatives and their cruelty. She slipped out of the massive bed.

Ghosts. They'd shared their ghosts tonight, Olana thought as she closed the nursery door behind her. She was startled by the sight of Patsy coming around the corner.

"Miss Olana?"

"No. I mean, you didn't see me. Here. Now."

The maid smiled, trying to hide her teeth. "He's come home?"

"Yes."

"That's good. Good night then, miss."

"Patsy?"

"Miss?"

"Mr. Hart and I—we didn't. I mean, it wasn't . . . as it appears."

"I wouldn't tell on you, either way."

Then Olana did a thing she hadn't done since her nurse left the household. She hugged a servant.

eleven

Matthew Hart opened one eye to a gelatinous mass that didn't look any more appetizing for the fine-cut crystal glass that contained it. He groaned. Mrs. Cole poured drops of the rum into her concoction.

"Lastly, a small amount of the offending brew, which, I see, is all that's left, Matthew."

He closed the eye and groaned again. Her hand cupped the back of his head. She held the glass to his lips. "Drink it all in one swallow if you can, sir, before your head leaves the pillow."

He managed in three swallows, which still seemed to please her. It tasted vile, but in seconds the soreness of his ribs was dominating the churning in his stomach and pain in his head.

"Better?" she asked softly.

"Miraculous." It was his own voice—submerged, but sober.

The woman smiled. "I've written up the remedy's ingredients for your book, in my best hand."

"Thank you." Matthew rolled to his good side and squinted toward the slit in the heavy drapes.

"What hour is it?"

"Just past nine."

"Nine?"

He sat up, yanked the covers aside, but the cook held her hand against his chest. "Miss Olana says you need some care," she said, deftly gathering his nightshirt as if she'd done it every day of his life. Matthew didn't even remember putting the shirt on. It smelled of lilies. Olana. "She's been downstairs all morning," the cook continued, "tearing sheets right alongside the rest of us so I can bind—Sweet Bridget, you look like someone took a mallet to you, sir!"

The ugly bruises brought the night's events through Matthew's mind in jumbled succession.

"Mrs. Cole, did a boy come by? Named Seely, or Seldon or—"

"Selby, sir. Here since first light, yes. Olana's been keeping his presence a secret like the rest of us. Never thought she'd do that, after you deserted her parents' dinner party last night. Do sit back, Matthew, she says I'm to take no grousing from you."

He gave himself over to her care, the way he had for the claw marks on his back. "If this keeps up, I'll owe you my fee, Mrs. Cole," he managed to gasp out as she wound the swaddling cloth.

"Nonsense. That boy's saying you got damaged in his defense. Poor lamb, he's just eighteen, lost his mother to pneumonia, then preyed on by those waterfront jackals."

She wiped his forehead with her apron, and discovered the effect of McPeal's first iron strike. "Glory be, a goose egg on your comely face as well? The vipers! You are a fine man, Mr. Hart."

"I'm a drunken idiot, Mrs. Cole. But you have a favorable impression of the boy?"

"Oh, he's so eager to be showing you his worth! Wouldn't touch a morsel of food until he'd worked for it. Patsy's feeding him half the larder now! There's even some bloom back in her cheeks."

"Is there? Well. Maybe this wasn't such a fool idea." Matthew Hart smiled for the first time since he'd opened his eyes on the day.

He watched Olana pace the length of the servant's dining table as he sipped Mrs. Cole's strongest coffee.

"But, Matthew, where is this Selby boy from?"

"Ireland, I think."

"You think? And his references?"

"Listen, darlin', the folks down here are doting on him like a prodigal son. Your father's looking for someone to replace the footman, isn't he? And 'Lana, Patsy likes him."

Her fine brows arched. "And why is that so important?"

"Patsy needs someone. She and the footman—"

"Had been engaged two years! This boy walked in this morning. First impressions—"

"Are the best. Why, the first time I saw you, I thought you were the most beautiful—"

"Liar! Your trees already hold that place." She turned on her heel. "And I first thought you an ill-mannered boor."

He grinned. "There, see?"

"Matthew!" But she was smiling.

"You'll talk to your father?"

"Yes. Only do go away. Wait for Papa in the library. They will not understand why I'm not furious with you."

He studied her face. "Why aren't you?"

"I don't know. Last night you trusted me. Didn't you, Matthew?"

He slipped his fingers through hers and brought their clasped hands to his lips. But his eyes closed before he let her see the faint suspicion cross his mind, suspicion that she was looking to launch her journalistic career by turning what was left of his family to ashes.

"Matt!" James Whittaker greeted him with an outstretched hand. "My wife sends her regrets. One of her ill mornings."

Matthew Hart winced as Olana's father reached into his cigar box, hoping he wouldn't light up. He was having an ill morning himself.

"Olana tells me you have a prospect for my missing footman!"

"Yes, sir."

"An Irishman?"

"Yes."

"That won't win Mrs. Whittaker's favor. She's determined to Frenchify the whole staff, but she keeps getting the Irish. This isn't the East coast, I tell her, where she can pluck them out of French Canada. Has the lad experience?"

"No. But he means well, and is very hardworking, according to downstairs."

"Well then, let's give him a go." He discarded his cigar, sniffed at another. "Now, tell me why you deserted us last night?"

"I apologize—"

"Oh, save your apologies for the ladies, or shall I say for my wife, as you already seem back in Olana's good graces. You should have seen her playacting you last night! Most amusing, a convincing twin! Right down to that perplexed look before you say—"

"Sir?"

"Exactly!" James Whittaker roared out a laugh that reverberated inside the ranger's aching head. "How do you do it, Matt? Keep that daughter of mine sweet-dispositioned?"

"We have our moments."

"But they are just that—moments, not eternities of recriminations and demands."

"What can she demand of me?"

The cigar he'd been rolling stilled between James Whittaker's fingers. "So it's my wealth responsible for her difficult nature?"

"I didn't say that."

"Or is it how I use my money? Do I spoil her as I spoil land, as I waste your precious trees?"

"I never—"

"She did it for you last night—my own child, lecturing me."

"Mr. Whittaker—"

"I see how you look over the acres of stumps, how you cringe at the sight of the mills."

Shit. This wasn't fair. What had Olana started without even telling him? "It's more the sound. I'm not used to much noise, vibration. I mean no disrespect."

"Disrespect be damned! What would you do with my land?"

Matthew met the man's direct gaze with one of his own. Think first, then speak calmly, he reminded himself, wishing for the life of him that he'd gone easier on the rum. "I wouldn't harvest every tree, Mr. Whittaker. That would reduce the risk of flooding, of losing the topsoil. And where I cut, I'd plant."

"Plant what?"

"More trees."

"You'd have me bankrupt in a year's time!"

Matthew grinned, despite the pain it caused. "No, I wouldn't. You'd never trust me with such a hare-brained scheme to begin with."

"Damned right! Damned—" James Whittaker hooked his thumbs in his vest, and laughed. "I don't believe I want to knock any business sense into you, son. You're a great relief from the likes of that stiff-necked Moore, no matter what new markets he's opening up." He bit off the end of still another cigar. "And who, while you were out breaking skulls up and down the Barbary Coast, asked me for permission to court Olana."

"Oh?" Matthew Hart felt the cloth around his middle tightening.

"Surprised?"

"Yes."

"Do you think it would prove a good match?"

"It's not my decision."

"I know that, son! I'm asking your opinion, advice."

"No, then."

"And why not?"

"I don't think Moore likes women." James Whittaker leaned toward him, looking baffled. "And 'Lana shocks him." More. More reasons. Think. That one was no good, it'd made him smile.

"My daughter shocks everyone, Matt. I'm afraid that has limited her prospective marriage partners. Even her . . . adventure with you has tarnished her in the sights of some."

"Those that ain't worthy of her consideration, sir."

"Perhaps. But the world is not as . . . uncomplicated for her as it is for you, son."

Why? Why in hell not? Matthew wanted to shake the man. They weren't talking about trees and timber. They were talking about Olana. She wasn't one of his holdings, part of his complicated business.

"Perhaps Olana's trying to be the son we lost," James Whittaker continued. "Why doesn't she understand she's ruining her chances?"

"Chances of what?"

"Providing me a grandson, of course. A male heir to carry on!"

"Carry what on?"

"The family, the business. That's her place, of course, if she truly means to please us. Even an obstinate, free-thinking girl like Olana must calm down, put away silly notions and take joy in her home and family."

"And give you an heir."

"Is that so terrible?"

"No. If it's her choice too. If she's happy."

"Choice? There is no choice!"

"You don't think Olana has her own mind?"

"Of course, of course she does. It must be guided, that's all." He laughed uneasily. "You make me sound the complete tyrant, Matt! This match has advantages. Moore manages all of Mrs. Whittaker's charitable trusts without taking a penny in salary! He's a seasoned traveler—has sold the products of my mills the country over. Soon it may be the world over. Grateful buyers have provided the specimens you dote on in the solarium.

"Now, as to Olana's attraction to him, or her lack of it—I'm not insensitive that every young girl has a heart's desire in these matters. But I can't put him off forever, can I? Especially now that her independent notions and behavior have parlayed her into a tightening circle of prospects, despite the dowry she brings to—"

"Damnation! Why does it always come down to money?"

His shout hurt his bruised muscle wall so much he clutched inside his vest. James Whittaker watched him in the deafening silence.

"And what should it come down to, Matt?" he asked quietly as his wife entered the room.

"Ma'am," Matthew whispered, reaching for the brim of a hat that wasn't there. As he closed the door behind him, he heard her scandalized tone.

"James, what on earth—"

"Ha!" her husband trumpeted, "I finally found a subject that fires out Mr. Hart to undisguised anger, madame!"

Matthew Hart let his hand drift inside linen, press cool against his aching ribs. He looked around the servant's parlor. Both Olana and Sidney Lunt waited patiently. But he couldn't get his mind past the conversation with her father. Did she know Moore wanted her? Olana had more in common with Sidney Lunt than Darius Moore. They were closer in age, too. And, hell, he liked Sidney. Why doesn't she marry him, if it's so all fired important? He'd never hurt her, she'd be safe with him. The boy standing between them shifted feet. Seldon? Selby. Matthew felt too much the hypocrite to be as stern as he'd planned.

"If we can clear your debts, get you started in the position for a trial period—"

"There won't be any end to my thanks, master."

"I ain't your master. And what I did last night was for me, you understand?"

"No, sir."

He exhaled, then felt Olana's hand cover his, forgetting her usual decorum before the servants, before her editor. Something had changed since he'd come to San Francisco. She'd become his friend. She mattered, beyond their diverse backgrounds, beyond the beliefs wedging them apart. He would always care what happened to her. And Darius Moore must not happen to her. Damn. It was still not his business. Why had he shouted like a madman at her father? Could Olana be pressured? No. She would never marry Darius Moore. She had too much sense. That should be contenting him.

He cleared his throat. "You're to talk with Miss Whittaker, Selby. About what you know of the waterfront. Especially those men like McPeal who the ships hire to shanghai folks like you. Which ships still do business that way. Who owns them." He tilted his head toward Lunt. "What else, Sidney?"

"When."

"Yes. When they do their dealings. And where they meet, is that right, 'Lana?"

She nodded. He liked the fire in her eyes. But the boy looked from him to Sidney, finally settling on him as the less mad, Matthew Hart surmised. "But Miss Whittaker—she's a lady."

"She's a lady with a mission, Selby. You want to help her and Mr. Lunt and their newspaper to put an end to what almost happened to you?"

"I do, sir."

"Answer their questions. I'm going back to bed."

Sidney Lunt caught up before he'd reached the first landing of the backstairs. "Matt. You're not angry, are you?"

"About what?"

"Me. You know, following you down there—"

"Scraping me off the floor?"

"You never hit the floor. And Serif did that."

"He was real then, the crocodile man?"

Sidney Lunt laughed. "Real? Yes!"

"Introduce him to 'Lana, will you? She thinks I cracked my head harder than I did. And thanks. You two and that deadly rum allowed me to annihilate the effects of my foolishness."

"That foolishness was calculated, not born of any whim to raise hell instead of swallow Salmon Victoria all night."

The ranger's eyes went cold. "So?"

"So tell me how some backwoods forest ranger knows Wharfside Inn, then walks into an innocent being shanghaied? How did you know where to hit McPeal? That he had a glass jaw?"

"That's not your story."

"It's a hell of a story, though, Matt. I smell it."

The ranger stood. "Do something useful, will you, Sidney? I thought that's what you wanted for your damned paper."

Matthew Hart waved off his following steps. But when trudged up to the next landing Sidney Lunt was still at his heels.

"Here," he said, putting the morning edition of the Gold Coast Chronicle in Matthew's hands. It was folded over on the editorial page. Matthew pulled his spectacles from his pocket, eased down on the step, and read.

"I was at the paper at three A.M. to get it into the morning edition." Sidney waited, pacing. "What do you think?"

Matthew raised his head slowly. "Mr. Parker says there's not a newspaper in California brave enough to take a stand like this—"

"Bravery be damned! It's bound to sell papers! So there you have it. Olana's got her start."

"Olana? I thought you said you—"

"Look at the byline."

"Who in hell is O. Lanart?"

"That's precisely what I hope all of San Francisco is wondering this morning! When you didn't take your place at table last night, and her mother was about to put her next to Moore, Olana took your seat. She became you, Matt. Hence her *nom de plume*. They are your ideas, but they've gone through her, you see? It came out of her in a way that puts a whole new slant on the debate! Most stimulating!"

"She wouldn't sit beside Moore?"

"Matt, I want you to encourage her to keep up that fine-edged anger, that challenge to their very masculinity!"

"Masculinity?"

"Yes! That's her angle! Oh you should have heard her last night! And the old fools were so taken with her rendition of you that they paid no heed at all at the insults she was hurling! They'll be storming about my new essayist without ever connecting O. Lanart to James Whittaker's amusing daughter."

"Appears I missed more than Salmon Victoria."

"Well, you were out dredging up waterfront scandal."

"I'll get you for leaving my carcass out in plain sight," Matthew promised.

Sidney laughed. "We couldn't budge you from under that damned sassafras tree!"

The ranger sighed. "Sit down, Sidney," he said. Matthew watched the delight enter the man's eyes as he took a place by his side. Why? Damned if everyone in this house wasn't doing strange things lately. 'Lana's editor, whom he didn't think could be still long enough to take in a sunset along the Pacific, was perched on the backstairs beside him, not displaying his wit, but listening.

" 'Lana's got a place there now, at your newspaper?"

"Hell, yes!"

"Good."

Matthew Hart put his hands on his knees to rise, but knew the pain inside his head would stay there unless he opened the subject somehow, with someone.

"Sidney, you've known 'Lana a long time, haven't you?"

"Since we were children."

"And you came after her, out there in the cold I mean. And before that, you visited her clear across the Atlantic, didn't you?"

"Well, yes."

"So you're fond of her."

"Matt—"

"I'll be going away from here come Christmas. You'll look after her, won't you? I mean, steer her away from bad decisions and such?"

"We're not talking about trees or the Barbary Coast anymore."

"No."

"Damn. How is it you know before I do? Dora's won, hasn't she? The old man's given Moore permission to court Olana."

"Yes."

"Probably part of a package."

"What?"

"Keeping you on till the end's part of the arrangement, and hiring Selby. Maybe letting Olana pretend she's a writer, too. Until the wedding divests her of all her silly notions."

The ranger put his head in his hands. He'd contributed to Olana's predicament? "Damnation, Sidney, what's going on in this house?"

He felt the editor's hand on his hair. The gentleness of the gesture startled him. When he lifted his head, Lunt was smiling his usual cynical smile, relieved by a touch of sadness.

"Layers, Matt. It's the layers you're not used to. I don't think she'll have him, do you?"

"No. But if she should come to you, for advice—"

"Done, my friend."

The men rose, shaking hands. Sidney Lunt was shaking his head too. "Damned if you two don't look after one another, as you say, too. But you'll drive me out of business, between your reticence and her daring."

"Daring?"

"This story. It could lead us all into some very hot water."

"How?"

"Matt, the Barbary Coast has been flourishing since the Spanish trading days. And the middlemen like McPeal are the dangerous ones. They stand between petty criminals and their contacts. Those contacts are sometimes among the most powerful men in San Francisco. And the city government looks the other way."

"Wouldn't the city want it stopped?"

"If there's money to be made?"

"What? How?"

"Graft? Corruption? Bribes? Ah, you are an innocent about some realities. Go. Get your rest. We'll talk about it tomorrow."

twelve

"Sidney, how can you think in here?"

"What?"

"The noise!"

"Oh, yes. Invigorating, isn't it? Watch your step Olana, there's a missing floorboard."

Matthew steered her around the hole. "If I couldn't dance come Christmas due to my being here, Papa would—" She didn't bother to finish. Sidney was already out of hearing, and pulling a disheveled man with a huge red mustache over to them.

"Matt, Olana, you must meet Alisdair Dodge—best shutter in the city!"

Matthew Hart put out his hand. "Shutter?"

"Photographer," Alisdair explained. Olana could barely tolerate the burnt and chemical smell emanating from his clothes. It was worse than the cigar smoke, the printer's ink, and turpentine scents that pervaded the entire *Chronicle* building. Matthew Hart seemed less bothered by this or the large room's continual uproar as Sidney sent them off to the photographer's darkroom. He steered her into his office. There, at least, it was quiet.

"Tea?" he asked her.

"That would be marvelous."

He sprang to a door and knocked twice, poking his head inside. "Three for tea, Serif, there's a good fellow."

Olana stared in wonder when the mammoth servant arrived. Matthew, she realized, wasn't inebriated enough to misrepresent this giant.

"Does he speak, Sidney?" she asked, her eyes following the tray with what looked like a doll's tea service in the massive hands.

"Not much. But he understands every other form of communication—from the whines of the building's cats to the rumbling presses."

She smiled. "And he does tea?"

The giant took the linen napkin from the tray and artfully placed it in her lap. "Oh, do excuse me, Serif. I mean you do tea, very well. I'm sure this will settle me nicely."

When he bowed, Olana saw a tiny tuft of braided hair sprouting up from the top of his head. He left the room noiselessly.

"He sees me as a bit of a savior," Sidney Lunt explained as he poured her cup. "Never liked circus work—the thing he was born into. We understand each other that way."

"Whatever do you mean?"

"Olana. You and I—we go back a long time together. Thousands of garden parties. When my parents bought me the *Chronicle* they thought it was a whim, like the dozens of projects I'd started, never completed over my life. They'd buy it, loose a few thousand, I'd move on, and we'd all be closer to the time I'd settle down, take on the life of a gentleman. I was born into leisure, like you, and as sure as Serif was born into the circus. My parents, the dear old bores, expected me to stay inside my class. But the paper's teaching me daily how much else there is! And I think someone is performing that feat with you now."

Olana longed to talk about her feelings for Matthew Hart. Sidney would be a perfect confidant, if she could trust him. Was Sidney inviting himself into that position, or still looking for her wild man's story?

"Why did you send Matthew off like that?"

"I merely took advantage of his enthusiasm. I want to talk with you about your work here."

"Oh?"

She sipped at her tea. Olana didn't want to do this part without Matthew. The notes from her interview with Selby were in her lap. Now he'd abandoned her. And Sidney was speaking too gently. She knew something unpleasant was coming.

"Olana, I wish you'd take time. To develop your editorials. You need to acquaint yourself with the preservationists, conservationists, Sierra Club, history, plants and animals indigenous to California. Matt can help Alisdair identify, photograph the giant trees north of the city. Your pieces will be illustrated from life, from the best photographer in the city. Matt can help you, too. Isn't he always hauling around plants from your father's—"

"Now I must write to please him?"

"No. But you can't cut your teeth on a story of waterfront corruption, woman! Reconsider."

"Matthew thinks I can do it."

"Your bear fighter is an innocent in the ways of men. And of this city. It almost cost him his life the other night. He doesn't understand where it could lead."

"And you do?"

"I have some notions." He took her hand. "Olana, Serif is a splendid bodyguard. But he can't look after us all."

"Who in heaven's name is asking him to?"

"Heaven might be our only protection, you silly girl!" He rose abruptly and began pacing the length of the small office.

Olana made her chin stop quivering, made herself stop thinking *not you, Sidney, not you too.* She stretched her arm along the dusty sofa's back. "I realize you have to flair dramatic for your readers, but surely we're talking about common criminals, not a beast—"

"We're talking about a many-headed beast, Olana. And an instigator who will be taking his leave back to a simpler world soon."

She stood, adjusted her hat. "Sidney, if you haven't the courage to pursue this, perhaps the *Sun* or the *Times* will."

Matthew Hart and the photographer bounded into her as she reached the door. Olana could see the pandemonium of the main room reflected in Matthew's spectacles. And now both men smelled horrid.

" 'Lana, Alisdair's taken photographs of animals at night, in flight! And Chinatown, on festival days! You've got to see—"

"I don't have to do anything!" she snapped, then strode past him. He didn't catch up until she was outside the building, and had her hand on the carriage's door.

"Hey, 'Lana," he urged. "Let's walk. The sun's out. You know what a miracle that is in this city." He waited. "All right?" She nodded, waved off the carriage then let Matthew guide her through streets swollen with people. Even strides, slowed for her benefit. She didn't look up until she realized there was green around them, and the street noises were in the distance. He had found Golden Gate Park.

His pace slowed further on a walk lined with trees. "A bad start? With Sidney?"

"He took the Barbary Coast story away from me."

"What? After he told me—"

"You don't have to bully me into my assignments, Mr. Hart!"

"Aw, 'Lana, I only just—"

"I'd prefer you didn't."

"Oh. All right, then." His voice softened. "What are you going to do now?"

"Walk."

"Good."

They did.

" 'Lana," he finally said, "I'd like to think breaking a few jaws would cure the waterfront, but Sidney knows better."

"Then why doesn't he want to use his knowledge to stop what almost happened to Selby? What did happen to you years ago?"

Olana saw a vein appear, ugly and distorted around the bruise on the side of his head. He stared down the walkway that led to the Mechanics' Building. "Did I tell you about—that?" he whispered.

Olana was glad his eyes weren't on her. "Don't you remember?" she asked softly.

"Not real well, no."

"You said they took you on one of those ships, when you were a boy. Did they really, Matthew?"

"Yes." The vein in his head disappeared. "Sidney's your friend, 'Lana. He's looking out for you."

"Is that why he put that ridiculous name to an editorial I never even saw, never mind wrote!"

"Wasn't he writing down your dinner convers—"

"Was he looking out for me when he sent me to Sequoia? No! He was looking to keep me out of his hair, for as long as possible.

Like all the rest! Out of sight, unless I'm doing my duty, like a good little girl. For him in editorials, behind a name that's not mine, now that he's all on fire with your cause. For my father, who, if he ever found out—Oh, he'd forgive even that as long as I stay attractive to rich men who'd like the chance of getting richer!"

Olana picked up her skirts and ran, but he caught up with her under a bower of bare grapevines. He touched her back. She whirled on him. "Go ahead," she challenged him. "Tell me I'm wrong, spoiled, ungrateful!"

It was too public a place, but he didn't know that. And Olana didn't care, not once his arms were around her, his heated breath warming her. "You're not wrong."

She turned, touched his face. "Just spoiled and ungrateful?"

Instead of the teasing she expected, he closed his eyes and kissed into the palm of her hand. The shiver of delight rode up her arm, burst through the secret places he'd opened in his treehouse in the woods. His hands took her hips.

"I wish—" His eyes left her, followed a seabird's flight.

"What do you wish, Matthew?"

"That you were not your father's daughter. That I was not my mother's son. That there was nothing between us."

He lifted her hat netting and kissed her, there, under the bower, kissed her desperately, hungrily, as if she'd disappear. His hands searched for the end of her corset, searched for a part of her not reined in. Olana's breath quickened. She gulped great doses of the city, her father's cigars, the photographer's flashpots. Her thighs warmed, her breasts hardened, her knees became, suddenly, unreliable. She was lost in kisses that touched her temples, cheeks, lips, neck.

"Oh my darling, not here," she warned softly. He raised his head from her neck. They both saw the couples strolling on a parallel path.

The back entry to the Golden Dragon was dimly lit. Incense heavy with jasmine was winning the battle with urine and rendered grease of pressed duck as the dominant stench. As McPeal climbed the stairs, it was hard for him to listen for signs of danger because of the noisy, shuffling footsteps behind him. He hated doing business in Chinatown.

"Walk on your toes!"

"Don't have many, sir."

"What?"

"Lost seven between us, my brother and me, after the ranger took our boots. Ever been frostbit? It's fearsome pain."

McPeal shook his head. The choirboy had, indeed, grown up. Made enemies. They made his job much easier. "Wait here," he told Ezra Carson before he entered the room lit only by a bottle-green, glass-shaded oil lamp on the desk. His client, the man sitting behind the desk, was not lit at all. McPeal could barely see the white cuffs of his shirt.

"Mr. Hopkins? That you?"

"Sit."

McPeal did, smelling both profit and revenge, a rare and glorious combination. "I brought one of the brothers, sir."

"One?"

"The other's still nursing his injuries. I figured we could strike a better deal with the idiot, eh?"

"We?"

"Mr. Hopkins," McPeal said, "we are men of the world. You're working on one side of town to keep an honorable family honorable. I'm working on the other, seeing that the rabble stays in its place when it wants to make life unpleasant for you and yours. You're a middleman, same as me, right? So we should understand each other. We're both in noble, serving, and profitable positions."

The rolled wad thudded at McPeal's chest. He'd been shot at close range twice in his fifty-four years. The shock he felt now was close enough to those two instants to make him hate Hopkins. He'd remember that hatred, when the time was right. The projectile fell into his lap. Now was not the time, McPeal decided, as the fingers of his left hand felt the unmistakable texture of money.

"Let him in," the man behind the desk said.

McPeal rubbed the sore spot at his sternum with his iron stub. Then he rose, opened the door.

Ezra Carson stared into the darkness, mystified. "Where in hell are you?" he bellowed, blindly stumbling forward.

"Ah, Mr. Carson. Poacher, prospector, sheep herder, thief, whoreson, and general *persona non grata.*"

"Now, now, you got it backwards, Mr. . . . Mr. Hopkins! It's me come to do some name calling! Of that crazy ranger and his woman!"

"Woman?"

"The Whittaker woman, doing Hart's wash half naked, all cozy and snowed in! Now if Cal and me talk to the papers . . . the ones who didn't get her story of rescue and deliverance, about what really went on—"

"Shut up!"

McPeal smiled, leaned forward. Ah. A kinswoman, this woman who belonged to Hart? How mad was he over it? Enough to maim the lover, perhaps? Slowly? Still no hint of his client's features, but the tone of his anger was somehow familiar. Didn't he like young, virgin China girls, this Mr. Hopkins, when he was going under another name? They were often like this, these gentlemen. Hypocrites about the women inside their own class.

Hopkins recovered his icy calm. "Who would believe you?"

"You did," even the idiot brother observed. "Who is she? Your sister? Cousin? We got what's juicy enough for them papers she don't work for, Cal says. Don't have to hold up in court."

Remember, McPeal told himself, without his brother lording over him, this one did quite well.

The man in the shadows shifted in his chair. "What do you know of the park territory?" he asked.

"Know that place as good as any government man save Hart. Know one thing he don't, too. A winter passage. A back way, around Indian Falls, to Hart's altitude, to his station in that blamed tree. That's how we surprised the little missus at her wash. Few more minutes, we'd of—"

"So you could get in, once he's returned?"

"Not this winter! Even to break his neck and fuck the shit out of his woman both!"

The wooden chair his client sat in creaked. "I require only half of your proposal."

McPeal leaned more forward still. "The game is changing," he observed aloud.

"How much did you and your brother want to shut your story up?" Hopkins asked. Wait. This was going too fast, McPeal decided. He was the middleman. He'd do the asking.

Ezra looked around the still room. He took a deep breath. "Five hundred."

"I'll give you two thousand."

"What?"

"Now. Two more when it's done. Done my way."

McPeal scraped the side of his jaw slowly with his iron fist. "I don't think Mr. Hopkins is talking character assassination anymore, Ezra. How are you and your brother at the real kind? You can get to Hart when he's alone at his post. Can you kill him?"

"Kill? Needed to kill a couple women after—But that's women. Hart's . . . well, Hart's strong, and crafty-like. I don't know."

McPeal leaned toward the shadow of his client. He didn't want to lose him. And he wanted Hart. Badly. "Why not do it here, sir? I might take it on myself, as a special favor, to a valued customer? A repeating customer? One who likes interesting games with China girls?"

His client bristled. McPeal smiled. Yes, he never forgot a voice peaked in its rage.

"No. Not here. It must be at his post. An accident, happening because of his stupidity. You understand, McPeal. To ease her grief, the foolish girl. My cousin. She loves him, you see. Unfortunate. But nothing else will do."

"Consider it done, Mr. Hopkins, sir. Come on, Ezra."

"But, Cal didn't say—"

"Leave Cal to me. You did very well."

thirteen

Matthew pushed his spectacles up against his face and scanned the bottles in Mrs. Cole's top cupboard. Extract of vanilla. Might make the boy sick. Rum, there. No, that was just flavoring.

The cook tugged at his coattails. "Come down from there, Matthew!" she chided. "You'll get your finery mussed!"

He closed the cupboard's glass doors, then sat on the counter, his legs dangling, making her smile. She was thinking of Leland, Matthew realized. He used to invade her cupboards, too. He pulled off his spectacles.

"It's time for me to talk with Selby, Mrs. Cole. I'm looking for something alcoholic."

Her voice hushed reverently. "Would sherry do, sir?"

"Sure." He jumped to the floor.

"It's here, waiting for the fish." She set two glasses on the long table, and curtsied. Why is she doing that, he wondered. I thought we were friends. Must be the damned clothes, all choking, formal, black. He was weary of his betwixt position in the Whittaker household, neither a servant nor a guest, but something of both.

In a moment the new footman was standing at attention before him. Selby's time here had already done him some good. He had more heft, and was cleaner. The first was thanks to Mrs. Cole's cooking, the last his affection for 'Lana's maid. His face was open, innocent, freckled, though his hair was dark. Had he ever been that young?

"You married, Selby?"

The boy blanched red. "No, sir."

"And you've taken to Patsy?"

"Oh, aye."

"Were she to need a husband—say she were going to have a baby and the father ran off . . . are you that big a man? Could you care for her and another man's child?"

The new footman's eyes registered shock. Damn. Matthew didn't know any other way to say it, other than straight out. He was wondering if the boy could speak at all when he did.

"Wouldn't be his no more, would it, sir? Not if he gave a jewel like Patsy up. I'd be the daddy, wouldn't I then? Mr. Hart, is this all what if? I mean, is Patsy—"

The footman had so far exceeded what Matthew Hart would settle for, that he struggled to keep his face stern. "You'll do your courting after, you hear? You don't take her until she's ready, I don't care what any blasted paper says, or any idiot notion you have about your rights as a husband. And you'll do no tomcatting after. You ever hurt her you'll have me to answer to, you understand that?"

"Yes, sir. Mr. Hart?"

"What?"

"You think she'll have me, then?"

Matthew smiled. "Ask her."

"Aye. Well, then. I'd best be about it. Hadn't I?"

Matthew pushed a glass of sherry in the boy's direction. "One swallow," he advised. The footman gulped down the prescribed amount, then almost knocked over Mrs. Cole on his way out. Matthew steadied her tilt with a touch of his hand. How he would miss her gruff tenderness, her scent of gladiolus and flour.

"Where's Patsy?" he asked her expectant eyes.

"Steaming the last wrinkles from Miss Olana's gown." She nodded her head toward the laundry room.

"Ah. Then it should come, right about . . ." A shriek. "Now," he finished, grinning.

Patsy burst through the doors, catching up Mrs. Cole in a wild dance. Matthew backed himself against the cupboard. She approached, took up his hand. He kissed her cheek. He liked the close look at her shining face his small intimacy afforded. He liked the scent of starch and sweat about her, and the glow in her face now that her sickness was past. He hoped Selby would prove worthy of her and her child. Patsy pressed his hand beneath her still small waist so that he could feel the bulge.

"I hope I can do as much for you yourself some day, sir," she whispered, then sailed out of the kitchen. Matthew's fingers warmed with the feel of the life within her.

"Why, that little mouse! What notions!" the cook exclaimed.

"I'll count myself lucky to have Patsy standing by in my need, ma'am." Matthew Hart raised his glass to her. "Done, Mrs. Cole," he said.

She pulled the steaming platter from the oven and poured the remaining sherry over its contents. "Done, sir," she agreed.

The wine cellar was extensive, cool, reminding Matthew of the way a pine forest closes in after a misty late summer rain.

"I must show you my prize winners, Matt!" James Whittaker's walk took on a younger man's jauntiness. He found the section of bottles, pulled one from the shelf. "Champagne," he explained. "The finest to welcome my daughter home! I'm opening ten magnums—to demonstrate how honored is tonight's occasion!"

Matthew gazed down the rows of bottles. "Looks like you bought the crop, sir."

James Whittaker thumbed his vest pockets, laughing. "Enough for my lifetime, perhaps. I'm planning on many more happy events."

Matthew shook his head, in frank awe of the rich thinking they could plan happiness. Then something happened. To the very air. The coolness of the cellar evaporated. His own voice turned grating as it spoke of the scene going on behind his eyes.

"What . . . if you needed them in an emergency?"

"The champagne?"

"Yes. Say, to save the house."

"Save the house? From what?"

Stop it, he willed his own voice. "Oh, fire?"

"Magnums of the best champagne are the last things I'd use to put a fire out!" James Whittaker laughed.

"Yes, the last. Mr. Whittaker?"

"Matt?"

"I feel . . . terrible."

Matthew watched the man's hand reach out. "Lean on me, son" he said, his voice far away. Matthew closed his eyes. Then they were sitting on cold stone steps. The older man loosened Matthew's tie, pulled his collar open. "There you are, your color's coming back."

The ranger tried laughing away his embarrassment. "It's hard on a man, being a slave of fashion," he said.

James Whittaker took his shoulder. "You gave me a start!"

Stronger. A vision of chaos. Matthew watched James Whittaker's movements, listened to his speech vaguely, as if he were underwater. "Come, we'll be needing fortification before my daughter sends us both twirling," he was saying, pulling a key from his vest, opening a glass cabinet full of glistening bottles. Didn't the man hear it—the sound that existed in the two worlds, splintering both? The fluted glasses and the magnum of champagne slipped from James Whittaker's hands, hit the floor, exploded. The cabinet shook, began to topple. Its owner stared up at it, terror freezing even his eyes.

Earthquake.

fourteen

Matthew Hart's worlds united with piercing clarity. Now. He sprang, caught the man's legs. He heard the crash as they landed on the stone floor, under the curved arch. *"Tohiuha!"* he called to the spirit of his grandfather, a Cherokee plea for serenity.

The roar subsided. He raised his head slowly from the floor sizzling in a sea of champagne and shattered glass.

" 'Lana?" he whispered.

Her father's voice came out of the darkness. "Go on, see to her," it said, "I can manage."

Matthew met Selby on the stairs, a lantern in his hand. "Take that down to Mr. Whittaker," he urged, passing him.

He bounded up each stairway, sensing her higher. His eyes caught a swirl of white by the grace of the moon's light, rushing toward his rooms on the third floor. He yanked Olana into the doorway, tucked her in beneath his heart as if the ground was still shaking.

Her hands clutched his shoulders, traveled down his arms. "A tremor, Matthew. We get them all the time!" Her voice was high-pitched, giddy. "Strong, but . . . Why, our daily almanacs read, 'Occasional shakes, followed by light showers of bricks and plastering!' Oh Matthew, I was so afraid you . . . you were—"

They laughed together. He realized she was still in her underclothes, and without a corset. Her hair flowed over her shoulders, down her back, its red glints fiery in the moonlight. Her hands traveled down his shoulders, his champagne-soaked clothes. She smelled of the same starch Patsy did, and of lilies.

"Stop that, I'm all right." When he took her wrists, her eyes focused on his. Wide, dark eyes, the lashes moist. Her breaths, lengthening now, tantalized his chin, his neck, made him feel his own pulse in his head. She rose to her toes, pressing her softly swaddled leg through his.

The sleeve of her camisole slipped off her shoulder. He heard it—expectant, like the air around them. He drew it lower, kissing a path from that shoulder to her ear, taking pleasure in her gasps, in the feel of her breasts rising, warm. She could have died, those breasts alabaster and cold, in the cave where he found her. She could have been ravaged, gutted, in the tree. The sea could have burst through the floorboards, swallowed her, tonight. What in hell was all the holding back about?

The sight of her made his joints ache. Her toes were glowing in the moonlight. He wanted to start with her toes.

"God almighty, 'Lana." He turned her gently into the shadows of the doorway. Her smile broadened, and he saw her eyes spark with remembrance of their time in the woods.

She lifted his coat from his shoulders. It fell to the floor. Her thumbs found their way through his hair to stroke the scarred, leathery remains of his ear lobes, the part of himself so ugly he hid. She stroked feeling into them as she kissed his mouth, tasting of the raspberry tart she was eating when the tremor came.

" 'Lana, I've got to have you. I've got to have you now."

"Yes," she gasped out in between her soft cries.

He couldn't make her that promise from their night in the woods. Because he wouldn't stay without, content in watching her rise to her own pleasures. She was a virgin and so this first time would hurt her, somehow. Did she know that? He had to tell her, but he didn't know how. It was something he'd never asked his grandmother, when he was young. Or Lottie, because he had no interest in any beauty but her own teaching, experienced kind. But he would be hurting Olana, somehow. Men in the Klondike bragged about piercing open virgins, making them bleed, scream. He didn't want to hurt her. He wanted her open, aching, welcoming so he could release inside that wet, red, life source's caress. He'd never mistreated a woman in his life but he wanted her, now.

His hands traced her spine, widened out around her buttocks before he kissed her deep, pressed her against the door, letting her feel the strength of his passion between her thighs. They might not make it to the bed.

"Olana! Where are you? You'll catch your death!"

Her mother's voice evaporated his ardor. It was close, perhaps two doors down, and searching. He couldn't move. Olana said "Shit," breaking it into two syllables like he did, but with her soft, ladylike tone intact. Matthew had barely managed to cover her shoulders with his retrieved coat before he felt her mother's icy stare at the back of his head.

"The danger is quite past, Mr. Hart."

He turned, careful to keep Olana before him, like an offering. He couldn't find his voice. Her mother's frown deepened.

"Give her the robe, Patsy, she's shaking."

"I'm not cold, Mother," Olana said. "Mr. Hart has provided, see?" She embraced the empty sleeves of his coat. It wasn't just him, Matthew realized. She'd been agonizingly frustrated too, but was in a better humor about it.

Patsy hid her smile as she draped her mistress's robe over his arm, as if he was her assistant. Then she sniffed the air. "Why Mr. Hart, your coat is wet! And smells like a distillery!"

He smiled with one side of his mouth. "I guess it won't do?"

"I should say not, sir!"

He and Patsy replaced his coat with Olana's robe as Dora Whittaker looked on, astonished. They worked carefully, so he'd see only flashes of white were he looking, which he wasn't. Patsy placed Olana's hair gently over the robe's lace collar.

Dora Whittaker pushed the maid aside. "Mr. Hart, what exactly were you—"

Her husband, smelling the same as he and with a fresh magnum of champagne under his arm, interrupted her.

"My darlings!" he hugged Olana and smacked a kiss on his wife's cheek. When she bristled, he patted her rear. "I'm raising tonight's champagne allowance to twenty bottles—no, make it two dozen!"

Olana stepped forward. "Papa! Might we still go on?"

"Go on with the celebration of my daughter's return, her restoration—" he looked at her blushing face more intently and smiled, "Nay, the enhancement of her beauty after her ordeal? Haul out the gaslamps, the candles if we must! San Franciscans will not be thwarted by a little rocking!"

"Have you gone quite mad?" his wife demanded.

He laughed. "Forgive an old fool, my darling," he pleaded. "I'm so happy to be here—happy to be anywhere!" He rested his hand on the ranger's shoulder. "This lad may not be quick with numbers but he's quick on his feet!" The smile left his face suddenly. "I couldn't move, Matt. And I thank all that's holy that you could."

Both women's fingers touched their faces in the same spot, just under their right cheeks, as they looked from one man to the other. Matthew saw a resemblance between Olana and her mother, and finally had something that endeared Dora Whittaker to him.

The library was cool and dark, its knowledge ever more enticing. Why hadn't he put himself in here at every possible moment, once she was well? Why hadn't he told her to go back to her room, put her hair up? Here, in her father's house, he'd almost stolen her flower. Here where the very walls told him he had no right to her.

Was it the tremors? He was ashamed of his fear of them. He had to get out of this city that shook him senseless. Matthew Hart shoved the envelope into his vest pocket.

"Aren't you going to count it?"

"No."

"Some would call that a bad business sense."

"Others, trust."

He'd twice refused any more than their agreed price. Now James Whittaker's words were threatening the return of his solitude. "I wish you'd stay on. You seemed to have eased all the aches and pains of this house. Even enough of Dora's that she's begun a renewed interest in . . . ah, life."

"Then I'd better quit before one of you starts feeling poorly."

"Seriously, Matt. I could start you at the mill."

"You're not indebted to me, sir."

"This has nothing to do with tonight. I've watched you with people. You have a way of making your will known, carried out."

The younger man winced, remembering the gentle curve of Olana's hips beneath the thin muslin of her chemise. "Considering what my will is, I wouldn't think you'd want that, sir."

"Well," James Whittaker was forced to smile, "maybe a bit of your forthrightness—if not your opinions—will rub off on the others. As for your ideas . . ."

The back of her neck now, its downy hairs wet against his tongue. "Ideas, sir?"

"Perhaps I'd consider them. In time. On a small scale."

The timbering, you great fool, Matthew reminded himself. The man is talking about the trees. Was he finally succeeding in what Mr. Parker had sent him to do? Concentrate. Matthew took in a deep breath, past her scent of lilies at twilight. "I hope you will. And I'd be glad to consult with you on it. But I already have a position."

"I could make it worth your while."

"No sir, you couldn't."

"Honest to the end. Very well. Here," he pulled another envelope from his vest.

"I'm not taking any—"

"This isn't money, son. It's the acreage your Mr. Parker wants."

"What?"

"The additional land. I bought it. For you to do with as you will. You have three months to decide. You may transfer it out of your name on March twenty-fifth. If you wish to start one of your new ideas, there's your playground. I'll back the enterprise."

"Enterprise?"

"One of your tree farms. If it's successful, we can join forces, work together. Your status will be quite different in this household."

"But sir, we need that land for the park."

"That's your superior talking. I'm giving you an opportunity. A position of power, influence."

"You're giving me an impossible choice. That land is a forest, sir, a connected world. It's not suited for tree farming, or—"

"Suit it. Mold it to your vision of the future!"

"You don't understand, sir. It already is my vision of the future."

James Whittaker sighed. "You have three months, Matt. And I have a daughter waiting. Impatiently, I think. And a rival who is ahead of you on every count except winning her heart. My wife is back in my arms at night. I understand the importance of your advantage, believe me. Take the time to think. To, I hope, get your affairs in order. Now. I have only one more order before you're free to return to your trees."

A shy tap at the door and the ranger forgot his trees. Olana Whittaker's gown was the deepest red he'd ever seen. Her skin shone like porcelain above it. Her hair was swept up and dressed with a single white silk lily. There was only one way he'd seen her lovelier.

"Wear out her shoes," James Whittaker whispered before he put his daughter on Matthew's arm.

Olana's face pinched in distress as they reached the ballroom floor. Now what? Had he put something on backwards? "Matthew, what did Papa say? You look like your world's been shattered!"

" 'Lana, I—"

She laughed. "Come, it won't be so bad! I promise not to step on your feet. Wait. Oh, Matthew, I'm sorry. I never thought to ask!"

The guests were looking only their way. "Ask what?"

The musicians struck a Straus waltz. Matthew took her waist. Olana lifted the train of her gown. They sailed off around the room's periphery. "Why, Mr. Hart," she gasped as he swept her into the air. "You can!"

"Can what?"

"Dance!"

He frowned. "This is walking. The fandango, that's dancing."

* * *

Hours more. A few hours more. Surely he could endure it all for a few hours more. The ballroom's varied polished woods glowed softly in the candlelight. But the room's beauty was diminished by the cacophony of sound, overripe color, talk. At the center of it all was 'Lana, smiling, radiant. This was her world, one in which he'd never have a place.

Was that what was bothering him most of all? Of course not. Still, his eyes tried to memorize her, a swirling image to call up when the intimate ones tormented him. Then she looked over her partner's back and spoiled it with a smile that was his alone.

James Whittaker had his shoulder. "You saw the tremor coming—tell them, son!"

Darius Moore's eyes ignited. Matthew didn't care for the endearment either. He was no man's son.

"Saw it? No, sir."

"So literal! Felt it, then! Why else does a strapping man go white in the cool dampness of a wine cellar?"

"My tie—"

"Wasn't that tight."

"Mr. Whittaker, if I had powers of prognostication, I'd of been under that arch *before* the ground started shaking."

Darius Moore raised his champagne. "Moreover, had you second sight you'd be mining the vast stores of wealth out from under your wilderness, not charting endless forests, eh, Hart?"

Matthew tried to keep the smile on his face. Impossible. Olana had promised him. She couldn't have told anyone about the marble in the cave's stream bed. She was not part of all this scheming, all these layers. Moore was fishing, just fishing. Matthew made his tight smile go slack. "The forests are anything but endless. I would think a modern man of science like yourself would know that."

Amused eyes, even the women's, were cast as one toward his adversary.

"Now, now, do not seek to turn the attentions of these illustrious guests on me, sir! I am a mere middleman! It's of you we require knowledge."

Matthew Hart looked from the gold brocade of Darius Moore's vest to the greed in his small eyes. What had Sidney said about middlemen? That they were the most dangerous of all? He didn't understand, but he knew Moore's look from his own mining days. This man had it for his trees and 'Lana both.

"Mr. Hart knows exactly how to add to his mystique. The less he speaks, the more he's spoken about." Sidney Lunt made his appraisal languidly. He drew amused nods.

Matthew Hart didn't give a damn about his mystique. Why didn't Sidney dedicate as much time to his attacks on corruption as he did on his wit? Conversation swirled around him. Pay attention.

"—Mr. Hart?"

"Ma'am?"

"I asked if your hair is worn in emulation of the lamented General George Armstrong Custer, your fellow guardian of the land?"

"Custer? Hell, no!"

Olana was returning to his side. She'd heard. It was time to turn backwoods clown again. His stance eased, his speech drawled. "I keep my hair this way to spare you the sight of my ears. Now my blasphemy has offended yours. I beg your pardon."

Olana was hiding her growing smile behind her fan. But her mother was not amused.

"Are we to understand, from your extreme reaction to being placed, however superficially, on the plane of the late General, that your sympathies lie not only with the rough-hewn natural landscape, but its savage inhabitants as well, sir?" she demanded.

"The Indians don't need our sympathy, Mrs. Whittaker," he replied softly. "It's we who need their forgiveness."

"Forgiveness?" Darius Moore could scarcely disguise his delight as he took up Mrs. Whittaker's cause. "For fighting hard-won campaigns to free the wilderness for settlement? For bringing them the opportunities of salvation and democracy, only to be thwarted by laziness, drunkenness, and, if the ladies will excuse me, unspeakable violence?"

A slow smile spread across the ranger's face. But his eyes stayed hard. "Your description fits an outpost army garrison perfectly."

Olana's eyes closed slowly. Sidney Lunt sat up straight in his chair. How in hell did he get into any of this? Dora Whittaker faced him, a steel rod running through her already upright figure, her anger causing her carefully powdered face to glow pink. Darius Moore was her knight beside her.

"I take exception to your remarks, sir," she said. "Were I a man, I would extend a challenge!"

"Were you a man, I'd have to remind you that dueling is outlawed in the civilized society you prize so highly, Mrs. Whittaker. Ladies," he nodded, then hoped he was walking out the right door.

Olana found Matthew wandering on a stairway, his tie loosened, his collar opened. He'd been doing so well, until Darius Moore pulled him into an argument. But it was he who'd offended the guests.

"Matthew, really!"

He glared past her. "Just show me how to get out of here."

"Not until you apologize to Mother."

"Apologies even you won't prompt from me this time."

Olana inhaled slowly. Nothing was going to spoil her evening. She smiled. "Never mind. Papa will tend to her. Only do come back! It's such a lovely—"

"For you, maybe," he said like a truant boy deprived of his supper, "you've been dancing."

She tapped his chest lightly with her fan. "And you've made every woman wild with jealousy because you've not asked a single one."

He took up the card at her wrist, scanned the names. "I don't understand all this."

She felt herself softening further. How he could do that? "Of course. Of course you don't. Dancing is more straightforward where you come from, isn't it?" Tell me anything from that place you come from, Matthew. But he only looked beyond the warm amber wood as the frosted glass doors opened.

Mrs. William Hunt, her diminutive husband in tow, came through them. "I was sure I recognized—there!" she called, her eyes lighting on them. "There he is! Matt! Is it you?"

"Coretta?" Matthew whispered.

Mrs. Hunt reached out for his hands. "I knew it! No one else could put such life into a waltz! What are you doing here? Wasn't it you who said nothing short of a divine command could get you into the city limits of San Francisco again?"

"Was . . . something like that. You look real fine, Coretta."

William Hunt tugged on his wife's sleeve.

"Darling!" Mrs. Hunt laughed that full, hearty laugh that had kept her off Dora Whittaker's A list of guests until tonight. "William, I'm so very pleased to introduce you to the man who is the reason I'm alive and on your arm!"

Soon a swarm of people entered, and Olana was pulled away by the mayor of Sacramento's son. As they danced, she watched the Comstock silver baron's wife and Matthew in the room's shadows. Olana suddenly hated the candles' lesser brilliance, longed for the electroliers to be restored. By the time the dance ended, Matthew and Coretta Hunt had disappeared.

Sidney Lunt tossed his head toward the small door that led to the servants' stairway. Dear Sidney. Her spy. But her mother urged Olana onto the floor in the grip of another man with eyes brightened by her father's champagne and his own importance. Olana made sure they finished dancing near the servants' door, quickly excused herself, and slipped through.

The kitchen was a steamy factory of rushing. At another time Olana might have been fascinated by the turmoil, having never been below stairs while a social function was going on above. But now she was only grateful that it was easy to descend the stairs unnoticed. The servants were busy in furious conversation that matched their activity. Mrs. Cole had the room's attention.

"I never met a gentleman who could joke, be respectful to me after he'd tied a good one on. But that was—"

"Whist!"

Silence. Olana looked down at her crimson skirts and how they'd swirled into the kitchen staff's sight. She raised her head and turned the corner. "I'm sorry," she found herself saying, "I'm looking for Mr. Hart. His name is next . . . on my card, and I—"

How dare they make her apologize to them, in her own house? And now, what was in their eyes, pity? The sound of Mrs. Hunt's raucous laughter. Olana strode to the downstairs parlor doors, knocked lightly, before she opened them. On the small table papers were scattered, white papers that blurred behind Coretta Hunt's fingers caressing Matthew's face as they kissed.

fifteen

Olana couldn't move, as much as she wanted to. The woman's lips left Matthew's. She took his hand, squeezed. "Hellfire and damnation," she muttered. "Olana. Child, listen. I want—"

Olana turned, not at all interested in what Coretta Hunt and her too bright, too clinging gown wanted. She rushed madly through the door the delivery men used.

It put her out, confused, almost on the street. It was cold, damp, so dark. She walked, shivering, until Matthew's formal coat dropped on her shoulders.

"Where you going?"

She turned and slapped him so hard his face yanked toward the moon and his mouth froze in pain. But there was no anger in his light eyes.

"Feel better?" he asked.

"No. My hand hurts."

"My jaw's had better days as well."

They stared at each other a long moment. She didn't know if she started laughing or crying, but she found herself doing it into his chest, as if he were someone else, someone who had not been the cause of her humiliation. And he held her quietly, patiently, as if he were that someone else.

"I'm sorry," he whispered into her hair.

"For what?" she asked, yanking herself out of his hold. He shifted his feet, as he always did when she confused him.

"Don't put the burden of it on Coretta, now. She'll be your friend, if you let her. Help Sidney look after you when I'm gone."

She spun out of his arms. "I hardly need looking after! And certainly not from a disreputable, fortune-hunting—"

He took her arm. " 'Lana. Stop that."

"She was a whore!"

"Stop," he warned again.

"It's common knowledge. She was one of your whores, in the Klondike, wasn't she?"

He turned away from her. Olana stared at his back, at the way his vest harnessed his broad shoulders. She'd known, from the first, there were others. She'd begged him to tell her about them. But she never wanted to meet one. She wanted them all to be dead, like Lottie.

Inside, another waltz started. Matthew turned, touched the card on her wrist. "Who's this one for?" he asked.

She checked. "Darius Moore."

"Come away. Dance with me."

"Where?" A laugh she meant to be wicked escaped girlish, giddy.

"Not far."

Her dancing shoes were not meant for city streets. He led her to one she'd never been, even in passing. A large ramshackle wooden building vibrated with the force of the music inside. Its doorway erupted with color and laughter.

"What place is this?" she demanded, wondering if his face still smarted from her slap.

"Where we can do some real dancing. You game?"

His eyes held a fierce challenge. He was smarting, all right. Was this his revenge? Olana wanted to go home. But Matthew Hart knew how to get her to try something that she had no desire to do. A Dance Hall. Is that where they were? She nodded. They entered a cavern of peeling paint, rough floorboards, music. And dancers who did not have the advantage of skylights to keep them from getting overheated.

She looked around. "We're overdressed."

"Nobody will mind." The dance ended and several of the patrons waved as he lifted his coat from her shoulders.

"Matthew, they know you. How—"

"I do have Thursdays off."

The band, as heavy with brass instruments as her house's was heavy with strings, began to play again. Matthew took her hand, drawing her on the dark wood dance floor.

She had to shout above the music, the further din of couples dancing in coarse, cobble-heeled boots and workshoes. "I don't know how!"

"Follow me!" he shouted back.

He held her close. She stumbled, then yanked up her train defiantly. The music had a rollicking rhythm she'd never heard before. It was as if the piano player's right and left hand were arguing, no, challenging each other to stay within the same tune. The other musicians did not bring any order to the chaos, they echoed it.

Matthew danced with her the same way, much closer than was proper in her father's house, and challenging her to find the elusive rhythm. He arched his arm so she had to sail under it, then pulled her in tighter. He skipped through a beat, she matched it. He stepped, then hopped, she followed as he watched. He held the small of her back and made her bend so far she saw the ceiling's garish blue paint and gaslight burns. The dance got faster, the figures around them fewer, until the music stopped. They were surrounded by smiling faces pointing down to a crudely chalked number—forty-two, at their feet. Other couples crowded in, laughing, clapping. Olana clung to him, her corset stays hampering each breath.

"Matthew, what was that?" she asked.

"Ragtime. And we've just won the cakewalk."

"That was walking?"

"Naw, the waltz—"

"I know," she breathed harder against his chest, "that's walking." Laughter mixed with the fading applause. When she turned, his arm remained around her waist. Now all but the women's eyes were on a man in a chef's hat and drooping mustache. He held a confection piled high with whipped cream. The women's eyes were on Matthew Hart, just as the women's eyes at her house had been. This was, the thought birthed in Olana's mind, something that wouldn't change were she to spend her lifetime with him. She felt his warm breath next to her ear.

"Take it, or you'll hurt his feelings."

"The cake?"

"*Oui, le gateau!*" the chef explained, as if she were the immigrant.

"But what in heaven's name will we—"

"It's the prize, 'Lana. Take it."

She reached out her arms. Matthew made no attempt to help her, though the whipped cream was soiling her gloves.

"*Merci beaucoup,*" she said.

The chef took off his billowy hat and bowed low. The dark curls that framed his face were absent from his head. It shone like a billiard ball. Matthew gave her waist a squeeze.

Outside, he finally took up his half of the burden. "Now perhaps you'll tell me what we're to do with this *objet d'art?*" Olana demanded.

"You've got cream on your nose."

"What?"

"Right there." He pointed, as he always did, with his chin. "Very becoming."

"Get it off."

"Please."

"Please."

He leaned across the confection between them and licked the side of her nose with one swipe of his tongue. "Delicious," he pronounced. "How do you say that in French?"

"Almost the same," she heard herself answer. "*Delicieuse.*"

"Delicieuse," he repeated, drawing the syllables out, making them dip as he'd made her dip when they were dancing.

"My nose is cold," she said vaguely, her irritation evaporating like the high peaked cream.

"We're almost there," he assured her.

"Where?"

"The Dunstan Home."

"Where?"

"It's one of your mother's charities. There," he backed her into a doorway. "The bell's right behind you. Give it a tug, darlin'."

"I'm not your—"

"Aw, 'Lana, get off your high horse. It's Christmas."

"And I've been abducted from my own gala, and forced to dance to barbaric music, then labored like a slave through dark streets to a destination—Matthew Hart, don't you dare!"

But he had already lost a firm hold on the cake as he doubled over with laughter. She lowered her side to match his collapsing grip, but he stepped on her foot, as he hadn't once done during their strange dance. Not hard, just enough to startle them both into sitting on the sidewalk with their legs splayed out beneath them.

Matthew's shirtfront was dec_____
nouncing the cakewalk event. Ti_____
with the cream in Olana's hair. But _____
laps. They looked at each other and _____
door's sidelights. A woman in her nigh___

"Mr. Hart? Is that you?"

Matthew scrambled to his feet leaving_____
tween Olana's knees.

"Yes, ma'am. Mrs. Mack, this here's Olana _____
taker's daughter? We were wondering if the _____
some cake."

Mrs. Mack looked from Matthew to Olana to th___
already been put to bed. But this I think we could ro___

Even with a few silver nonpareils left in her hair, th___
the Dunstan Home stared at Olana as she ate, giving t___
of her mortality. With Matthew, even in his formal clo___
were much more at ease, so much that Mrs. Mack had to sco___
for interrupting themselves to talk to him.

"Did Santa Clause give you the cake to bring us?"

He leaned over and whispered a question in Olana's ear befo___
he answered. "A fellow named *Pere Noël* did," he explained. "Clos___
relative to Santa. Curly hair, big drooping mustache, bald head. If
you see him around, you'd best be good."

"Tell us a story."

"About what?" he asked the one, a girl of about seven, who had
been brave enough to make the request.

"About her," she said. "The queen."

He closed his eyes. "All right," he agreed. Olana watched, from
her place closest the fire, as the children gathered around him,
some of the older ones pulling the younger under arms of their
identical threadbare sleeping gowns.

How many Thursdays has he been coming here? Why didn't he
tell her about these children? They needed new nightclothes. They
needed Christmas presents, not a bashed-in whipped cream cake.

"Her name is Snow Woman," he began. "I found her in a cave."

"A cave?"

"Yes. She was so white. The ice sparkled like diamonds from her
hair, her face, her clothes. I was afraid."

m the word as the girl said

raight through, that she was
k Snow Woman home, found
e. And she found mine."

"Why?" Olana heard her

it.

"I was afraid the co.... And Mrs. Mack says you wear
ice, right down to he....ild in his lap, casting a sideways
her heart beatin...

"That's no... an older boy pulled him back into
it on your ...ours. Eating, reading, helping each

"Is ...other with you when you leave this
...ght. Mrs. Mack's hand on your head
...th you lend each other as the nights
...Woman now. See how red her dress is?
...ness in the dead of winter. Her heart is as
...t flows beneath the ice in her cave. It flows
...rble almost as beautiful as her own skin. When
...ack to her father, living in his castle of warm woods,
...e the cave, the marble. You can come and see it, it's yours
, too."

cake. "They
...use them for
...e orphans of
...em proof
...es, they
...d them
re

Olana enjoyed the silence between them as they walked. The empty streets were almost like his woods, where she'd once been contented to spend this Christmas Eve night.

"Olana," he said quietly. "Mrs. Mack. She's got a cancer. She's dying, and is trying to place all the children in homes, or other places before she can't take care of them anymore. Would you tell your mother? Maybe she'll help?"

"Of course."

"Thank you. I'm sorry we didn't get along better. I'm truly sorry."

"There's time, Matthew."

"No, darlin', there isn't." Then he looked down at her shoes, frowned. "We'd best get a cab."

"I'm not cold."

"Your shoes are ruined."

"I have others. Matthew, did my father really deed you the cave?"

"Yes."

"I'm so pleased."

She closed in deeper against his side as they walked up Russian Hill. Light blazed from every window of her father's house, the beacon crowning it, crowning all of San Francisco tonight, Olana decided.

"I'm giving the land to the park, darlin'," Matthew said.

"Of course you are."

"You understand that it's got nothing to do with how I feel about you? You understand why?"

"I've been up there with you, Matthew, remember? I . . . I was just wishing we were there tonight, snug in your bed," she admitted.

He caught her up in an embrace that lifted her off her feet. "Stay, please," she whispered.

"I can't. I have to go home. My home. 'Lana—"

"Look. We're almost there."

He stared at the twinkling lights in the Japanese lanterns of her father's solarium. At its edge, his hands on a windowsill, his face distorted through the glass, was Darius Moore. Olana felt the muscles in Matthew's arms harden. Did he sense her pleasure in it?

"Don't flirt with him. Anyone else, not him."

"Why?"

"Because he wants you. He wants you like he wants the trees—to conquer, to enhance himself."

"Matthew. I believe you're jealous."

"Of course I'm jealous. Go on and gloat, laugh with your friends about it."

"I'd never—"

"Listen to me! Stay clear of him, 'Lana. I know his kind. Your mama don't but I do!"

"What has my mother to do—"

"He's been wiling his way into her grace with his manners and laudanum. But it's you he's after now."

"After? You make it sound like—"

"A hunt? It is a hunt, Olana. And you are in his sights, as sure as any defenseless woman or child ever was on one of his glorious Indian War campaigns."

"What are you saying?"

"I'm trying to be your friend, damn it!"

Olana wondered if it was the moon that made his face look so free of guile. "You are my friend, Matthew," she told him.

Inside, the band struck up another waltz. Matthew exhaled, held out his hand. "Then dance with me. Not the rest of this blasted city. Me. Then I need to go, darlin'."

BOOK THREE

sixteen

San Francisco/St. Pitias, California
Winter 1904

The clothesline was still strung out across the hearth. Fogarassy must have used it, as he looked after the place and his animals for the month. He'd seen the sky, the snowstorm coming, and was in a hurry to get back to Three Rivers, and give Matthew back his post and his solitude. But he could have stayed for coffee. Matthew brought the last trunk into the back room, pausing to lift the lid and take up his grandmother's book. His fingers caressed the worn cover fondly. Now it reminded him of Olana. He slammed the lid back down and kicked it deep in the recesses of the ancient sequoia's trunk.

On the mantel she'd left Seal Woman's comb and mirror, shining clean. And what else? He lifted the hair bracelet she'd fashioned from her nightly brushings. Olana had decorated it with tiny dried seeds, berries that complemented the glints of red woven in intricate, swirling spirals. It was like Olana herself, strong and delicate at the same time. Had she left it for him? It was so different than the gift waiting for him in San Francisco after he'd taken her dancing, and to Mrs. Mack's orphanage. He'd climbed up to the third-floor nursery to find it crowded with a camera and equipment, festooned with ribbons. With what else? A job on Sidney's paper so he'd stay? Her father wasn't the only one good with the bribes. He'd been so angry he'd left it untouched, and without saying good-bye to any of them. His women wouldn't approve of that. They'd call him rude, not worthy of them. But they didn't have to know.

Matthew slipped the hair bracelet on his wrist. Comfort, warmth spread through his weary muscles. He fell into the narrow bed's confines, too tired to remove either his clothes or boots.

When he awoke the fire was low, he was cold. The clothesline was gone from the hearth. A shadow moved behind him. Then something pulled taut around his neck. The clothesline. The room went out of focus.

"Damn your eyes, bring him back! I want him to feel, to plead, after what he and his fine lady put us through. Hart! You hear me?"

Matthew opened his eyes to the rotted-toothed grin of Cal Carson, then was yanked to his knees. Cal kicked his middle. Hard. Cal's oath punctured the darkness. Then, laughter. "You lit into him with the selfsame sore foot he caused you! Sometimes I wonder which of us is truly brainless, Cal!" Ezra exclaimed.

The gun barrel came down on Matthew's head, knocking him to the floor. These were murderous blows, he realized somewhere in the back of his scrambling mind. They were trying to kill him.

Ezra's one hand grabbed his shirt, as with the other he brushed away spattered blood with an almost delicate care. "Now, Cal, don't go damaging the ranger too bad. No bullets, no foul play, or no pay," he reminded his brother dutifully.

"Pay?" Matthew whispered.

"That's right, you got a price on your head, Ranger, can you beat that? Went to San Francisco to blackmail your ladylove's people, and found ourselves a whole new line! Mr. Hopkins is paying us good money to—"

"Shut up!"

"Why, Cal? Ranger's got a right to know he's of value, don't he? He had us in his sights last time, but he let his pretty lady spare us to take advantage of this more profitable opportunity. That's how I got it figured."

Matthew Hart struggled to keep his head up, his eyes focused. He didn't know anyone named Hopkins. "Wasn't our choice," he garbled out painfully.

Ezra came closer. "What?"

"My rifle. Was broke."

"Broke?"

"Clean—" Matthew tasted blood, swallowed it. "Clean in half." He smiled, then fell over.

Ezra brought him back to his knees. Stay. If he could only stay upright. "No foolin'?" Ezra laughed. "You hear, Cal? Was a bluff lost us our run through his fine lady and seven toes between us! Now, you got to admire—"

"Will you shut up!"

Cal pushed his brother aside. Matthew swayed, but struggled to stay on his knees without Ezra's support, though the cut over his eye was swelling it shut. "Your lady wouldn't find you so appealing now."

Ezra laughed. "He does look a touch peaked."

Matthew realized his chance while the brothers transferred the tether of the clothesline. In his second of freedom he went for the low slung holster at Ezra's leg. He aimed the pistol with his one seeing eye, and fired.

Cal looked surprised through the smoke, as if the ranger had somehow shot him without a weapon. The hole in his side turned red.

Matthew Hart felt his head in a vise. He fired another shot that ricocheted wildly off the hearthstone. Something clicked. It was either his neck breaking or the gun's hammer striking an empty chamber. Damned Carsons couldn't even load firearms properly, he thought. Ezra dropped him. He landed hard. The gun skidded out of his reach. It was all right, Matthew made a quick peace with himself. He'd gotten her out. He didn't have to suffer her death as well.

"I . . . broke him. But I didn't mean to, Cal!"

The ranger thought of his animals, who would care for them? He felt warm blood in his throat again and coughed.

"Look at him," Cal said with disgust. "I wanted him to plead. Now he's heaving up his insides!"

It was not his insides, Matthew realized, but blood from a dislodged tooth. He looked at his arm, still reaching for the gun. It was stretched out, the hand shaking uncontrollably, vulnerable. If he could draw it in, protect it, if he could slow down his breathing . . . Cal Carson's boot heel crushed the last two fingers. It hurt. Matthew didn't think it would have hurt if his neck was broken. Under it, he told himself. Every bone in the hand will break if you can't get under it. He exhaled, adding to the pool of blood beside his mouth.

"Shit. He don't even squirm."

Cal fisted his hair, but Matthew had a dim sense of the wounded man's grip weakening. "Come on," his brother pleaded. "Don't hurt yourself more. He's dead. Let's get you mended."

They set fire to his bed, his charts, and journals on the table, before turning their torches close enough to singe his eyebrows. Matthew fixed his still eyes on the flame.

"Let's watch him burn."

Fresh adrenaline coursed through Matthew's veins. Not burn, not that way, please, he asked a God he'd given up half his lifetime ago.

"That'd make me sick, and I wouldn't be able to take care of you, Cal," Ezra apologized.

"Close your fucking eyes!" The torch waved away, then dropped. Cal Carson fell on Ezra's supporting arm. The two hobbled through the doorway, Ezra still apologizing for spoiling his brother's good time.

The searing of his throat yanked at Matthew Hart's fading consciousness. His lungs cried out for air. He rolled to his side, then onto his hands and knees. The room was so dense with smoke he couldn't see the door and had to rely on memory, feel. A flaming rafter hit his back, igniting his shirttail. By the time he'd rolled it out, he was so disoriented he crawled deeper into the sequoia's trunk, where death waited for him. He rested his face in the cool dirt. When he heard the sound of his trapped animals' screaming, he set out again.

He peered through the darkness, flames, and red glows and found the window. One. Too high. If he got to rebuild, he'd put windows everywhere, he swore to himself. He crawled along the room's edge until he felt the door. He pressed his face against the crack and inhaled frosty air.

He exhaled weak, helpless laughter. His good hand fumbled with the latch. He leaned against the door. It moved. Water trickled in beneath the doorway. He pushed harder. It gushed. He breathed in more air from the doorway's crack. Once more. Harder. It opened.

He crawled outside, coughing the snow crimson, then staggered to his barn. Its roof was in flames. He lay back in a snowdrift, soaking his clothing, then entered. He led his horse, rasped for the others to follow.

The animals scattered into the woods. Matthew watched them through the steam rising from his clothes, through the snow, now falling hard, there at the base of a sequoia. He watched the blackening destruction being held in check by the storm's fury. He thought it was a wonderful time to die.

But Lottie stood over him in her most flamboyant dressing gown, her hands planted firmly on her hips.

"Can I come with you now?" he asked her.

"Aw, Fandango Man, you're hurtin' too much to be dead, you know that."

"Shit."

"Now don't go and get yourself froze. Think what she'd make of that, after all your grousing at her. She'd laugh herself silly."

Darius Moore sent a roomful of flowers every day. When Olana sought to go out on her own, or with her mother or Sidney, he happened to be at the adjoining opera box, table, booth. She'd acknowledge his presence, then retreat home early. Olana had always known Darius Moore to be a proud man, and she was sure he would look elsewhere for his strange amusement. But the next day, more flowers would come, precise in their language. He was courting her.

"You play the game well," her mother said.

"It's no game. I feel like a prisoner. I shall tell Papa to make him stop."

"You'll do no such thing. Your poor father is quite busy enough trying to keep up with all these business expansions that Mr. Moore is engineering. Besides, imagine your father's surprise to learn that you, after your . . . forest adventure, now require his assistance against a perfectly proper man's attentions."

Olana turned her head toward the bright spring morning past her bedroom's curved turret windows. The scent of flowers—red carnations, bemoaning his poor neglected heart, set in canary grass speaking his perseverance, and crowned with tulips, dozens of red tulips declaring love
assaulted her.

"Olana?"

She did not turn. She felt the heat of her mother's hand hover at her shoulder, then draw away.

"Do come this afternoon. You have not been yourself this season. We can both be fashionably late, making an entrance that will rival the tableau that horrid Mrs. Simpson has planned of 'The Last Days of Pompeii'!"

What would Matthew Hart have thought of these grown women dressing as ancient Roman matrons and standing still as statues? Olana suppressed a smile.

"No, thank you."

Her mother sighed. "You think we're a pack of silly old hens, don't you?"

"No, Mother."

"Well, sometimes I do. But it's a benefit for the Christian Ladies' Ethiopian Fund, and it's the first interest Mrs. Simpson has chosen to take in charity work of any kind, and Darius says we must indulge her."

Patsy appeared in the doorway. "Coach is waiting, Ma'am," she said, handing the woman her gloves and hat. Olana followed her mother to the door.

"What about the orphanage?"

Dora turned. "Orphanage?"

"It's your only charity located here in the city. Dunstan House, remember? Why don't we go there sometime, perhaps read to the children who have not yet been placed? They're short of help now that Mrs. Mack—"

"Olana, the place has my generous funding."

"Then why don't the children have more—"

"The matron makes judgments on where the money goes, not ourselves! She had her job, we have ours! Going there. Reading. Honestly, your notions. I didn't have the time to read to my own."

"Better late than never."

"And what is that supposed to mean?"

"It might be fun."

"Fun? That's a coarse word, Olana. One would think—"

"Mother. You suffer through these ridiculous events for the sake of the unfortunate, why not try—"

Olana saw Darius Moore emerge from the coach below and look at his watch. Instinctively, she stepped back from the window. Her mother touched her arm.

"What are you frightened of, Olana?"

"N-nothing."

"He's very fond of you, you know," her mother said quietly. "Quite determined and patient. Well. I'd best be off. Our Darius is a punctual man. That's tedious of him, I'll grant you."

Olana watched at the window as the coach departed. Her fingers danced against her waist at the prospect of a free afternoon to work on her latest O. Lanart piece. She was finally learning to make sense of the arguments between the ideals of groups like the Sierra Club and the conflicting mining, lumber, and herding interests. As she wrote she strived to find out what she was thinking, just as she had while Matthew was away in their tree house. And she'd actually found some common ground upon which to form her own opinions.

She did know how to think, Sidney said so, though she worked harder at her blasted typewriting machine than she'd worked on anything in her life. Sidney was a patient but hard taskmaster, and only three of her efforts had appeared on the *Chronicle*'s pages. One of them "The Park in Winter" was largely descriptive, drawn from her notes when in exile. But even that one drew angry letters, accusing "the poetic but misguided Mr. Lanart" of "using his artful prose as a propaganda tool for radical conservationists." The letter went on to rail against a government that wasted money on a place which could be open to visitors less than half the year.

Sidney loved the controversy. And he was right, using the pseudonym helped her to express her views without worrying whether her father would ever forgive her. Let Sidney have his waterfront corruption, his exotic bodyguard. For now, at least. She had her own secret that none of the Nob Hill Society knew. Olana didn't as yet know if she enjoyed writing more than the intrigue of getting her words into Sidney's hands. But she was becoming a newspaperwoman, even if no one knew but herself and Sidney. And Matthew, she realized, for Sidney had shown him that first O. Lanart piece. Was Matthew yet down from his mountain? Would he ever see the results of her efforts? Why had he left without a word? And without the gift that might have made them partners?

"Miss Olana?"

She turned to the maid whose eyes had grown brighter since she became Mrs. Selby. There was something brewing in those eyes today.

"Well, what's got you eating the canary, Patsy?"

"Canary, miss?"

"You couldn't wait to get mother off to her *soiree.*"

Patsy came closer. "It's a visitor!"

Olana inhaled the jungle of blossoms surrounding her and shivered. Darius Moore had not come back? "I don't wish to see any—"

"He left this, and as he was one of my own, my very own countrymen, I told him I'd try my best."

The maid handed Olana a laundry receipt with a few words scrawled across it.

"Farrell!"

"The bearer waits," Patsy announced formally, then giggled. "We tucked him away in the back sitting room until Missus was off."

"I was plowing up Mrs. Goddard's north field for spring planting when I saw him tramping down from the mountains, Miss, with his animals following after, unbidden. He looked like a forty-days-fasting-in-the-wilderness saint to me, I don't mind telling you! Especially with his beard and hair grown bramble wild and that great burnt-edged remedy treatise under his arm. I crossed myself three times before I saw him grin and knew if nothing else about him belonged to Matty, that grin did!

Farrell chomped into another slice of raisin toast and swallowed from the cup of tea that looked so small in his workman's hand.

"Soon as he was fit, the boys and I wrestled him down long enough so now he sports a pure gold tooth where his missing one was. Looks mighty fancy when he smiles."

"Does he smile, Mr. Farrell? Is he well?"

"He only frets over his lost notations. He's been trying to write them all from memory again. That's contented him a bit."

"And infuriated him."

"Ah, course, you remember him and his combustible relations with pen and page, don't you? But his eyes caught fire once, Miss Whittaker—when he made notation of your cave."

"My cave?"

"The one that was your discovery, miss."

"Discovery? I'd hardly call stumbling into a shelter a discovery!"

The Irishman filled the small sitting room with his laughter. "Most discoveries are made just exactly that way! Anyway, he's gone and named it for you."

"Named it?"

"Sure enough. Of course, the land it's on was disputed, until your father went and bought it, gave it to Matty, for that tree farm."

"Tree farm?"

"Sure. When we heard about his present, and how it wasn't all officially his until the spring, well, that made us extra glad the Carson brothers didn't scorch him along with his place! He . . . Miss Whittaker, he did tell you he was giving the land to the park?"

"Yes, he told me."

Farrell shifted uncomfortably, watching her face. She didn't care. Her father had offered her to Matthew Hart, complete with a dowry, and he'd refused. Why? The marble, of course. She understood that, now that she'd researched for her writing assignments. They would want to mine the marble in her cave. He would not let them do that in his wilderness. It was not her. He loved her. Why didn't he explain it all? Why didn't he tell her that he had to return, to guard her cave until spring? Her father's gift had almost killed him.

"Miss Whittaker," Farrell called her gently, "sometimes I think I talk all together too much."

"Not at all." She smiled. "Mr. Hart talks too little."

"Well, the men, we're getting the cave ready to show folks, come summer. So we thought, and put it to Mr. Parker all official, that you ought to be invited for the grand unveiling of your namesake, as it were. Would you like that?"

Olana flung her arms around Farrell's neck. "Oh, Farrell, do rescue me from this hothouse of tulips!"

"There now, miss," he laughed. "A little more protest, if you please! I told them I had to come here personally on account of it would take the Devil's own tongue to get you to come back."

seventeen

"What did you come here for?" Thomas Parker demanded. "To personally escort him off government property?"

Olana lifted her head from her struggle with the complicated document. "What does this mean?" she demanded, out of patience.

Mr. Parker rose slowly from behind his desk and stood at her shoulder, jabbing at paragraphs with his pewter letter opener.

"Here I'm told what a bad choice I made for my head ranger in the first place. Here's why." He flung the letter opener across his blotter. "Solid research, Miss Whittaker—among sixteen-year-old, closed file documentation."

"I don't understand!"

"Army security during the Indian Wars! Dishonorable discharge for one Private Matthew Hart. I could petition till my last breath and never get to the bottom of it."

"I had no part—"

"Of course. You don't have to work at it yourself, do you? You can buy anything. Well, you got your money's worth."

"Mr. Parker—"

"I told him I'd refuse to do it. His donating the land, that's got to count for something, I said," Parker continued as if she hadn't spoken, "so he resigned his post. 'You know they'll just keep firing folks until they find someone to do it,' he said. Matthew remembers the army well enough to know that's the damned truth."

"Mr. Parker, surely you don't believe—"

The director snatched the letter from her hand. "It hardly matters what I believe, young woman!" He exhaled and his voice became quiet. "He warned me when I sent him off to San Francisco. I was asking too much, he said. Why didn't I listen?" He looked up, seemed surprised that she and Farrell were still standing before him, and frowned. "Now, unless you want to assemble for a ceremony of one at your blasted namesake cave, I suggest you get the turn-about coach for Fresno."

Olana shielded her eyes and stared out at the expanse of small farms and abandoned mining towns along the train's route. This was insane. Even if the address was an accurate one, even if they found it, under what pretense could they present themselves?

"We've got the advantage," Farrell said. "We're but one train behind him, and he doesn't know we're giving chase so—"

"I'm not chasing him!"

But what else would she call pleading with Mrs. Goddard to give them the name of the town he returned to each spring? She was clearing herself. And Sidney too, he and the *Chronicle* needed their good name cleared, too. Every ranger and roadman believed Sidney had the discharge revealed that had lost Matthew his job. That couldn't be true. Sidney was her best friend. He wouldn't keep anything so vital from her knowledge, would he?

Olana was shocked to learn Matthew Hart lived anywhere besides his tree. He was such a part of the forest. Why hadn't he told her he had people? Who were they? He knew everything about her, including Leland's name for her. Why had he told her so little about himself? Or had he told her, and she wasn't listening?

It was dusk when they engaged fresh horses at the railroad station at St. Pitias. There were only two coaches waiting, so Farrell asked the driver about the passengers he'd taken from the previous train.

"Tall Anglo? Light hair, eyes that send the ladies sighing?"

"Sounds right."

"Odd looks, even among his own folk."

"Did you take him home?" Olana asked.

"No, he don't ever ride coaches, that one. He walks. Not on the fine new road, either. He breaks off from the road, goes through what forest we got left."

Farrell beamed. "Now I know we're talking about the same man. Would you bring us there?"

"I can likely get you there before him."

* * *

From the nearby mission, the bells began to peal for evening vespers. Closer, a soft voice filled in the spaces in between with an older song, one Olana could feel more than hear. Once the bells stopped, the song went on, wilder, with the nearby Pacific's waves as accompaniment.

The horses' pace slowed further as the farmhouse came into view. Unlike the adobe dwellings they'd been passing, it was built of weathered graying clapboard, in a Southern style, right down to its double-story porches. A wooden swing creaked lazily in a night heavy with natural electricity. The very air was charged.

Farrell paid their fare. The affable coachman left them.

The homestead was surrounded by an iron fence that Olana imagined had once offered protection, but now was so uncared for it lent a sad, neglected air to the place. The remaining parts were rusting away in the salt-sea air.

The singer stopped. More electricity filled the void.

"Shall we present ourselves as weary travelers?" Farrell asked behind her.

"Listen," Olana cautioned as she heard sounds of underbrush in the scrub pine forest across the road.

Matthew Hart stepped off the trail quietly, in his high laced moccasins. He crossed the dirt road and stood before the highest part of the rusted iron gate. When he touched it, the lamps inside lit the windows with a golden glow. The door opened next, and a tall, dark-haired woman stepped out on the porch.

"Supper!" she called, though not to him, for the sight of him then halted her next word in mid-syllable. Her hand shielded her eyes, as if the sun was bright. "Matthew," she said, stretching out the "a" in endearment. Olana heard Farrell take in a pained breath behind her.

The ranger let his cloth bag slip off his shoulder. He met the woman as she stepped off the porch, took her waist between his hands and lifted her in a swinging arc. She hugged him as he buried his face in her neck.

A small, raven-haired girl in a red pinafore darted out from the side of the house and hid herself in the woman's skirts. Matthew Hart removed his hat, and went down on one knee. He spoke gently, but the girl did not detach herself from the woman. Then he opened his bag and brought forth a doll Olana recognized. He'd lingered outside the toy shop's window where the doll was displayed until she had to tug at his arm. Now the doll, the woman's encouragement, and his own patience finally yielded him his prize. The girl took his present in one hand and touched his clean-shaven face with the other.

Olana watched the woman's hands stroke through Matthew's hair, as hers had the night after the grizzly bear and the Carson brothers. He'd called her Mrs. Hart then. No wonder he'd smiled his amusement—she'd been a child playing this woman's part.

Olana couldn't hate her. She couldn't even hate him. He'd tried to tell her that he was not free, she realized in the blazing clarity of hindsight. If he could have told her of these two when she was only infatuated, perhaps she might not have grown to love him with the passion she now felt tearing her apart. She should have known. Even when he'd touched her the night long he didn't do what might have put a child inside her. He had a child. And this tall, piercingly beautiful wife, whose arms now circled them both.

Another woman, her gray hair shining silver in the darkening night stepped onto the porch.

"Storm's coming, Vita. Where's the child?"

"Mama—look. Matthew's home."

The older woman's face lit with a delight. One hand glided to her hip, the other touched the back knot of her hair like a girl.

"Well," she said. "Come inside, the lot of you."

Olana didn't turn away until the house's warm amber light had absorbed them all. The sky flashed suddenly, and she heard Farrell struggle for the words.

"I'm sorry, Miss Whittaker, God's truth I am. I didn't know, not a single one of us knew—"

Olana pushed away from his hands, his pity, and stumbled blindly into the woods from where the ranger had emerged. She ignored the sky's flashing, and the thunder that obliterated Farrell's call.

When he tried to pull her out of the ditch, she forgot how small a man he was and yanked him into the brambles beside her. Somehow, in the space between a lightning flash, they heard Matthew's approach above them.

All was silent except for the rain pelting the wide brim of his hat, and the Pacific's surf there at his back. Olana could only see Matthew Hart's silhouette as he raised his rifle.

Farrell spoke softly. "Matty. It's us, lad. Miss Whittaker and myself."

The ranger's eyes opened wider. He lowered his weapon. "Christ almighty. How in hell—"

"By train, coach, and tramping, same as you." Even Farrell was made succinct by the storm. At least he had a voice.

"Well you can damn well find your way back then, can't you?"

The tall woman appeared beside him. She held a spidery black shawl around her and raised a lantern that illuminated them all. Matthew turned.

"I told you to stay—"

"Move aside."

To Olana's amazement, he obeyed. The woman knelt beside Olana and took her hands.

"Cold, even through your gloves."

"Oh?"

"I'm Vita Hart."

"I know. Yes. Of course. I know."

She began to rub the life back into Olana's hands, and looked to Farrell. "You're friends of Matthew's?"

Farrell took off his hat. "Would've counted ourselves so, up until a moment ago, ma'am."

Vita Hart glanced up over her shoulder, but received only a growl. She shone her lantern closer to Olana's skirts.

"My tablecloths," she marveled.

"I'm sorry," Olana stammered.

"Why, you're the girl Matthew found in the snow, aren't you?"

She bit down on her shivering lip and nodded.

"And you, sir?"

"Farrell, Mrs. Hart. Your own, your very own, Farrell. I fed him back when we were building the road."

"Well." She smiled. "You must allow me to return the favor." The woman cast another dismayed look behind her, where Matthew was digging his boots in the mud. "Please forgive the inexcusable rudeness of my son, and come inside."

"Son?" Farrell scrambled to his feet. Olana felt the crushing weight lift off her chest. "He's your . . . Bless my soul, woman, you're his . . . ?"

"Yes." She laughed, reminding Olana of the mission's bells, were they rung with humor instead of solemnity—full, deep, joyous. Vita turned to Matthew, and held her hand out impatiently. "Give me that firearm and show your friends some hospitality!"

As Matthew surrendered his rifle, Farrell rushed to the woman's side. "How'd Matty get himself a mother with your disposition, ma'am?" he said, taking her lantern and offering his arm.

Matthew lifted Olana to her feet and steered her toward the house, all without meeting her eyes.

"You never told me." He did not respond, but slowed his stride when she stumbled. She tried again. "Your mother. Matthew, she is so—"

His brows knit in anger. "What?" he demanded.

"Beautiful," Olana said softly.

"Yes," he said, annoyed, as if she'd told him something obvi-ous—that it was raining, which it was, that they were getting wet, which they were. But his face finally showed signs of a thaw.

Vita Hart turned Olana's hat in her long slender hands. His hands, Olana realized. "This is so lovely! Is it what they're wearing in San Francisco? If I can reblock it while it's wet, then iron the netting, you'll only need to replace the feathers." The small bedroom's oil lamp picked up the silver strands in her dark hair, less silver than Matthew's hair had. It was still hard for Olana to believe she was his mother.

Vita placed the hat on the night table, and looked down at the edition of *A Connecticut Yankee in King Arthur's Court* that Olana re-moved from her bag. Olana placed it in the woman's hands.

"It's signed. For Matthew by . . . by the author."

"My parents and brother met him, the first time before I was born. They were visiting the Hudson River Estate of Frederick Church."

"The painter."

"Yes. And Mr. Clemens and his family were welcomed from their home in Hartford. My father enjoyed the stay so much that when I was born some months after, they named me for that house, Olana."

Matthew's mother smiled. "That's like a fairy tale."

"I wrote to Mr. Clemens, about Matthew reading me *A Connecticut Yankee* while I recovered. He sent me this edition to give him. Do you think he'll accept it, Mrs. Hart?"

"He'll be drummed out of this family if he doesn't!" She laughed, clutching the book close. "Mr. Twain, he's the first to give us folks our own voice. I don't know if . . . forgive me, but if someone of privilege can understand how important that is to us. And now, Matthew's name's on one of his books, in his own hand. My."

No one Olana knew held the writer in such esteem as the woman before her. Vita Hart went gliding toward Olana's wet skirt spread out by the stone fireplace. "What a marvelous design this is."

"A compliment to the material's quality, my dressmaker said. Where did you get such cloth, Mrs. Hart?"

The tall woman turned and the fire threw lights and shadows across the richly textured weave of her own crimson skirts.

"Vita, please. I wove the cloth, in the attic," she said with a soft pride. "I've been weaving my life long. My mother does the spinning and the sewing. Matthew must look like his own granddaddy to you—Annie hasn't changed her patterns in fifty years. He came home in store-bought clothes this year. That must be why. Finally fed up with us and the old ways."

There was a hint of desertion woven through the woman's accented speech. "Oh, no. He's proud of his clothes," Olana protested, gathering up the soft folds of her borrowed muslin dressing gown. "And the first thing I noticed about him was the fine weave."

The older woman's eyes searched hers. "What's happened to them, Olana? There's almost nothing in his bag."

"There was a fire."

The woman's eyes went wild. "I knew. Something. From his eyes. He was hurt? And you?"

"No, no, I was home by then." Olana explained the circumstances as Farrell had told her. When she was finished, Olana felt the woman's long, strong fingers cover her own. "Forgive me. But he never tells us anything."

Olana smiled. "Me either," she said.

Vita Hart threw back her head and laughed, the same way her son did, however rarely. "You're going to be good for this house, Olana."

Olana looked at the intricate star quilt on the bed. "Thank you for not yet asking why I've come."

"We don't question blessings. This is going to be great fun. I've never seen Matthew in love."

"Love? He'll scarcely look at me!"

"That did not escape my notice."

As she entered the simply furnished parlor, the gown she'd borrowed from Vita Hart floated a train behind her, making Olana feel like a child playing dress-up. Her only consolation was the similar effect the ranger's clothes had on Farrell. Matthew was already sitting at a sturdy oak table, and did not even look up from the pieces of his rifle laid out before him. He methodically began to wipe them dry and oil them.

Vita frowned before taking each of his guests by the arm and bringing them to the old woman in the bent wood rocker.

"This is my mother, Annie Smithers," Vita said.

Farrell shook the woman's hand vigorously. "Mighty pleased, Ma'am." He grinned. "But it's my sacred duty to inform you your grandson's a blamed fool."

Matthew Hart grunted and adjusted his spectacles. His mother laughed. "Why is that, Mr. Farrell?" she asked.

"On account of he spent the last three meanest winters on earth in a tree at eight thousand feet when he's so rich in beautiful women."

Annie Smithers snorted, but Olana saw a faint blush rise to Vita Hart's cheeks. Did she not know how beautiful she was? Matthew's mother took Olana's hand and put it into Annie Smithers'.

"Olana Whittaker, Mama—the lady Matthew took care of in the storm."

The strength in Annie Smithers' fingers belied her age. "I'm very happy to—" Olana started, but her hand was abruptly released.

She looked over Olana's shoulder. "Yankee, Matthew," she called to her grandson. "Her folks won't take to you no how. Money's all they think has value, Yankees."

Vita frowned. "Mama, behave yourself," she said.

"Should I now? I did when you brought yours home, then I kept a civil tongue. Would to God I'd of spoken up!"

Matthew Hart dropped his oiling cloth and bounded there, between the two women. He knelt before his grandmother.

"Easy. I ain't brought her, Gran," he said.

Her blue veined hands riffled through his hair. "Liar," she whispered and pushed him away. The woman's clear brown eyes found Olana's and she knew the mind behind them was sound.

Olana knew something else as well. "You wrote the book—the one Matthew consulted to make me well."

Annie Smithers frowned exactly the way Matthew did. "No one deserves credit for the wondrous nature of the body to heal itself. Don't tell me he's taken on doctoring airs."

"No, no. He told me the same thing."

It was a houseful of echoes of him. No, he was theirs, their echo. Matthew Hart left them as quietly as he'd come, and went back to his firearm cleaning.

The little girl appeared, putting her hand on Matthew's leg. He smiled and lifted her to his lap.

"You smell something?" he asked her softly.

She nodded solemnly.

"Something good?"

Another nod. When he pulled off his spectacles, she touched his shirt's pocket.

"Go on," he said.

She pulled out a rod of peppermint candy and began sucking on it.

Olana had quite forgotten the child. Seeing her closer, there was no resemblance between the girl and Vita Hart. Her hair was black and shining. The shape of her eyes, the high-set cheekbones said she was an Indian, probably from the mission of St. Pitias nearby.

The ranger took her hand. They walked to the women.

"This is Possum," he said, with only little growl left in his voice.

"Wesoma," Vita Hart corrected him. "Her name is Wesoma, but she won't answer to anything but Possum now."

Olana lowered herself to the child's level. The little girl's sticky fingers reached timidly for her freshly bound-up hair. There, Olana thought. She wasn't doing so badly in this household, was she? Surely Matthew Hart could see that.

"And whose little girl are you?" Olana asked. The child continued to pat her hair. "Cook's?" she tried. The small face looked puzzled. "The gardener's?"

Matthew Hart swept the girl back into his arms so suddenly some of Olana's hair tore from its bonds. His eyes narrowed at his mother, then bore into Olana.

"She's mine," he said. "She's my daughter."

"Yours?" Olana's laugh was high, giddy, broken.

Matthew Hart left the room and the house with the child clinging to his neck.

"Oh my," Vita Hart said. "He really didn't tell you anything about us, did he?"

eighteen

"Matthew! Come back here!"

He stopped, waiting for his mother to catch up with him. She drew a small red bonnet from her deep pocket. Matthew remembered thinking those side seam pockets endless when he was a child. He wondered if Possum saw them that way now. He smiled absently at the thought, but knew his mother was in no humor to discuss pockets as she tied the bonnet under his daughter's chin.

"Your lady doesn't know any better. She can't help the folks she came from any more than you can."

"She ain't—"

" 'Isn't,' Matthew."

"Am I supposed to let her treat Possum like—"

"The only one treating anyone rudely is you."

"Me?"

"What do you call looking at her down the end of your rifle?"

"Prudent."

She exhaled, ran her finger down the back of her granddaughter's dimpled hand, a gesture of both tenderness and common sense, checking if the child was cold. Shit, these women could distract, then disarm his anger, he thought.

"Matthew. She wants to set something right between you, I can feel it. And she finds herself in a place she's never been, among people entirely different from her own. I think she's doing splendidly. It's you who shames me."

"Mama," he tried, "Her people treated me like a servant—"

Her fine brow arched. "What's wrong with serving?"

"Nothing. If you're acknowledged as a member of the human race."

"Oh, Matthew. You already know that."

"But they didn't, don't you see?"

"Then feel sorry for them, not yourself."

Damned woman. Try again. "Mama, I'm used to my own company winters. All I've wanted for months was to get back to the woods—"

"And those terrible men burned you out of your home there, almost killed you! When were you going to tell us that?"

"Shit."

She turned away, pulling her shawl tighter around her strong, straight shoulders.

"Who told you—"

"Don't blame her for anything else! Talk to us, we love you!"

Possum clung to him tighter. "Mama, that's over," he lied softly, knowing it wouldn't be over until he threw dirt into the graves of both the Carson brothers, and whoever hired them.

Possum tugged at his sleeve. "Why does Mana cry?" she asked.

His mother took the child into her arms. "Because you and your daddy are all I have to leave this world," she said.

Matthew didn't understand her devotion, didn't know why she even tolerated him. She loved Possum, of course. He had, in the most accidental way, helped make her a mother again. Maybe that was it. He rested his arm lightly on her shoulder and looked out toward the sea.

"I been thinking—"

" 'I've', Matthew." She sighed. "Please. I don't want to be Possum's sole source of proper English while you're home."

Matthew doubted his daughter would remember his improper English tonight. Her head was already surrendered to his mother's shoulder. How much she'd grown from last year. How splendid she was. "You're right, Mama. And I wanted to talk to you about that. Being home. I've let the place go too long."

"What do you mean, Matthew?"

"I mean, up at the park, the road's all built, you know? And I left all my notes with the folks there. I want to come back year round, Mama. If you think y'all, uh—you all could stand that."

Vita Hart pressed the sleeping child between them as she embraced her son. "This is your home, Matthew. Stay. Watch the stars," she advised, "while I put Possum down into her dreams."

Olana had wanted to run. But Farrell held her anchored beside Annie Smithers. "I'm sure Miss Whittaker here meant no disrespect—" he began.

It was not hatred that sparked the old woman's eyes. What was it? Curiosity? "Can she learn different?" she asked Farrell.

"Learn? Why you should have seen her slinging hash at Three Rivers, without never having to at home, I'll wager."

A soft grunt. "Hard times ahead for these two. Bad blood mix."

Olana stood. "I have no intention of—"

"There, see? Always with their 'intentions,' Yankees, as if they mattered any."

Farrell smiled uneasily. "I'm from Ireland myself," he said.

Annie Smithers took Olana's hand in a gentle hold. "What is it you want, child?" she asked.

"Possum's mother—" Olana heard herself, in spite of intentions.

"He lost her three years ago, to the sea. Full-blooded Yurok. Came out strong in Possum, excepting her build. She'll be tall, like him and his mama.

"He found her on an island out there, beyond the channel. Abandoned after some sailors stole her from the mission, long before. They raped her, cut her tongue out, and threw her overboard when they were done. She'd been living wild with the seals for years. That she didn't kill Matthew on sight for the sin of being a man, I'll never understand. Then, we did raise the child right and respectful, his mama and me did. And a few other good women had a hand in his education by that time, I imagine. He was bringing Possum and her mama home to us when they were wrecked. That's when he went inland, after Seal Woman drowned."

"To us, the road building, and the trees!" Farrell exclaimed. "I knew he was carrying a burden when he first came to us. Didn't I tell you that, Miss Whittaker?"

Olana thought of nothing but her mistake, and a damaged woman who'd been his wife, and the gentle way he held his child. Vita Hart entered with the little girl asleep on her shoulder. How gracefully she walked. Farrell noticed it too. He watched the stairway long after she was gone.

Suddenly the front door opened with the force of a blow. Matthew Hart charged in. He ran his hand through his hair and focused on Olana. "Any of your fancy education make you conversant in Italian?"

She stood in her excitement. "My music lessons last year, in Italy. I sang arias from operas."

"Come see if you can understand all this fuss then," he demanded, catching up her hand in his.

"But what—"

"A whole carriage full of folks. Needing help. I think it's Italian they're speaking. Opera," he muttered over his shoulder to Annie Smithers.

His grandmother grinned, showing a full set of strong white teeth. "Well. Ain't been this social around here since the last big storm blew a few of the lowlanders over," she proclaimed.

Outside, they were beset by a hail of conversation. Children were speaking in English and Italian and translating for each other. One thrust a large grapefruit in Olana's hand before she'd been able to decipher any of it. They pulled like a tide to the black carriage.

Inside the long, low, coach was a mustached man and an enormous woman. Her head was on his shoulder and she panted high in her chest.

Olana looked to Matthew and saw the night's tensions dissolve from his face. A calm serenity took over. When the woman heaved a long sigh, he grasped her hand gently.

"How do you say 'good,' 'Lana?"

"*Bene.*"

"Bene, Señora."

"Signora."

"Oh, yes. *Signora,*" he corrected himself.

The woman's face beamed back at them both before she rested her head again on the man's shoulder.

"*Signora Amadeo,*" the man completed his wife's name while shaking Matthew's hand. I am Antonio Amadeo. This is Smithers?"

"Yes."

"My wife. None came like this, before time. We thought travel safe? Please—in the town—they say to come here. You can help?"

"Yes. Come in."

Together the men eased the woman out of the carriage. They began walking, again swarmed by the children. Olana finally realized where Mrs. Amadeo's enormity was centered.

"Matthew, is she—"

"Very." He smiled.

"But what on earth can we do for her?"

"Not much. She's got the hard part."

"But—"

Mrs. Amadeo stopped the procession following her by standing stock still. She reached out her arms. Her husband, who was a head shorter than she was, took one hand. She grasped the empty air with the other. Olana wanted to run away from the desperate, groping fingers.

"Hold her," Matthew Hart commanded.

Olana caught the hand, felt the grip tighten. Matthew Hart placed his hands somewhere inside the woman's worn black cloak. Slowly, the grip on her hand eased.

"*Bene, bene,*" he said. He turned to Mr. Amadeo. "Olana. Ask him how long have her pains been coming this close."

"Ah—Quanto tempo—ah, *allegro spirito?*"

"Un'ora fa."

"He says for an hour. What does it mean, Matthew?"

"Means we'd better get this lady inside and wash our hands."

He was enjoying her confusion. Why had she ever come here? She wanted to go home, not be thrown into this strange woman's agony.

Once they were in the house, Annie Smithers pointed the way to a small room off the kitchen. Mrs. Amadeo reached the room's doorway just as another of her pains started. She knelt, waving everyone else away furiously. Olana heard round, full words that sounded like a prayer. When it was over Mrs. Amadeo looked around the tiny room as if she'd been brought to the Taj Mahal. *"Grazie,"* she told them all.

Matthew Hart's mother and grandmother smiled. Then Annie Smithers spoke. "Vita, help her with her clothes. Matthew, fetch me the things in the bottom drawer. And you, child—shoo these useless men into the front parlor. Tell them to keep the children quiet. And put the kettle on."

When she returned from performing her tasks, Olana saw the room transformed into a workplace. Mrs. Amadeo was dressed in a white nightgown. Pillows were piled high behind her. Both her attending women had full white aprons over their homespun clothes. Matthew was different only in his rolled-up sleeves. They showed the strong forearms she knew well, but still gave her a shiver of delight to see.

He and his women were talking softly as he put on his spectacles. His grandmother was clearly in charge, though she kept her hands nested in the pockets of her apron until she pushed her grandson toward Olana's steaming kettle.

He held out a low basin of scissors and instruments.

"Pour," he said.

She did. The steam rose up between them, misting his spectacles and the laughing eyes behind them. The task done, Vita Hart pointed to a chair beside the bed. "Talk to her for us, Olana," she asked softly.

Olana slipped into the chair. Mrs. Amadeo's breathing changed again. Vita climbed up on the small bed and stroked the laboring woman's head with a wet cloth. Matthew and his grandmother sat on either side of the bed's foot. The sheets widened. Annie held them higher. Olana swallowed hard. That meant they both could see—

"Crowning!" came Annie Smithers' triumphant whisper. "Your baby's almost here, ma'am."

The woman's tormented face turned to Olana.

"Quando?"

"Yes, soon. *Si!"*

Annie Smithers handed her grandson a small brown bottle.

"Can't depend on my hands anymore, Matthew."

"But Gran—"

"I taught you well."

"It's been years."

"You didn't forget. Don't fuss now. Make me proud."

Olana watched a battle of opposing forces waging war for possession of Matthew Hart's face. Finally, it reflected the pride in the old woman's eyes. With Mrs. Amadeo's next pain, he poured some of the bottle's amber liquid onto a cloth and put it somewhere inside those spread sheets. The woman pulled back into Vita's arms.

"You'll thank him for it later, Mrs. Amadeo," Vita said in a soothing voice, "when you don't count a torn bottom among your miseries." Then her hand probed the woman's bulge. "Still high," she said with concern.

Annie Smithers nodded, though her eyes stayed intent on her grandson's hands.

"Good, Matthew. Steady now."

Mrs. Amadeo gave out a powerful groan and fluid exploded forth, soaking Matthew's shirt. He blinked, but didn't flinch.

"Tell her to stop, breathe easy," Annie Smithers commanded Olana.

"Andante!" sprang from her lips, as she remembered the vocal guidelines of her sheet music. *"Andante tranquillo!"*

Olana locked her eyes on the woman's and blew out soft, long breaths. Mrs. Amadeo followed her example until her time was past. Then she laughed suddenly, and reached up to touch Olana's face.

"Musica sito?"

Olana giggled.

"Bene," the woman approved.

Matthew gave Olana a cocked smile. "What are you two chatting about?" he asked. Before she could tell him that she was translating this birth into a concert, something he saw in Mrs. Amadeo's face made him attend back to his work.

"All the strength you can muster, ma'am," he urged. "But slow."

"Allargando," Olana translated.

Olana heard another splash, then saw Matthew Hart holding up a purple, squirming baby boy.

"Che bellezza!" his mother sang out.

Matthew Hart stared at the infant between his hands. His voice had a misty quality Olana had never heard before. "What does she say, 'Lana?"

"She says this is wonderful."

"You got that right, ma'am." He smiled at Mrs. Amadeo as she held out her arms for her son. Then she closed her eyes in pain, and leaned back into the pillows, groaning.

"Mrs. Amadeo, it's over. Look at your baby," Vita said softly. The woman kept panting, straining. "Olana, tell her that—oh, my Lord," she looked between Mrs. Amadeo's breasts. "Matthew," she called, "there's another."

"What?"

Olana found the wiggling baby boy suddenly thrust into her arms.

nineteen

Let it be the head, he thought, but Matthew Hart had his spectacles on, and had attended enough births to know better. The second child was coming buttocks first. With the woman's next pain the tiny round bottom emerged. The legs squeezed out from under it. Matthew looked to his grandmother. She smiled at him, at the tiny half child in his hands—purple, warm, perfect.

To help ease the waiting he slid his fingers between the baby's legs.

"Girl."

"Bambina," Olana translated.

Mrs. Amadeo grunted hard and the child slipped out to her neck.

"Good, that's fine, ma'am," Matthew Hart said softly, as he checked the child's intact, pulsing cord. It's all right, he told the panic rising up his throat, she doesn't have to breathe yet, she's getting what she needs through the cord. Yet as he heard the child's brother sputter and nuzzle in Olana's arms, he prayed fervently to whatever forces were making the room glow red, to whatever was making so many people so silent it seemed the house was holding its breath. *You're straddling two worlds, child. Come out.*

Mrs. Amadeo moaned. The baby started, her tiny arms and legs stiffening, reaching into the air around her. *No,* his mind cried out, *don't try to breathe yet.* "Gran—" he called, and felt her cloth wipe the sweat from his eyes.

"Clear the way to her nose," Annie Smithers advised softly.

He willed his stiff fingers to move, to go inside the woman and make a breathing passage for her daughter. But they felt broken again, crushed under Cal Carson's boot, though they had long since healed.

"Go on, Matthew."

He transferred the child to his left hand, and with his right, began.

"Ah!" Mrs. Amadeo sighed out her pain.

"I'm sorry," he whispered and went deeper, found the tiny mouth, nose. A sound. Dark, red. The baby was choking. He looked up.

"Push. Push hard with the next one, Mrs. Amadeo," he urged with more calm than he felt. What he felt was another woman dying in his hands, sliding out of his reach, this one before she was even born. *Damn. Damn them all to hell.* He couldn't breathe. The muscles around his middle constricted. Then he heard Olana's voice.

"*Bene, Signora—energia,*" she urged. Her eyes were shinning as she nodded. "I think another one's starting, Matthew," she told him. The knot in his stomach eased. Olana was so beautiful, how could he have pointed his rifle at her? Her cheeks flushed pink as if she'd heard his thought.

Annie Smithers poured the almond oil over the taut skin of the mother's perineum. It stretched more. A deep cry from Mrs. Amadeo and the chin, ears, the head. Free.

"Well, hello," he said as if the baby had just knocked on the door. She opened her eyes wide, gazed into his soul, and defecated a tarry black in his hand. He threw back his head and laughed. Then the room filled with more quiet laughter, intensifying the glow, warming the new life among them.

Olana and Vita bundled Mrs. Amadeo with her children while he tied and cut the cords, then waited for the afterbirths. They came forth soon after the infants began to suckle, and with only a little grunting effort from a mother distracted by her new children.

"Two trees of life," Annie Smithers pronounced as Matthew's hands explored the veined membranes that did indeed spiral forth like an ancient tree.

"Whole?" Annie asked him.

"Whole."

"Long life," she predicted for the twins.

"Long life," he repeated. "Tell her, 'Lana."

Olana didn't answer. He raised his head and found her watching the babies at their mother's breasts. Her eyes were as wide as Possum's when she'd first seen the sea.

He finished his work, then drew Olana into a corner of the room. Her gown and hands were stained red from the little boy she'd held. He pulled down the damp towel from his shoulder and wiped her fingers.

"It's going away," she whispered.

"What is?"

"The glow. And the smell of roses." He savored that look on her face, memorized the brilliance of her eyes, the winsome slant of the brows above them. "It was real, Matthew? The roses? The glow?"

"Red?"

"Yes."

"It was red for me this time, too."

"It's too early for roses."

He shrugged. "Always smells like roses at births Gran attends."

Her hands pressed his through the cloth. He brought them to his lips. They were as soft as the babies were, and smelled of the heady brew of new life. They were both startled by the laughter and a torrent of Italian language behind them. He released her.

"What does she say?"

A high color came into Olana's cheeks. "Isn't it time her hus—band and children came in?" she asked. "I would think they'd like to see—"

"That's not what she's saying."

Mrs. Amadeo expanded her thoughts.

"I'm not getting it all," Olana protested. "And she doesn't understand . . . us, Matthew. She thinks—"

"Olana, what does she say?" he pressed.

"That I will make you fine children."

"Oh."

Her eyes went brighter still. With anger. "That's all? 'Oh?' No laughter? Surely the notion amuses you. Taken for your wife again, a stupid, unwelcome Yankee?"

He grinned. "You can't help being a Yankee. And you ain't the rest."

"That's as close as you'll get to an apology," his mother advised from behind him. "He takes after his grandmother that way."

Vita Hart knocked her son playfully on the side of his head. "Go tell that poor man to come in and meet his new children," she commanded.

They all knelt around the hearth. The oldest two boys were already half a head over their father's height. The youngest was a girl about six years old. There were four in between. The babies were going to have seven pairs of loving arms to hold them, besides those of their parents. A good time for twins in this family, Matthew judged.

Only Farrell, kneeling there among them, did not have a string of rosary beads gliding between his fingers. Matthew Hart watched the mouths moving in soundless devotion. Then he saw himself putting his wife's rosary in her grave at the mission. She'd blended her Catholicism with the lore of her people. Perhaps he should have saved the beads for Possum. They finished the Hail Mary. Mr. Amadeo raised his head.

Matthew smiled. "They're all fine."

"All?"

Matthew touched Olana's back. "You tell him."

Olana held up two fingers. *"Due,"* she said, *"bambino, bambina."*

That set off a gasp and a stream of questions from the man and his children. Olana kept nodding. Finally, Mr. Amadeo lifted her off her feet and smacked her cheek with a kiss. Farrell looked to Matthew and shook his hand.

"Always knew you were a doctor, Matty!"

He frowned. "I ain't nothing of the kind. I get to catch babies every now and then, is all."

"Catch babies, cure snakebite, and heal frostbite—"

Mr. Amadeo and his children surrounded them. "Go in, go see them," Matthew urged.

But the small man locked Matthew Hart's shoulders in an embrace first, then smacked his face with an only slightly less invigorating kiss than he'd bestowed on Olana.

"Damn," the ranger groused as the crowd passed. "I thought letting you tell him would save me from that."

Olana laughed. "It's very Continental."

He wiped his face with the back of his hand. "It's very mortifying."

The room was empty. She came closer. He righted Possum's little chair, knocked over in the rush.

"Matthew?"

"Hmmm?"

"I . . . don't want to wash any of it off."

He smiled. "I know. Maybe we should walk out on the beach? It's stopped raining."

"All right."

Matthew had always done this part alone. He tried hard not to resent her presence. When they reached the sand Olana drew closer.

"Matthew, your hands are shaking."

He looked down at them. "Always do, after. Gran says there's no shame in it." He laughed randomly. "Hope it won't be twice as bad, that's all."

"You love her very much, don't you?"

"Gran? Sure. I didn't think I was worth anything when she started bringing me to her birthings. Let me into a world of women's secrets. Told me I had a gift."

"You do."

"Naw. But I needed to think so then, until I got better at watching her. Doing what she does. Did. It must be hard on her not to be able to bring them in anymore."

"She didn't look to be suffering tonight."

"No. How could any of us? Two, 'Lana. Two!"

The rush of pure joy that always followed the shaking began. He didn't want to frighten her. But he didn't want to miss it. He looked from her perplexed eyes to the stains on the ivory gown. Blood. Panic threatened his joy. The stains had to go.

Olana protected her middle as she backed away from him. "I can't swim."

"Now that's a shame."

He advanced, lifted her over his shoulder and bolted into the water. She laughed, pounding his back lightly. He spun around once then dropped her. Her flailing arms made a great splash.

Matthew left Olana standing, sputtering, the water swirling around her waist. He dove deep, swimming along the bottom. The height of the rush came like a great, crashing wave, fed by his own awe of how circumstances had come together so that he'd held those two new lives in his hands. Matthew Hart's world, for a shining moment, had been in perfect order, and he knew enough to give thanks for it. He wished he didn't have to breathe, and heard a tinkling laughter inside his head in response to the thought. Her laughter. Piercing his aching lungs, finding its mark where it always did, his heart.

Matthew let his own buoyancy carry him to the surface. Moon-illuminated strands of seaweed and glistening sand caressed him as he rose. Like her fingers. Stop. The desolation always followed those memories.

He surfaced, dove again. Stay, he told himself. Stay here cold, deep. Then Olana's cry came through to his ears. He'd forgotten her. Completely. He surfaced. She was standing where he'd left her in the water. Crying. Why was she crying? He swam to her side.

"What's the matter?" he asked, his voice sounding strange, distant, even to him.

"I didn't see you. For so long. Oh, Matthew, don't do that!"

"I'm sorry," he said as she shivered, wept, grew more beautiful. He took her into his arms, held her close. Not the same. "Stop. Olana, stop, now."

"I'm trying." She choked, hiccoughed, sputtered like the newborn she'd held in her arms. Different. Full of airs, properties, this one. Not that powerful woman he'd loved, then killed.

"Bones in this water?" he teased, which only made Olana sputter more. Her sputtering turned lower, deeper. He licked salt the sea had left from her earlobes, chin, neck, and feasted on her soft moans of pleasure. Her fingers raked through his hair, flinging strands of seaweed back to the water. His hands found her, not obstructions to her, everywhere.

"Why, Miss Whittaker," he said, "you're quite corsetless this evening."

She smiled wide. "How rude of you to notice."

He thought he'd earned a slap at least, but he got only soft, deep laughter against his neck. "I missed you, Matthew," she whispered.

He kissed her then, kissed her mouth like it was the first food he'd had in months.

twenty

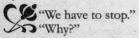 "We have to stop."

"Why?"

"Because you're the women's guest. Uninvited, but—"

"You've made that clear enough!" Her anger finally flared, annoying Matthew in its timing. She could have waited until the soft curves of her breasts weren't so transparent through the weave.

"Stop that," he warned.

"What?"

"That infernal pouting. I ain't your father, it won't work with me."

He watched her level, measured gaze. Was she wondering if she could get a clear blow at him? The night's birth exhilaration had left them both sharp. No. She picked up the dripping train of his mother's gown and turned away. Somehow that hurt worse.

Once on shore, the wet muslin choked her shins. His sharpness was so far gone that he could not even catch her as she sank onto her knees in the sand.

"What am I doing here?" she whispered.

He leaned over her. "That's what I want to know."

"I came to save you."

"Save me?"

"Didn't I? And what do I find? I find a wife—"

"Wife?"

"Who is really your mother . . . a whole houseful of women, and Italian people, and this beautiful, beautiful baby . . ." She stared at her arms, outstretched as they were when he'd thrust the tiny boy into them. "Two babies," she corrected herself.

He knelt beside her.

"I'm not crying," she maintained, though the tears were dripping off her nose.

"No, 'course not," he whispered, lifting her into his arms. Clinging skirts now threatened his own steadiness. "You're just real tired, darlin'."

"Matthew Hart," she murmured.

"Hmmm?"

"You're always telling me how I feel."

"I am?"

"Yes."

He smiled. "And I'm always right."

"No. Not always."

Her head stilled against his chest. He only allowed himself to lower his face into the wild nest of her hair once, to savor the scents of the sea and new life combined.

When they reached the porch, Annie Smithers flung the blanket over Olana and began pulling out hairpins. "Swimming this early. And when the moon is full. Don't you know that makes you daft?" Olana's wet hair slapped across his arm. Annie sighed. "Best introduction she could get to this family, I suppose. Sit. Your mother's getting the rest of them abed. She'll want to do the same for your grand lady."

Matthew half fell into the porch swing. His burden didn't even stir. "She's not my—"

"Always sleep this sound, does she?"

"How should I know?" he said, too quickly.

"Looked after her through the winter, with no knowledge of her habits?"

He felt himself coloring. She hadn't meant . . . or maybe she had. Damnation. His grandmother was the only woman who could make him blush. He tried getting interested in the floorboards of the porch, two of which needed replacing. No good. She waited.

"I been trying to steer clear of her, Gran. You didn't raise a fool, I know what's trouble."

"Never made you sidestep any, not in my memory. Why'd she track you here?"

"Some notion she's got of saving me."

"She bible toting?"

"No!"

"Well, what do you know, Matthew?"

Olana stirred, brushed her face against his chest and sighed. Matthew looked into his grandmother's eyes. Trapped. His voice became a fine thread of a whisper. "She makes me feel—"

"Makes you? This bit of a girl ties you up helpless, does she?" she spat out.

He stared at the moon. "I feel," he corrected himself in a desolate whisper. "I feel whole again, Gran. Just when I was getting comfortable in the part."

Annie Smithers yanked the hair back from his brow with a gruff tenderness. "You're all of a piece, child. There's pain, but you get useless without living whole."

Her eyes joined his in their survey of the clearing night sky.

"You did well tonight, Matthew," his midwife grandmother told him.

"For a man," he finished.

"No." She smiled. "When your grandfather started helping me with the birthings I'd only give him that he did all right for a man. Wasn't so. Ain't now. You both have the gift. My pride ain't such that I'll keep it from you, like I done him."

Matthew always knew when the grandfather Annie meant was his mother's father, not her last husband, Joseph Fish, who was the only grandfather he'd known. Vita's father was the one they all said was the outlaw. All of them but Annie. She called him her darling boy, like she sometimes, rarely now, called him.

"You're mashing her nose, Matthew."

"What?"

Annie Smithers laughed softly, then looked up to the woman who'd appeared in the doorway. "Best get these last ones abed, Vita, before your boy dents his lady's face permanent."

"She's not—" he began to insist again.

"She did well too. For a Yankee."

Vita led them inside and upstairs, past what had been his uncles' bedrooms, now full of children's deep breathing. Someone had set out a jar of hyacinths in his room, beside his bed. His mother motioned for him to set Olana down.

Hell, he needed to keep watch anyway. He did her bidding without protest.

"Poor child." Vita Hart sighed. "What have you done with her?"

"Me? I only—"

"Soaked her to the skin when the nights are still cool," she fussed at him as she laid out Olana's damp hair across the pillows.

"It was her—"

"Go now." She waved to the adjoining door. "Take your rest."

"You're damned peas in a pod with Gran, you know that?" he said in a furious whisper. It only made her smile. "Now there's two women won't let a man finish a sent—"

"Shoo."

He grabbed a pillow from the empty half of his bed. The movement caused Olana to stir and sigh deeply. His mother's warning look returned. Matthew tucked the pillow under his arm. "I'm going," he said, retreating.

twenty-one

Olana woke to soft breezes blowing in from the open casement windows. She stayed still, wondering where she was, until she smelled the salt-sea air, heard the rush of the ocean, its pounding against the shore. She rose slowly from the abundant feather bed. She was dressed in a nightgown of light blue with delicate embroidered roses on the placket. It had not been Matthew who dressed her, she knew that from the careful attention to the ties and buttoning. On the chair beside her bed were her traveling clothes, pressed and clean, and the white nightgown she'd worn last night, also cleaned and yes, she realized as she drew it up to her shoulders, shortened to her height.

She walked to the window and drew the lace curtains back. Below her a child was weaving a string between her fingers and those of the doll Matthew brought her from San Francisco. What did they all call her? Possum. Matthew Hart was a father. Possum's father. A fresh pain stabbed through all the wonder from the night before. Would Matthew forgive the assumptions she'd made?

"Stay still!" Annie Smithers' exasperation exploded from the next room. Olana went to one of the three pine panel doors and opened it a crack. Within the adjoining room, Matthew was trying to free himself from his grandmother's grasp. She pushed him into the curved back chair.

"Now let me get a decent measure."

"I'm the same size I always been."

"You're thinner."

"I'll eat."

He tried to rise again. She finally stripped the shirt off him.

"Oh, child. Darlin' boy." Her voice's tenderness was as naked as his back. "I knew you weren't going all modest on me for no reason."

"It's not—"

"Now, don't you go wasting your mind on a lie, Matthew," she scolded softly. "I know the marks of a bear."

She touched the scars. "How did you treat it?" she asked.

" 'Lana packed it with snow, then greased it."

"The Yankee?"

"Olana's her name, Gran."

"Well, appears she is good for more than sleeping the morning away and showing off feathers and satin enough to turn your mama green."

"She catches babies all right, too," he reminded her.

Olana could feel the rush of pride warm her. Annie Smithers only grunted, and continued studying his back. "Any infection? Fever?"

"Some—at 'Lana's place." He swung around in the chair and Olana could see excitement in his eyes. "This lady, the cook? She made a good healing concoction. I wrote it in the book. Along with a fine recipe of hers for curing a morning after."

"Bears and the demon rum. You had an eventful winter."

"Aw, Gran."

She touched his cheek. "Was it hard for you? Being back in that city?"

"Sure," he said softly. "Sure it was."

Olana longed to know everything they knew about each other. Her fingers touched the door.

"Stand up," Annie Smithers' no-nonsense voice was back, ordering a man Olana didn't think could be ordered. But he stood, as she unrolled her worn tape measure.

"Gran, I ain't grown taller since last year."

She made him hold the measure at his waist as she knelt and brought it to the heel of his boot. "Living 'mongst them towering trees so long," she mused, "you never know."

Annie finally finished measuring, recording her calculations. How nimble she was, Olana marvelled, this spidery grandmother of Matthew's. Her own mother would look tortured and old beside this woman. Annie Smithers flung a soft shirt from her sewing basket at her grandson. He pulled it over his head, but stopped suddenly at the third button, and snatched up the old woman's hands.

"This shirt's new. This season. And it's your work, not Mama's. Ain't nothing unsteady about your hands."

"Didn't say there was."

"But, last night, the babies . . . you made me do it."

"Seemed like you needed to." She smiled. "You put me in mind of when you first came to us—all lost, beaten down. What's made you so?"

He walked to a window, bracing his arm against the frame. "I want to come home, Gran."

"Why? You ain't stopped loving them trees, with or without the bears."

"No."

"Ain't known you to turn from anything needing your protection."

"I got my own family needing, don't I? And the place here? With Grandfather gone—"

"The place is looking worn down. And Possum older," she continued for him.

"Yes."

"None of that's the reason. Oh, you've fooled your mama. Through the night we shared vigil with the babies, she gushed on about you being home to stay. Never was suspicious enough, that girl. And she's so happy she don't see you got pushed back into our lovin' arms."

"Pushed?"

"You heard me." She waited. Silence. "By whoever occasioned that gold tooth?" He was still not forthcoming. She shrugged. "Tell me now, tell me later."

Olana found herself taking a strange, secret pleasure in knowing something these women whose blood he shared didn't know. That made it easier to watch the beauty among them. Annie Smithers straightened the garment, which was more like a farmer's smock than a shirt. Her hand lingered on his shoulder.

"Your mama, she frets, Matthew. Ain't no need to tell her about the bear, is there?"

"Weren't no need to tell you. And if you weren't so blamed exact in your measurement—"

"That was Vita's doing. Also says I got to chat with your lady there on pattern changes to make modern your clothes."

"What?"

He pulled his suspenders hastily up over his shoulders, then grabbed his vest from the chairback on his way out. "Mama!" he called. His grandmother followed at his heels. "Matthew Hart! Them babies!" she hushed him furiously.

Olana used the commotion to mask her closing the door. Annie Smithers entered from the corridor as she was doing it.

"You'd best get some breakfast before showing me how to yank my boy into your century," she advised, then strode off.

Olana had barely time to look at her watch, her morning had been so full of people and tasks. But now it was growing quiet, even here, outside, where the ocean was always in hearing distance. The children had gone down to the beach. The babies were nesting quietly with their mother. Matthew Hart had barely been in her sight, and then he was awkward and distant.

Vita Hart had patiently absorbed Olana into the household. Annie Smithers was more tart, but in her own way, thankful for what little help Olana could render, given her ignorance, her need to be taught the things the women did so easily.

Olana took her cup of fruit-scented tea and the large wedge of raisin cake and sat out on the back porch steps. She did it quietly, so that the sharp-eyed little girl went on playing with her doll.

"Do you like her?" Olana asked.

Possum looked up. She didn't run away, as she had with the Amadeo children's attempts to include her in their afternoon play. She nodded. Olana smiled. "Why are you called Possum?" she asked.

"Because I am still. The possum must be my spirit animal, he says."

"Your papa?"

"Papa?"

"Father?"

"Daddy. Matthew is my daddy," the little girl explained patiently, although she could not yet pronounce the "th" in her father's name. "No. Grandfather gave me the name. He died. We all cry, sometimes. But I dream of him then. In my dreams he's on his way to Seventh Heaven. He's in the mountains. With Daddy and the trees." She began to rock her father's gift on her knees.

Matthew Hart's daughter was as strange as he, Olana decided. Confusing. She didn't talk like a child at all.

"Have you named your dolly?" Olana asked quickly.

"Mama."

There, better. Olana laughed. "That's what she says, doesn't she? But that's not her name!"

"Says?"

All of the dolls in the window of the shop where Matthew'd bought this one had the device. Olana thought that's what had fascinated him, as he'd been fascinated by Alisdair Dodge's photography. At last. Her turn to be teacher. "Didn't your daddy show you that she can talk, Possum?"

"No, miss."

"May I?"

She took the doll from the child's embrace and turned it to make the mechanism work. No sound. She tried again. The child looked fretful. Her fingers reached. Olana placed the doll on her lap, examined its back. There, beneath the velvet coat and lace bodice, the muslin body was ravaged with an indentation. And clumsy stitches. Matthew's stitches.

"He took that clever device out. He took her voice out," Olana said, stunned by the realization. "Why in heaven's name did he do that?"

"My mama had no voice," Possum explained, then gave her doll to Olana. "She's pretty?" the child asked.

"Beautiful."

"I am not. I am a damned Breed."

"Who calls you that?"

"People in town. They say, 'Look at Vita Hart. That beauty saddled with a damned Breed.'" The child smiled. Olana felt Possum's quiet tolerance. "Do you think gardeners are ugly?"

"No!"

"Give her the doll," she heard Matthew's hard voice command, before he threw his toolbox on the porch. He watched, steel-eyed, as she obeyed. Then he walked off toward the apricot grove.

"He's hungry. Feed him," his daughter advised, putting Olana's forgotten raisin cake into her hands, before she skipped into the house. "Mana! Gran!" she called. "Cook!"

Olana found him in the grove of apricot trees, leaning on a gnarled trunk so dwarflike compared to his sequoias. He was watching the Amadeo children below.

"Matthew—"

He didn't turn around. "She can play without the doll squawking back. She doesn't need everything done for her. Not my daughter."

"Not like the Whittaker daughter."

"I didn't say that."

"No, you didn't. Coward."

He turned quickly, almost knocking her offering from her hands. She shoved it against his soft shirt.

"Here. Eat," she commanded.

A smile stole across his face. "Hell," he said. "Now you sound like them."

She looked into the distance, bit her lip. He touched her arm as shyly as he'd been bold the night before.

"Aw, 'Lana. Have mercy on a man used to his solitude."

"No more swearing!"

"Sure, all right, only don't start bawling."

"I don't bawl!"

She heard him make several further attempts to speak, but they ended up odd, exasperated noises. Then he sat, and the sounds changed. She stole a look. He was eating.

"Want some?"

"No. Thank you."

He reached up for her hand. His was swollen, nicked with the work he'd done all day. "Sit. Please. Let's talk."

"Yes. How could you leave Three Rivers without—"

"About you going," he changed her course.

"I see. Which you would like to be—"

"Yesterday. But it's not for me to say."

"Why not?"

"This is my grandmother's and my mother's home. You're their guest, not mine. And against my advice they've accepted your offer to help out with the Amadeos. You won't be tossing feed to chickens at your leisure here. You don't yet know what work is, Miss Whittaker. But you'll find out. And you'll leave with the Amadeos."

"I thought you said that matter was up to—"

"You'll leave!"

Was this the same man who'd held up those babies in the rosy glow last night? Who had made her cry out in joy under his loving hands? He rested his forearm on his knee now. Tension showed in his long fingers, in the line of worry across his forehead.

"Listen, 'Lana, I don't mean it like that, exactly. I just can't catch my breath, you know? So much is happening. You—you don't know anyone named Hopkins, do you?"

"Is this someone from San Francisco?"

"Maybe."

"No. But perhaps, if I wire Sidney, he could—"

He took her arm. " 'Lana, you need to listen to me now. Nobody knows about this place." He rubbed at the line on his forehead and gave out a short, helpless laugh. "Nobody but you, and Farrell, and the Amadeo family."

"And Mrs. Goddard."

"Mrs. Goddard?"

"It would take wild horses to get it out of her, Matthew. And it's not an exact address, it was just the town's name on an envelope you once left behind."

"God almighty, why did I come here? It all seemed so right last night, with the babies. Even you and Farrell seemed right where you were supposed to be. Well, listen. If you stay here, you got to stay without contact. Sidney, your parents. Anyone."

"On that subject I can reassure you. I've Aunt Winnie'd this excursion."

"What?"

"I didn't think Mother would approve of my returning to the park, so she thinks I'm shopping with my aunt for the next social season. She approved of that and was, frankly, glad to be rid of me, I think."

"Damnation!"

"Matthew, you promised."

She made it sound tart and prim, like in the days they wintered together, to make him remember, smile. But he didn't smile. He stared off toward the house, and the child playing with the ringlets of her new doll's hair.

"How old is your little girl, Matthew?" she asked him quietly.

"Not yet four. Last year she was still a baby, barely talking. Someday she'll be as crafty and stubborn as you. This fathering business is terrible hard."

"Terribly. It's an adverb."

That got her a look so sharp she held up her hands in supplication. "Vita made me promise to correct you—honestly! It's part of my official duties."

"Like telling her my clothes don't suit me?"

"I didn't do anything of the sort! It was she came to me. She asked me to describe how men's apparel is fashioned now and I only—"

"We prefer simple ways here."

"I've noticed." No. She didn't mean to ice the words. He was so sensitive to that difference between them, the one that was mattering less and less to her. She wished he would say anything, no matter how blunt, how cruel. But he stood and walked to the house without looking back at her.

"Well, it would've been just a visit to the cave. Then we ran smack into—into your other troubles, lad."

His eyes iced. "I resigned, Farrell. That's all. To come home." The last word brought on a thaw. "My little girl's growing up without me. I don't want to disappear again," he whispered, leaning his head on his arms.

"Is that what you been doing since the court martial, Matty?"

Farrell lost his friend's eyes to the sea again. "The women need me, don't they?"

"I could go up to San Francisco. Make some inquiries myself."

Matthew raised his head, smiled. "Not without the women's leave you're not going anywhere. We got guests. And you're useful, with your wild Irish stories and 'Lana's Italian translations. But maybe, after, if you're willing. But no one can know about this place. If ever the women got hurt on my account—well, it'd kill me. Then they'd be left with no protection at all."

"Draw up your mama's quilt, Matty. I'll take the first watch."

"Lay your head back, like on a pillow," he urged.

"It's not a pillow."

Damned woman, why did he offer to teach her to swim? Because she could drown, for not knowing. What if she went on one of those cruises her San Francisco friends were always coming or going from? His patience returned.

"Still, it will hold you like a pillow. Better. It will hold all of you. Take a breath, a deep one, come on, with me."

He put his face beside hers in the water and inhaled. She watched him, smiled slowly. She was enjoying his torture in seeing her soaked to the skin.

"Breathe!"

"You don't have to shout."

Her hold on his arm loosened. She took a deep breath. And there, yes, she was floating on the surface of the bay. Her hair soaked and resting on the water gave her face the look of one younger, a child. She was a child, reveling in the power and beauty of her body. Why shouldn't she? He'd been the same way with Lottie, after all.

"Matthew. It feels like I could stay here, and rest."

"You can."

He remembered floating like she was now, while his wife dove deep and far to play with the seals, even in the days when the baby was heavy within her. He grew to love her strange, guttural sounds, to pick it out among the seals and know her. He didn't have to teach himself to love this woman's voice, and that shamed him. It was a betrayal, somehow, of his wife.

"It's as if you're not even holding me."

"I'm not."

"Of course you—" She tugged on the light muslin of her underskirt he'd slipped into her hand instead of his sleeve. She panicked and sank before he could recover her. She came up sputtering and screaming.

"Blow the water out your nose. It will feel better."

She obeyed, then hit him a glancing blow to his shoulder. "You lied! You said you'd hold me!"

"I didn't say forever. 'Lana. You held yourself. I might not be beside you in the water, sometime."

"I hate the water."

"Maybe. But you're not helpless in it."

He turned toward the shore, avoiding those wide eyes, those soft, curving shoulders. But when he was waist deep, he felt the tug at his sleeve.

"I'm sorry. More, please?"

He smiled. "You sound like Possum."

"Will I ever swim as well as Possum?"

"Possum will swim better than I do, soon. She has her mother's gift. No one will match her."

She was pouting that infernal pout. He dared not try either of their patience anymore today. He took her hand.

"Come out. I don't hear the voices anymore, do you? I wonder where they've drifted off to."

The scream of the child made their hands lock together before they ran together up the shoreline.

twenty-three

Matthew counted their heads as they ran. Only five, no, six, one was two-headed—Joseph had Louisa on his back. Missing was another sister, Cara. Possum took hold of his suspenders and nodded toward the shoreline's caves as Constantine, the oldest boy, spoke.

"She follow the music—there, Matt."

"Music?"

"We go, forget. Now, look. We call, call. No Cara *mia*."

"High tide. That cave's closed off, will flood."

"Che cosa?"

Matthew looked beyond the boy's worried face and lifted Possum higher, pressing her against his heart. He closed his eyes, listened. He heard breathing. Even, slow, breathing. He gave his daughter to Olana.

"Cara's asleep. I'll get her. Tell them, 'Lana."

He turned back once, when the water reached his waist. The children had closed in around Olana and Possum. The sight of them he'd remember his life long, were he now successful. If not, it would be the sight he'd take and hold onto as long as he could.

He hit his head on the underwater ceiling of the cave twice before he finally found the surface. He came up gasping, but the sleeping child did not even stir. He touched her arm.

"Cara mia?" he repeated her brother's affectionate name.

She opened her eyes, smiled her recognition of him. Matthew liked her lively, intelligent face, the tender way she held Louisa up to see the babies. Cara looked to where the entrance had been. Her face contorted into a young mirror of her mother's in childbirth.

"Insidia!"

She pulled away from his reach, her eyes wildly surveying their disappearing pocket of air. "Easy, Cara. Breathe easy," he urged.

"Ee-see?"

"That's right. High tide fills this cave. But I got in, didn't I? And we can get out. Together."

"No! *Non oltre,* Matthew!"

Her panic echoed off the glistening walls. He ran his hand through his hair and took in a long breath of air. Precious air. Would Possum remember him? Will she mix him up with that other face on the mantle if both their likenesses were there? Would Olana turn to Darius Moore and forget him, forget how his child had once clung to her neck? Stop it, he ordered the voices in his head.

"Seal Woman will help us, Cara. Maybe it was her music drew you inside. She used to sing, you know? Couldn't speak, but she could sing. Like a flute. Clear-throated melodies of her people. If we need breath getting out, she'll help us, I know she will."

He reached out his hand. She took it.

"There's the girl, Cara. Come. Play with me in the water. Watch your hair swirl around like hers, like a mermaid's."

As she floated in the rising water, Matthew took out his knife and began cutting a strip of fabric from the hem of her skirt. He tied one end about her waist, the other around his wrist. He looked into her eyes and saw the panic subsiding, replaced by a puzzled stare.

"There. Until we're outside we'll be attached, like the twins were to your mama. I'm your mama."

She giggled softly, hiding her new second teeth behind her fingers.

"Hey," he said, pouting. "I thought you didn't know my language!"

Olana saw the child first, her head bobbing over the surface, then disappearing. She screamed her name and tore into the water, going as far as she dared, then sending Possum out from her. Possum found her father, who came up sputtering with his burden under his arm. He stumbled and let her brothers relieve him of the child. They lay her on the sand. His voice was clear and deep as he sliced the remnant of cloth between them.

"Leave her be," he told the children. "She's doing fine. *"Bene, Cara mia."*

She continued choking out seawater, but her head tilted toward Matthew and the corner of her mouth spasmed into a smile. He sat back and rested in Olana's arms.

That night he sat on the porch steps, staring at the stars and absently picking at the piece of cloth still tied to his wrist when Olana appeared above him. She held out the steaming cup of tea. "Your grandmother says to drink it all."

He let it warm his hands and inhaled the sweet scent. "Sassafras. She thinks my blood's gone thin, does she?"

"Has it?" Olana smiled, he could feel it, though she kept her chin low, her face in the shadows. She resisted only slightly as he raised it.

"The outdoors suits you. It suits you something fine," he whispered, sweeping his hand behind her neck as he kissed the patches of moonlight that played between those of the tree branches on her face. Then he kissed the shadow places. She leaned her head back and let him continue the pattern on her neck.

"What did you put in that tea, woman?" he teased, biting her earlobe.

She laughed, drawing him close. His hands gave her hips a dancing massage and his kisses deepened, sweetened by his grandmother's sassafras.

"Come back with me, Matthew," she urged.

"What?"

"Back to Three Rivers."

A wall of ice came between them. "Why?"

"To clear yourself from these ridiculous accusations."

"Does your Mr. Lunt think they're ridiculous?"

"It wasn't Sidney who—"

"No? Are you sure?"

"I work for the man, Matthew."

"Oh? You've taken to staining your fingers with ink?"

"You don't know anything about it! My pieces have a . . . a following. And between Sidney and myself, I assure you, we will reinstate you in your position."

"I have no position."

"Because you won't defend yourself!"

"I have no defense."

She laughed high, nervous. "Matthew, there's been a terrible mistake. You mustn't let your pride—"

"It isn't."

"Not pride then! Hurt? Whatever is keeping you—"

"Olana. It isn't a mistake."

She laughed again. His face stayed sober.

"The man who swam in after that child today, the one who came after me in that snowstorm, the one who stood up to those horrible men—he wasn't discharged dishonorably from the army."

"But he was."

"Why?"

"I was a traitor. During wartime."

"They'd have had you shot!"

"Hanged. Mustn't waste bullets on somebody like me. They were building the scaffold. I watched them for three days."

"Stop it!"

He took her arms in his steely grip. "I warned you. Told you I wasn't your silly dream of me. But you wouldn't leave me be. Now you've invaded my house, my work, my skin. Well, you won't cause my women to go through that hell again, you hear me? Go home, Miss Whittaker. To your blasted social season, your foolish—"

"I don't fit here, do I?"

"You fit too well."

"How? I'm not one of your pampering women who never ask the difficult questions, who keep you at the center of their lives, even though you shut them out whenever it's your whim. The women who care for a child you abandoned—"

"I think you should be quiet now," he said in a soft, unworldly voice she'd never heard before. It triggered a peak in her rage.

"Quiet! Of course, darling boy! I must be a terrible annoyance. You prefer your women without tongues!"

Olana was on the ground before she realized he'd hit her. She felt no pain, not even a sting. Where had he struck? She didn't even know that. She didn't remember going down backwards over the root of the apricot tree, but there she was.

She remembered the look on his face. It was the look that brought tears to her eyes, not any pain. She watched him stare at his right hand. Was that the one? She watched him open, close the hand. Then Matthew Hart did something he'd never done in all the time she'd known him. He ran away.

twenty-four

Farrell left Olana's side to hitch the horses to the wagon. She'd said her good-byes to everyone, except the two women. And Matthew, of course. He hadn't returned.

Vita came from the side of the house. She ran to Olana and took her hands. "Wait. Don't go until I come back."

Olana nodded. Vita disappeared in the soundless glide of her skirts. Another ten years at finishing school would not give her that much grace. Vita returned with Annie Smithers at her side.

"We're beholden," the old woman, prompted by her daughter's elbow, declared.

"I was glad to earn my keep."

"We didn't keep you," she snapped, then sighed. "Look here, child. You sure you two can't talk this out between you?"

"Quite sure."

A small sob erupted from Vita, which touched Olana to a degree she didn't expect. Annie Smithers continued talking for them both. "We know now we got him spoilt something awful. We don't know how to fix it. We were counting on your help in that."

"Spoiled?"

"On account of he's our only child left, and our heir. His nature's good and true—you know that, down in that part of you pure of manners, that part that's like him."

"I am nothing like him."

The old woman's jawline tightened, like her grandson's had right before he hit her. But she took in a deep breath that freed her voice of anger.

"If you feel the least affection for us, know this. You're leaving a parcel of troubles on our hands if you leave us now."

"The Amadeos understand enough English—"

"It's your understanding that troubles me, Olana Whittaker."

"Mama, don't." Vita Hart's voice cut through the tension. She stood between them, offering something. Olana was circled in the women's cinnamon scent, their soft brown eyes. They put in her hands the folds of Vita's wondrous cloth, Annie's sewing. It was the gown she'd worn on the night of the birth. Don't look at it, Olana told herself.

"Please," Vita Hart entreated. "It's the only way we'll have to touch you. Remember we're your friends and here, waiting if ever you need us."

"Got nothing to do with him, you hear?" Annie said. "It's 'mongst the three of us."

Olana turned to Farrell and the waiting wagon. She didn't look back.

Matthew Hart watched the friars leave the fields for evening vespers. The older ones ruffled his hair as if he were still fifteen as they put their hoes in his hands. He wanted to follow them into their adobe mission church, and give himself up to a religion of mysteries and obedience. But he needed Olana's forgiveness first. He hoisted the hoes to his shoulder and headed toward the shed.

"She's gone. You can come home now."

He turned to see Farrell. "Gone?"

"I'm just getting back from the train station."

"I never hit a woman before in my life Farrell, I swear it."

"You hit her?"

"Didn't she say?"

"She didn't say more than two words together at a time, even to the women. But I didn't like the look about her. What possessed you, Matty?"

"It was like watching someone else do it. I wanted to kill whoever's hand—"

"Easy, lad. I'm fond of the girl, but you're not the first man who's lost his temper with a difficult woman. Some even feel it's a good thing to give them a regular—"

"I ain't one of those!"

"No, no, and me either. I'm just saying the urge is human nature, poor blighted souls that we be. I suspect even ladies like Miss Whittaker understand that. I don't suspect that was all turned her homeward, neither."

"What?"

"Not used to feeling outnumbered, I think."

"Outnumbered?"

"By doting women. You've got yourself a paradise here my friend. You must know that."

Matthew turned west, to the open sea. "I know that blizzards and tall trees can be more peaceful company."

"But you have a family. And a fine woman."

"I don't have any woman. I don't want any woman!"

"Why not, son?"

The evening wind, the vespers, the bell turned Farrell's voice into his grandfather's. Under the spell of that voice, he couldn't lie, even to himself. He drew in a breath that rippled under the strain of the truth. "Because it hurts too much when I lose them."

"Miss Whittaker is a young, strong woman, Matthew. What makes you think—"

"If I love them, they die."

"That's foolish."

"Hasn't been."

"What would your mama, your grandma do under the burden of such thinking?"

"Do?"

"They'd have to disown you."

"Why?"

"On account of all them pictures on their mantle. All the husbands, fathers, brothers. You're the last of their men, ain't you?"

"I . . . suppose."

"Well, don't they worry about you dancing with heiresses and grizzlies all in one season? But nothing keeps them from loving you."

"I hadn't thought of that."

"You think you're the only one whose life's been touched by

misfortune? Why those women put up with—"

"Don't you go badmouthing my family, Farrell!"

"There, you feel something for them, that's a relief. They're more than your handmaids."

"Handmaids? The way they badger me?"

Farrell laughed. "You foolish enough to prefer peace to these women? That being so I'd gladly take your place."

Matthew Hart slammed the last hoe into its pegged place on the wall, then joined Farrell walking to his grandmother's farm. In the grove of apricot trees, at almost the spot he'd cuffed Olana, Farrell did something Matthew had never seen him do in the three years he'd known him. He removed his hat when he wasn't anywhere near inside.

"Matty? I mean it. About taking a place with you here."

"What?"

"I'd like your permission to court your mother."

Matthew's stride broke, and he almost tripped over his own feet. The Irishman stopped, hit his hat against his leg.

"You quit making this so hard on me! I know you got troubles of your own, and my timing's not the best, but hell, I can't wait any longer to let that woman know my feelings toward her fine and glorious person."

Matthew struggled to keep his voice even. "My mother is happier here than I've ever seen her. She's Gran's only surviving child and partner. And she's the only mother Possum's had since she was a baby."

"I know that. I don't want to change any of it. I'm not looking to divide your family, son. I'll even adopt little Possum as my own if that would—"

Matthew cut off his friend's air before he could utter another syllable.

"Possum's mine," he said between his teeth.

Farrell yanked himself free. "You're telling me you want your peace, your solitude. You can't have both! Miss Whittaker might decide she does or don't want that piece of you you'll part with, but that child needs a daddy! She's only got herself a seasonal gift-bringer, as I see it."

Matthew's arms felt suddenly strange, as if the bones inside them had turned to iron. "Get out. You and your two-bit philosophy."

"That ain't for you to say, Matty."

"Goddamn you, Farrell."

"Maybe he will. But not before I do all I can to make your mama feel some affection back for me. I'll be going to San Francisco with the Amadeos, see what I can do for them in their fruit business. But I'll be writing your mama regular. And I'll be back to check on you and your mood, and hers as well. I aim to wed her, son, with or without your goodwill."

Farrell scuffed his worn hat against his leg again and placed it on his head. Both men turned toward the lights of the house.

Vita Hart was waiting on the porch. Matthew could see her clearly, even in the settling dusk. There was a smudge of cinders on her cheek. She nodded her thanks to Farrell, then walked to where Matthew felt riveted, quarantined outside the circle of light cast by his grandmother's house.

"Mama—" he tried, but was startled by the harsh, distant sound of his own voice.

She smiled. "It will keep. Supper's on, darling."

"Won't keep. Mama, I hit her."

The shock in Vita's eyes changed to grief. No anger. Where, he wondered, was her anger? "Supper's on," she said again.

From his grandmother Matthew got what he was after—punishment. By the woodshed. She'd never struck him. She always waited until he'd chopped enough winter wood to feel good and pummeled by his own effort. Then she yelled.

"You shamed me and this house!"

"I know that."

"You ain't fit to carry on the looks, the life of your granddaddy!"

Matthew laid down the ax. "I ain't him."

"You're his heir!"

"But not him. So don't talk to me like your Georgia friends, woman! I ain't your outlaw saint come back!"

She looked stung. He had her. Was he winning a battle with his grandmother? He didn't want to win. He only wanted her to understand. He followed her into the dark shadow of the woodpile, touched her back.

"I won't bear that burden, Annie. I got plenty enough of my own."

Matthew's grandmother sighed. "You didn't kill Seal Woman, Matthew."

"Good as did," he whispered. "Wearing her down until she'd leave the island with me. Thinking I knew what was best for her, for all of us. Not knowing, even on the island . . ."

"Not knowing what, Matthew?"

"How happy I was. Always was a late bloomer, wasn't I, Gran?"

She smiled a wan smile. "Excepting for that quick-to-sprout length of you. Which caused its own bit of wreckage some years back. Did you tell your lady about that, Matthew?"

"She ain't my lady, and opening my mouth at all's got me in my present state!"

"No. Not your mouth," she turned away from him, "the back of your hand. You ain't raised toward such, Matthew. Where'd it come from?"

He saw his mother appear again on the back porch. "Ask her," he whispered, surprising himself with his own bitterness. What was he doing? Blaming her for loving his father? Stupid. Unmanly. "Mama?" he called.

She turned. There. Forgiveness had joined the grief in her eyes.

"Is Possum asleep yet?" he asked.

"In bed, but not asleep." She smiled. "Go on. One more story won't do her any harm."

He entered the softly lit home and climbed the stairs. Matthew looked at Possum as she slept on her back, her arms outspread. The moonlight made a shadow dance across her face, her deep copper skin, her blue-black lashes and hair. Had he anything to do with this child's beauty? Did Seal Woman make her in some way that had nothing to do with him?

The tranquility left Possum's face suddenly. "All broken!" she cried out, sitting up, then blinking him into focus. "Daddy?"

"Yes. What's broken?"

"The Dumpty—in the book."

"Humpty Dumpty?"

"Yes, the round man."

"Not a man. An egg. An egg with a face painted on."

"Egg?"

"Sure. Like we break, eat all the time. Like tomorrow, for break-fast."

"Will you be here then?"

"Yes."

"Not with the friars? Not with the trees or bears or the Yankee lady?"

He sat beside her on the bed. "We could gather the eggs together, if you'd like."

"Would you paint on a face?"

"Sure."

She nuzzled in against his chest. He leaned back into the pillows. Possum looked down the length of the bed. "Daddy, you got your boots on!"

"Do I?"

She started a giggle that careened and tumbled into laughter, over the same circumstances her mother would find amusing, something that tied him to the earth, even in his sleep.

He sat up, pulled off one boot without difficulty. Possum scampered to his aid, tugging his remaining foot free, falling over in triumph. Again, laughter. Matthew couldn't abide the sound of it. He stood, went to the window. She followed.

"Don't cry," she said, a touch of fear in her voice. "I'm sorry I'm a damned Breed. That there is no sun in my hair."

He looked down. "Possum, you ain't . . . sun?"

"Even in the night yours has the gold. Mine is all shadow."

He knelt, though he feared his swollen eyes would frighten her further. "You are your mother's gift to me, brilliant in your beauty. I love you."

"Why do you go away dancing with bears?"

He smiled. "They dance with me. There's a difference."

"What difference?"

"Of choice. I'd rather dance with you."

She laughed again, but the sound didn't hurt as much this time. He lifted her high in his arms. Matthew found himself swaying back and forth to the rhythm of the waves below, the way he used to when she was an infant in his arms.

"Sing, Daddy," she urged.

He obliged with the first song that came into his head.

Go to Joan Glover and
tell her I love her and
by the light of the moon
I will come to her

His daughter listened to the words once, then took up the second part as they waltzed before the window. It astonished Matthew at first, her pure, flute voice knowing the song his mother had taught him as a child. Then he laughed at himself, because his mother was also hers. Of course she knew the old round as well as he did.

Why did he leave this child? Why did he think he couldn't care for her? She now completed the triumvirate of his badgering women. They would not part with her, not while she was still a child. He could only dream of climbing the Sierras with her on his back, far away from the talk that made her feel anything but beautiful.

BOOK FOUR

twenty-five

San Francisco/St. Pitias, California
1904–1905

Olana collapsed on the sofa. "I won't be allowed out of the house. I'll miss the social season! I need this season, Aunt Winnie!"

"Oh, I'm afraid that's neither here nor there with your parents now. You'll be living under your mother's demands from this day forward, your father agreed to as much. Oh, lovey, I tried, but after the first few days, and with no communication, except your infrequent but perfectly delightful mental images . . . well, Olana, even I couldn't go on pretending I'd misplaced you like a forgotten piece of luggage! And that horrid man is so persistent."

"Man?"

"Mr. Moore! He treated your disappearance as a military expedition! And he upset your parents so thoroughly that my own brother called Mr. Trap the most horrible names!"

"I'm sorry, Aunt Winnie, truly I am."

"Oh, we'll survive."

"If I could get my hands on Darius Moore this minute I'd—"

A deep voice interrupted her. "And I'd welcome any opportunity to get a safe hold on you."

Olana whirled around. He was dressed like a railroad detective, all black and gray, starched and polished. He smelled like the oiled iron of his weapon. It was time to get Darius Moore out of her life forever. "You sir, are an interfering, loathsome—"

"And despite weeks of worry, I do not return your sentiment. Miss Whittaker, would you allow us to converse in private?"

Her aunt stiffened. "Not without Olana's—"

"It's all right, Aunt Winnie. There is no one with whom I'd rather converse at the moment." She stared hard at his hip. "Though you might surrender your weapon to my aunt's safekeeping. I might be tempted to empty it into your skull."

His face reddened before she turned and rested her fingers lightly on the tea table. When her aunt closed the door she faced him again. Darius Moore had regained his composure.

"What business of yours is my whereabouts, sir?"

"The business of concern, of protection, of enduring regard."

"Regard? Look what you've done!"

"I've invested time, energy, and expense seeking a treasure so recently returned from misadventure. Returned in delicate condition. I was not going to lose you again."

"Since you never possessed me that was hardly a possibility."

"I wish to."

"Mr. Moore?"

"Possess you. Keep you safe from danger, want, disloyalty." The words stung her. All the things Matthew Hart had failed to do. "I wish to marry you, Olana."

She looked directly into the dark, steady eyes that were, at last, impatient. When he took her into his arms, she didn't resist. This man had a different strength than what she'd known from Matthew Hart. Disciplined, taut, steely, where the ranger's hold was fluid, giving, even pushing, pushing for her to float, to swim, to think, even to rise to pleasure.

"If you were mine—"

His kiss was intoxicating in its strength, as Matthew Hart's first kiss had been. But it was different, too. Its passion invaded, requiring nothing of her. He brought her lower. He was not all flowers and smooth surfaces. Darius Moore had passion, after all. Olana felt swallowed whole as he pressed her deeper into the cushions of her aunt's Turkish sofa, as the steel of his gun bruised her hip, as his watchchain raked across her blouse.

He released her suddenly, stood, and paced.

"That was an inexcusable breach of conduct. I have the highest regard for your family, and belief in your own womanly integrity. Against all reports, I would defend you! Please. When you have recovered enough to see fit to forgive my churlish be-

havior, I will renew my efforts to win your hand. Until then I withdraw—"

"There is no need to withdraw, Mr. Moore." Olana sat up. "I am
quite recovered. And my answer is yes."

"Will this be a case of Petruchio mastering his shrew?"

"If he ever gets her to the altar tomorrow!"

"What have you heard? Why, it would kill her dear mother!"

"Leave it to Olana Whittaker to turn every disaster to her own
advantage. Faced with being excluded from the social season by her
latest scandal, she becomes the social season!"

The gleeful voices disappeared down the corridor. Olana hugged
her knees, leaned her face into the folds of her dressing gown, and
inhaled the rosewater of her bath salts. Why had she chosen rose-
water over her lilies? It reminded her of the two babies. It reminded
her that the two weeks she'd spent at St. Pitias were real.

"Olana, there you are! Why look at you, your hair's not even
begun!" Her mother took her sleeve as she would a forgotten parcel containing yet another wedding present, and steered her up the
stairs.

"I'm tired, Mother."

"Tired? With the most grand party thus far about to begin? It's
I who should be resting, I've had the burden of so many details over
the last weeks. All you have to do is dance, go to fittings and teas
and parties, then dance again. Now, do get out of public sight, some
guests have already arrived."

"I know."

"They didn't see you?"

"No."

"Thank heavens for that. Well, you mustn't try their patience any
more than is warranted just to make a late, head-turning entrance.
Olana, your hands are so cold."

"I'm afraid."

"Afraid? You? Is it the trip? Seasickness? I'll have my physicians
make up a box of preparations—"

"Not of the trip, Mother."

"Well, thank goodness for that. You'll be serving as a sort of goodwill ambassadress for your father's new expansion to the Far Eastern marketplace, you know."

"I know."

"Well, if it's not—"

"It's the wedding, Mother."

"The wedding! I can assure you, given the short notice you and your betrothed insisted upon I did my best—"

"Not the ceremony. What happens after. The marriage."

"Oh. I see. I was rather hoping—perhaps Mrs. Cole would speak to you about . . . that." Her mother's face brightened. "You'll find joy in the children, and your new social standing, I know you will. You're such a resourceful girl. Well. We're chatting here on the stairway like a couple of old fishwives! I think I can get your father to open up more than a thimbleful of his prized champagne tonight—shall I send up a glass? It will warm you, settle your nerves. Such a peculiar man, becoming parsimonious at this, the crowning moment of his daughter's life!" Dora Whittaker saw Patsy. "Do bring some order to these tresses," she handed her daughter over.

Olana looked at her maid's gentle, honest face.

"Patsy—is it a burden, being married?"

"In my circumstances, the burden would have been far greater if I'd not taken Mr. Selby as my husband." She glanced at the widening middle beneath her apron.

"Of course. How foolish of me." Olana continued down the hallway with her maid at her heels. Patsy touched her arm shyly.

"If you mean to inquire of Christy Selby's character, miss, it's nothing less than sterling. He's making good his promise to Mr. Hart."

"Promise?"

"He courted me. I mean even after we tied the knot all legal. Courted me like I was some treasured dew-eyed girl, instead of what I am. I think I cannot help loving him forever for that, even if he should stop treating me so decent as he does now."

"Do you . . . Patsy, do you think Mr. Moore will treat me decently?"

"I—I couldn't say, miss."

Olana closed her eyes. How stupid she was being.

She stood outside after Patsy opened her door, staring at the pale blue gown laid out on the bed, at the two giggling servants ready to truss her, put her into it. She'd given up even her love of deep colors. Why?

"Miss?"

"I can't. Patsy, I can't endure another night of this. It's all wrong. A mistake."

Patsy shooed away the other maids, closed the door, and took up her mistress's hands. Olana saw sympathy, and a spark of mischief in the girl's eyes.

"The three-way mirror, it's still in the nursery rooms since Mr. Hart left us. It's lovely and quiet up there, Miss Olana. I'll do your hair there tonight—would you like that?"

"No!"

"I can bring up the gown, too, so that it's just the two of us. We might talk. You're wanting to talk, aye, miss?"

"I'm so confused, Patsy."

"Sure you are. It's a new path your life is taking. You need to talk. And have a little quiet, for once, to think."

Olana climbed the stairs behind her maid. That was what all the parties were for, she realized. To keep brides from thinking.

"Go on, miss," Patsy waved her in at the nursery door. "I'll fetch your gown. And more pins for your hair."

"Yes, all right."

After the brightly lit hallway, the room appeared dark. There was no dressing table, nothing set up. How could Patsy do her hair? Olana turned back to the door to call her servant back when she saw Matthew Hart.

twenty-six

He entered from the bathroom, a towel slung over his shoulder, a basin of water between his hands. He looked like he'd been days in the saddle, despite his freshly scrubbed hands and face.

He put the cloth and basin on the bedside table and faced her.

"You can't marry him," he said.

"And what have you come to do about it? Hit me again?"

His feet shifted weight. "I'll never do that again. I'm sorry."

"Please go."

He breathed deeply. "You won't then? Marry him?"

How could she explain about the importance of the wedding trip, her father's business, her mother's pride and health, her own strange new attraction to Darius Moore and his hunger for her? She laughed. High, nervous. "Why not?"

He came closer. She smelled brandy and elderberries. They stared at each other in silence, close enough for Olana to feel the mounting anger rush into his breathing, to smell the leather of his saddle, the dirt of the road mixing with his intoxicant, his berries. "You love me, damn it!"

Olana threw back her head, but never got to make a sound. His mouth was over hers. His hands slipped inside her dressing gown and pulled her camisole against the rich red weave of his shirt. She tore at his hair, then pounded his back, even where the scars from the bear's claws were. But he only growled low, explored her mouth, drew her deeper into the spaces left between them. Then he stopped, released her. They were both breathing hard, staring at each other, still so close their clothing touched.

It was her fingers to blame, she thought, later. It was her fingers she couldn't control. They had to touch, be sure it was a tear there, streaking down the left side of his rough, unshaven face. She struggled to speak, but her voice failed her next, and she uttered only soft, idiotic syllables. He lifted her with the grace she now knew was his mother's gift, and placed her on the bed that had been his when he'd lived here in her father's house. There he quenched, then heightened the ache in her mouth, breasts. He said nothing, but she felt him watching her even when she retreated into the deep reds and purples that painted themselves, then burst once, twice, behind her eyelids.

His hand slipped between her legs. Wet. From the first sight of him she'd been wet there. "Oh—" she said. He nodded. "Good, darlin', that's right, open for me, sweet girl," he purred into her ear. There. Slow. Yes. Deeper. Was there that much room inside her? Olana took his steaming face between her hands and laughed softly, trusting him, he would know. He began to move. Even more exquisitely than he danced.

She responded to his long strokes. Moving under him, squeezing his thigh. " 'Lana, don't—" he gasped, looked panicked, then gave out a cry of pleasure that delighted her in her own power. He came crashing down, suddenly gone, with a soft blasphemy at the pillows. Olana thought she would die from the yearning, when she felt his face against hers. "I'm here," he whispered, turning her onto her side, kissing her. His hand reached up between her legs and sought, found the way to complete one more delight.

It came to her only slowly that she was lying on her brother's bed with a man she'd convinced herself she despised on the eve of her wedding to his opposite. Matthew Hart nuzzled between her breasts, draped his arm casually over her hip. He was falling asleep. She shook his shoulder. He nuzzled deeper.

"Come away," he murmured.

"Where?"

"I don't know. Anywhere you'd like."

"When?"

"Now. Tonight."

She sat up, hoping that might keep her from weeping out in her embarrassed confusion. But a soft cry still escaped. It woke him. He looked at the blood on his hand, then at her, with what, surprise? But knowing, of course knowing she was supposed to bleed, the first time. He knew everything her mother had never told her. Her color heightened as he reached for the basin's cloth, squeezed the warm water through, gently touched it to the inside of her thigh. A shiver of passion rode through her, despite her embarrassment.

"Don't," she said.

He relinquished the cloth and dressed quietly as she finished blotting up the blood from her leg. Then he sat beside her, made an awkward gesture for her hand. She pulled it away.

"Stop looking so d—so damned sorry!" her furious whisper came from nowhere.

"I'm not sorry," was his even reply. "Are you?"

"I—I can't think about it anymore. You'll have to go now, Matthew. I have so much to do."

"Do?"

His face reminded her of a stunned little boy's. What boy? Leland? Her voice erupted again in that silly, nervous laugh.

"Matthew, please understand. This overpowering—"

He stood. "Overpowering?"

"It was not entirely unreciprocated. And I could never have, I mean what you, what we did was based on the genuine affection I feel for you since our unlikely paths crossed. But I'm getting married tomorrow."

There. That was the one sentence she'd practiced. But in all of her dreams of him coming back, he'd now be on his knees begging for another chance, pledging his undying love. Not lording over her, looking annoyed.

"Christ, 'Lana, I'll marry you if you're so blamed set on it."

"You still don't understand."

"No. You don't understand. Exchange grooms. You do it all the time with your damned hats." Suddenly he was on the bed with her again, his hand pressing against her ribcage. "What happened between us, just now—what was that?" he demanded.

"You know better than I." She tried lowering her eyes, but he lifted her chin with his hand.

"Don't start your games, woman! I deserve better!"

"You deserve nothing! All you've done is take! You tell me how I feel, you offer me disgrace and the open road to nowhere!"

He looked stung. He released her, his eyes scanning the bloodied water in the basin. "Shit. Oh, shit," he muttered.

There, at last. She had him. She went giddy with her power, that was the only way she could see it, after. Get him to his knees. Why was she so intent on that? "Matthew," she summoned his eyes. The hope there almost made her lose her resolve. No, he'd made her suffer, hadn't he? She would turn the screw just one more time. "I wouldn't dream of troubling you to marry me because of this . . . assignation. But I was frightened of only one part of my wifely obligation. Now I can look forward with even greater expectation to the abilities of a devoted husband."

His eyes went slate cold.

He grabbed his hat from the bed, kicked past the French doors of the balcony, and disappeared.

* * *

Matthew rode hard. Nothing made sense, no matter how many times he ran it through his mind. Why was Olana so maddeningly half herself, half that pompous facade? She'd made her choice, what did he go there for in the first place? Why did he let Farrell and the women convince him? He had only meant to kiss her, kiss her so she stayed kissed a good long time, yes, but not what happened, in her father's house. And the blood. What had he offered her when it was done—a cut from her folks, the way of life she cherished in her own way, as powerfully as he did his.

He slept on the beach in the rain, still so addlebrained from the drinking he didn't have sense to take refuge in the caves. He woke to the gentle Angelis bells of St. Pitias, then to the impossible clarity of his women's eyes.

"Did you tell her you love her, Matthew?"

"That's what I went there for, ain't it?"

"Well, did you?"

A moment's hesitation. To think. And they were on him, like wolves on a downed elk. "Don't you remember?" prodded one. "Were you drunk?" the other.

"No!" he called them off. "Not . . . not before. I had one shot of brandy at the boarding place. Then, when I got to the house, Mrs. Cole, the cook, she gave me a half glass of something tasted like your cough remedy, Gran. That was all. I—hated having to sneak around, just to see her."

"But you got to see her, alone?"

"Yes."

"Then you told her you loved her."

"Yes, goddamn it, I told her—" The words he'd used finally came back to him. "I think I told her that she loved me."

"That's not the same thing, Matthew." His mother breathed out her despair.

"I know that! But she was going to laugh, laugh at any notion of love between us. I couldn't let her laugh, I couldn't take that, not from her."

Vita took his arm in her strong grip, and locked her eyes on his. "Matthew, you didn't force yourself on her?"

"No. 'Course not."

"She was already confused, pulled this way and that, then neglected by you—"

"Neglected?"

"Then you . . . you . . . overwhelmed on the eve of her wedding!"

He'd never heard his mother so angry. He responded with a childhood tact, silence, for the rest of the day. At supper he sat sullen beside his daughter, and without his grandmother between his mother and himself.

"You haven't touched the pole beans, they're your favorite."

"Ain't hungry."

"Daddy's sick."

"I'm not sick, Possum."

The child pointed to his sore abdominal muscles. "There."

"Two of you got her spooked, you know that?" He meant it to sound light, but it came out through a growl of displeasure. He stabbed the plate at his mother. "I told her I'd marry her!"

"Told her you'd marry her, not asked her to marry you!"

"It was the best I could—"

"And it wasn't good enough, was it?"

"You don't have to ram that fact down my throat with your damned beans!"

He flung the plate. Not at her, past her. It broke into three pieces against the wall. The pieces shattered when they hit the tile floor. Possum ran to Vita's arms. Escaping him. He felt Annie Smithers' presence in the doorway, but couldn't take his eyes off his mother as she shielded his child. The look on her face was too familiar.

"We're not afraid of you!"

He struggled for a response, and finally managed "I am," after they'd already gone up the stairs.

Matthew waited for his grandmother by the woodpile, drenched in his own sweat.

"I'm getting on, Matthew. Can't be patching things up twixt you and your mama forever."

"I don't know how either of you find the strength to tolerate me at all."

They were walking along the shore before Annie Smithers spoke again. "You bedded Olana, didn't you?"

"Yes."

"And you're not sure she wanted to."

"I was sure. Then. I just wanted to kiss her. Something happened, to both of us I would of sworn." He inhaled deeply. "Gran. There was blood. I didn't hurt her, did I?"

She stopped. "Were your ways loving?"

"Uh . . . sure."

"And she didn't act hurt?"

"No."

"She was a virgin, is all."

All. "I knew that," he insisted. Hadn't he heard enough male boasting of burst cherries in the army and the goldfields? "It's just . . . the women before her weren't, and I need to know if it hurt. I don't want her to remember me that way."

"It didn't hurt."

"Well. That's good."

They stopped on the cliffs, their favorite place to watch the stars come out. She was waiting for him to speak. How did he know that? The silence between them was full, rich, a time to gather his thoughts, his strength.

"Mama's right. 'Lana's young and I went and confused her more—telling her what she feels, demanding she be what I want her to be."

"Well, maybe."

"But I ain't what Mama fears. I'm not my father. Tell her, Gran."

"You got to tell her yourself, Matthew."

"I know when she's thinking of it. I see him between us again, with his strap."

"Tell her."

He climbed the ledge that brought them closest to the stars. He reached down for her, trying to hide the strain she was on his sore muscles. What was the use? She spread her healing hands over the ache. Then she yanked his left eyelid open and peered into his body workings. She shook her head.

"Matthew Hart. Did you consume half the rotgut in San Francisco?"

He touched his sore middle. "It was only on loan," he assured her, coaxing a smile that relieved her look of general disgust.

"Some good may come of it," she said. "Biggest problem I could see between you two was your determination to keep your hands off each other. Ain't good, all that holding back."

He felt the laughter rise in his throat, and with it a new surge of energy. Was there a way out of this?

"So. What now?" his grandmother demanded.

"Now? She's married. Gone steaming across the goddamned Pacific. I just hope my past record holds true and I'm as wrong about the nature of the man she married as I am about everything else." He let the laugh out, as humiliated as it was. Annie said nothing, but put her hand on his shoulder. He pressed his face against it. "Gran, it eats me up to think on it, but I hope he's everything she wants, including being better at the loving of her."

twenty-seven

Olana's hand ached from shaking hundreds of other hands.

The day was a blurred memory. The oppressive weight of her gown's train and veil, of the orange blossoms that hid her trembling hands. Leaving her father's arm to take the arm of a stranger in scrupulous morning dress, from his Prince Albert frock coat to the pale lavender of his gloves. Her father's sad eyes when he danced with her, she remembered that, and Sidney so drunk Serif took him home. She deserved it, she deserved it all, along with the pounding between her eyes now.

Olana thought of her father's last conversation with her new husband, there, on the ship, as she stood on the other side of the stateroom door.

"She is my pride, Darius. And delicate, under all that spirit. I've accepted her choice, accepted you into my family. You'll allow me to tell her mother I've secured your promise to be gentle with her."

There was an unnatural silence. Then her husband's voice. "Your time is over. Your spoiled and willful daughter will come home my wife. *I* expect—"

The blast of the *Mariposa*'s horn had invaded then. It made Olana's ears ring through her parents' last good-bye. Her father's arm shook as he lifted her hat's veil and touched her cheek. He said nothing. Was he ashamed, she wondered, for bargaining her away? She was angry, so angry with him. Now she remembered his silence better than her mother's nervous prattle. She lay on a wide bed in the *Mariposa*'s most luxurious stateroom, surrounded by dozens of rapidly fading white and yellow lilies. And her maid's sob. Olana sat up.

"Are you ill, Patsy?"

"Oh, no. I was hearty on the Atlantic crossing, so I don't expect this ocean will be any worse. It's you, Miss Olana. Forgive me but I never seen a sadder bride."

"I'm tired, that's all. You can go."

But Patsy fussed with her hair, insisting it was not quite sitting right over the dressing gown collar. Finally, she put down the brush.

"Use this, miss." Patsy handed her something powdered, slippery, that had a rosy glow.

"What—"

"A sheep's bladder."

"What in heaven's name—"

"It's got the blood inside. I don't know how to say this except straight out, miss. Mr. Moore, he will need to know he got what he bargained for. If you file one of your fingernails sharp, and keep this under the covers with you until the right moment, he should be none the wiser."

Blazing clarity. More life lessons from her servant. "Thank you," Olana whispered and slipped the small bladder into the pocket of her dressing gown.

"Shall I sit with you? Until he comes?"

"No, no. Find Selby. He was balancing a trunk and three valises up the gangplank. I expect he'll need your tender touch."

"If that's all then—"

"Yes."

She turned at the door and rushed back, taking up Olana's hands in hers. "Tell me if I done wrong, miss? Letting Mr. Hart in? Tell me, and punish me!"

"You did nothing wrong. Go on, Patsy."

Later, much later, the sound of her husband's groans woke her. Olana tapped at his door.

"Darius?"

No answer. She opened it. The sour smell assaulted her first. His coat was on the bed, but he was sprawled on the floor of his small bathroom. His face and hair were wet, his eyes closed. She knelt beside him.

"Darius, are you ill?"

"Go away."

"You are, let me—"

His eyes opened. "You never wanted me!"

"What?"

"But you had to have your parties, your social season. And now the groom is dispensable?" His eyes went small in their contained rage.

"Whatever do you mean?"

"Is this your latest amusement, my little bride? Poisoning?"

"Perhaps . . . if we took some air—"

"Get Wallace."

"Of course. But let me—" She reached for the stack of wash-cloths on the shelf, but he caught her wrist and twisted.

"Now," he said between his teeth.

"Darius, you're hurting me."

"I know."

Olana stumbled back to her own room. She hastily donned her raincoat. Wallace. Where had they put him? She knocked at Patsy's room. Selby came to the door. His sleepy eyes came to attention when he recognized her.

"Don't wake her, Selby!' Olana whispered. "I'm very sorry to disturb you at all, but I've forgotten where we put Wallace!"

"He's first door left of the master's, ma'am."

"Yes, of course, thank you. Mr. Moore is ill. I'm going for the ship's doctor and—"

"I'll call Wallace for you," he offered.

"Good. Thank you."

"Button up, Mrs. Moore. Feels like a storm's up to shake this grand vessel, and make us all queasy."

Olana fumbled at her raincoat's collar, thinking of the sweetness in the footman's concern as she struggled through the corridor. Her wrist hurt where her husband had twisted it. Like when Cal Carson did. No. There was no resemblance. Her husband was a proud man, who did not like to be seen ill. That's all. Poisoning. He was distraught. He would apologize for the accusation once he was well.

Passengers and crewmen hovered around Doctor Phillips as he stood in his office doorway, his black bag in his hand. He was a different man from the laughing, pleasant-faced gentleman to whom the captain introduced Olana at the reception. Drawn face, near panic in his eyes. Something was wrong. Something beyond the swells buffeting the ocean liner. Doctor Phillips saw her and raised his arm.

"Mrs. Moore! I am on my way at your urgent summons!" He cut through the other passengers and took her arm. Three crewmen followed.

"Say nothing, please," he advised in a low voice as he led her down a stairway. Then he stopped. "Is one of your party ill?" he asked quickly.

"My husband, but it's the seasickness I think. If there is a more urgent need—"

"There is indeed. There has been a fire below, in the engine room. Under control now, I assure you, but there are some rather serious injuries I must attend to. Without causing panic. I'm afraid I used you as a ploy, Mrs. Moore, for the needs below."

"May I be of help?"

"Help? But your husband—"

"He has his manservant."

Doctor Phillips looked to the crewmen with them. Two nodded, one scowled. "I appreciate your generous offer," the doctor said gently, "but the injuries are burns. And the sight—well, look."

He opened his coat to reveal his vest smeared with blood.

"I have had some experience, sir," Olana said quietly. "And my health is quite robust."

"If it becomes less so, you will have to attend yourself."

"Fair enough."

The acrid smoke combined with their continual descent made a feeling of panic rise from the pit of Olana's stomach. But she continued downward on the doctor's arm. Why her offer? Was this better than spending the rest of her wedding night in her husband's company?

The jammed quarters had been turned into an infirmary. There were seven sailors on bottom bunks, and one more brought in on the broad back of a boiler man as they entered. This was a different life, with many fewer comforts, than the one above. Olana sensed no panic, only a desperate vigil being kept over the crew's burned comrades.

"This is Mrs. Moore," was all the doctor said before he handed her his coat and leaned over the latest victim. Olana draped it over an upper bunk, put her own beside it, and looked around the room. The ship rolled, knocking over a pitcher. Her first task became clear. They were all calling for water.

Hours later a man whose scalp was burned off clutched her hand. His skin was so blackened Olana could tell neither his age nor race. He opened his eyes. Young eyes.

"You smell like roses."

She smiled. "My cologne."

"What's your name?"

" 'Lana," she whispered.

"Sounds like the sea at rest."

His eyes followed the swirling motion of her hair as it swept through her ivory comb. Then they stilled in death. The man sitting on the patient's other side began to weep. Olana draped her macintosh over his shoulders.

Hours later, Olana heard the doctor call from the vague, fragmented forms that waltzed across her eyelids.

"Mrs. Moore."

Automatically, she held out her hand for the heavy mug of coffee he'd put there twice earlier that night. "We've gotten five of them through the night. Get some rest." He walked on.

Olana stood, took a step. The ocean's churning knocked her against a bunk. The bladder in her pocket burst. Its blood soaked the browning parts of her gown bright red again.

A voice. From someone new to the room. "Good God. Doctor—here, Mrs. Moore!"

"I'm quite all right," she insisted, trying to clear the hair from her eyes. "I mustn't be any trouble. Please, don't." But she couldn't stop the man who picked her up. Her protests couldn't keep Doctor

Phillips from lifting layers and examining her side.

He shook his head. "A small cut, and some bruising, that's all. I don't know why it bled so much," he marveled.

Then it was cold. She was on the deck, being carried. Olana panicked. "If I'm any trouble, the doctor will not allow me back!"

"You may go back. After you've rested."

"You don't understand."

"I understand, Mrs. Moore."

Inside again. A cabin. Warm smells of blackberry tobacco and ink soothed her. "Doctor Phillips said—" she still protested.

"I will pull rank on the good doctor, if necessary."

"Pull rank?" She looked around the quarters, then more closely at the burly sailor's ribbed sweater, his white bearded face. "Why, Captain Brewster, I beg your pardon! I didn't recognize you without your—regalia!" Her hands made a vague motion at his chest, as she giggled helplessly.

"That's quite all right, Mrs. Moore. But now you know you'll come to no harm here, so please close your eyes."

"Yes. No harm. Please," she murmured.

His lips pressed her forehead gently. The way her father's did. Before he'd sold her to the highest bidder.

The room's tobacco and ink mixed with the scents of Matthew's house on the ocean—pine woods, the loom, the salt sea. And she was waltzing with him again, there behind her eyes. When the sea lurched, she hit the side of the bunk, then sat up straight.

"Matthew, help them!" she called out.

Patsy leaned over her. "Oh, miss, did you really go down to the burned sailors? Did the captain of this grand vessel really carry you here himself?"

Olana looked around. "Yes. I think so."

"The whole ship's abuzz with it, Miss Olana! Doctor Phillips is singing your praises as well."

"The men—"

"Holding their own, miss. All asking after you."

Olana leaned back. "Patsy. The bladder burst. Down there. At a most inopportune time. One might even be tempted to say I entered my matronhood in the absence of my husband and the presence of a dozen sailors. How shall I describe this event in my memory book, do you think?"

The two giggled, their heads together, until the doctor's soft knock announced his presence. "Well, I'm happy to see my head nurse is rested and ready to report back for duty," he said.

twenty-eight

Matthew took on his mother's work, the things that left her hands calloused, her face weathered—mending fences, tending the corn and apricot trees. It gave her more time for weaving, now their only cash source besides the apricots.

Matthew accompanied his grandmother when people were sick or families birthing, content again to be her apprentice, to watch her write her learnings in the burnt-edged book. He taught himself from it, and from his grandmother's years of experience. They talked deep into the night, while his mother took advantage of the cool air to bake bread and his daughter sat snug in his arms.

He loved his mother's doting, his grandmother's gruff wisdom, both their forgiveness. Best he loved his daughter's growing limbs, her able mind. Possum began reading a few simple words of his newspapers and books at her place in his lap. He borrowed readers from the friars at the mission school. She watched the words glide by, absorbed the woodcut pictures as he told her the stories.

By day she was still her mother's water child, racing him to the ocean every afternoon when his chores were done. Her broad-shouldered strength allowed her to swim rings around him, to stay under the water deep and long, so long that Matthew scolded her about it at the dinner table. Her eyes grew wide and indignant.

"But I will not get drownded, Daddy!"

" 'Drown,' " her grandmother corrected. "It's 'I will not drown.' "

"I'm not so sure about you, Mana."

Vita raised her eyes to heaven. Matthew faced his daughter. "What makes you so sure about yourself, Possum?" he asked.

"The way I was born. In the sac."

He frowned at his mother. "Who told her that story?"

"First I've heard of it."

"Is it true? Did she come into the world that way, Matthew?" Annie asked.

"Yes. But I don't remember telling you. Did I, Possum?"

The little girl tilted her head. "Maybe. Maybe I dreamed it."

"Dreamed it?"

"Sure. You dream, don't you, Daddy?"

"Yes. I . . . dream."

His mother smiled. "Now who's two peas in a pod?"

Matthew did his best to scowl. "You're raising a child who won't mind her elders."

His mother shrugged her graceful shoulders. "It's all I know."

"House of anarchy," Annie Smithers agreed.

Possum's small fingers patted Matthew's cheek. They drifted to his hair. He still marveled at every display of affection. "Why do I have no gold here, or sky in my eyes?" she asked.

"All the colors play in your hair, your eyes."

"Do you love her still, my mama?" She pronounced the word carefully. Not "mana," but "mama."

"Yes." He saw Seal Woman bringing home the bundle that contained their new daughter, walking slowly, but so straight, tall. He saw her hands tell the lucky birth, promise that she was giving him a child who would never drown the way she herself, impossibly, did so soon after. Matthew allowed the memory of the birthday linger. He'd never done that before, he realized. What did it mean?

"Will you take me to the snow mountains this time, Daddy?"

He saw Olana now, raising the red wineglass shyly, without airs. Strong arms, like his wife's. "I'm not going back, little one," he said, and saw the glass shattering. He shook the image away.

"You go, when the rains come."

"Not this year. I told you."

She looked at him sideways. "Promise?"

"I promise."

* * *

The scent. A strange scent. What was it?

"Wake up."

"Darius?"

"Bridegroom, my darling. Your bridegroom at last."

The panic rose in a bitter bile to her throat. Did she think this night would never come? "Are you feeling well enough—"

"Now you inquire after my health? When you no longer can play Florence Nightingale to the crew of the *Mariposa?*"

"You wouldn't allow me near you on the ship."

"You found diversions soon enough! Including the captain's bed."

"Darius, you—you're joking."

"I am in deadly earnest."

"Then you've been drinking."

He laughed. Cold. Hard. Brittle. "Not from anything you would pour, Lucretia."

"That's not the least bit amusing."

"I agree. Marriage is such a deadly serious business, isn't it, Mrs. Moore? Here we've been husband and wife for six weeks without my being well enough to claim my conjugal rights, thanks to your manipulations."

"I did not cause the storm at sea that made you ill. And I am glad for your recovery. But if you no longer care for me, could we not behave in a more civilized manner toward each other? Darius, we've both made a mistake. Shall we discuss an annulment?"

"No longer care?" he said, his voice arch, but as calm as water in the pond of the stone garden behind their rented house. "I never cared for you, Mrs. Moore."

She fought the lump forming in her throat. Good God, did he drag her halfway around the world to tell her that? Out. It didn't matter how. Or what price. She needed to get out of this marriage.

"I see. But my freedom will cost my father."

"No, no. Not your father, Mrs. Moore. I've had your father exactly where I've wanted him for years. This has nothing to do with freedom. I wish to ruin you."

"Ruin?"

"Make you worthless. No longer . . . respectable? If it's not too late. If it is, I will kill you."

"Darius, why are you saying such awful things?"

"Because I can. Here. Now. After years of playing the fool. Of underestimating you on the ship. That will never happen again, little wife."

"I must insist you leave."

"No, no, no. You must not insist. Ever again."

He hit her hard across the mouth. Her startled scream brought Patsy into the room.

"Miss Olana! Are you—"

"Mrs. Moore has had a nightmare. I'm here with her. Leave."

Patsy came to Olana's side, went into the drawer, brought out perfumed powder, dusted it along her mistress's arms, chatting away. "It's the very strangeness of the place causes her nightmares, sir! If she could have a little outing tomorrow, perhaps? The air, the higher air of these beautiful mountains will surely revive her."

Olana heard her husband's teeth grinding. She felt the cold of the sheep's bladder being placed in her hand. Her maid had found or concocted another replacement for her maidenhead, here in Japan. "Thank you, Patsy," she said through her tears. "You—may go."

Darius Moore followed the servant, and locked the ebony-panelled door behind her.

"If she does that again, I will leave her and her bastard brat in this country to take their place among the beggars on the street."

"But Darius, she was only—"

He took hold of her braid and yanked her head back into the pillows. "Shhh," he hissed softly. "Lesson one: No more contradicting me." He released her. She didn't move. "There. Better. Now unbraid your hair."

When she did his eyes softened. He took the strands between his fingers, then pressed it against his face. He turned down the lamp and disappeared in the darkness. Then he was on top of her.

"Spread your legs."

"But Darius, I'm not ready."

"What?"

He wound her hair around his fist and pinned her against the pillow. "What do you want? Kissing?"

"N—no. This is a mistake. Isn't it? Darius, what is it that you want? If you'll leave me alone—"

"No more bargaining, don't you understand? Now. Kissing is for courtship. Say it."

"Darius—"

"Say it!"

She did, her fear overcoming her fury.

"For naughty little wives—honor, obey. Spread."

He turned another knot in her hair. Her throat strangled when she forced it to silence. He thrust himself inside her. Again, and again. She clawed at the bladder and finally slashed it open. An animal's blood came between them, finally relieving the dry torment. It was more welcome than he was inside her.

He collapsed, heaving and sweating. His sweat had the scent of her mother's room when she'd been ill for days. Opium. He rolled over, put on his dressing gown, and turned up the light. Then he yanked back the covers and ripped her gown down from her shoulders, leaving her naked and shivering. He inspected the sheets as she wept.

"Well, then. Your wild man didn't have you first after all. You were mine to burst open, my ripe little wife. What did he do? Bugger your maid in your stead? Well. No scouring by an oriental medicine man to make you pure or kill you, then, my lovely bride. But you can thank your ranger for the hell I'm about to make of your life."

Olana closed her eyes so he would not gain further power from the sick revulsion she felt.

"Do clean yourself. You smell like a pig," he said before he left.

Olana lay shivering in the cold, hard silence. Darius Moore had her locked away, far from home, and responsible for her only friends left, Selby and Patsy. Olana wished she'd died of frostbite, there in Matthew Hart's tree. He would not have mourned the silly heiress who barely knew enough to come in out of the cold. But she would have died in peace, and in his arms.

There wasn't enough air in the room, suddenly. Vita came in from the kitchen, took his hand.

"What is it, Matthew?"

"N—nothing. Mama? Could we open a window?"

They stared at him. Every word he said took more air than it should have. He got to his feet, reeling, but walked out onto the porch, waving them back. It was no different there, though he could feel the cool night's breezes against his skin. Then, as suddenly as it had come, it was gone. He pumped water up from the well and into his hands, over his face.

"Tighter," Darius Moore said.

"But, sir—"

"Measure."

Patsy anchored the ties against the corset hooks and brought the tape around her mistress's waist.

"Eighteen and one half, sir, and if that's not the smallest I've ever seen it—"

"I like round numbers. Allow me."

"I will not, sir!"

He lifted an eyebrow and turned to his wife. "Mrs. Moore?"

"It's all right, Patsy."

He took the ties from the maid's hands and pulled. Olana muffled a small cry.

"There, eighteen. Even. Mrs. Moore understands. This is business. A man of influence in a crowding market has a taste for small-waisted women. We all must do our part to compete."

As soon as the door closed, Olana walked to the window. "What did you and Selby do today, Patsy? What did you see?"

"No. No more filling your head with stories to live in."

Olana turned. "Don't be angry with me—"

"You've gone pale and sickly! He hasn't let you out of this bleeding house except trussed up on his arm. He's a monster!"

"My husband is very busy. And the customs here, for a woman of my station, are different."

"But Miss Olana, ever since we got off the ship—"

"I was selfish, on the ship. Leaving him to Wallace while I—"

"Endeared yourself to everyone aboard with your devotion to the burned sailors!"

"I did not keep a proper vigil—"

"Vigil? Paugh! When he—"

"Stop it!" Olana turned her head, breathed deeply. "I mustn't cry. He knows it when I cry. It puffs my eyes so, and my eyes are a very valuable asset—"

"You're sounding like him, miss!"

"Patsy," she whispered. "I want to go home. He says if we can just get this last contract, my father will not be ruined."

"Ruined? Is that why you married him? Did he tell you a bold and vicious lie such as that?"

"He showed me the papers, Patsy, that night, after . . . after Mr. Hart left. I was determined to marry no one, the night before the wedding. Swear not to tell!"

"Of course, miss, but—"

"It will be over soon. And we can go home. To America. We'll get you and Selby away, far away from him and his threats."

"Does he dare to be threatening—"

"Then I'll figure my own way out, somehow, and things will be better. In America. Won't they?"

It came back. Each night. But Matthew hid it, putting Possum to bed earlier, fighting it alone in the darkness. Then it would trick him, come later, just as his dreams began. He paced his room, or climbed up on the roof, or dove into the pounding surf.

But he couldn't hide his hollow eyes, his thinning frame. He waited until Vita had taken Possum to the beach one afternoon, then approached his grandmother as she stirred the stockpot.

"Gran?" he called her softly. "I think there's something wrong with me."

"At last." She sighed, directing him to sit up on the table with a wave of the wooden spoon. "Talk, Matthew."

"Nightly. A feeling. That I can't breathe."

"Where?"

"It starts here, around my ribs."

"Let's have a look at you." She signaled. He took off his shirt and felt her healing hands explore, thump at his chest.

"Then?"

"Then?" he echoed.

"What happens then, child?"

"Oh. Goes away. For three nights now I feel it traveling, both lower, deeper, at my gut, and higher like it . . . like it wants a hold of my heart."

"How long does it last?"

"Quarter hour. Sometimes longer."

He rested from the weight of telling her as she continued to look, thump, listen.

"Can't find a source," she pronounced, "not inside you."

He climbed off the table, pulling on his shirt. "What now, Gran?"

"I best be on hand when it seizes you tonight."

She stayed by him, reading *David Copperfield* aloud, the way she did for him when he first came to her, after the court martial. Her reading filled him with such peace he didn't think anything would disturb it. But it came.

"Gran!"

"I'm here, Matthew."

"Here—" He fanned his fingers out over his chest.

"Easy."

"Can't."

"What do you need?"

"Out."

"Go, then."

"Where?"

"Where it takes you, darlin' boy."

There was a cry in her voice. Was it hurting her, too? Irrational thought. But what was rational about this malady? Matthew hurried past his mother's room, sensed her lamp brightening.

He went down to the sea's roar, heard the gasp, the soft dig of his grandmother's footsteps as he fell to his knees in the sand. He saw his mother behind her. On your feet. Stand, he told himself, but when he tried, he fell face down.

His mother's pained cry made him open his eyes, force back the black. His grandmother rolled him onto his side.

"Cut," he said.

"What? Cut what, Matthew?"

"Don't know. Tight, too tight. White."

"Matthew!" He had a distant sense of his grandmother's and his mother's shaking hands ripping the taut, white material between their hands. "Look!" they both demanded as they tore. Release. He was released from the torment. He breathed long, full, not yet believing he could. He lay on his back, watching the ink-black sky, the shredded remnants of their petticoats flying about the beach.

"Now I've made us all mad," he whispered in disgust.

"It's not you, Matthew," his grandmother said.

"What?"

"You're taking on another's burden."

He didn't argue. It felt too good to breathe.

"Still in your dressing gown? I won't have any more of this honeymooning now that you're home!"

Olana turned and laughed out her excitement. "Sidney!"

"Run up and get some togs on, I've got the steps down to the most wonderful new dance!" He turned to her machine and began to unload the Edison cylinders from under his arm. She stared at his back, afraid to let him out of her sight. He turned and regarded her curiously.

"Well? Go on, go on."

"It . . . was good of you to come, Sidney."

"I don't stand on ceremony. Been turned away three times by your new staff. 'Mrs. Moore is unwell,' he imitated their sour butler perfectly. "Where in hell is Patsy?"

"Still in Japan! Oh, Sidney there was the most dreadful mixup as we were leaving. I've sent out numerous inquiries to get her and Selby back since. She must have had her baby by now and—"

"No wonder you're unsettled! Why didn't you ask my help?"

"Could you help?"

"Of course. Done."

"Done? But—"

He put his finger to her lips. "The power of the press. Or rather my cousin who knows the American Ambassador. He'll scout them out. Done. I'll have them steaming home in a week, promise."

"Sidney, you're a treasure."

"Well, that's better!" He pressed her cold hands. "Unwell, indeed, why you're a vision, ready to take her place with the H.R.H.'s professional beauties, not that you haven't got more Yankee good sense to do that!"

She arched her brow. "What's this? Anglomania? Is there a British noble family invading our city with eligible second sons and homely daughters?" she teased, then delighted in the way his cheeks colored. "Why, Sidney, there is, isn't there! How exciting!"

"Exciting? It's what we complained about all through Europe, remember? I can't believe I've got myself caught up in——"

"But you are, quite! My darling Sidney——in love! Details, if you please," she demanded.

"I can tell you, can't I?" he asked, suddenly serious.

Olana touched his face. Sidney. Home. Could he help her form the path out of this nightmare? "Of course." She affected a pout. "If you promise to always love me, too."

"I will, Olana. We will, the both of us. Olana, I was a miserable friend to you after you announced your engagement, but——oh, be a sport now, you divining witch, and jump to. Come, come, you're no Japanesey geisha girl now——proper attire, if you please! The steps to this new dance are a little tricky and I need the practice."

"You'll wait?"

"I'll chain myself to your recording machine if any servant tries to bully me out, promise. Now, off."

Olana flew about her dressing room, grabbing a simple blouse and jumper that was part of her old wardrobe, not her trousseau. Rather than call up a parlor maid that her husband had selected, she hastily tied back her hair in a green ribbon, and ran down to the small sitting room. Sidney was still there.

"Record time, you must have missed me!" He grinned.

"I did, I missed everyone, everything! I never felt so alone in my life!"

"Alone, on your wedding trip? There's a story there!"

"Sidney, don't tease me!"

"Well, why have you holed yourself up so? Even your mother remarked that you're taking your matron's role too seriously, only entertaining your husband's business prospects, not accepting a single invitation since you've returned!"

"It's all one business. I'm not their little girl anymore, am I? I'm in service to their fortune."

"Now there's a grim thought!" He laughed uneasily.

"I'm sorry Sidney! Don't be angry with me!"

"Angry? My dear sport——Never mind, what a bore I'm being! Let's dance."

He put the needle on the cylinder and took up her hands. The music coming out of the machine reminded her of the dance hall and the cakewalk. She tried to remember the funny two-step dance Matthew taught her.

"That's it! Don't tell me they're doing this in Japan! Or have you been sneaking out nights without me? Now swing out and back, and circle, isn't it the liveliest damned thing?"

She breathed in the pressroom and cigar smell she'd once found so oppressive about Sidney and his obsession. She lost herself in the lively music. He swung her too fast and she slipped, falling against the sofa's arm. Olana collapsed, pulling him down beside her as the cylinder finished.

"Sorry!" He laughed.

"Oh, it's not you, darling! I'm a little off balance these days." Olana realized that she'd fallen against his hat, and crushed its brim. She pulled it up, but her look of dismay turned to unbridled mirth at the sight of it.

"You could have just said it wasn't to your taste," he mocked offence, then joined her laughter until they both put their heads to the sofa back and stared up at the ceiling the way they had as children. He took up her hand. "Are you happy, sport?"

The lingering smile disappeared from her face. He squeezed her hand nervously. "There now, never mind. We have all afternoon. Want to hear another?"

"Very much. Sidney? You won't forget me? If you marry into your damned English royalty?"

"Don't be absurd! I'm going to be the eccentric uncle to your children, remember? It's not I who have abandoned our plans to be the perfect society matron! And I'll be gallant enough not to mention who is forgetting who for almost an entire, dreadfully boring season!" He went to the machine, chatting on, because he was afraid, she knew, of her eyes. She was afraid of them herself, and rarely looked in the mirror. "This one's from St. Louis," he changed the subject abruptly, "a ragtime piano player named Joplin named it after the place he played it—"The Maple Leaf." But it was the rage of Paris first, can you beat that?"

They'd hardly begun when the music stopped.

"Now, what the devil—" Sidney turned, then thrust his hand toward her husband. "Moore! I've been bringing Olana up to date on the social scene. Welcome home!"

"Thank you."

"I was wondering if I could borrow my correspondent back for her record of certain heroic actions that the captain of the *Mariposa* has already given to the *Times*? Shame on you both for not coming to me first! And her impressions of Japan, of course. They'll be better than the accounts of Alice Roosevelt, I'd wager."

"Olana is much too busy with her own obligations."

"Oh? Are you, Olana? Even if I bring a new typewriter over next visit?"

Olana opened her mouth. She must say something, anything, but in the presence of her husband, her mind seemed to be freezing, as sure as her body was before the cave found her. Darius Moore took her hand, brought it to his lips as he regarded Sidney Lunt.

"Perhaps you'd like to see Mrs. Moore in her new element? Why not join us for dinner tonight?"

"I'd like that very much."

"Eight o'clock."

"Good, then." Sidney took up his hat, and brushed it off with exaggerated indignity as Olana stifled a small smile behind shaking fingers adorned only by her gold wedding band.

"Your recordings," Darius Moore reminded him as he reached the parlor doorway.

"Present for Olana." Sidney pointed at her. "Practice, clumsy," he commanded, before he left them.

Darius Moore turned back to her as she busied herself re-designing flowers in a vase. "You invited him here?"

"No. He dropped by."

"Dropped by? Do you know what that signals?"

"Signals? Darius, Sidney and I are friends since childhood."

"I see. His tastes are plebeian." He broke a cylinder against the marble tabletop. She rushed to his side.

"Stop that! They're mine!"

"And you, blushing, dancing bride, are mine." He took up her hair and wound it around his fist. "A matron, not a schoolgirl. You will keep your hair pinned up."

"But—"

He yanked her head back. "Only I get to take it down, yes?" Her eyes teared. "Yes?"

"Yes," she whispered.

twenty-nine

Olana stumbled, thrown both by the heat of the night and weight of her Worth gown. Her husband took her elbow and snapped her up with a jerk.

"What's the matter with you?"

"I'm a little dizzy."

"Hold on to me for now. But I'm placing you at that ancient Hunt's arm all night, so don't go leaning on him or you'll both topple."

She saw her reflection in the oversize gilt mirror, was frightened by that look in her own eyes. What was happening to her?

"Darius, I can't."

"Can't?"

"Not tonight. Please."

"Stop talking nonsense."

"I'm not well."

"You were well enough to dance like a bordello queen this afternoon with your childhood chum. Turn around." He stepped back. "Let's have a look."

She hated those words. He used them whenever he inspected, before displaying her for his business associates to envy, glower, admire. He never looked at her face. Now he pulled down her gown's neckline too far, exposing the nipple of her right breast.

"Hmm," he considered. "That ought to loosen the investment dollars of the old tightwad." He pinched it hard as he set it back in place. Olana cried out softly and a yellow substance came forth.

"What in hell—secretions, my little heiress?" He spread his hand against her ribcage, tightening the hold of an already tight corset. "Does this mean you're beginning to enjoy my tastes in marital bliss?" he whispered close against her ear.

"Go to hell," she breathed before he pushed her to her knees. He yanked her head back, then gently cupped her neck in his hand.

"I'm glad you have a little fight left. I would lose interest in you entirely and when I lose interest in a woman . . . well, then, you're not just any woman are you, Mrs. Moore? I must remember the charms of that long, ivory neck, and full, such full breasts that a man might loosen his purse strings for a glance, a touch. I need a few willing investors in my latest enterprise tonight, Mrs. Moore. Perhaps it's time you began to take the next step in our partnership."

He stood above her. She watched him harden, become angry at her, for being so. "Remove your gown," he said in the flat voice he always used when he made that demand of her.

"No."

He turned the inside lock on her bedroom door.

"No?"

"Please—no."

"Please, no, that's better," he purred as he unfastened her gown. He broke a shining, polished fingernail in his haste.

"Damnation! Finish!" he commanded.

She did, stood the heavy gown against a chair, and turned to him. When she opened her mouth, he pushed her back on the bed. His breath reeked of expensive scotch whiskey. She felt the familiar pressure against her ribs.

"Open your eyes, little wife. You'll not have your dreams this time, but me."

She didn't have the breath to say anything before he was inside her, plunging hard and merciless, and then gone. Did he know that even with her eyes open, she was not seeing him? Suddenly, he yanked down her petticoats, examining the small bulge below her corset line.

"What's this?"

"I—"

"Not a fondness for sweets, I think. Never mind. Rest, Mrs. Moore. I'll make an appointment with Doctor Gaston. A very discreet fellow, who has wanted a little slice of you since your wildman embarrassed him."

Olana shuttered, remembering.

"I will not let him hurt you too badly. But you're right, perhaps I'd better watch. To make sure he does a proper job. I need you,

Mrs. Moore. I need you full, buxom, beautiful. Not a thick, mis-shapen matron. And I will not share the fruits of my labor with any brats you make for your father. You have work to do. My work."

He kissed her earlobe gently and rose from the bed.

"I'll help you this time. But you must learn how not to inconvenience me further. Then you will do as you're told, with whom you're told. But you will never take your hair down for any of them, do you hear? Your hair, and its streaks of red, virgin blood, is mine."

Olana swallowed the bile that swelled up her throat.

"Are you ill, Mrs. Moore? We'll end early tonight, after they've had a good look, perhaps a well-timed, accidental brush with your enticing breasts."

The men all faded into formal, black and white duplications of each other, but pushing through them, her seven-month pregnancy on proud display, came Coretta Hunt, her arms ladened with flowers woven into a circle.

"I know these are not the exotic blossoms of the Pacific, but Sidney and I thought up a welcome home," she spoke so loudly even the men took notice. She placed the necklace of flowers over Olana's head and it framed the low neckline of her gown with roses and baby's breath. Olana gave Mrs. Hunt a grateful smile, and squeezed Sidney's hand. The guests applauded. Sidney quieted them with a wave of his hand. "I have a toast," he announced, "an old English toast for a wedding and now a welcome home:

Love, be true to her; Life, be dear to her;
Health, stay close by her; Joy, draw near to her;
Fortune, find what you can do for her,
Search your treasure-house through for her;
Follow her footsteps the wide world over,
And keep her husband always her lover!

She didn't care what price she would have to pay later, Olana pulled Sidney to her side and kissed his cheek.

"That was lovely, thank you."

"I let you down sport," he choked out softly. "I'm sorry."

She leaned on his arm. "You are my only friend left. Don't forget Patsy, Selby, the baby. I don't care about my parents anymore, about the business. But I'm obliged to that little family. Bring them home. Please, Sidney."

"My God, Olana. What about you?"

Dinner was announced. They were separated, Sidney placed down toward the long table's foot. He could only raise his glass to her from there, looking miserable, lost. But Coretta Hunt took her arm once dinner was done and the men lit their cigars to talk business.

"But—" Olana protested once Coretta steered them to the empty dressing rooms.

"I doubt even your husband provides spies in the company of women," she said, loosening the ties of Olana's gown.

"Mrs.—"

"We're alone, my name is Coretta, and you're going to faint if we can't get you out of this!"

"But we'll never get it tight enough again."

"So?"

"He'll know."

"You've already been put on display."

Olana looked in the woman's eyes, then down at the ring of flowers gracing her neckline. "I felt so naked," she said softly.

"I know."

"You're kind."

"Oh, kindness be damned," she said as she unlatched and un-laced. "We're both women in a man's world. The deals are being worked on now. They won't see us again until we're under wraps. And their heads will be swimming with numbers. Please, Olana. I know we didn't get a very good start back at Christmas. But I can see you're hurting. Sidney is anemic with worry. I'll wager Matt is too."

"Matt?" she whispered.

"Let me give your feet a rub, shall I?"

"But you're the one—"

"Oh, I haven't been sick a day, though this little rascal does some mean tumbling."

Olana let the woman remove her shoes. Her massage brought back the smell of the sea outside her Aunt Winnie's house.

"Your touch is as gentle as Matthew's," she breathed.

Coretta smiled. "Well, that's a high compliment. Olana, please, talk to me."

Olana's eyes darted to the door, the windows, the room's picture frames. She began to laugh, a strange new laughter, but addictive, as Coretta wound her own shawl around her shoulders and held her close. "What can I do for you?"

"Tell me a story," she whispered, "About the Klondike. About Matthew."

Coretta Hunt stroked her cheek. Olana had almost forgotten that simple gesture could lead to nothing else, could be done without piercing her elsewhere, somewhere no one could see. Coretta moved back to the opposite end of the couch. Olana felt the woman's fingers kneading her feet again with sure, deft strokes.

"Well, back then Matthew Hart, he was an overgrown boy, about the same as he is now," she launched them into the past she'd shared with Matthew. "He'd followed his partner McGee into town the first time they had a strike and had enough for our . . . entertainments. McGee went upstairs right off, but Matt stayed by the piano player, sipping his drink, listening, watching, in that quiet way of his. Some of the girls liked his eyes and tried to get him, because a few of the clients, well, they were unpredictable, and he seemed steady. He right enough had the hunger for our delights, you can tell by the eyes, so we knew he wasn't after the piano player. Still, he shook his head, all bashful, getting more and more discomforted. I went over, asked him to dance. Well, he twirled me through a fandango that pretty much peeled the gold leaf off the picture frames! That's how I met Matthew Hart."

Olana smiled, leaned back, losing herself in the woman's words and touch.

"We got interrupted by a cry from upstairs. Bad cry. We knew how to tell the difference between them and the . . . the good ones. Lottie, that was our . . . our mother, went flying up with Matt at her heels. He took care of the brute misbehaving himself in such short order that Lottie crowed, 'Well, Fandango Man,' you got a job any time you're in town.'

"Well, I never saw a man's eyes go from enraged to delighted in such a short span. And he took her up on it, whenever he and McGee were weary of each other or their diggings. He was the best of our strong men. The others got out of hand when they sensed our reliance on them. Sooner or later they wanted free drinks and time with the girls, that's if they were the better ones. The worst tried to arm their way into the business. Lottie had to shoot two of them rascals cold dead.

"Matt was a different sort. He never laid but a tender hand with his remedies on any of us. He never even asked for a single thing beyond our company as conversation or dancing partners. He pretty much joined our family when McGee kicked off of the frostbite."

"That's when you were lovers?" Olana whispered.

"Child," she said gently. "Matt and I were never lovers."

"But that night, in my father's house, he was kissing——"

"I was kissing him, Olana. There's a difference. Listen. I wanted a child, and he knows all that women's wisdom. He was helping me figure out the best time. See, after all the wild young men I'd had in the Klondike, I wanted to marry me one who was rich and not so demanding of me that way, you know? But I lost a child up there, and that was a hard thing, even though she was a mistake and I didn't have a clue who her daddy was.

"Well, it was Matt got the bleeding stopped then, who let me cry into his shirt, so I made bold that night, years later, to tell him I wanted another one, to keep me company when Will goes. And he went busy with his calculating when the best time of the month would be. He knows that from studying with that grandma of his. Well, didn't we find that very night I was ripe and ready. I laughed out my joy and asked if he would mind a kiss, sort of to prime the pump, you know? Well, he was obliging a soon-to-be-with-child old friend, Olana, and it broke my heart that you took it the wrong way."

"It was only Lottie then?"

"Lottie was a formidable 'only,' child."

"And he loved her?"

"Loved her so much he lied to find out how to love her."

"Lied?"

"Told her he had a girl, waiting back east. Told her that he wanted to know how to please this girl, how to make her feel as good as Lottie made him feel. Well, that moved her more than I'd ever seen diamonds and gold mines move that woman, and she'd been offered both. But there was no girl, it was Lottie who Matt loved. He was smart enough to know that she'd been so used by life that she would not believe him. How he knew that, is still a mystery to me.

Young as he was, he must have been used a bit by life himself, I reckon. He finally told her the truth when she got the gangrene. Did no good. She died saying she was happy to deliver his bride such a well-mannered lover. Olana, he wept bad as we did when we lost her.

"Afterward he brought us girls—his seven sisters he called us down here to San Francisco, and did exactly what Lottie asked him when they married."

"They married?"

"Now don't you believe any of the gold digger stories! Matthew Hart was not taking advantage of a dying woman old enough to be his mama! It was Lottie asked him to tie the knot, on account of he was the only one she trusted with her money, to take care of us. And he did just exactly that, without taking so much as a cent!

"He brought us down here to 'Frisco, set us up, gave us our share of her inheritance, then disappeared until I saw him with you on his arm at your fancy ball last Christmas. Olana. I feel responsible for whatever happened between you. And I want to be your friend."

"That would be . . . wonderful," Olana realized as she said it.

"Good. Now, how far along are you, sweetling?"

"Along?"

"How many months?"

"Months?"

"I know you haven't announced, but the physical changes—"

"What changes?"

"Your breasts. You've noticed they're real full, more tender?"

"Yes, so is my—" She touched her middle and began to feel ill.

"Olana. You mean you yourself don't know—"

She tried to hide her tears from this experienced, full-bellied woman. "Didn't you ask someone the signs? Your mother?"

"No. I—I used to talk to Patsy."

"Your maid?"

"Yes. But Darius stranded her—there in Japan. She and Mr. Selby, her husband. I didn't know about it until we were already out of port. He tried to make it look like a mistake. I've felt so strange, so lost. But I don't think I could possibly be . . . that way, Coretta. I mean, so soon. He was seasick the whole crossing, and in Japan he was so angry with me, for tending the sailors, for thinking I poisoned him, we didn't c-consumate until—

"What a considerate bridegroom."

"I didn't mind being left alone all those weeks! It's better than now," she blurted.

"Moore's hurting you, isn't he? Shit, I know his kind! I could carve his precious manhood out! Now let's put our heads together on this. When was your last flow?"

Flow. Matthew's word. It warmed her toward this woman. "Why, before I got married. Two weeks before."

"Olana, that was four months ago! And you never suspected—"

"I thought it was the strain. On the ship. In Japan. It stopped once before, when I was in the snow, with Matthew. I accused him, Coretta, of . . . you know, when I was sick, unknowing. He was so good, so patient with me, explaining that it can stop for reasons other than—"

Olana began to cry, not the silent screams of her nights with her husband, but a sloppy, blubbering, heaving cry from deep inside the little girl she felt like in Coretta Hunt's arms.

"You'll have to tell that idiot soon. Perhaps, when he knows, he'll be kinder to you," she offered.

Olana sat up, and took the older woman's hands in a white-knuckled grip.

"If I'm as far along as . . . as four months, then I'm carrying Matthew's child, Coretta."

"Matt's? Olana, did you and Matt—"

"Only once!"

"That's all it takes, love! When?"

"The night before the wedding."

"I knew it! Wagered Sidney on it, though I doubt he'll remember, sober. I knew Matt would come back, try to stop you."

"But I drove him away with my stupid—"

"Never mind. Don't look back just now. You've got to take action on your future. Damn. Moore will figure out your baby's not his if it comes early. But you've got time before—"

A cold fear invaded Olana's heart. "No!" she cried out. "No time. There's a doctor, coming tomorrow. He'll not have me a misshapen matron, Darius said, Coretta! What does that mean? Are there doctors who—"

"He'd cut out his own. That son of a bitch."

Olana felt suddenly giddy, lightheaded, and unbearably tired. "I can't endure it anymore," she whispered. "I don't know how I thought I could." She gripped Coretta Hunt's arms. "Coretta, I can't lose this child, it's the only decent thing I have left."

"You have friends, Olana. Who will help you. We'll get you out. Tonight."

thirty

His eyes were red-rimmed from the cigar smoke. He was very drunk. Still Darius Moore came into her room, locked the door. It would be quick, Olana told the panic rising up her throat.

"You loosened your corset, after dinner."

"I didn't think it would matter. Weren't the deals all made?"

"The deals? The deals? What do you know of dealing? What has that whore been telling you?"

"Why, Darius, Mrs. Hunt—"

He cut off her air with a grip around her throat. "Is a whore." He knocked the back of her head against the bedpost. "Say it."

"Is a whore," she whispered.

His anger, his violence toward her had been quiet, subversive. Olana's mind reeled, trying to figure out how to protect herself and her child from his new, explosive ranting.

"Displaying her sin proudly," he continued, "with her cuckold husband standing by, as if that whore's bastard were his! Damned blind fool, he loves her."

"Yes," Olana whispered.

"I don't love you!"

"I know that," she said.

"You don't know anything! You don't know the years of patient, calculated waiting, before your father loosened his hold on you. You don't know the flattery, the idiotic, chaste court I paid your mother! To gain control, to have control, the way I never could in the damned army, in business, in any whorehouse. You're stealing it, Mrs. Moore. Because I can't control the way you make me feel! No. It's not you, it's only this, your hair."

He yanked pins and combs, then held her braid around his fist as he rifled through her drawers. Olana's eyes stung with tears but she did not cry out. He'd awakened the servants, she was sure, but she could expect no help from any. They'd been selected by him, for their discretion. The metallic flash, reflected in the lamplight, paralyzed her, the way the glint of Matthew Hart's knife had, long ago. She was safe then, only thinking herself in danger. With Darius Moore she'd thought she'd be safe. Now both she and an innocent were in danger. Scissors, not a knife. He yanked her hair harder. The cutting was a relief. Still, Olana cried silently for the loss. You don't need your hair, a sassy, practical voice, one like Matthew's grandmother's, told her. What you need tonight is your legs.

Matthew learned to handle the attacks on his own, stumbling into the sea caves nightly for relief. But his suffocating nights made him more reclusive. He never left the farm.

Then the worst night came. Moonless, cold. If a night could be forsaken, this one was, he remembered thinking as he stumbled along the wet sand. The wind howled to match the severity. It deadened his call to the women when he realized he might not make it to the caves without their help. Would he die here of his phantom illness then? He'd always wanted to die here, on the beach. But not like this, confused and helpless. Not with a small daughter to raise, the women depending on him, even that small help his physical strength was. He slipped on the rocks, and fell into the pounding surf. Then rose, lurched into the cave. There his breath returned with a surge of strength.

When his eyes adjusted to the dim light he saw Olana, huddled against the wall, her ragged clothing wet and gleaming like scales. A bright green scarf was matted around her head, over her shoulder. Her eyes were unworldly bright. When he held out his hand, he thought she was going to will herself into the gleaming rockface of the cave.

"I need Annie, Vita."

"I'll take you to them."

She stood slowly. Her ill-fitting clothes could not disguise her pregnancy. The scarf slipped off, landing in a briny pool. She got on her knees, groping for it. Failing, she found the ends of her hair, hacked off just below her ears. She pulled. Harder, until he thought his heart would burst.

" 'Lana! Stop it!"

She obeyed him, covering her mouth. Something broke inside him. Something useless. A burden. But he mourned it anyway.

"Matthew?"

"Yes?"

"Why are you crying?"

"I . . . I'm so glad to see you."

"We're friends, then?"

"Sure."

"He took my hair."

"It will grow back," he promised.

"My shoes are ruined."

"I'll carry you."

Matthew picked up the scarf from the glassy pool, offered it. She took the scarf, the tips of his fingers, then his hands.

"You're safe now," he said, lifting her, trying to block the wind as he walked, trying to lend her and her child within all the heat his body could give. In return he felt assurance that his night wanderings for air and sanity were over.

Once he'd given her over to the women a blinding rage filled up Matthew's need to hold her. He shoved bullets into chambers of his rifle to relieve the rage. He put the cartridge belt over one shoulder, strapped his rifle over the other. His grandmother blocked the back doorway. He walked past her. Off the porch, into the pale quarter moon's light. She followed.

"What are you doing?"

"I'm going to kill him."

"You won't have a chance. The powerful, they surround themselves with protection."

"Take care of her."

"You trust the women and orphans you'll leave behind?" she hurled at his back. Sense. Damnation. It would not prevail against his need. He walked toward the barn. Annie Smithers didn't follow, but he knew she was not yet through with him. Faster. He had to be faster.

He only wanted to look back at the house, but it dimmed behind the three of them, three women in white. His mother's keening wail made his hands shake. He mounted. He'd never get past them. He turned Little Coy for the beach. The wail came again. The horse reared, throwing him. She ran riderless along the Pacific shoreline.

"Spooks, these women are spooks," Matthew muttered, hauling himself to his feet. Olana stood before him, out of breath from running and the burden that widened the flowing pleats in his mother's nightgown. Her hair haloed her pale face. Her eyes looked frozen in a nightmare. But she spoke with a strength that amazed him.

"Matthew. Don't make me regret coming here."

His grandmother took his rifle, his mother removed the cartridge belt from his shoulder. Olana gave herself back to the women's care. They led her to the house and left him to find his horse on her path to the sea.

"I'll take care of this house's defense," his grandmother informed him later, in the hearth room, as she put the steaming cup of chickory root coffee in his hands.

"What's my place then?"

"Help us."

"You don't understand, Gran. I feel a steel cold need inside me. I got to kill him."

"Now who's the spook?" she accused. Then she sat beside him, taking his hand in hers. "Matthew, listen to me. I know you're pulled that way, but putting a bullet in a man don't take half the courage it does to tend the living. We got a big job ahead. All of us."

He doubted his grandmother's words every time Olana flinched at any unexpected sound or sight of him. He took to rising before dawn and tending to crops, fences, and apricots for them and the friars of St. Pitias until after she was bedded. Sometimes his only look at her all day was as she slept.

Olana changed his routine just as he was realizing it was one. He was deep in the cloistered recesses of the mission, mortaring a chink in the friars' walled garden.

"I want you to come home, Matthew."

"How did you get in here?" he wondered, knowing that this was the most restricted part of the monastery besides the sacristy itself.

"I asked," she said.

"You must have a way with words."

He lost himself in her lovely, blossoming form, in the pink health returning to her cheeks. The frightened look was tamed by a new light in her eyes. Was she happy? He wiped his hands on the rag in his pocket and dusted off the stone bench. "I don't mind it here," he said softly as she sat.

Her brows came together. "Possum misses you."

"She brings me dinner. And we meet at the beach every afternoon for—"

"It's not enough."

"I'll talk to her."

"Matthew, please try again. To tolerate my presence." Her head bowed, her request was like a prayer from a madonna.

"I thought it was you tolerating me," he whispered.

"In your own house? Among your family? Even I was never that presumptuous."

"Then why—" he said, reaching his hand for hers. She yanked back. "Hey," he whispered softly, "you afraid of me, 'Lana?"

"No." She turned away. A dark silence came between them.

"I thought we were friends," he tried.

"We are."

"Friends can talk. Touch." His finger swiped her elbow.

"Don't!"

"Talk to me, 'Lana. Please. I can't come home to your silences. Not even for Possum."

"Then I'll go."

"Stop that. You are a guest of the women."

"I don't expect you to understand."

"He raped you." A steel rod rode up her back. He took a deep breath. "I hated being touched, for a long time after," he whispered to her, the stones, the budding flowers of the friars' garden. She turned back to him.

"After what?"

"After. W-when I was a boy—" Say it, he willed himself. It was so many years ago, say it. He received help in his stumbling efforts from the most unlikely source possible.

Olana touched the tips of his fingers with hers. "The ship, the one that shanghaied you out of San Francisco. Did someone—"

"Several."

"Oh, Matthew."

He struggled to keep his eyes on hers. "It wasn't my fault," he said gruffly. "It wasn't yours."

"You warned me," she whispered.

"When I should have—"

She shook her head. "No, no shoulds. Only now. It's hard enough, hour to hour, isn't it?"

"Yes."

"Matthew. When will the pain go away?"

He smiled sadly. "I'll let you know."

He looked out toward the ocean. He felt her hand come to rest in his open palm. He smiled, but didn't dare to look at her. They sat for a long time in silence, their fingers loosely twined.

"Come home," she urged, finally. "Make peace with your little girl."

"Will you come with me?" he asked. "After I put away the tools?"

She smiled. "I'll help you."

The sun shone brightly, a taste of summer as they walked. Matthew worried, though she was steady, and the women had provided her with a wide straw hat. Olana stopped suddenly, and an otherworldly look gentled her face.

"My," she said.

" 'Lana?"

"I must sit."

He led her to a grassy spot where she watched the waves beat the shoreline. Her fingers hovered above the light merino wool of her loose gown.

"I thought it was my overindulgence in the stewed apricots this morning, but now . . . I believe . . . Matthew, the baby is moving."

Instinctively his hands went to her middle. Resting, then probing. He looked up at her shining eyes. "There?"

"Yes! I have—what is it Vita and your grandmother call it— 'quickened'?"

"Yes."

"Alive, then? The baby is alive?"

"Yes, darlin'."

She stiffened. "It's not yours, Matthew."

"That don't matter none," he said.

"It doesn't?"

"Oh, right," he corrected himself, "Doesn't."

As she shook her head Matthew delighted in the way her free, short curls brushed her neck. God, it would be hard to watch them grow without touching her. "Child's an innocent," he tried assuring her.

"Matthew, do you mean it?"

"Sure I do."

"I don't believe you."

He shrugged. "You don't have to, not yet. We got us some time. I'll show you."

thirty-one

Matthew got used to Olana's silent presence among the women. As the days grew warmer they all brought his dinner when he was pruning the apricot trees. Sometimes they walked to the shore with him afternoons. They spoke among themselves as he swam with Possum. He even caught them all laughing once, but Olana blushed and Annie shooed him off on another task when he asked to be let in on it. He went about their bidding without complaint, but wished he could earn his way off his elders' probation lists sooner.

He and Olana were not alone until Possum's fourth birthday. The women took his little girl into town for some finery, leaving Olana in the house alone. They charged him to look in on her, but not when. Matthew tried to concentrate on the trees, but after nicking his knuckles the third time, and hearing the gracious sound of the noon Angelis bells, he put down his tools. Noon, that was a good time, wasn't it? He wouldn't scare her if he came home with the bells, would he?

Olana was in the kitchen, on her knees, weeping, her apron smeared with the same dark matter that was dripping from her fingers. Not blood. God, please, not blood. He couldn't will his limbs to move. She raised her head.

"I'm so clumsy!" she yelled at him, pushing the curls off her forehead with the back of her hand. "I wanted everything perfect."

"Perfect?" he repeated, stupidly.

"Everything went together fine. Then I couldn't get the stove fired up properly, then I knocked over the bowl of c-cake batter—stop it! Stop laughing, you hateful man!"

But he couldn't stop, even as she flung fistfuls of flour at him, because he was so flooded with relief. Cake batter. Not blood.

"I'm useless, ignorant, ungainly, stupid—"

"You are the envied woman of this household," he told her sternly, dodging the assault unsuccessfully.

"What?"

"You heard me. Envied! With a sacred trust. We are honored by your presence among us."

She looked stunned. Didn't she know that already? He smiled, wishing he'd told her sooner. The delicate blush complemented her already heightened features.

He knelt on the floor amid the flour and chocolate batter and broken crockery. "Let's see what we can salvage, shall we?"

"All right," she whispered, joining him. He took her wrist in a gentle hold and brought it to his mouth, licking the batter dripping from her fingers. "Hey. This is good!"

"Really?"

"Sure. Look. There's enough left in the bowl. We can rescue a little cake for Possum out of it. Would you like that?"

"I like . . . this," she said softly.

"What?" His tongue stroked along her finger more slowly. "This?" She giggled. Like the girl who still lived inside her. The one her husband had damaged badly, but hadn't killed. Matthew feasted on her laughter as well as the sweet chocolate. He dipped her finger in the batter and started again, his tongue harder as it glided along her palm's lifeline.

"No . . ." her protest ended in a deep sigh. His heart thumped wildly. She wasn't pulling away. He caught the faint scent of rose-water from her skin. She returned her hand to the bowl, sighed again, then skated her batter-drenched fingers along the contours of his face, down his neck. He kissed into her palm.

"Matthew." Her voice burst over the syllables of his name. She leaned down.

The commotion at the front door made her leap like a startled deer, knocking over the sack of flour. He looked up through the white dust to see his grandmother's familiar, fisted-up waist.

"Well, well. Who won?" she asked.

She came to his room that night. From deep in a dreamless sleep Matthew saw only her face edged in darkness. His eyes adjusted, and the outline of her nightdress appeared.

" 'Lana?"

"Yes."

"Are you hurting?"

"No."

He sat up, then remembered he'd forsaken his nightshirt on this warm evening. She came closer.

"Would you kiss me, Matthew?"

"Sure."

He did, tenderly, his fingers hovering under her chin. Then he waited. The way Lottie waited for him when he was coming alive again. He pulled the covers aside. She slipped into the bed. Shivered.

"Cold?" he asked.

"My hands and feet. Why is that, Matthew?"

"Takes longer for the blood to get there, now that you're sharing."

"There's nothing wrong?"

"No." He breathed into her hands. "You tell Annie and Vita your worries, 'Lana?"

"Not all of them."

"Why not?"

"I don't want them to think I'm as ignorant as I am."

"But—"

"You already know." She laughed. Embarrassed, high, her eyes skittering across the room's braided rug. "I thought," she whispered as her cold toes contacted his leg shyly, "that I would never feel like . . . like I did when you came in with the noon bells' tolling. Not again. Matthew, do you—"

"Oh, yes." Stop that. Jumping on her words, he chided himself.

She took a deep breath. "Could we, I mean would it hurt the baby if we—"

"No, darlin'." Shit, again. But she didn't seem to mind.

"Could we, then?"

"When you're ready."

"I am."

He resisted the urge to tell her she wasn't, that he could feel her fear in her voice. But trust had brought her to him, hadn't it? Trust and that courage of hers, leading. So he lost his face in her short curls, his hands in the new curves beneath her gown. He tasted her tears. Why was she crying? It unnerved him. He stood, pulled on his nightshirt, and went to the open windows. He leaned into the ocean's sound, felt her hand on his arm.

"I'm too ugly now?"

"No." He drew her close. "Honest to God, 'Lana, I have never wanted you more."

He felt the heat of her blush and took pleasure in it. She turned her attention to the night sky. "So clear," she said. "Like when the twins were born."

"Yes."

He lifted her onto the deep windowsill, beside the vase his mother had filled with yellow roses. She dangled her legs, making a soft breeze.

"Olana, I love you."

The dangling stopped. "You only love broken things."

He inhaled deeply. "I don't believe you're broken, 'Lana," he whispered. He took a rose from the vase and touched her bared shoulder with it. Olana shivered, but not with the cold. He kissed between her breasts, then led the rose up to her throat. She plucked it from the stem. Matthew felt the petals shower his hair. Their scent intoxicated him. His tongue stroked her nipples as her little gasps and raking fingers urged him on.

She peaked, melting her body in that delicious way Matthew loved. He lifted her from her perch and carried her to bed. Once down, the catches in her throat.

" 'Lana—I can wait."

"No, please, Matthew. Don't turn away from me tonight."

He placed more pillows behind her back, then slid his hand between her thighs. She was moist. Smiling bravely as if she was at the gates of Hell.

His mouth took hers, delving deeper. He slid inside her. She gasped.

"You well, 'Lana?" he asked.

She nodded, blushing, but her hands urged him on. Again, again he entered, burying himself between her thighs as she laughed musically at his ear. The tears only started when they were done, when he was falling asleep in her arms.

He took her hand. "What is it, love?"

"It didn't hurt," she breathed.

The dread circled his heart. " 'Lana, did I hurt you, that first time, at your house? I did everything so badly, when I wanted—"

She pressed her fingers against his lips. "That night has been the thread to my sanity, Matthew!"

"It has?"

"I thought I'd somehow dreamed it, after—" She closed her eyes. "It was like being under a waterfall, that night—feeling so full, rushing, powerful, beautiful. What came after . . . oh Matthew, my cruelty toward you, who were—"

"Rude, and demanding, and confusing—"

"I deserved it. I deserved everything."

" 'Lana, don't."

She drew herself and her childspace away from him. He coaxed her back into his arms and held her there, gently, as the pre-dawn light began to filter into the room. She stirred against his chest.

"Innocent," she murmured. "That's what you said my baby is, didn't you, Matthew?"

"Yes."

"I want a name that means that."

"The women, they know those things." He kissed her temple. "Ask the women."

When he woke she was gone, but her scent remained, and the sheets were strewn with rose petals. His grandmother knocked the last one out of his hair at breakfast. Olana giggled behind the cream pitcher.

"Cal limps for the bullet still in his side, and can't eat no fried foods either. All for nothing? Damn. That ranger sure as hell looked dead."

"Shut up, Ezra," his brother growled.

"Mr. Hopkins recognizes your effort. That's why he's willing to engage our services again." McPeal rubbed the stubble of his chin.

"Where is he? We'll get him this time."

"Unknown, at present. This job is simple robbery. To show our Mr. Hopkins that we're serious about getting back in his good graces. He's looking for traces of his kinswoman, the very elusive Olana Whittaker Moore."

"Find one, you'll find the other, if you ask me," Ezra claimed. "All set up in housekeeping again."

McPeal had learned to listen to the dull brother. "If this escapade leads to them both, we'll have a chance at those thousands again."

"Who do we rob?" Cal asked impatiently.

"Seems there was a shadow woman, the night Mrs. Moore slipped off her matrimonial rigging, who led the distraught husband on a merry chase to a big house, along the shore. She delivered something besides a false scent."

"We can get her to tell us what, don't fret yourself, Mr.—"

"No violence, this time! You'll get me in, take whatever you'd like. Now. Mr. Hopkins has arranged easy access. But I'm told the house is confusing."

thirty-two

Sometimes Olana went to his room, sometimes Matthew went to hers. Sometimes they met in the hallway, laughing. It was one of those nights that Annie Smithers caught them. She sighed.

"Will you two settle yourselves in one bed so we can all get a good night's rest?"

Matthew colored to the roots of his hair as he "Yes, ma'amed" her. His grandmother was the only person alive who could embarrass him, and Olana realized that doing so was the old woman's chief vice.

Her grandson never ceased delighting Olana with lover's variations, were they playful, passionate, or tender. He encouraged her attempts to give him pleasure. He made her feel beautiful again, though her hair was shorn and her middle soon would not allow even Vita's largest apron to keep her shifts protected.

She helped the Smithers' household bring in the apricot crop, and often went with Matthew and Possum for their daily swim in the bay. The summer grew so warm Olana walked out into the water herself and floated on her back while they swam around her. Once, while Possum napped in the shade, Matthew brought her over the hill and made love to her gently, sweetly in a place he dug out of the sand to accommodate her growth.

He and his women never grew impatient with her questions. If she were shy about asking the women, he would ask for her. How big was the baby now? How would she know it was ready to come out? What would it feel like? She thought that in the women's care, and with him beside her, she could face even the agony she had seen on Mrs. Amadeo's face.

It was after the birth she had difficulty imagining. She didn't think of it much, only when a stranger rode down the road and she'd seen fear in Vita Hart's eyes. Or the night she woke up screaming.

"He's coming," she finally whispered through clenched teeth.

Matthew caressed the seven-month bulge her waist had become. "I won't let any harm come to you, I swear it."

She touched his face, which seemed to glow in his conviction as well as the full moon's light. "It was a dream, Matthew."

"Listen to your dreams," he said, settling her against his chest. "Especially now."

The next day she found his Colt Peacemaker in the drawer beside their bed. His rifle was ready over the mantle. Even Annie's old Dragoon pistols came down from the back room's cupboard and rested in the drawer under the pastry cloth. And Olana heard the two women arguing.

"Mama, he's a powerful man, her husband. He could make it look—"

"Ain't time to worry about that yet. Let's get the child through her confinement."

Vita's troubled face brightened when she saw Olana. She held up the tiny baby gown. Olana took it from her hands. "Will he be this small?" she asked.

"She'll be, yes," Annie proclaimed.

"She? How do you know—"

"She doesn't know, just fancies she does," Vita spoke, irritated.

"Tell me my business when you've brought in over a thousand babies," Annie scolded her daughter.

"A thousand?" Olana marveled, happy even in the midst of these two women's quarrel.

"One thousand, one hundred, three."

"You remember exactly?"

"Don't have to. Got a record."

"May I see it?"

The old woman's face betrayed pleasure before she fetched the thick book from an undistinguished place beside the Bible and Sears Roebuck catalogue. She placed it on Olana's dwindling lap.

The opening pages of the text revealed a handwriting related to the one in Matthew's book of remedies, but more childish, full of too hard pressing and ink blots. Olana ran her fingertips over them and felt the buckling efforts of a young woman pioneering to be her family's first literate.

"My first seven years ain't in there," Annie explained as she stood over Olana's shoulder. "Those I did apprenticed to my mama. Before Michael Barnes taught me my letters. I wasn't much of a student, as you can see."

"Michael—"

"Barnes. The husband with the vest and watchchain," Vita explained which of Annie's men she was talking about. Olana nodded, remembering the old photograph of the graying man with sad eyes. The first baby written in the book was born in 1843. Olana's fascination grew as she read on. The women worked silently around her. She found Vita, written in more detail than the rest. Empire, California, 1850. Gold Country. Annie Smithers was a forty-niner. Olana drifted through time, distance, and children until Vita nodded down at a new page.

"There's Matthew," she proclaimed softly at a drawing of her and a wrinkled, peaceful baby in her arms. "My second stepfather drew us."

"Joe Fish. Who was taught by Sequoyah himself."

"That's right."

"Matthew told me he made wonderful likenesses."

"You are getting to know us all, both living and passed on!"

Olana stared at the drawn, shining face of the young mother. "Was it a difficult birth?" she found the courage to ask.

Vita smiled. "I was very frightened. Mama and I were estranged at the time, because of my marriage. I was the only woman at the garrison. There had been some Indian trouble. I sent for Mama, but couldn't be sure she even got my message, or would come if she did. She had little ones of her own then."

Annie snorted. "Joe Fish knew there'd be no stopping me once I set my mind to going. He got me through."

"And once I saw Mama and Joe, the burden of my loneliness and fear had lightened along with my pains. I never saw a more beautiful sunrise than the first one I saw in my son's eyes."

"Oh, I must read—"

Olana discovered the next page had been brutally ripped from the book. Though carefully replaced, it was smeared with an ugly red ink stamp-marked "Property of U.S. Army."

"What is this?" she asked the women.

"This stood between Matthew and a rope some years ago."

"His court martial."

Vita raised her eyebrows. "He's told you?"

"Not him. It was the reason he lost his commission at the park."

"Lost?"

Annie Smithers' mouth narrowed into a hard line. "Didn't I tell you, Vita? Didn't I tell you he got pushed back on the farm?"

There were tears in his mother's eyes. "The documents were supposed to be sealed. His father promised me. I stayed with him the rest of his life because he promised me those records were sealed!"

Olana took her hand. "They were. Mr. Parker didn't know why he was ordered to dismiss Matthew. And he wouldn't follow the order. So Matthew resigned."

"He loved those trees," Vita whispered, "they were healing—"

"He was shutting parts of himself down," Annie contended. "Permanent hibernation would have come next. He needed to come home. It was for the best, Vita. Quit coddling the boy."

"Tell me about the court martial," Olana asked.

"He was tried and found guilty of desertion in 1890, during the Conner's Ridge Campaign," Vita began.

"Massacre," Annie corrected her sharply.

"1890? Why, Matthew was—"

"Born June twenty-fifth, eighteen and seventy-six. During the Battle of Little Big Horn, that changed everything. Or maybe just speeded things up. Leastways, his birthday made Matthew fourteen in ninety. Fourteen. Exactly how we got him freed, though they should have not wasted the rope and put it around—"

"Mama," Vita scolded. "His father had lied years before, in order to get him enlisted. Matthew was always a little tall for his age."

"He never had no business in uniform, and I told them such at the trial."

"I don't know why the Apache didn't kill him," Vita fretted.

"I do. Even in their beaten state, them Indians had the sense to recognize a child as good and pure as his superiors were filthy in corruption! He refused to kill women and children at Conner's Ridge. He defended them against the murdering savages who gave the command for slaughter. A few even managed to slip away because of it, with their babies on their backs. That was both disobeying orders and aiding the enemy, as the army saw it. The soldiers beat him so badly it was two weeks before he could stand trial."

Olana's head hurt. "Mama," Vita cautioned, placing her hand on Annie Smithers' arm.

"So," the old woman finished, "now you know for what crime Matthew lost his place among the trees."

The book had gotten too heavy for Olana's lap. It slipped to the floor, notes and recipes flying out of the pages. It had something to do with her, his losing his place in the trees. It wasn't Sidney that found him out, she finally realized. It was Darius.

thirty-three

The women helped her rise from the chair. "You have a good lie out on the hammock before dinner."

"But the pole beans—"

"Get!"

Olana closed her eyes the moment she put her head back on the roped swing. When she opened them, she saw Matthew, his spectacles down on his nose, snapping pole beans and rocking her with one bare foot caught in the open weave of the hammock. She saw somewhere in his determined concentration, a teenaged boy refusing to obey. She touched his face.

"You are a fine man."

He frowned. "Tell that to the women when they see the mess we've made of these beans." His daughter appeared, still and waiflike, from her place under his arm. Matthew grinned. "Take these to your mana, will you, Flibbity-gibbet?"

He leaned over and kissed Olana full on the mouth, even with his daughter rolling her eyes as she sailed off, munching and leaving a trail of their handiwork.

He climbed into the hammock with her. His clever hands were soon dancing beautifully with the places that brought her delight. Why had she told him the child wasn't his? Her increasing size was saying it was. If the baby came, full term, in two months' time, she would be sure. Then she'd tell him.

Annie rang the dinner bell.

"We should—"

"Stay a little, 'Lana," he urged. "I got to ask you something."

"What?"

"I'm wondering if you'd like to get away a bit."

"Away where?"

"Just outside the mission. They have a festival. I crate up the apricots, sell them. I'd like your company there for some . . . business of our own as well."

"Business, Matthew?"

"Yes. On account of it's a holy place, you know? Back before the Spanish friars set down on it. Maybe that's why the friars chose it, you think?"

"I don't understand."

"You will. It's me should understand how to do this better, ain't like I never . . . nerves, I guess, darlin'." His fingers danced along her side, as they had that first time he'd touched her, against the sequoia. "Got to figure it some more, you know? I ain't done enough, gathered enough. Say you'll come with me to the festival, 'Lana."

She lifted the summer gold hair back from his face, as intrigued by his drawl and slip into backwoods grammar as she was by his invitation. "Of course I'll come, my darling," she agreed.

The apricot festival was huge and welcoming. Olana clung to Matthew's arm as they stood among people with loud voices, speaking in half-English and half-Spanish, only a smaller fraction of which she could understand. He kept his arm around her, leaning down often to translate.

"They are happy for you, 'Lana."

"Oh?" she heard her own voice. Thin. Frightened.

"They want to know how many."

"How many what?"

"Months along you are."

"Why?"

"Good fortune. Luck that you'll bring to the festival for every month. They believe—"

"I don't know!"

Matthew lifted her into his arms. "She needs to rest," he explained softly. Everyone bowed and Friar Malcolm led them into the mission.

"Matthew, put me down. I'm much too heavy," Olana protested.

"Hush," he whispered, then set her on a couch of pillows in a cool, quiet room bathed in shade. The cowled monk handed him a basin, pitcher, and white cloth, and left. Matthew poured, took up the cloth, dipped it in the water, and touched it to Olana's brow. He was so like the friars in his stillness, she realized.

"Matthew, I'm sorry. I don't know what came over me."

"The women warned me about keeping the spaces around you open."

"Do you think that's all it was?"

"Sure. You won't tell on me, will you?"

She took a sip of cool water. "My silence might cost you."

"Why, Miss Whittaker," he planted a kiss on her shoulder, "Whatever do you mean?"

"I . . ." she tried, but couldn't keep up the playful facade. "Oh, Matthew, the festival people, the holy men at the mission. If they knew what I really am. What a burden I've been to you and your—"

"Are you going to start that again? Listen, I think we'd best do something official."

"Official?"

"Get married."

"But—"

"Shit, I'm doing it all wrong again, ain't I?"

"Matthew, I'm the one who did everything wrong."

"You nap now, I'll get to work on this. Meet you after you take your rest, after the feast. Promise?"

"All right." She was too tired even to argue with him.

* * *

Matthew was so gracious and Olana tried to match him, raising her glass, admiring the fierce dance he did around the daughters of neighboring sheep ranchers. They snapped their wide skirts in an angry passion that he did not seem to notice beyond its sensuality's enhancing the dance. Olana wanted to tell the women that she should not be the object of envy.

The evening's waltz was not the Viennese one of her Christmas ball, but a soft, slow dance that was done close. As Matthew brought her to the floor, he lowered his lips to her ear. "Olana Sarah Whittaker, would you do me the honor of becoming my wife?"

"Yes," she whispered.

"Good," he said, his voice tinged with surprise, as if her answer would have been anything else.

As Matthew negotiated with the friars, wool for apricots, Olana sat waiting. She touched the back of her head. Her hair was still in place. It had just grown long enough to pin the back strands up, giving the illusion of length. Olana did not want any to see how her husband's wrath had been visited on her on his last night of abuse.

Shifting the folds of the white gown his women had presented to her this evening, she felt a sudden need to show Annie and Vita that she might, someday, make Matthew happy. Their gift's high waist and ample material made her feel unconstrained by her pregnancy, almost pretty. When Matthew returned, handing her the spray of succulent blooms, she felt what he called her, beautiful.

"Walk?"

"All right," she answered, sure he would explain the canvas sack he slung over his back.

A clear three-quarter moon and stars blazed from the August sky. Matthew headed toward a grove of scrub pine guarding an outdoor travelers' shrine beside the mission's walls. "We can do it there," he told her.

"Do what?"

"Get married."

"Matthew!"

"I asked you proper, didn't I, when we were dancing?"

"Why are you doing this?"

"What?"

"Mocking me."

"What?"

"I want to go back."

"Cold feet. Goddamn it."

"Don't you blaspheme at me, Matthew Hart!"

"I apologize. To you. To the lady in the sack. Now will you marry me?"

"Lady?"

"If you'll—"

"Matthew, I'm already married."

"I know that. That's why we're having the divorce first."

"Divorce?"

"I'd rather make you a widow but the women made me promise not to go after him. Shit. You ain't Catholic, or against divorce on principle, are you?"

"No."

"Good. Come on."

She tagged behind his long strides rather than display any more of her bewilderment.

There was a bench at the grotto, made of the same stone as the mission walls. Olana sat there and watched him unload the first of his treasures. It was a long gray-green bundle wrapped in red yarn. He buried one end in the ground and lit the other. It smelled of sage.

"The divorce will be a Cherokee one, if that's all right with you, on account of it's the only one I know. See how the smoke goes straight up tonight? That's a good sign. Now you're going to be on your own here, Olana. You say who you are and who you're divorcing. Into the smoke."

"Into the smoke?"

"Yes."

"Matthew—"

"Yes?"

"I love you."

"So divorce him."

Olana stood close to where the smoke ascended skyward. She felt a strength coming from the women's gift, or maybe from inside it as she spoke. "I'm Olana Sarah Whittaker, and I divorce you, Darius Moore."

A warm breeze swirled the gown about her legs. The sage smoke followed, then rose high, toward the stars. Olana threw back her head and laughed. "I did it!" she shouted. "Matthew, I did it!"

"Perfect. That was perfect, love," he said quietly.

She felt curiously light as he rummaged through his canvas bag again. He drew out a mesquite wood carved Madonna, one with a belly still distended like Mrs. Amadeo's from recent childbirth, and full breasts, one of which the infant Christ was latched onto like any mortal newborn. Matthew held it before her.

"This is *Nuestra Señora de la Leche y Buen Parto*. In English, Our Lady of The Good Delivery and Bountiful Milk," he explained. "I figure she can be our witness." He put the statue into the grotto's niche, then lit blue votive candles on either side. The scent of beeswax mingled with the sage.

"Now for this, I'm going to try to remember, from when I married Lottie up north, before a preacher who was mostly sober, if that's all right with you."

"Matthew, aren't we being . . . sacreligious?"

"No. Seal Woman, she was the Catholic kind of Christian, like the friars and the Amadeos and Farrell. I don't suppose I'm any kind of anything, Olana, but that don't make me disrespectful. Well, that wife and me, we married ourselves, on an island. After she died, I brought Possum to the friars. To see about making her legal and baptized and all? Well, they told me that we did right under our circumstances. They told me a priest or minister doesn't marry people, that people marry each other. That's what we'll be doing now. In our circumstances."

"You've thought about this very carefully," she said.

He took her hands. "Not at first. I need your forgiveness for that, Olana. For letting my own fears, my grief over the lost women fight my love for you. It's cost us. It's already cost us both something awful. But I mean to change, if you'll have me. Will you have me?"

"Yes," she said.

He brought her to her feet. "Well, then, I take you, Olana Whittaker, for my lawful wife, to have and to hold, from this day forward, in good and bad times, for richer for poorer, in sickness and health, and nothing except death can part me from you now. From this day forward. Oh, hold on, I already said that part, didn't I?"

Olana nodded, her face beaming. He shrugged. "I think that's close to it, anyway."

She repeated his words, without letting him know that he'd omitted the vow Darius Moore had never let her forget: obey.

Then he reached into his pocket and brought out a ring she'd admired on his grandmother's finger. A simple gold band, studded with garnets. It fit.

"With this ring, I pledge you my fidelity," he said softly.

Olana thought of all the gifts she'd tried to give him. Her father had purchased the parkland, she and Sidney had been ready to launch his photography career with expensive equipment. He had always been richer than any of them. And now, she had nothing. The child within her thumped against her ribs. "With this kiss, I do the same," she answered, and raised her lips to his. They kissed as the last waltz began at the trading fair.

"There," Matthew pronounced, his voice gruff.

"There," she agreed, smiling at the tear flowing down his guileless face. She wiped it away with her thumb. "Stop that now," she imitated his accent, "or you'll get me going."

They sat together on the stone bench for a long time. The wolves began their nightsongs from the distant hills.

"Matthew?"

"Hmmmm?"

"How old are you now?"

"Twenty-eight, I think. Wait. Almost twenty-nine."

"And I'm the third Mrs. Hart?"

He winced. "Well, yes. Only second, consumated."

"Second? Do you mean to tell me you didn't—with Lottie?"

"Not after we got married. She was too sick by then. Just before."

"I see."

"Do I scare you, 'Lana?"

"No, Matthew."

"That's good. I'm scared enough for the both of us."

"Too frightened to consummate this marriage?"

"Well, no."

"Good."

He took her hand and they returned home. They did not drift off to sleep in each others' arms until the sunlight rose over the eastern horizon.

* * *

Winifred Whittaker was lighting another cobalt blue glassed votive candle in the Transcendental Hall when she heard the scurrying above her. That was the room where Olana slept when she visited. Was it a sign? She listened carefully, but the sound had no set rhythm. It spelled only gibberish in Morse Code. Miss Whittaker decided to try for contact.

She took Olana's nightgown from its red velvet cover, then its original wrap of butcher paper, the wrap it had hastily been tied in when delivered by that woman in Olana's clothes. A tall, strong woman. Olana was lucky to have such friends. She didn't need to bring this assurance that her niece had escaped her dreadful marriage all on her own. But Winifred was glad to have it. Glad to help her niece keep another secret.

"Dear child. Send me some news, to comfort your family. Your father is ill, your mother having her nervous spasms. That man you married pokes his finger in my face and calls me a meddlesome old woman. Well, I am a meddlesome old woman. One who loves you, and can keep a secret. Don't come back until the time is right, only tell me if you're well and happy?"

Miss Whittaker sat back in the teakwood chair, the one that once belonged to a high priestess of Bali. She put the ceremonial sword in her lap. She took up the nightgown and held its fine weave to her face. She waited. She caught the scent of burning sage. Burning sage and contentment.

"Extraordinary," she marveled. "Good girl. Happy. In his arms. Tell him I haven't forgotten. I'll keep looking for the train."

From the upstairs room came a crash. One of the cats, that's all, Winifred thought, annoyed at the interruption.

When she reached the room, she found it ransacked. A cold chill, then someone ripping Olana's nightgown from her hands. Someone who had already caused harm, great harm. "Mr. Trap!" she screamed before swinging the ceremonial sword. "Help me!"

thirty-four

Matthew's grandmother threw Olana's cloak at him. "Get out. A walk will do you both good!"

"What's gotten into her today?" he groused, climbing above the first rise.

"Slow down," Olana called. But he was lost in his annoyance. "Matthew, please," she tried, louder.

He stopped, turned. She slipped down to her knees. She felt his hands cup her elbows. What right had he to move so fast? " 'Lana—"

"Get away from me!"

There. The power of her voice could still stop him. When the circling pain was over she touched his face. "Matthew. I think it's started."

They didn't have to say anything to the women. Even Possum, peering out from Vita's skirts, knew. Annie flashed a triumphant smile at her daughter.

"Told you. Before midnight we'll have ourselves a guest. One who won't use the front door."

"A bet," Matthew fumed. "A damned bet. Is that what's had us walking the county around, and put you in a snit?"

Olana leaned on his arm. "You think so, Annie? Tonight?"

"If you keep moving."

Olana raised her shining eyes to Matthew's. He kissed her full on the mouth, in front of his daughter, mother, and grandmother.

"Some of that won't hurt progress neither," Annie Smithers observed.

Matthew left her once, when she insisted he take his afternoon swim with Possum. While he was gone, she held onto the women's arms and breathed against the folds in Vita's apron.

"What was Possum's birth like?" she asked them in between her pains.

Annie smiled gently. "There's no one left who knows, child. Possum was born out on the island. Seal Woman drugged Matthew senseless so he wouldn't worry at her cries. Broke his heart."

"I can't be like that, Annie. I need him."

" 'Course you do. And he needs to help. Don't put yourself in her shadow."

Olana screamed as the pain hit a sudden peak. She felt the cool cloth against her forehead. "Down," Vita urged, "send the cry down."

Easy for them to order her about. She yanked in an angry breath. "How?" she demanded, holding on to the "ow," until it ground between her toes.

"That's it!" Vita laughed. "That's it exactly!"

Olana smiled faintly and closed her eyes. When the next pain drove her lids open, Matthew was rubbing her back whispering, "Yes . . . wonderful," against her ear. She smiled to see his gleaming wet daughter come out from under his arm.

"Would you teach my baby to swim, Possum?" she asked.

The girl's smaller fingers followed Matthew's path. "Sure," she said.

Time became fluid, the house hushed. The small fingers massaging Olana's back disappeared.

"Where's Possum?" she asked.

"Mama took her to bed an hour ago. Said she was just resting in between them, like you."

"I didn't scare her, did I?"

"No." He smiled. "You're being splendid."

"Am I?"

"You dazzle me, Miss Whittaker," he told her.

The resting time in between her pains lessened from minutes to what seemed like seconds. The intensity grew so that she did not have time to catch her breath, even to scream. Another. So soon?

"I can't do this anymore!"

"All right. Give it to me."

She laughed. Where did she find the breath to laugh? She

breathed. Deep, deeper. The pain lessened, was gone. "How did you do that?" she demanded.

"What?"

Olana felt a surge of energy. "I want to walk."

Matthew lifted his head. "Gran?" he asked.

"Let the lady do what she wants," Annie Smithers gave out one of her rare, full smiles. "Go on, we'll get the room cozy."

When they reached the shoreline, Olana tried to memorize the sky, the position of the quarter moon. She hung onto Matthew's shoulders as the pains came. They climbed the dunes, watched a single lit window at the mission.

"Do you think the friars pray for us, Matthew, though we're sinners in the eyes of the world?"

"Let's not give a damn for the eyes of the world tonight, shall we?" She loved his voice, even when it rumbled low in his displeasure. The moon's light couldn't hide the weariness in her lover's eyes. "Would you kiss me?"

She urged him on even as her belly hardened between them, even as the pressure, the pain mounted along with their passion. At the peak of both, something broke. Olana felt a great gush between her legs. Her knees buckled. She called, but he'd already caught her, laid her gently on her side in the sand.

"That's so much better," she murmured, feeling him gently place his coat over her shoulders.

"Your water's broke, Olana."

"Oh? Good."

"This is what the women have been waiting for. You got to get up, darlin'."

"Why?"

"To have the baby."

"Baby? Not now, Matthew. I'm so tired. I'll have it tomorrow."

He knelt back in the sand and rubbed his eyes with the heel of his hands, like a weary little boy. Then he took her arms.

"No," she protested. "I have to get down."

"Down?"

"Down, yes. You know, dowwwn . . ." She heard sounds coming from inside her. Deep, guttural sounds that felt almost as good as the pushing she couldn't control.

"Oh, my," she said as it finished. "That felt fine. Almost as fine as when you're deep inside me and—"

"Olana. We got to get home," Matthew said against her ear.

She smiled. Her hand tugged at his suspenders. "You've got too many clothes on," she said. "So do I."

"Behave yourself," he groused, taking her full weight up gently in his arms. "The baby's coming, 'Lana."

"Really?"

"Don't want the women to miss this, do you?"

She circled his neck and breathed in his piney cedar scent, heightened by salty sweat. "No," she admitted, licking his ear. He stumbled.

"Jesus, 'Lana!"

"Don't you dare blaspheme at me, Matthew Hart!" She giggled as he brought her through the last gate. She saw the lights of home and the women pacing the length of the porch.

The borning room was clean and warm and waiting, like the night the Amadeo children were born. How many others were born here, Olana wondered. The thought seemed to fill the room with cries of pain and new life. Olana added hers—deep, guttural, driven by a force she'd surrendered to.

"Matthew?"

"I'm here, love."

"Will it be soon?"

"Very soon."

He wiped her brow. She rested her face against his. Olana felt secure in his arms, and under the watchful gazes of the women at the foot of the bed. She'd never heard Annie Smithers' voice so soft.

"I'm pouring on the oil, Olana. You remember that part?"

She smelled cloves mixed with the roses' scent. "Yes. Annie? Vita? Another—"

"Yes, we see your pains coming now too, darling girl," Vita assured her. "That's it, good . . ."

Olana pulled herself up and groaned until she thought she was coming apart. Something finally passed through.

"The head!" Vita proclaimed.

"Help me," Olana breathed out, closing her eyes, forgetting everything except that she was split apart and open, vulnerable, forever.

"Feel," Annie Smithers urged, bringing her back. "Feel your baby's head, Olana, it's almost over. Matthew, help your lady!"

Vita brought Olana's fingers, twined in Matthew's, down to touch the slippery hardness between her legs.

"The baby," she remembered. "Matthew, is that the baby?"

She heard his choked sob before the rushing urge took her over again. The women's voices were chiming echoes of each other. "All right . . . easy now, Olana. Good, good. Perfect, little . . . girl!"

A squirming baby. Again. Alive. So alive. In her arms. Her own. And the pain darting out to the farthest corners of her memory, leaving only shudders of joy in its wake.

"Matthew!" she called out. His face was buried in her back.

The baby lifted her head from between Olana's breasts, blinked back even the dim light of the borning room.

"Matthew," Olana coaxed softly, "Lavinia's here. She's looking for you. She knows your voice, your hands. Come meet her."

He raised his head until she felt his chin at her shoulder. "Olana," he said in quiet awe, "she's you all over again."

Annie Smithers snorted. "Best find your spectacles, Matthew Hart. This child's got hair as light as a wheatfield in August."

James Whittaker stared across the table at his son-in-law. It was so difficult, keeping focused on this new calamity. Since Olana's disappearance, he left more and more to Darius Moore. The business, the stolen payrolls, the unrest at the timber mills, the accusations. But not this. Winnie was his sister. His only family left. He had to concentrate. He had to help Winnie, just as he had to keep his wife well, had to find Olana. James Whittaker knew, finally, what was important, now that he was losing everything.

"The dead man was named McPeal, sir. A waterfront character."

"Waterfront? Does he know anything of Olana? You remember how she had such an interest in the underside of the trade after Matt brought Selby home?"

Moore bristled. "There is no connection, sir."

"But he was stealing Olana's nightgown—Winnie keeps saying that!"

"Your sister says a lot of things, Mr. Whittaker. That she put herself in her Mr. Trap's care, that he killed McPeal for her, kept the Carsons locked in until help came."

"Mr. Trap. We thought him harmless within the family, you see?"

"Never did, sir, no. Neither will the investigating authorities."

"Oh, this is very unfortunate."

"More than unfortunate, Mr. Whittaker. Inadmissible, as evidence. What you have humored as her eccentricity, will now permit her assailants to go free."

Darius Moore never missed an opportunity to turn the knife. James thought that marriage to Olana might have warmed the man a little. Instead she returned from Japan almost as cold, as distant as he, except for her eyes. They were fevered, frightened, accusing. He could no longer remember her, even as a child, without those haunted eyes. Disappeared. Again. If only he could locate Matt. Matt would track her, didn't that lively Irishman say he could track anything that had the breath of life? Was she alive—his life, his hope, his future? Or was that why everything else was falling apart—his wife's always fragile health, his business, now Winnie?

Did Darius Moore mourn Olana's loss, James wondered bitterly. Not the way Dora and he and Winnie did. But yes, with a determined intensity that made him a force, a force to lean on, now. Now that he was feeling so damned peculiar himself.

"A trial will call your sister to the stand. Will you have her humiliated?"

"What is my choice? These are dangerous men. The court might understand—"

"Perhaps. At the expense of any sanity your sister has left."

"I resent that, sir!"

The fine, manicured fingers passed over his son-in-law's face. If only he could change that face. If only Olana had married Matt. Why didn't she? Why didn't he ask her that before she went steaming off to Japan? None of this would be happening.

"I've overstepped my boundaries, sir," the man before him said. "I apologize."

James Whittaker exhaled. Warmth, yes. There in his eyes. His son-in-law loved Olana, as much as a man like him could love. "What are we going to do, Darius?"

"I have a proposal."

"Yes?"

"I will talk with the attorneys privately. About an insanity plea."

"Insanity?"

"We can offer to house the brothers in an asylum for the criminally insane—tell them it's a delicate, family matter. They will be put away. Your sister can have a quiet recovery. Mrs. Whittaker and yourself can put it behind you."

"But the criminals themselves—they'll never agree."

"I will endeavor to convince them."

"The family has been very generous about this."

Cal Carson smiled. "Have they, Mr. Hopkins?"

"My name is Moore."

Cal Carson smiled, showing his canine teeth and his advantage. "Of course, sir. The grieving husband, looking for his runaway wife."

"Disappeared. She has disappeared. Not run away."

"Like a lost lamb. A tragedy."

Darius Moore's fingers itched for the feel of the prisoner's throat. "Do you two want to hang? I can see to it!"

At last, silence. "Cal—" Ezra finally called, nervously. "We are the ones in jail. We should listen."

Cal sat as straight as his crippled side would allow and stared Darius Moore down. "Sure. We're good at listening. Our previous boss told us mighty good, useful stories. And maybe you want Mr. Hopkins to die, sir? In Chinatown? Maybe after he pushed that crib girl out the window? With Mr. Hopkins and his filthy little habits departed, the respectable Mr. Moore can come up out of that dead soul to find his beloved wife, yes?"

Moore exhaled. A bargain. He was good at bargains, before the heroin and that woman's hair took over, made him stupid and careless. Made Hopkins stupid and careless, not him. He could have kept them separate, could have made Olana a good husband, even, if it weren't for her wildness, if she hadn't brought home Matthew Hart. Or if these two imbeciles had killed him properly in the first place, so that plan . . . her turning to him in her grief, would have worked. Now everything was coming apart. "What do you want?" he asked the brothers impatiently.

"The four thousand we already risked our necks for. Each, now that we've lost our middleman to that woman's damned sword. And of course, our freedom."

Cal Carson watched Darius Moore slump back in his chair. Even he would have sworn he looked like a beaten, grieving man. Did he want the ranger's woman still? This badly? Was it the money? Maybe he should have said two thousand. Were they all going to go down together?

"Her hair is gone," Moore whispered.

"What, sir?"

"I have to find her. I'll give you ten thousand if you'll help me find her. You kill him. You'd like that, wouldn't you? But help me find her. I have to have her back."

God almighty, she was a sickness in him. Cal Carson leaned close. "Sure, sure, we'll find her. The nightgown, that must be what McPeal was babbling about, why the woman fought so hard for it. Just get us out of here, Mr. Moore, and we'll help you track her with it."

"The nightgown?"

"Yes, sir."

"Good. We'll do that. Exactly that. First, you must sign yourselves over to me as your guardian."

"What?"

"Then, when you plead yourselves insane, I can get you out."

"You can?"

"I've already convinced the family, who want to spare the old woman. I'll take you to the hospital myself, then Whittaker will wash his hands of you. I'll return in a week's time to grease you out."

"Not with any of our ten thousand as greasing!" Ezra roared.

"You drive a hard bargain, Carson. McPeal warned me about you. All right. Not with any of your ten thousand. Help me to find them and the full amount is yours."

The attendants of Agnews had never seen such a joyful locking up. The new inmates, dirty, ugly, and raving, had been almost comical in the way they hung onto the finely dressed gentleman, calling him "dear guardian," thanking him for their deliverance, asking him to

write and take them on outings as if they were children being sent
off to school.

Only when they were being led to their cells, the well-dressed
man's demeanor changed. He took the warden's arm.

"They are dangerous. Murder is not beyond them. I want your
staff to be very careful."

"Of course, sir."

"I resent this duty my family has required of me. They should
be swinging from the gallows. I don't believe in coddling."

"We don't coddle here, sir."

"If anything should happen to them, because of their own violent natures, of course, during the three-year term of advance
payment, I would not want any of the money refunded. I am that
grateful to you for taking them in. So very grateful."

"Ease your mind, Mr. Hopkins. And your good family's, sir."

Darius Moore sat back in the cab's privacy. Done. He would
never be so stupid again. What made him think he needed any of
them? He could work alone. He would always work alone, now. He'd
get the nightgown. He would find out why the old woman fought
so hard for it.

thirty-five

On the Sunday after Lavinia's birth they walked the path to
the mission at St. Pitias to have her baptized. Olana had
never been in the small mission chapel's painted adobe walls. There
were few symbols she knew of as Christian, a cross here and there
punctuating the more prevalent spiral designs in deep blues, reds,
turquoise. When the sad-eyed friar began, Olana gave up her child
to the women who were her godmothers and to Matthew, who was
Lavinia's godfather and father both. Matthew was so solemn, smiling only when Possum nuzzled under his arm.

On the way home, his sharp eyes darted above the ocean, watching.

"Osprey," he whispered.

The brown and white hawk gleamed slick and powerful as it dove into the water. Matthew took Olana's hand, pulled.

"Come with me!" he said, breathless.

"Where?"

He pointed, as he always did, with his chin. "Closer to him. On the rocks above the caves."

His mother spoke, a gentle counterbalance to his excitement. "It would be a hard climb for Olana, Matthew."

Olana felt the burden of the cloths between her legs, still catching the afterbirth blood. "I can carry you and the baby, 'Lana," he offered.

She looked for her midwives' nod of approval, then echoed it, making his light eyes lighter. Or did the sky do that? Matthew caught her up, not only in his arms, but in the exhilaration of his voice, his quick, even strides, that slowed only when his grandmother and mother, with Possum on her back, fell behind. When they reached the rocks, Matthew was drenched in a glistening sweat. He placed her on his discarded coat and took the baby from her arms. Then he took Possum from his mother's hold and led her to the edge of the rocks. The women watched, drawing close to either side of Olana like sentinels.

The osprey flew in circles over the clear water, over the rising thermal wind currents. *"Tsi:sghwa! Du!"* Matthew summoned. The circles narrowed, spiraled closer. Matthew lifted Lavinia higher, then brought Possum's hand up until their clasp pointed to the sky. His voice rang out across the water.

> *Look at my children!*
> *They are daughters!*
> *New!*
> *Born in this new century!*
> *One as beautiful as the Scarlet Tananger!*
> *One as beautiful as the Hummingbird!*
> *Now! I am as beautiful as the Red Tsugv:tsala:la!*
> *From where my feet stand, on upward, I am beautiful.*
> *I truly am a man!*

He began the chant again, then a third and fourth time as the osprey's circles came closer. Olana's wonder mixed with fear. Her fingers ached for her cooing child, caught fast in her father's song. What would happen now? The power that his words had over the massive bird seemed so much stronger than the water of the baptismal font at the mission. Olana shivered there, in the bright sunlight. She felt the women link their arms behind her.

"What does he call himself?" Olana asked them.

"A rainbow," Annie Smithers answered. "A red rainbow. He is making himself whole again, beautiful again, through his children. He is out of *gv:hnage,* the black. He is out of mourning!" she exclaimed in a voice as excited as a young girl's. "At last. At last, Matthew."

The bird glided above their heads, his wingspan the length of a grown man, still playing the thermals, and hardly flapping those wings. Olana could see the glint of water on his feathers, the blood on his talons. Then he caught a northwest wind and headed up the coastline.

Matthew returned. He put the baby back into Olana's arms. Possum scrambled into the warm spot left vacant against his heart. Olana heard the women arguing behind them.

"Are you sure there's no Cherokee in the boy, Vita?"

Vita gave out a small, ladylike snort. "You would know better than I, Mama."

Was it the water's spray that put more glints of silver in Matthew's hair? What made his eyes so full of the sky, the sea, it appeared he'd stolen a slice of each?

"Come down," Olana whispered, taking his hand, pulling him toward her earth, toward the browning blood between her legs.

"I can't," he said. " 'Lana, I'm so happy."

They lay together on the beach on the fading afternoon that their lives changed. Possum chased the tide. Olana watched the baby's golden head rising and falling there against her father's chest. Lavinia loved lying that way, his even breathing tickling her downy head and making her smile in her sleep. Olana felt her breasts swell with milk at the sight of that smile. They were a family, she realized. A small, perfect family inside Matthew's larger one.

"I need to go in now," she whispered. "To help Annie and Vita with supper." He shifted. She touched the baby's head. "Stay," she urged. "The sun is still warm."

He smiled. "I could stay here forever."

"Well, don't do that. Bring the baby in when she needs me!"

He caught her hand, kissed the finger's joint, just above her garnet circled ring.

Olana only wanted to think of how happy the month since the birth had been for them. She was drunk with the power of her body to bring forth someone so perfect, and then be able to nourish her, help her grow to be the soaring delight of her father.

Did Matthew know he was Lavinia's father? Olana'd been so frightened that day she'd told him otherwise, frightened that he would never love her for herself, that he would only care for her out of obligation to his child. So foolish, how could she be so foolish? Matthew loved the baby asleep against his heart with a measureless devotion. But if she told him now would this magic season disappear? His women knew, but they were waiting for her to tell him. She must tell him. He was so without guile himself. He would not doubt her word, not even if Lavinia grew into his boots and slung a rifle over her shoulder to protect her father's sacred grove of sequoia trees. Suddenly, in her mind's eye, Olana's daughter did exactly that. She saw Lavinia like she sometimes saw her brother Leland, from behind. She was tall, and as golden and beautiful as Matthew. She hoisted the rifle higher, then disappeared in the shafting light between the giants, before Olana could ask her advice.

Why was she feeling cold, Olana wondered, as she stepped into a house that had never given her anything but warm acceptance. She heard a voice behind her.

"My darling prodigal."

thirty-six

Olana closed her eyes, heard the women working as usual in the kitchen. She opened them again, hoping he would have disappeared.

"You're looking well. Even beautiful. Not for long. You've been very naughty. Made people laugh at me. Still, I've missed you. Had only your hair. It fell apart, disintegrated I caressed it so much. And your nightgown, your favorite one, that I took from your silly aunt? It was woven from a very select herd of merino sheep, the sheep of the mission at St. Pitias. Do you know it? There's a monk there, who, upon hearing my sad tale, was happy to tell me where I might exert my claim for my prodigal wife."

His eyes were sparked with yellow. Matthew's firearms were ready, but where?

"Olana? Is that you?" Vita called from the kitchen.

"Answer," her husband directed.

She spoke in a breathless whisper. "Couldn't we go? Now? Darius, I'll do whatever you want of me—"

She would have. She would have left them all without a word, without a sign, if she could have prevented what the ice around her heart told her was coming. Darius Moore pressed the cold barrel of the pistol into her spine. Olana heard Matthew's familiar step on the porch.

" 'Lana! You should see how she takes to the water!" he was saying as he came through the door. As she screamed. As Darius Moore lifted her off her feet, crushed her ribcage with one strong hand, and with the other, fired once, again.

The shots. Loud, so loud even Matthew falling, even the grind of his boots against the floorboards, were silenced in the ringing aftermath.

Vita lunged. Moore raised his weapon, shot again. Hit again, although Olana shoved his aim off. Now even the ringing in Olana's ears silenced. She heard nothing, though Vita Hart went down on the hard floor, skidding into Matthew's side without any grace at all.

Darius Moore dropped Olana in his fury. His hard boot smashed the side of her head, blackening the room. When it came into focus again, he was circling the Harts slowly, deliberately pointing the smoking gun at Matthew's temple. He went to one knee beside him. Matthew was shaking except where he held Lavinia against his heart. His eyes closed as if he were one of the friars at their holy vespers, which seemed to infuriate Moore, because he was shouting. What were the words? Olana couldn't hear. Another shot. Matthew stilled. But Darius Moore fell over, blood emptying from the side of his head.

Annie Smithers stood above them, one of the family's old Colt Dragoons in her hand. She kicked the body aside as if it were a fallen log on the path to the beach and bent over her kin. Vita rose slowly, pressing her sleeve to her seared cheek.

Olana sensed everything now, from the acrid gunpowder, to the desperation in the women's voices. Annie's shot had restored her hearing as surely as the others had taken it away. She approached.

"Give us the baby, darlin' boy," Annie Smithers whispered.

Matthew twitched, managed only drowning, guttural sounds that his grandmother somehow understood, answered. "Your mama will be all right, won't you, Vita?"

"Yes. Matthew, please. Give us the baby."

He sputtered blood that streaked his mother's sleeve. When his wild, suffering eyes found Olana, his mouth quivered into a smile. He cradled the baby closer against him.

"Please," Vita Hart wept. "Matthew, please."

Lavinia was still. Not minding the blood soaking her blankets. Whose blood? Hers? His? Theirs? Theirs, surely, there was so much of it. Both women continued pleading with Matthew, though he was now as still as the baby. Dying. Lavinia was dead and he was dying.

Olana touched his hair. It was moving, but only because of the breeze from the kitchen. "I'll take her now, Matthew," she said.

His arms released their burden.

Vita walked Olana to the sofa. She helped her open the blankets.

"There's nothing we can do for her," she said. "I have to help Annie with Matthew now. Do you understand?" Her face was wet with tears that exposed the ugly cauterized slash beneath the powder burn on her cheek. Only Darius Moore could make this woman ugly, Olana thought.

She swayed her knees back and forth, which had elicited the baby's first smiles, on the day she was born. Milk soaked her bodice front, as if the baby were crying to be fed and not still, so still. "Don't take him with you," she whispered. Not to the dead child in her lap, but the golden, grown woman, walking into the shafts of light between the sequoias.

The tube his grandmother had inserted into Matthew's throat spurted blood, then air.

Matthew sat up. He saw what none of the others noticed, Possum huddled in the fireplace. He knew those vacant eyes. She was in shock. He stood, walked to her side. He touched her shoulder.

"Darlin'?"

"How are you here, Daddy?"

"I'm worried about you."

She traced her hands along his side.

"Are you dead?"

He smiled. "I don't feel dead."

Tears. That was a good sign, he told himself. The shock was leaving her.

"But you're over there, too." She took his hand, pointing to where Annie and Vita were frantically huddled over someone with his boots on. The floorboards were stained with blood. His joints started to ache. There was a searing in his throat.

"I'm . . . confused," he admitted to the child.

"Stay, Daddy," she pleaded.

He caught sight of Olana, sitting apart from the women, with Lavinia across her knees, reciting words that sounded like the litanies the friars prayed on the feast of the Blessed Sacrament. He circled Possum's knuckles with his thumb to loosen her hold on him, and to savor the soft beauty of her small hands.

"I . . . I'm supposed to take Lavinia for a walk on the beach."

"You just came from there."

"Did I?"

Olana's litany turned into sobs. "Why's she crying? Possum, what's happened?"

"It's all right, Daddy," the little girl said. "Go on, do what you're supposed to do. But come back. Promise you'll come back."

She finally let go of him. He turned and felt her strong, small hand against his back, pushing.

He leaned over Olana, touched her cheek. "How's our hummingbird?" Lavinia was smiling her familiar, well-fed smile. And this was his favorite time to walk her. "Are you two finished? Is she all full?" he asked.

Olana didn't answer. She didn't even look up. But Lavinia reached her tiny hands to him. He took the baby and left the house.

Matthew walked her along the shore, a part of the shore he didn't remember. It was beautiful, the sand white and warm under his feet. All the pain, even the searing at his throat disappeared. It stayed twilight somehow, the sun hanging red and still over the water, without moving. It was home, and yet not home. He was walking beside a man with his own coloring, and a little younger than himself. A stranger he'd known for a hundred years.

He began hearing Olana's voice, pulling him out of the conversation with the man. She was dressed in finery again. Black silk. She was weeping, with her eyes and her breasts both. "Matthew," she said, "my father's ill. I have to go home."

He wanted to tell her that he would go too, and help care for the baby so that she could care for her father. But his voice wouldn't work. It worked on the other side, where he still felt the man's hand on his arm. Why wouldn't it work with her? Why did it hurt so with her, and not on the other side? She was going to leave. She was going to leave if he didn't talk. He made his fingers close around the silk of her sleeve. Even that hurt.

"I've got her, 'Lana," he rasped out.

She screamed then, a scream so loud it sent him back to the other side with such force he almost fell over, he almost dropped the baby. The man steadied his arm.

"My throat hurts," Matthew told him.

"It will pass. Give me the child. She's heavy for you, isn't she? There's a woman here. She's been waiting to take care of her."

"But 'Lana's crying, and her breasts are full of milk."

"Give her to me, Matthew."

The man's eyes were as blue as his own. He seemed so utterly without guile that Matthew trusted him. He put Lavinia into his arms. The man looked into the green quilted bundle. "So beautiful."

"Yes."

Matthew's mind eased a little. The man held her gently. He walked into the shadows, gave Lavinia to a woman in a rocking chair. Matthew was soothed by the red and blue spiral patterns on the hem of the woman's dress. He even closed his eyes, rested. Contented coos, silence. The woman must be gentle, too. The man returned to him.

"If she cries—" Matthew began.

"Don't worry. Let's walk."

"I can't stay."

"No, you can't," he agreed. "Let's walk."

They did, and Matthew noticed the cut of the man's clothes were the same as his old ones. One of the braces of his suspenders was damaged and fixed with a small piece of rope.

The stranger stopped. "I want you to tell Annie something," he said, looking out to the sea.

"Annie? You mean Gran?"

"Hard to think of her as anybody's grandma." He brought one of his long, graceful hands up to the brace, and fingered the frayed piece of rope. His accent was like Gran's hill country friends' back east. "Tell her it won't be long," he said. "Tell her I'm waiting, I'll help her through. I won't let her down this time."

"You know my gran?"

"You have to go back now."

"No. Talk to me. Did I have a brother? Are you my brother?"

"No. But we're blood. Matthew. You can't bring Lavinia. She belongs with us."

The weakness was coming over him again. His throat was starting to hurt. "No. You tricked me!"

"It was the only way."

"The baby's crying!"

"No, that's you."

"Don't send me back without her. Please."

"I'm sorry. There's nothing I can—"

Matthew swung. The man was faster. Matthew punched only air before he fell to his knees. "Damn you," he said between his teeth, as his body betrayed him further, convulsing with fever. The man was pressing his chest now, killing him.

"Help me, he's so stubborn," he called behind him.

"I told you." Matthew heard a familiar voice, his grandfather's voice. "That's from her side of the family, not ours."

Now two young men, brothers, their coloring night and day with only their blue eyes matching, were pushing, pushing.

"I can't breathe," he told them.

"Yes you can, Matthew," the one with his grandfather's voice said.

Their faces turned into two friars, with brown eyes and brown robes damp with sweat.

"Dear Lord," one said, "we've killed him."

"No," Annie Smithers said behind them. "He's back."

thirty-seven

Matthew Hart closed his eyes against the pain every breath was taking. The next time he opened them, he saw his grandmother slumped in a chair. She looked frail for the first time to him. She was getting too old for this, he thought. He was cold, but too weak to even pull up the quilt. The green quilt. Lavinia's.

"Gran," he called with the rasp that was left of his voice.

Annie Smithers woke. "I'm here, darlin' boy," she whispered, tucking the coverlet into the empty space against his heart. The woman in the shadows, the one with Seal Woman's blue and red spiral hem. Why hadn't he looked at her? He shuddered, coughed. The rattle was moving up from his lungs. He felt like he was breathing through broken glass. He would not always feel like this, he realized. He was not dying. He would recover, if he wanted to.

His eyes scanned the narrow bed, the small cell for signs of how long he'd been there. The small mission room was full: bedding, Annie's tinctures, salves, decoctions, his mother's woven nightshirts in a stack, photographs and drawings of all the men from their mantle. A crucifix. No mirror. His hand went to his face. Expecting stubble, he felt a beard.

"How long?"

"Six weeks."

Her voice broke over the two words. Tears. He could count how many times he'd seen his grandmother weeping on one hand. Fractured images flooded through him, then left him empty.

"I'll be all right. Go to bed now," he demanded, afraid that if she didn't, he'd lose her as well to this cold, dark, night.

Matthew came home to the bed in the borning room, to his daughter's haunted eyes, his mother's marred beauty. Farrell was doing his work for him, and proceeding with his patient, tenacious courtship.

Farrell filled in gaps of his lost weeks, when Matthew had questions he couldn't bear to ask the women. He'd come soon after the shooting, willing to bribe the local law so that his grandmother would not have to leave his side for an inquiry. "But it never came to that, Matty. Your sheriff, he stood over her there at the mission watching you wheezing what little life was left to you. Stood concocting a story full of an unknown assailant laying siege. That man's as honest as the day is long, and there he was, spinning tales. Good Lord, Matty, you've got a powerful family!"

"Town owed Gran a few favors," he explained. "After all the good she's done, the sheriff wasn't in time to stop a band of vigilantes from hanging her boys."

"Boys?"

"My uncles. The sons she had with Joe Fish."

"How many?"

"Five."

"When did this happen, Matty?"

"Years back, when I was in the Klondike. They were none of them angels, but they were not killers."

"Well, the sheriff, he made it so your women could pull you out of the dead, and your lady could go home and bury that snake husband of hers and tend to her father, all without a sidestep to a hearing."

Matthew closed his eyes, felt Farrell's hand on his shoulder. "Matty. Let me send Olana word that you're—"

"No!"

"But son—"

"Nothing. Swear it!"

"All right."

Matthew leaned back in the pillows, worked on making his breathing regular again. The alarm began to recede from his friend's expression. "Farrell? I don't think my gran's looking well," he whispered.

"Annie? That lady's built of iron, son."

"Around the eyes, I see it. She's caving in."

"Matty, the woman's nearing eighty. She's entitled to a little caving in!"

"Goddamn it, Farrell—"

The coughing. Again. "Now, Matty. Your mama's only allowing me to chat with you while we 'remain serene and without blasphemy.' " Farrell tilted his head as Vita's form glided by the open doorway.

Matthew smiled. "So. She's made you keeper of the grammar and morals, has she?"

Farrell filled many silent, lonesome nights with stories that brought even Possum away from her favored spot by the fireplace. He pressed San Francisco bank statements into Matthew's hands. Their numbers made his head ache, as did talk of the prosperity of his and Mr. Amadeo's fruit market business.

Farrell brought in Mr. Amadeo himself. The small man stood at Matthew's bedside, filled with plans of expansion and further investment. Farrell and Amadeo overlapped each other's explanations of a new enterprise—a bank for people who wanted homes for their families, and for small, useful businesses, not for those seeking favors from fellow members of the club. Matthew understood that much. But when they talked of loan interest rates, land appraisals and surveys, he couldn't even find the questions that might cut a path through his confusion. All he wanted to know was how the Amadeo children were thriving in San Francisco.

Matthew's first walk was to the gravesite on the hill above the mission. He sat, exhausted, by his mother's side as Possum kept spiraling away from his grandmother's care.

"Why is she doing that?" he asked.

"I don't know. She's been wary since—" Vita touched the scar on her cheek absently. "She saw, Matthew."

"What?"

"Everything."

"Christ, Mama."

Vita didn't chastise him for blaspheming. She even leaned over and loosened his collar as he felt his breath tighten at the vision of bloodstained floorboards, and his little girl's stunned eyes. Vita's scar was still red, ugly. He took her hand.

"It's been hard on you, I know," he whispered. "I'm sorry."

She shook her head, bit her lip, then regarded the small gravestone fondly with him. "We thought Seal Woman might like a little one to look after. Was it all right to bury her here, Matthew?"

"Wasn't for me to say."

"Why not?"

"Vinnie was 'Lana's."

"She was yours, too."

He looked at her. " 'Lana said—"

"You couldn't see? Couldn't count the days in the Yurok way, from that night before her wedding?"

"I didn't think to. 'Lana said, back when she first came to us, she said—"

"She lied to you! Why? Why did she lie?"

"I don't know, Mama."

"She didn't give you the pleasure of knowing that baby as your own child for the little time we had her!"

Vita turned away, weeping in that silent way of hers. Matthew looked for his grandmother. She'd finally gotten a hold of Possum's hand and was walking toward the shore. Hands full, no time to mediate between him and Vita. He touched his mother's arm.

"Mama. It doesn't matter now. I couldn't have loved her any more if I'd known. Could you?"

"No."

"There's enough pain already."

"You're right, of course."

"I ain't right, I'm just . . ."

"What, Matthew?"

He tried to escape her eyes, but in their new intimacy, she was becoming as hard to evade as Annie. "Lost. Mama, I've never felt so lost in my life."

She squeezed his arm gently. "I'll tell him it's not a good idea for me now. There's so much need here, between keeping up the farm, and Possum's aversion to Mama, and, Matthew, you're not nearly well enough—"

"Wait. Tell who what? What's not a good idea?"

"Marrying Mr. Farrell."

He smiled slowly. "So. That's why he keeps showing me his receipts. You love that blarney soaked scoundrel, Mama?"

"Yes. But I've been alone so long. And he wants the wedding trip to be a cruise."

"Cruise? Where?"

"Around the world."

"Around the— Is his business that good?"

"Oh, Matthew. Mr. Farrell has been a gentleman of substantial means since before you were born."

"He has? But why—"

"He didn't wish it to spoil all his fun, he says."

"But he'll use it to foster his intentions on my mother." She was not fooled by the growl in his already rasping voice. She laughed behind her hand, like a girl.

"Matthew Hart, you're failing miserable as your mama's daddy," Annie Smithers announced.

"That's what I been telling you for years, Annie," he countered, successful enough at putting a Georgia crack in his voice to make her narrow her eyes.

"I'm losing her to that tale-spinning Irishman, ain't I?"

It had been such a long time since anyone in his household had laughed, the sound his women made together sounded foreign.

"The cruise will take a year I should think," Vita said, still worried, "and I couldn't bear—"

"You always wanted to see the world."

She cleared the hair from his forehead. "Oh Matthew, I don't know."

"This family could use a wedding," he said.

Matthew gave his mother away, trying not to think of the other times the house was full of roses, trying to stand all day on his slack muscled, atrophied legs. He was barely strong enough to ride with them to the train station, to hold her a moment before she and Farrell set off. The shade of green in his mother's hat almost trapped him then. It would have, if his grandmother had not begun to cry once the train pulled out.

"She's still my little girl, Matthew."

"They'll take good care of each other, Gran."

"I know. But she's still my little girl."

"Sure she is."

He released his walking cane, put his arms around her. How did she get to be so small? Where was Possum? He called out for her, turning, stumbling.

"Shit," he muttered, as the purple spots appeared before his eyes.

A man took his arm. A man with iron gray hair, like Olana's father's. "Here's a seat for you, son, and the lady."

"My daughter—"

"My wife's gone to fetch her. Rest a moment."

"Thank you." Matthew closed his eyes and wondered how he was going to be able to get these two females home, never mind pulled together as a family.

It was that day, when the house was so quiet, so empty of Vita and Farrell and their few wedding guests, when Possum refused to come in for supper, that he grabbed up his stick, and went out along the sand to find her. She was in her mother's cave, clutching the doll he'd brought her from San Francisco.

"Possum? Want to eat?"

She looked away. "Not her food."

He sat on the rock beside her. "You'd get sick of mine pretty quick, even if Gran were to let me near her pots."

"Why did Mana leave? I can't watch you by myself! I'm only a little girl!"

"You don't have to watch me, darlin'."

"What if Gran hurts you again?"

"Gran didn't hurt me."

"She did! She did!"

Her voice echoed off the glistening walls of the caves. Matthew caught his daughter's wrist, felt her rapid, birdlike pulse. Then it all came back to him. His own firstborn had started him on that journey. He held her now against his heart, stroking her glossy hair as she stroked her doll's.

"Listen," he spoke the first words that came to him, trusting them. "When I was little, like you, I lived in the desert, in a horse soldier's fort."

"Where was Mana?"

"With me, taking care of me, like she did for you. She loved me. I could feel the strength of it. But she couldn't keep bad things from happening, Possum, like I can't for you. My father was a horse soldier. And he was at war. I saw things sometimes, terrible things that come out of war. Like what you saw, the day the man came, the day you were inside the fireplace."

She broke from his hold, staring. "He said he was your friend, Daddy, said he brought presents. But I would not get mine if I spoiled his surprise. I'm good at keeping still, that's how I got my name, I told him. He did not speak the truth. He brought hurt. Gran made him dead, then she caught his madness and cut you open."

"Gran was helping me, Possum."

"To go on your spirit journey? To come back?"

"Yes."

She regarded him curiously, then spun away, behind him. "Did you see my mother on your spirit journey?"

He looked out the cave's blurred opening. "Almost. She was hiding. She liked to hide."

"I do, too."

"I know."

She circled around, faced him again. She took his hand. "I'm hungry," she said.

* * *

He offered it to Annie that night, as a gift for her loyalty, her patience with his slow recovery. She'd bundled him into his bed, where he stared into her fish soup. "I met your blamed outlaw," he told her, "back when I had the fever."

"My—"

"Says he's waiting, that it won't be long. And he'll help you, won't let you down this time. There."

"Matthew."

"I got a message back to him. He tricked me and I won't forget it. I want a second chance to knock him off his feet. You tell him that."

She reached to feel his forehead, but he pushed her hand away. "I ain't fevered! Swear it!" he demanded.

"All right, Matthew."

"I got to be the only man in creation bested by two grandfathers," he groused.

"Joe? You saw Joe, too?"

"Yep. They both flattened me, sent me back to you. I hope you're happy."

"I am."

"Well I ain't. And give me something with a morsel of meat in it will you, woman?"

She trumpeted a sound that was a laugh and cry together. He took her arm, drew her in against his chest. "Gran. How did you stand it, losing all of them?"

"I didn't, child. I only just salvaged what was left. Went on. Me and Joe, we thought we were not long for this world, the crush of losing the boys was so strong. Then you came back to us. You and Possum. You were our salvage, keeping us out of hell a little longer."

He smiled. "Well, I don't know where I was. But you'll like it. It's just like home."

She looked out the double window, watching her great-grandchild.

"I love it here. I love my home, Matthew. I hope when my time comes to die, that I can get into my bed and die there. I don't want to be any trouble to you or Possum. I want it to be a clean thing.

I'll have my bath and get into my shroud, then into my bed. There's a good picture, ain't it?"

"Yes, ma'am," he agreed.

"But I ain't going anywhere until you're set up with that damned Yankee woman."

He looked at the moon, winced as if its light were bright. "Annie, I think 'Lana and me, we must be finished now."

"Why?"

"How can she forgive me?"

"Forgive what?" she demanded.

"That I couldn't protect them. That I was holding Lavinia when— That's all she'd ever see if she'd look at me. It's all I ever see."

He touched his clean-shaven jaw absently, grateful he'd asked her to leave the mustache so that the face that stared back at him mornings was almost that of a stranger.

The old woman shook her head. "Do get yourself some sense, Matthew. I'm weary of this world."

"What? Hey, where you going?"

"To get you some meat."

thirty-eight

January, 1906

Matthew sat in the small garden behind the house. He'd carefully cultivated the ground, and through its bounty found seasons. The fragrant Tamarack pine he'd planted when they'd first come was now taller than Possum. He ran his finger along the dark green bundle of needles. Stiff, strong. He looked to the trellis he'd built and mounted against the brick wall of a neighbor's shed. The yellow roses were opening. There had to be something redeeming about a place where roses bloomed in January.

The early morning fog hung tight and low. It was more steady, reliable than the patches that often darted about square blocks of the city, making dogs and horses skittish. He'd dreamed of that fog the night before, only it had turned to fire, sweeping down those city streets, destroying everything.

In the distance, he heard the early morning cable cars starting down Market Street. In an hour he'd be on one, heading for his small office on the outskirts of Chinatown. The cable cars were like the morning fog—predictable, even at breakneck speeds they traveled down the hills. He smiled to himself. There was something he liked about San Francisco. 'Lana might find that amusing.

He allowed himself one thought of her each day, usually during this silent time before dawn. All the other times he didn't allow, though they came anyway, here in her city. Suddenly, his daughter was beside him, her nightgown glowing in the hazy pre-dawn light.

"What's the matter, darlin'?"

"Dreams."

"Bad dreams?"

She nodded. "Gran hurting you. Here." She ran her small finger along the knot of stitches in his throat. "Not hurt," she reminded herself softly. "She cut you, so you could breathe."

"That's right," he encouraged her.

She had seen more than he had that day and he was still as skittish as those draft horses caught in fog patches. Possum's dreams were what Annie and the Amadeos had predicted, growing fewer since they moved to San Francisco. She would still not let Annie touch her, though she spoke with her great grandmother now, and ate her food, two things she refused for the first few months. Matthew knew Annie's heart was broken, but she'd told him that it had so many scars she thought there must be room for another. Her patient understanding of his daughter stimulated his own. And he had someone to hold. That was more than Olana had.

"Daddy?"

"Yes, love?"

"Why do you look at the flower so hard?"

"To carry the beauty inside me all day."

"Even at work?"

"Especially at work," he told her ruefully. She laughed as his mustache twitched, making way for his smile. A miraculous thing, her laughter. Like roses in January.

"What was her name, the baby you sang for?"

He tried to say it without the catch at his throat, but as always failed. "Lavinia."

"And that lady?"

"Olana."

"You didn't call her that unless you were angry. Are you still angry?"

"I thought you didn't remember her name at all."

"She knew string games. Will we go home soon?"

"After Mana and Farrell get back," he promised.

At work Matthew found his desk cleared except for a copy of the *Gold Coast Chronicle* and a cup of steaming coffee. He looked up at the pleasant-faced woman in the doorway.

"Mrs. Fine. The first appointment?"

"Cancelled, sir, so have your coffee in peace before Freeman's Shoe Shine Emporium and Nickelodeon comes calling."

"Freeman's—"

"You heard me correctly, Mr. Hart. Should make a lively enough start to your day!" She closed the glass-paned door, muffling the ringing telephone and blurring the swirl of skirts and activity beyond.

Thursday mornings were forming themselves into this pattern, Matthew realized, mysteriously cancelled first appointments and all. He sat in the swivel chair behind his desk and picked up the newspaper. It was the day the O. Lanart column ran, the day Olana took the city of San Francisco to task on its shortcomings.

He opened to the editorial page. She'd launched herself into the Hetch Hetchy controversy. San Francisco's engineers wanted a site within the Yosemite National Park dammed for the city's water supply. A bitter debate was raging between "misguided, hysterical nature fakers" versus "greedy, arrogant temple destroyers." Olana's deft prose cut through the war of words and brought both sides to task for their pejorative caricatures of each other.

"Tell them, 'Lana!" He laughed and put his feet up on the desk, leaning back for his last swallow of coffee. He peered over the newsprint to see a diminutive black man, loaded down with papers and an intricately carved wooden box under his arm. He was shaking his head.

"A good grade of leather and fine fit—being ruined by poor maintenance. If I might be blunt, sir, those boots are exactly why the Lord has seen fit to place me on the good green earth!"

Matthew Hart kicked himself back from the desk and stood, thrusting out his hand. "Mr. Freeman, come in," he invited, looking over the man's head to the women outside his office's doorway.

"There, see?" one whispered to another, "I told you that, Southbred or not, Mr. Hart would hear out even the loan request of a nigg—negro man!"

"Ladies, I need numbers," Matthew admonished, closing the door.

By five o'clock his head was aching with numbers and he still had Sister Justina leaning across the big oak desk, laying siege.

"You have so much in common, I'm amazed you haven't met her before, Matthew!"

"Met?"

"Lady Hamilton! Now you haven't forgotten? You promised to come and have tea this afternoon, to meet her? You did forget. You're not wearing the trousers I suggested, the ones with the thin stripes."

He looked down at the worn weave of his brown pants. He wasn't used to thinking about clothes. His mother had done that for him.

"Well, there is a nice shine on your boots at least!"

"He made me!" Matthew protested.

"Who, dear boy?"

"A client. Demonstrating his business."

"Really? How very colorful. We must tell Sister Gertrude."

"I think you'd best send my regrets, Sister."

"Oh, no. Gertrude has been baking all morning. Any regrets offered will come from you, yourself. I'll not face her wrath!"

He smiled, overwhelmed by this woman. And her prodigious energy doubled in the company of her fellow sisters of Dolorosa Mission.

He'd found lodging close to the mission to remind them all of home. Soon his daughter was skipping about within the old stone walls, delighting the sisters with her lively mind. But the sisters were not like the quiet, reclusive friars of St. Pitias. They were another order entirely, much more in the world.

". . . Matthew, are you listening to me or having a vision?"

"Ma'am?"

"You must have been frightful in school!"

"I never attended school, Sister."

"Never?"

Shock. There. He had her stopped, at least. He decided to press his advantage. "I'm not sure I'll allow Poss . . . my daughter Wesoma to continue at yours, either."

She frowned. "Of course you will. God has placed a sweet, bright child in your care, Matthew Hart. And her formal education in ours at the mission. You don't have to get testy. I was merely asking if you read Mr. Lanart's column this morning, when you drifted off, lost in your own thoughts."

He sighed, giving up all pretense of sternness. "I read it, Sister."

"Was it peerless?"

He smiled. "Peerless."

"Better, better. Yes, you're ready."

"Ready?"

She poked him with her umbrella. "Get your hat. Let's not keep her waiting. Lady Hamilton has been almost as difficult to corral as you yourself!"

"Sister, if this duchess of yours doesn't have any inclination—"

"She's the wife of a lord, not a duke! She's to be addressed as 'your grace.' "

He frowned. "This here's America."

"Matthew, you must promise to behave. Lady Hamilton works just as diligently as you do for the children. Her benefits are becoming legendary! Why, one performance of *Tosca,* the one you neatly avoided last month, garnered—"

"If this woman's so busy charming money out of society matrons, why—"

"You both have wonderful ideas about the mission school's building plans. Some are in conflict. She thinks we need a new library building, for instance."

"What?"

"Now, now—"

"Knocking out some partitions and closets in the downstairs classrooms will be much less costly to—"

"Wonderful ideas! Both of you! You should talk them over." She touched his sleeve. "Matthew. We don't want to lose you both over your differing opinions."

He exhaled. "One hour. I will sip tea and be polite for one hour."

"There's the good fellow," she triumphed.

Matthew closed his ledger and pulled off his spectacles defiantly, trying to be stern, trying to let the brown-caped woman know that she'd never do this to him again. She took his arm before he'd gotten to the hat rack to fetch his wide-brimmed Stetson.

"Sister Justina, I'm coming," he said between his teeth.

"And I'm not letting you go until you're in Lady Hamilton's presence."

The pedestrian traffic was snarled by the rainfall. Through it all the indomitable woman held onto his arm, even handing him her umbrella and chastising him for not carrying his own. He was peeved enough to hold it over her head only. She was still railing at him about catching pneumonia when they entered the vestibule of the convent.

"Why, I thought you under the wheels of some dreadful vehicle!" Sister Agatha called down the hallway.

"Dragging feet were more the danger, Sister! And look at him— the fine Ulster coat we chose for him, soaked!"

Sister Agatha pulled them inside the warm gray parlor, laughing. "That's all right! Why Lady Hamilton has yet to—"

Sister Justina finally released her death grip on his arm. Matthew Hart had a peripheral sense of the two nuns, never at a loss for words, gone suddenly hushed. It was fleeting, overpowered quickly by the sight of a third woman, as rain-drenched as himself, more beautiful than on the best rose mornings, turning.

" 'Lana."

thirty-nine

She seemed smaller, but somehow stronger in her simple dark suit, trimmed in black, with a gored skirt. The lace of her high-necked blouse was dry; she'd had more sense than he and had turned up the flaps of her coat in the rain. But her straw hat hadn't protected her face. Drops still gathered in rivulets and fell unheeded off her nose. Her lips, parted since she'd taken in the sharp breath at the sound of her name, were as ripe and full as he'd remembered. And she wasn't running away, as she did in all his dreams.

He covered the distance between them in one long stride, took her waist between his hands. Kissed her. Her lips opened, her fingers swept up his back, into his hair. He lifted her off the floor.

The voices faded. Doors closed. Olana stood with a man as dazed as she, his blue eyes immeasurably sad. But sane, unlike his eyes in her dreams. When on her feet again, she held onto his lapel to steady herself. He took her arm.

"Listen. We've got to get out of here. Before this duchess woman comes. You hungry?"

"Yes. Yes, good."

The sisters reappeared, sent them back into the rain. Matthew lifted her umbrella over them both.

"Think we shocked them?"

"Oh, definitely." Olana giggled, a sound she didn't think she could make anymore. "But I don't associate with people I'd worry about shocking. I've learned that much." She leaned in closer, searching through the rain for his scent.

"Still, I thought they'd be in a spitting nails fury, us standing up that blamed countess." His walk slowed. "Here's a place I eat at sometimes," he offered quietly. "The food's decent."

They entered the dim, green-walled restaurant. Olana didn't remember what she ate, something savory, in a wine-based sauce. Matthew spoke softly in his new, rough-edged voice. Of his mother's marriage to Farrell, of their travels. Of his promise to help the fledgling business his new stepfather had formed with Mr. Amadeo. That was what had brought the trio of his grandmother and daughter and himself to San Francisco.

"We fought the whole notion of it at first. But, well, you know Farrell."

She stretched her hand across the table and took his fingers between hers. "I know you," she said. "And how much you love your mother. It was very generous of you to come here."

"Yes, well. It's a good business. And it runs so well I don't think even I could ruin it."

"What kind of . . . ?" she began, but was interrupted by a wiry man in white chef's clothes, who presented an etched glass tray to her with a flourish. "Tortes! For you, charming lady—raspberry mixed with apricots, new! Try, try!"

Olana tasted. "Delicious."

The man turned to Matthew. "So, you tell my brother I need bake oven, Matt? The bank will help us? Look at the papers, see?"

Olana watched Matthew pull his spectacles on, then study the document the man had shoved into his hands.

"Where's the price, sir?" he asked.

"Here."

"This is your monthly payment, Mr. Detrich."

"Yes. It will be mine, when I start payments."

"When you finish payments," Matthew explained. "Which, this document indicates, will go on through the lifetimes of your children's children."

"I don't understand."

"That's what they're counting on, Mr. Detrich. That and your passion for your tarts."

"Tortes!"

"Tortes. Listen. You know Christiano's Bakery, in the alley behind Howard Street?"

"Yes."

"They have this kind of oven. My grandmother buys her bread there. They bake in the early morning. Maybe they'd rent you the use of their oven in the afternoons. Maybe even sell your tortes, along with their bread."

The chef's eyes narrowed. "Italians like tortes?"

"We're all Americans now, Mr. Detrich. We taste everything."

"I will think on this."

"Good."

"And, Matt, you'll take these, all wrapped up nice, for the grandmother, the little one, and your lady?"

Olana looked at her hands.

"Sure, thanks." They shook hands and the chef backed his way into the kitchen. Matthew was putting his spectacles in their case when the thought dawned on Olana.

"Of course. The poor bank the sisters have been raving about. You run the poor bank!"

"It's the Bank of Naples. And Mr. Amadeo runs it."

"Mr. Amadeo finances it, from his fruit business. You are the loan officer, here in the Mission District!"

He frowned. "And I've just given you a poor example of how I drum up business."

She laughed. "You take the applications, walk the streets visiting the small groceries, bakeries, hardware stores. You look at a man's hands to see if they've seen work before giving a house loan!"

"The sisters—"

"Painted you perfectly! And kept you a complete mystery, once I shied away from Mr. Amadeo's name, and at you sounding . . . sounding exactly like yourself."

She saw the question in his eyes. No, not now. No whys. Not before she had him all to herself a little longer. "Are the Amadeos well, Matthew? Their twins?"

"Oh, they scurry about all over now. Possum calls them Deedle and Dumpling. Mrs. Amadeo has us over to supper Wednesdays. The two oldest boys? They're caring for the apricots at the farm for Gran."

"They were your farm's apricots, in the tortes?"

"Yes." He stopped suddenly, and reached across the table to touch her cheek. "This is too much, isn't it?"

"No. Oh, no."

"You haven't touched your coffee, finished the tart."

"I prefer tea."

"Tea, of course. At breakfast and supper. Coffee in the afternoon, wasn't that it? Except when Gran made you drink the sassafras instead, then the raspberry leaf." He gave out a fond laugh and shook his head. "Remember how you fussed?"

"Yes. I'm sorry!" There it was, the cry in her voice. He leapt to her side, his angry, ragged voice in conflict with the powerful eroticism of his lips pressing healing kisses at her temple. "What am I saying? Forgive me. Too much, too fast."

"No, no," she breathed, "but I do think your friends would like to close up for the evening, don't you?"

In the time it took Matthew to turn around, the Detrich family disappeared behind the kitchen's swinging doors. The restaurant was empty. He frowned. "It's late. Your mother will be worried."

"I don't live with my parents now, Matthew. What about Annie?"

He pulled a watch from his vest pocket. It was gold, but had neither fob nor chain. Farrell's watch. Farrell's gift, she was sure, to his new son, heading into a world that did not tell time by the seasons, by the sun's rise and fall over and under the horizon. Matthew's frown went deeper as the numbers made their meaning clear.

"Do you have a telephone?" she asked quickly.

"Our landlady does, yes."

"Good. You can ring Annie up from my house. We'll have our tea there, how would that be?"

"That—that would be fine."

Olana stole only quick looks at him as he pulled crumpled bills from his wallet and placed them on the table. He was smiling, even while calculating numbers, handling money. When he put her cloak over her shoulders, she touched his cheek. "This was lovely, Matthew. Perfect."

He leaned down, kissed her mouth. They didn't manage to stop until they heard clapping from beyond the kitchen door.

Olana's house was north of Market Street, just inside the part of the city he'd marked off for himself as forbidden. It was a small house, by her former standards, though still twice the size of the building where Annie and Possum and he rented a floor. Olana's house had three stories, with second- and third-floor balconies, stained and leaded glass windows. Its fanciful trim freshly painted in rich blues and purples set off the creamy beige clapboards. It ran deep into its lot, with a separate side entrance and a generous back porch. Overlooking what? A garden? Yes, there were trellises back there, like his own.

Olana walked up the steps with the pride of ownership that her nervousness, her quivering smile could not hide. He knew that pride, he'd seen it on all the faces at the house parties of his clients. Perhaps he should go, he thought. Go now, so he wouldn't put any more strain on the fragile thread that was once again being woven between them. But her face was so lovely in the porch light. She put the key in the lock. Before she turned it, the door swung open. Patsy.

"Miss Olana, you're home by the grace of God!"

"And you've got a full day tomorrow."

"Aye, but with a moment to give you a proper—Oh. Oh, my."

The blood left the maid's lips. He smiled. "Hello, Patsy."

"My," she said again, reaching out into the night air, touching his arm.

"I thought he'd disappear, too," Olana said, laughing softly. Did she? He felt lightheaded by the thought. Women. The things they say to other women. He felt lucky to be within hearing range of the words.

"Well, come up, come up, the both of you!" Patsy admonished, pulling them into the hallway.

"Matthew needs to use the telephone," Olana said, climbing the stairs, her hand so white and beautiful on the rosewood banister. She stopped, cocked her head.

"Well?"

"Well?"

"Patsy will show you where it is."

"What?"

"The telephone, Matthew!"

"Oh. Oh, yes."

But he still watched, until her feet disappeared around the curve.

When he fitted the receiver back on its cradle, Patsy stood beside him, a silver tea service in her hands. The tortes were joined by a few currant scones.

"Did Mrs. Cole make those?" he asked.

"She did indeed, sir! She's still up at the big house. What with all the care Miss Olana gives her father, it's like we're all still of a family, see?"

"No," he realized as he said the words. "She's told me so little, Patsy."

"Aye, well. It's been a good amount of time, sir. Be patient with her, will you?"

"Sure, of course. Here, give me that—"

"Nonsense! You're as bad about knowing your place as when you first come amongst us! Follow me, if you please." She skirted by him and began climbing the stairs. He stayed close behind.

"Patsy. How's Selby? And your baby—"

She turned. "A boy, sir, just turned two, he has. Born in Japan, before Mr. Lunt had us brought out, thanks be to God."

"A good birth?"

"A fine birth, bless you for asking. And it's a fine man that boy who married me has become, Mr. Hart."

"You deserved no less."

"Now, don't you be talking that way or that one upstairs will have at me thoroughly for ruining the sugar with my tears!"

"If she takes that brush to you I'll—"

"Ah, whist, now. Those days are long gone." She stopped on the second landing and raised a more intent face to his. "Our baby, sir? Hugh Matthew's his name, and Mr. Selby and I hope you do not take offence at it."

"I hope that poor child does not! Could I see him?" he asked.

She smiled. "Ah, you can give him a good bouncing in the morning. Come have some tea, some comfort by Miss Olana's fire." In the morning. That's what his grandmother had said along the crackling phone lines, "see you in the morning."

"Soaked!" Patsy pronounced, easing off his jacket, removing his tie, and detaching his shirt's collar with quick, deft fingers, once they'd climbed to a third-floor suite of rooms. "I'll just take these below stairs," she pronounced, "and press them nice again."

"Patsy, go to bed!" Olana roared from the room beyond.

She sniffed. "I should take orders from that one, who knows as little as yourself about coming in out of the rain?" Then she took up his cold hand and pressed it to her cheek. "Oh, stay this time, sir," she whispered. "Don't be leaving each other no more. Open your heart to her circumstances."

"Circumstances?"

Patsy cast a quick glance toward the sound of Olana's advancing footsteps, and raised her voice. "You'll both take some tea into yourselves this cold night, miss—"

"Go!"

Olana came through the laced French doors in a deep green silk kimono, shirred at the shoulders, and falling gracefully to the floor. She was still brushing out her hair, hair almost as long as when it had protected her face from frostbite. Already? How could that be? Her glance chased Patsy to the door. Olana closed it behind her. Then she turned, smiled shyly at him. Matthew forgot the fragrant tea steaming between them. And any questions about circumstances.

Matthew Hart looked like he had always been sitting there, in her rooms, drinking tea, smiling. He searched for safe territory like her O. Lanart editorials, phrases of which he recited to illuminate points about his own views. They spoke of Sidney, her house, parents, and the servants he'd taught her to cherish. And she'd woven stories about them all, rapidly at first, then more slowly, with more thought and detail, once she'd relaxed. Now she was even allowing silences—soft, easy silences to fall between them. And he was stretching out his long legs by the fire. How still he was. She was not used to his stillness anymore, after being around the nervous energy of Sidney and Basil. She stretched her hand, touched his knee.

"Matthew. Are you well?"

He smiled with one side of his mouth. Yes, she remembered that, but now the mustache accentuated it, made it more self-effacing, and sadder. It went with his rougher voice.

"Can't sing worth a damn," he admitted. "Then, I never could carry a tune in a bucket, could I?"

She fought the images of him singing rounds with Possum, then walking the baby, his lullabies softly, dearly out of tune. She would bring them back later, she promised herself, later. He was so afraid of tears.

"But you can dance. Tell me you still dance."

"Dance?"

"Yes!" She leapt to her feet. "Dance with me."

She wound her gramophone and put on a cylinder blindly. A Straus waltz began. She turned, expecting him to be gone. But he was standing there in his shirtsleeves, his open vest, as if he'd just steamed some sassafras for Patsy's morning sickness. His long, gentle hands were formally outstretched. Shaking slightly. Waiting. She went into his arms. They danced around the sitting room. He'd lost none of his grace.

Olana lifted her head. "With you it is as easy as—" Walking. She was going to say walking, but he'd covered her mouth with his by then. Before the machine wound down he was kissing her throat in three-quarter time.

He smelled of the rain, of the leather bindings of his ledgers instead of the leather of his saddle, and down beneath it all, pine. She caught it as he lifted her into his arms and brought her through the opened French doors to her bedroom. She slid her fingers through hair so thick it was still wet at the roots from the rain. A small, rough sound escaped his throat. He swayed, and for a moment Olana thought he would drop her. But he widened his stance. "I am for you," he said, "you are for me."

"Yes," she promised, pulling her eyes from the scarred knot of ugly purple in his throat—opened clumsily, like the back of his daughter's doll, and closed, stitched up in haste, cheating death. He sat her on the turned-down bed, and knelt behind her. He kissed the back of her neck softly. "Stars," he whispered, there against her ear, "colored stars. See them?"

"Yes," she said. The stained glass of her bay windows' transoms made them appear that way. He knew that was the source of their tones, but the childlike wonder was still in his voice. He was the same man she had loved for years, despite all his changes. He kept kissing her as his fingers discovered the pattern of the frog closures of her kimono, and opened each with an aching slowness. His hand reached inside, lifting the kimono and her gown from her shoulders in one motion. They fell into an ivory and green silk pool around her hips.

His right hand fanned out just under her breasts, steadying her as his kisses flowed down her vertebrae. She giggled when he reached the base of her spine. He emitted a gruff purr, glided over and bit her side so gently she could feel the tiny ridges in his teeth. She even knew the cold metal of the gold one as he smiled wide in response to her own deep, free, laughter.

Matthew lifted her out of the remains of her clothing and nestled her in her pillows. Then he was astride her, his own hardness melting back her thighs, even through the worn weave of his trousers. Clothes, too many clothes. She was much worse on his than he'd been on hers, tearing, pulling. He didn't seem to mind, he even helped her yank the damp shirt, shuck the trousers.

Olana leaned back then, admiring his firelighted, taut body, muscled thighs. She caught his scent again as he brought up the sheet like a white fogged night behind him. His tongue circled adamant nipples, stroking hard, stronger, guided by her breathing, her cries, her fingers dancing at his shoulders. Olana leaned back, took his head between her hands, and wailed softly at the stars beyond her windows as he entered her. This wild, tender man was pushing her again, over cliffs of delight, into beds of pine needles and roses. How had she lived so long without his pushing?

When she woke his side of the bed was empty. Olana felt around her wildly. Twisted sheets. A pillow molded into an hourglass shape and wet with sweat. The baby. He was still holding Lavinia, still plagued by that bloody afternoon. Olana raised her head toward the dim light, finally saw him through the French doors, sitting half-dressed by the fire. She slipped into her kimono and joined him. Matthew looked up. His eyes were red and swollen. He turned back toward the fire's light. "You weren't going to leave without saying good-bye?" she asked him quietly.

"No. Fire needed tending."

She placed her hand on his shoulder. He leaned his face into it. "I wish it had been me, 'Lana, I swear it."

She laughed hard, shocking him. "Listen to me," she demanded. "Darius Moore wanted to flush her out, back before I even knew she was inside me. That's when I ran away."

More pain in his eyes.

"Had it happened then, before I felt her, saw her, before the ocean and the women and the chocolate! Before you taking even the pain of my laboring time away—oh God, I think, sometimes, it would have been a mercy! I lied, because I wanted you to love me, not your obligation. Lavinia was your child, Matthew."

"I know that," he said quietly.

"What?"

"After you left, my mother told me. She and Annie learned the Yurok ways of figuring to the day of conception. They knew I went to your father's house, made such a mess of trying to stop you from marrying him, and that we got her started then." He bowed his head. "Damned women know everything."

She approached. "Matthew, don't you hate me?"

"Why? I told you it didn't matter." Olana saw his face struggle with incomprehension. "Does it make you feel better, that I know?" he asked.

She collapsed onto his shoulder. "Of course it does, you great, thick—" Her heaving sobs were loose now. He was not running away from them, though she could feel his fear. He held her close, stroking her hair. Olana heard a faint rumble. Humming. Her fingers, warm now, found the knot of stitches, touched them as she kissed behind his ear. His skin was warmed from the hearth fire.

"I love you," he whispered. "Lord, how I love you."

Matthew," she breathed against his neck. "It's not possible."

" 'Course it's possible. Anything's possible. We might even learn to forgive each other one of these days."

She slipped her hand into his. "Come back to bed," she whispered.

Soft, filtering light. Matthew was wrapped in softly swaddling peach colored comfort and Olana's scent. It was none of it a dream. He didn't need to dream when his night had been so full of her and the new heights they'd explored together. He wouldn't let her go. He'd never let her go again. He reached through the softness for her, but she was not beside him. He smelled coffee and oranges. He smiled, closed his eyes.

Then the footsteps. Not hers. Not Patsy's. A man's. Light. Sneaking. Watching him. The blood in his veins ignited, alert. He kept his face serene while his muscles tensed, waited. There. He felt the light weight of silk cross his hip. He grabbed the arm, twisted, sent the man sailing over himself on the bed. He pinned him there with a choke hold.

"What are you doing? Where's 'Lana?" he demanded.

The man's eyes were wild with fear.

"Coff—"

"What?" Matthew eased his grip. The man gasped, coughed. About his own age. Foreign, some kind of foreign. Bright, almost fevered eyes, indignant now. "I live here!"

Matthew followed his glance to the breakfast tray on the bed table, the blue paisley robe. "Shit." He breathed. "Sure. Right, 'course you do. But you oughtn't go sneaking around a man like that!"

"I'm—frightfully sorry."

"Well, ain't no harm done, is there?" Matthew tried to brush away the wrinkles in the man's vest. "I mean, there won't be any need to tell 'Lana, will—"

"Basil!" she summoned from the doorway, her hands on her hips, reminding Matthew of his grandmother in all her fury.

The man leapt off the bed, gestured to the tray. "I brought you breakfast," he tried. Stony silence. He went to Olana's side. "It's he. Your ranger, isn't it?" he said, then whispered something else against her ear. When her arms shook in response, he jumped. "I'm going!"

Olana didn't move until the doors closed.

"I'm sorry, Matthew," she said, the anger still making her quake. She sat on the bed beside him, her kimono opening to reveal a distracting blush between her breasts. "Aren't you cold?" she asked softly.

"No." He glanced down at his nakedness, back to her blush. He couldn't be the source, he reasoned. Men weren't beautiful. She couldn't feel the way he did, now, as he placed his hand on her knee, guessing she was bare too, under that one layer of silk. "Aw, don't be hard on him, 'Lana," he tried. "Fact is, I think I scared him half to death already."

"That would have served him right."

He slipped his hand inside her robe. "Since when have you got men servants at the meals anyway? Where's Patsy?"

"He's not a servant, Matthew!" She stood, but did not break free of his light hold. "I have to get dressed."

Yes, she was nude under the gown. He had a chance. Though her hair was already pinned up, she was responding to his caress. "Aw, 'Lana, have breakfast. It'll do wonders for your disposition."

"My disposition is perfectly . . ."

He eased her closer. "Let's start over. Good morning."

She sighed, touched his face. "Yes, of course. Good morn—oh. My. Matthew, I told you I have to—" Her head fell back. "Yes, yes . . . there."

Olana watched him pull up his suspenders as she nestled against the pillows. She wondered if the colors were too soft, if there was too much lace in the room. What was she thinking? He pulled on his vest, took out his watch and stared at it, then shook it.

"It's past ten?" he asked as he went to the shutters, cracked them open and stared out onto the street below. " 'Possum's used to me being home. Us sitting in the garden together a little before we go our separate ways. She even likes the lumps in my porridge." He took his forehead between his thumb and middle finger; a gesture so graceful, so familiar. "If she really needed me, Annie would have telephoned," he spoke to himself. Olana hungered to be included as more than the reason for his worry.

The half-smile was back as he sat beside her. "I make them both a little crazy, I think." He lifted the hair from her shoulders, and kissed the back of her neck. "I'll telephone from work."

"You're not so concerned about being late there."

He shrugged. "It's not far from here. And the women operate the place, truth to tell. It pleases them to make me feel useful. Annie's already told them I haven't been run over by a street car, I expect."

He took both her hands.

"I'd like to see your family, Olana. I'd like you to visit us. You should see how Possum's grown, and goes off to school, and recites her Robert Louis Stevenson rhymes—'Lana, if this is going too fast, you'll let me know, won't you?"

She nodded. He picked up the forgotten blue paisley robe, looked at it more closely, held it against his face. Searching, she knew, for her scent. Not yet, she heard the voice screaming inside her.

"This isn't yours."

"No. It's Basil's."

"Now I feel worse."

"Don't. He's very pleased. I told him about you, Matthew. He knows we found each other again. He brought the breakfast, the robe to show he approves."

Matthew glanced at the orange peels, the other remains of the breakfast they'd devoured together after their morning lovemaking. "Approves?"

"Of us, Matthew."

"Since when do we need your servant's approval?"

"I told you he's not my servant."

"No, you didn't."

She blushed, her eyes scanning plowed covers. "I was trying to."

"Well, whatever in hell he is—butler, footman—"

She took in a deep breath and needed all of it for the three words. "He's my husband."

forty

"No. He isn't."

"His name is Basil Edward Hamilton. He's the younger brother of the twelfth Duke of Spenser."

"You're married to me."

"Matthew, listen."

"Did you divorce me? Did you burn sage and divorce me?"

"No."

"Then you're married to me, goddamn it!"

"Please, listen."

"Then what? Be happy that I've shared Lady Hamilton's bed? That her lord approves? Should I be grateful that you've found a husband who brings me breakfast instead of bullets?"

He went to the window, flung open the shutters. Morning light flooded the room. Olana's tears stung, but she howled out her own rage. "Why didn't you send word you'd recovered, damn you?"

He swung around. "It was you left me, remember?"

"I stayed until—Matthew, the doctors said there was no hope! You had your women, you'll always have your women. Do you think it was easy? Watching you? I begged you to stop holding her and help me heal ourselves if we couldn't heal her. The doctors said you hadn't breathed for so long. That you would stay there, locked in that moment. They said your mind was affected, was gone. You were holding her last night, weren't you? You were still holding her!"

"Yes!" She saw a steel rod ride up his back as he stared down at her. "You afraid?"

"A-afraid?"

"That you gave yourself to a madman? Afraid of a child? A tainted child? Coming from us, from last night? Or do you have ways of flushing away all but blue-blooded children?"

"Stop it!" she screamed.

Even in the heat of his anger he knew he'd crossed the line to abuse. He stood still, finally listening. There was no hatred in her face. There was almost nothing at all. She was cut off from him utterly, there, in her separate grief for their child. He felt alone again, in this city. He wanted the farm, his daughter, and grandmother. His visions. Lost his mind. Was she like the others? Did she think his dreams were madness? He would not give them up, even for her. They had sustained him through everything, his visits with Lottie, with the grandfathers, with her own brother Leland. He touched his fingers to his closed eyelids.

"I held onto her as long as I could. I couldn't win against the ancestors," he whispered.

"What?"

"That's where I was, in that moment. I held onto her as long as I could, don't you understand? I would have stayed with her, even if the sun never went down. I would have stayed with her. They pushed me back. What for, I'd like to know."

He picked up his coat and left her house.

Matthew sat behind his desk, scanning the land survey, while the Mexican silversmith watched, holding his hat in his hand.

"What's this?" Matthew asked of a mark on the paper.

"A tree, sir."

"What kind?"

"A young ash. Marked for cutting down."

"Why?"

"It is too close to the house site."

"Move the house site."

"But then the road will have to be longer."

"The tree will shade the house in summer, keep the place cooler. And your children will not like you cutting down an ash, Mr. Lopez. That's a good climbing tree. We can increase the loan to cover another fifty feet of road. Agreed?"

"Agreed? You mean that's all?"

"Everything else looks in order. I'm sorry you had to wait for me this morning."

"Wait? Wait? It was nothing! I can go?"

"Yes, go home. Make plans."

As the man pumped his hand, Matthew watched his small garnet earring do a jig against the lobe. He wondered what Olana had done with his grandmother's ring. Was it in some forgotten drawer? Should he try to get it back for Annie? It had her outlaw's mother's name engraved inside, and a date: 1828.

When the silversmith left, Matthew turned to the window, leaned his head against the pane, tried to imagine the Lopez children swinging from the ash tree. He was thwarted by Olana's scent in his pores. Hyacinth. Not lilies anymore. He returned to his desk and sat, tried to concentrate on the survey for his next appointment. Then Sidney Lunt was leaning over him. When Matthew tried to rise, Serif anchored his shoulder.

"I'd knock you senseless if I weren't so glad to see you," Sidney grumbled. "Get your coat."

"I'm at work—"

"You have just been relieved. To do some catching up."

"Sidney, I think you should stay out of this."

"And I think you should be quiet until we're through." Sidney Lunt lifted his eyebrow in the direction of his massive servant. "Now you can get your coat, or I can drape it over your unconscious form. That's up to you."

The Whittaker house on Russian Hill looked the same and yet different than Matthew remembered. The neatly trimmed boxwood and forsythia hedges and ornamental trees were neglected. Inside, the impression persisted as the open spaciousness was diminished by sealed-off rooms and darkness. A lady's maid opened the door. She smiled at the trio.

"Mr. Lunt! Serif! We weren't expecting you today! Mrs. Whittaker will be so pleased!"

The servant had loaned the first air of brightness to the place, It quickly sank into darkness when she left.

"Sidney, what's happened here?"

"Darius Moore, Matt. He happened here too, remember? Drove them close to financial collapse—James from his business, Dora from the social register. Moore embezzled from every one of her charities. Olana took over the books, chased the charlatan doctors away from her father before the house went on the block, too. She knows that losing the house would finish the old man off, so she's managed to keep the great behemoth running, albeit in reduced circumstances. And she's working to restore her mother's philanthropic reputation."

"Sidney!" The woman in gray rushed to greet him, kissing his cheek tenderly. Matthew almost didn't recognize her from the life in her walk, the brightness of her eyes. Dora Whittaker didn't know him at all. She glanced in his direction, smiled politely, then addressed Sidney. "Isn't Olana with you?"

"No, Mrs. Whittaker, I've brought—"

Her hand went to her mouth. "Mr. Hart."

Matthew smiled. "You're looking right well, ma'am."

A sadness replaced her shock. "Winnie's been telling me about signs that you were coming—her stars and moon. I thought I was humoring her! She'll be so glad. And James. James will be ecstatic." She turned to Sidney Lunt and Serif. "Don't you think, gentlemen?"

"Anything is possible," Sidney conceded, grudging.

She laughed. Olana's mother was taking his part against men who used to be his friends, Matthew realized. And Sidney and Serif were now acting as his jailors. The world was upside down. Matthew's head ached. "Come." Dora Whittaker took his arm, when he hadn't even offered it. "Winnie's napping, but James is in the solarium."

The solarium was the only part of the place that looked better to Matthew in its overgrown, wilder state. James Whittaker sat with a woolen blanket across his knees, shrunken deep inside his clothing. One side of his face was frozen in a deadened, downward pull. The other side twitched as a colorful bird bounded from bush to tree to the glass dome of the solarium. A uniformed nurse sat at her patient's side. She too followed the bird's flight.

"Very good, sir. Yes, isn't she pretty?"

His face reddened, and garbled sounds burst from his mouth.

"Yes, I daresay, spring is showing her signs!" she chirped.

"Open the transom," Matthew Hart instructed.

She gave him a cold look. "I beg your pardon?"

"Let the bird out."

"Really, sir, I don't see how——"

He'd already found the pulley. The bird soon flew through the opened window. James Whittaker sighed in exhaustion. His head lolled against his shoulder. Matthew Hart knelt by his chair and took up his hand, over the protestations of the nurse.

"Is that what you wanted, sir?" he whispered.

"Mmmm," he murmured, nodding. Then James Whittaker's good eye blinked three times. He lifted his head with an effort that created beads of perspiration along his brow. "Mmmmatt!" he called, triumphant. "Matt," he said again.

"That's right, sir."

"Gracious. Gracious me," Dora Whittaker breathed.

Matthew felt a hand at his shoulder, and caught the scent of oat scones and remedies in the starched white apron. "Welcome home, Mr. Hart," Mrs. Cole said. "You look destroyed in your hunger, sir."

Mrs. Cole pointed him to the best chair in the servants' parlor. "Before Miss Olana came home," she continued, "I'd lost the downstairs staff but for Patsy and her Selby and the wee one. Selby was off hawking seltzer drinks outside the opera house to keep us fed, it was so long since we'd gotten regular wages!"

Sidney Lunt sat on the couch, stretching out his impeccably tailored, black and white form, then rubbing his temples. His voice was still pitched with anger. "Without Olana the Crockers or the Huntingtons would have lapped the place up, even if it's not as exclusive a neighborhood as Nob Hill! And her father would be dead, her mother broken. Dora's changes were forged in Olana's fire."

"Mrs. Whittaker seems almost . . . happy," Matthew admitted.

"She'd put him in a sanitarium," Mrs. Cole whispered, "and took to her bed until Olana came home. That's the change in her!" the cook pronounced. Then her expression saddened. "And you, sir. You've had your trials over this long time gone, have you not? Trials the good should not have to bear."

She cleared the hair from his forehead and planted a no-nonsense kiss on his brow. Matthew closed his eyes, welcoming the comfort that didn't require explanation. He felt pulled taut by just being here. Somehow she knew, and was not pulling. Matthew was not so sure of Sidney, and so wanted to call Mrs. Cole back when she took up their hats and left for her kitchen with Serif in tow.

Matthew waited. But Sidney Lunt seemed preoccupied with the way the sun's slanting rays made the side of the teapot glow. So stationary. So unlike him. Matthew stood, took up a raisin scone and began pacing the room's periphery.

"You're supposed to be suffering, not feasting on Mrs. Cole's confections!"

Matthew put the scone back on the plate like a schoolboy corrected. That drew an elaborate sigh.

"Will you sit down, man! You're making me dizzy."

But Matthew could not think as well sitting down. And he had to think. "So she married to keep the house for her father?"

"We just told you she's kept the house by her own wits!"

"Yes, but——"

"I thought you were dead! I was so sure you were dead! It was the only way any of it made sense!"

"Any of what?"

"How . . . how bereft she was."

"Olana never told you what happened?"

"Not me. Not her parents." He exhaled. "Coretta knew something of it, but wasn't telling. Sworn silent, I'd think. Listen, Matt. Spense is titled, landed, and cut off without a cent. Olana married him as a favor to me."

"To you?"

"He was facing his family's ire. He was supposed to find a rich bride, marry, and bring her and her millions to buck up the crumbling ancestral home. He intended to, he'd always followed his family's wishes. Please sit down, Matt, this isn't easy for me."

"For you? I'm the one—"

"No, you're not!" he called out sharply. "Not the only one, I mean. Basil's family was going to let the government deport him, don't you see? He was caught in a vise! Matt, before I even approached Olana with it, I asked if there were any hope for you and her. Olana said there wasn't a chance."

"Why did she say that?"

"How in hell do I know? Years ago I gave up trying to figure out this crazy dance you two do around each other. I only know I let you both down in not talking her out of that first marriage. Now I've done the same thing talking her into the second!

"Matt. The day she buried Moore, the grief surrounding her was like a fire. Hot, impenetrable. It was not for him, that grief. I was sure it was for you, that you were dead."

"It was not for me. We had a child."

"What?"

"A daughter, Lavinia. I had her in my arms when Moore came. The bullet, it would have gone straight through my heart, my gran says. But I was holding her, you see, so it frag . . . it, ah, fragmented." Matthew felt his throat constrict around the phantom bullet.

"Christ. Oh, Christ." Sidney pulled him down on the sofa, put the teacup in his shaking hand. "Drink, Matt," he urged.

"I can't."

"Sure you can. Here, I'll help you."

The contact between their fingers was warm, concerned. Matthew closed his eyes, swallowed. The bullet dissolved. He could breathe. He leaned his head back on the cushions.

Sidney Lunt spoke softly. "The closest I got was the day she buried Moore. She put him next to her brother. Why there, I asked her. 'Leland knows what he's done,' she said. 'Leland will keep him there.' Matt, Spense didn't plan to fall in love with the Golden West. Or with me."

"You?"

"Yes. Me. Yes, that love. The one that 'dares not speak its name?' Tell me you never once suspected . . . you didn't."

"No. I—I'm sorry."

"Don't be sorry!"

Matthew Hart stayed silent a full minute. Blocks. Everywhere, blocks to the thought of it. Damnation. Make it come together. He knew there were men like that. Not all of them abominably cruel. You idiot. There's the why. Why Sidney didn't marry. "Sorry that I didn't know, I mean," he finally said. "Sidney, listen. This is hard for me."

The smaller man flinched when Matthew Hart avoided his eyes. "It doesn't change the fact that Olana was doing me a favor, does it?"

"Favor?"

"Yes, I bought the house. I set her up with a piece of the *Chronicle* as it finally went into the black. I badgered her into writing that column to help keep her sane while you were God knows where recovering. And Basil did manage to change her name to something that doesn't make her twitch to hear. Olana and I, we've loved each other all our lives, Matt. Yes, she was doing me a tremendous favor I'll never forget."

Matthew looked into Sidney Lunt's eyes. "I can't pretend to understand. I don't. But if it helps, I don't feel any different. Toward you, I mean."

Sidney Lunt threw back his head and laughed.

"What's funny?"

"That's exactly what Olana said when I told her about Basil and me. Though I think she's always known. Woman's intuition and all that. Well, you must admit it bodes well. Look what I got her to do!"

"Damnation, Sidney."

"Listen, I'm married to Spense. We even changed Olana's name to mine on the certificate."

"What?"

"So you're only fornicating, she's not an adulteress."

"We ain't—"

"Oh?" Sidney's eyebrow shot up. "You're not?"

"I mean, we are, but—"

"Well, that's good!"

"But she divorced him, she Cherokee divorced him, and we got married. We married ourselves, in front of a statue even, before the baby came!"

Sidney looked down his nose. "Really, Matt. All we did was change the names on a perfectly legal document."

"We're legal, goddamn it!"

"All right! So you're engaging in holy wedlock, and Spense and I kept her from being a bigamist! How does that sound?"

Matthew yanked his hand through his hair, exasperated.

Sidney took his shoulder, his voice no longer caustic. "Come back, Matt. We'll figure a way through all this. Spense and I couldn't be happy without her. And the two of you belong together, when are you going to see that?"

Matthew sat very still. He raised his head. "Sidney, I made this awful mistake."

"Welcome to humanity."

He stood. "I need a loan."

"What?"

"Just until Monday."

"How much? What for? What kind of banker are you?"

"Ten dollars. Will that buy a lot of flowers in this godforsaken town?"

Sidney grinned. "All you can hold."

"Then that's what I need."

Matthew bought three shops out of the last of their day's blooms, then camped himself on her front porch. He wouldn't heed Patsy and Selby's entreaties to come inside, but did put down the flowers to take their little boy on his lap, then watch him pick the petals from three roses before Patsy retrieved him. It was dusk and growing damp with cold when Olana came up the walk out of a fog patch.

He hastily gathered up the bouquets the baby had scattered. When she reached the top step, Matthew faced her, tongue-tied, unable even to release the flowers.

"I'm sorry," he finally said.

She took his hand, led him inside, up the stairs, to her rooms.

He faced the windows, scanned the third-floor balcony of the house across the street. Through the loose-weave drapes, he saw a piano, a small man playing scales for a singing child. Sister Gertrude said Possum should have singing lessons. The scent of the flowers in his arms brought him back. He spoke to them. "Fact is, 'Lana, ain't none of my business, how you . . . what you . . . I mean nothing matters more than that we found each other again, and you don't hate me."

"Shh," she filled in the awkward space with the softest admonition, so soft he turned to make sure he had heard. That's when he saw the loose-fitting chemise that was the only thing left on her. Her skin glowed through its delicate weave. He took in a pierced breath.

"I'm trying to do this up proper. And you're—distracting me."

"Enough to let go of that jungle?"

She stepped closer. The chemise drifted off her shoulders and settled around her ankles. He dropped the flowers. But they'd been holding him up, somehow. Without them, he went to his knees. His hands gently traced the contours of her hips. He kissed along the blue-silver scars of her pregnancy's stretch marks. She raked her fingers through his hair. "Matthew—"

"Hmmm?"

"Your mustache." She gasped out her pleasure. "I like it."

"Thank you."

He didn't remember what happened to the flowers, but he caught their scent when they reached her bed. How much did he owe Sidney for them? He mustn't forget, he was better with numbers now, he must show them. And the city, he must tell her. "Hey, 'Lana?" he summoned as she straddled him, as her fingers moved at his stiff collar.

"Yes?"

"I like cable cars."

"Do you?" She laughed, pulling his shirt open. "Now that's a wonder."

Soon there was nothing between them, not even words. Her new grown hair sifted across his chest as she worked her hands, her lips, her limbs, toward pleasing him.

When she'd finally gone still in his arms, he breathed into her fragrant hair and kissed the pulse spot at her temple. "I visited at your parent's today," he said. "Part of my education from Sidney."

"Sidney?" She lifted her head. "But I didn't tell him anything. Of course. Basil did. They are both dear men, Matthew."

He was not ready to concede her that, but he grunted.

"Bear," she teased, resting her head against his chest again.

He did not know how to tell her of his instinctual fear of this stranger who held power, legal power over them. Let it go. It was so wondrous, her forgiveness, the feel of her in his arms again. Her voice led him away from that dark, confused part of his mind.

"The house is very different, isn't it?"

"Yes."

"When I came home Mother almost didn't know me."

"Me either."

"Oh, darling," she whispered, reaching up to kiss where the curve of his mustache met his lower lip.

He glided the back of his fingers along her bare shoulder. "So, we're both different. Doesn't mean we can't go on. Changed."

"Alone," she whispered.

"We're both alone, without her."

Olana shivered. He drew up the covers and pulled her close.

The day Dora Whittaker caught Matthew unawares was a good day, when her husband was talking in full sentences, about his joy that their family was all together again. He'd thrown away one of his canes, too, to walk triumphant between his wife and sister. And he'd opened a bottle of his prized champagne, and they'd all had a glass, even Dora. Perhaps the champagne had given her the courage to take Matthew's arm there, by the side gate that led to the streetcar line he took home to the Mission District.

"Mr. Hart. Please."

"Ma'am?"

"When Olana first came home, her dresses were spotted with milk. She had to bind up her . . . her bosom. There was a child?"

When he didn't answer she pressed his hands, insisting.

"Lavinia," he gave up that sacred thing, her name.

She would not break contact with his eyes or hands. Why, Matthew wondered. Why did women endure so much? "What happened to her?" she whispered.

He looked up the long block toward the bay, squinting as if the sun were pouring out blinding rays. But it was only a fog out there on the water, an afternoon fog rolling in.

"It was Darius Moore, wasn't it? He killed his own child."

Matthew didn't think anything could get his eyes back on her. That did. "Not his, ma'am. Olana's. Hers and mine."

He didn't expect Dora Whittaker's tears, or her hand taking his, lifting it to her cheek. "My poor boy," she said. "I'm so sorry."

"Yes, well. Leastways I saw her in. Knew her a little while."

He walked her back to the side door. "Matthew," she called him his given name for the first time, "I have something I believe you were looking for." She reached shaking fingers into her apron pocket and drew out the miniature doll of Olana, the one Leland had charged him to find years ago.

"I took his train from Winnie's house. I never told anyone, even James. I had to have a piece of my son, a remembrance. I didn't know this was inside."

"Give it to her," he said softly.

Trade. He had to offer her something in trade for this wondrous gift. Matthew reached into his vest and drew out the photograph. He hesitated only a moment, then placed it in her hands. She opened the holder, then cleared the thin tissue paper from the mounted image.

"There's the lot of us," he explained.

Her eyes scanned the faces. She gasped softly when she found the baby on Olana's lap.

"Lavinia?"

"Yes. We took good care of her, Mrs. Whittaker. We took good care of them both until—I couldn't get to my guns, you see? I never saw it coming." He willed his racing heart to slow down, his mouth to talk sense, this woman was Lavinia's grandmother, she deserved sense. But it didn't matter. She wasn't listening.

"She's beautiful. A beautiful baby. And Olana. How proud, how strong she is."

"Yes, ma'am. Like you."

"Who are the others?"

"This here's Vita, she's my mother. And Annie, my grandmother, is behind us. They helped Olana bring Lavinia in."

"Bring in?"

"Give birth. They're midwives."

"And this child?"

"She's my first daughter, Wesoma. We call her Possum. Her mother, she drowned some years back. Gran and me, we look after Possum, here in the city. Though some days it's the other way around."

"Where is your mother?"

"She's just married. Visiting with her new husband's folks, over in Ireland."

"How splendid for her. Your people have been very good to mine, Matthew."

"We were your family a little while. Imagine. What one little baby can accomplish."

"Matthew. I didn't encourage this second marriage."

"It don't matter, ma'am."

"It does to me. That you know. Basil is all I would have wanted for Olana at one time. He's what I sent her to the Continent to find, before you two stumbled upon each other. But I didn't urge it.

"After she married him she seemed more sad, more lonely than before. I know something of lost children, Matthew. I'm not quite as silly as the woman you knew." She smiled. "Would you bring your family next time you visit?"

"Sure, ma'am."

"My name is Dora."

Matthew was only dimly aware of the room's light fading. His fingers ached for the photograph. But he couldn't have taken it back from Dora. Lavinia was hers, too. Had he said good-bye to Olana's mother, back at the house? He didn't remember. He didn't remember anything but the need to have the photograph again, wedged against his heart. It had never been far from him. The tightness in his throat threatened to strangle him. He closed his eyes against it. Phantom. Phantom pain. Not real. Sidney stood before him, resplendent in his opera cape.

"Matt! What on earth happened to you?"

"Happened?"

"We were meeting at the theater, then Delaney's, remember?"

"No. I don't. I'm sorry."

"Well, put on some lights will you?" he demanded, then rushed around, a black and white blur, doing it himself. "Jesus, what a sight you are! Are you ill?"

"No, no. I just needed a favor of Alisdair and I thought he might be here at the *Chronicle* and he was and I am."

"What?"

"Waiting."

"Waiting?"

"For him to finish. Did I miss supper?"

"Matt, it's past midnight."

"Is it? Shit, I didn't leave a note for Annie."

"We told her we were going to see *The Importance of Being Earnest,* then to Delaney's. We told her this morning."

"Oh. That's right."

"We tracked you to the Whittakers', then to your place. Dora and your grandmother, they both said to leave you alone. I don't think it was such a good idea. Olana's worried herself into—"

The sight of the disheveled Alisdair coming out of the darkroom made Sidney's words faint, indistinct.

"I think this one is as close as I'm going to get to the original without going blind, Matty," Alisdair said, offering the print.

"It's fine." Yes, fine, distinct, he knew that even without his spectacles. Matthew raised his head. "What do we owe you?"

The photographer pulled down his sleeves, considering. "One of your grandmother's pies," he decided. "Peach." Alisdair returned to the darkroom as Sidney Lunt peered around Matthew Hart's shoulder.

"Good lord," he said.

"I gave mine to Dora. Gran had the only other copy. Photographer's studio burned down soon after, so there was no negative. I need it. On me. You understand?"

"Yes."

"Well. We got a new negative now. Alisdair made one, by taking a photograph of Annie's photograph. Plenty of photographs, until one was clear, almost as clear as the original. Everything will be all right." He stood, but the room would not stay still. "Sidney," he whispered. "I feel a little strange."

"Sit. Alisdair's used to breathing these infernal fumes, but you're not," he said, easing him down on the sofa. "I'll open the window."

"No!"

"What?"

"Don't open it! It will spread."

"What will—"

"The fire."

"There's no fire."

"A storm. A storm of fire. Nothing. Nothing you can do. Bring up the hand-cranked presses—the ones in the cellar."

"All right. I'll do that. Close your eyes, Matt."

But the firestorm raged there too, behind his eyes. Did he call out? Shaking. Is that why both men anchored him now? Don't, please. No. Different men. Kind ones. Not like on the *Madeline*, so long ago. He smiled at the shy, wild-haired photographer and felt, suddenly, immeasurably sad. "Peach?" he asked.

"It's the one I dream about each night, aye."

"Remind me tomorrow, will you, Alisdair? When I have more of my wits about me?"

Mostly the strange, fragmented firestorms captured his attention as he slept. They raged around a bull with red eyes, a gold chalice spilling blood. Sounds came with the dreams, strange unearthly sounds, the chattering of a thousand monkeys, the roar of deranged bees. He woke clutching Olana's waist. She spoke his name softly. Then the gentle, trilling purr of her desire would replace the bees. "You won't regret it, 'Lana," he'd promise. "You won't regret loving me."

But even nestled in her arms after, he'd lie awake, on guard for the dreams, and confused about his life in the day. What was he doing here? What was giving the poor and immigrants small loans, finding them homes? How did that compare to the Barbary Coast, the land and water rights plunderers, the monument to graft and corruption that was City Hall itself? Could he even help keep the bank afloat with his own denseness about numbers? Sleep. He needed more sleep, to sort it out so it didn't go around on itself, devouring its own tail.

City families started asking for his grandmother at births. Sometimes she allowed him to come. Those were the only nights he slept dreamless, after births.

When was Farrell coming home to take this weight off his shoulders, to give Possum her mana back? In the Fall, their latest letters promised. What if his mother fell in love with the green hills of Ireland? What if Farrell made his triumphant homecoming permanent? They would be in the cool breezes forever and he would be here in the city by a bay that offered no relief in this still, silent heat. This earthquake weather.

He sat up. "Earthquake."

Olana touched his back. "Do you feel a tremor?"

"Not a tremor. An earthquake. Where's Possum?"

"Just next door. We're at your house tonight, remember?"

"I have to see her."

"May I come?"

He took a gentle hold on the back of Olana's neck as they looked into Possum's room. He'd done it again, he realized. Awakened her to his phantoms.

"It's this weather, I think," she whispered. "It's got us all a little addled. So still."

"I can't sleep. I can't think. I didn't know what house I was in. What about your father? Who will help him?" Olana trembled there in the still, hot darkness. "I frighten you, don't I?" he charged.

"No."

"I do. I frighten you worse than when you thought I'd rape you."

"Matthew. Stop it."

"You think I'm going mad."

"Darling, listen. We can go away. When your mother and Farrell come home. We'll go to Aunt Winnie's, shall we? We'll open up her house by the sea. Just the two of us."

"The farm," he whispered. I want to go home, 'Lana."

Her body froze in its stillness. "Don't ask that of me, Matthew. Not yet. I don't have your courage."

He kissed her forehead. "You? Who does weekly battle with every pompous ass institution in the state of California? Who tames a hundred city rag-tag motherless ruffians with Louisa May Alcott twice a week?"

She smiled, relieved. "That's to counter your *Huckleberry Finn* the other two afternoons."

"Both of which may be found happy together on the shelves of the new library space at Dolorosa Mission."

"When it's not being hastily cleared for a German folk dance or blaring with Irish pipe music, Mr. Hart!" she imitated her tone when they sparred at the community mission meetings.

"Or the harp. Now, Lady Hamilton, I was the happy recipient of the overflow of your delight in that demonstration." He kissed her deep into the pillows, then glided his thumb over her brow's anxious line, erasing it. "Forgive me for waking you, darling girl," he whispered.

"Let's see what we can do about making better dreams tonight, Mr. Hart," she urged.

The next morning at the *Chronicle,* Olana sat watching the steam rise from the teapot's spout. Sidney and Basil's eyes were so focused on her face she knew there was no escape. She'd made a promise to them, and broken it.

"You didn't tell him," Sidney said.

"He hasn't been sleeping well. His dreams, his obligations— This is one more thing to worry him."

Sidney's brow arched. "Oh?" he said. "Is that what your news is?"

"No. I'm gloriously happy. But what if he's not as happy? I can hardly expect him to be, can I?"

"That's why we have to tell him. So we can work out what's best."

"What's best for us will hurt you and Basil."

"We shouldn't have gotten you into this." Her husband spoke for the first time.

"My eyes were open."

"You don't regret it?"

She touched his face, missing his usual animated banter. "It's very early for you, isn't it?" she said softly. "Have some tea."

A twitch started under his left eye. "Listen to her!" he hissed at Sidney.

Her editor frowned. "Olana's right. Have some tea, you're very out of sorts, nightowl." Sidney watched her as she poured. "He'll notice the changes in you soon, sport," he told her gently.

"You think knowing about the baby will make him give them up, you damned fool?" Basil accused sharply.

Olana put the teapot down. "Give what up?"

Sidney winced. "I thought we'd agreed—"

"I won't stand her taking all on herself! Worrying over his health, his sanity, as if he was some perfect being! Let's get the central thesis straight: she's the one carrying his child, and he's the one breaking her heart!"

"Matthew? Breaking my heart? How?" Olana tried entering their conversation, but they were whirling about each other now.

"Damn it, Spense! I said I'd talk to him about it first!"

"About what?" Olana demanded.

"But you haven't!"

"I haven't had the opportunity."

"You haven't made the opportunity! You're as blind to his deceit as she is!"

"Deceit?" Olana tried again. "What are you two talking about?"

"You love him!" Basil accused Sidney. "As deeply as she does! Well, I haven't forgotten Olana! I haven't forgotten my wife!"

Basil Hamilton had never before called her his wife, when they were in private, like this. Olana stood, then dropped the empty teapot. It shattered across the floor. Serif rushed in, on guard. She eyed each of the three men in turn. "Now," she said calmly. "You're going to tell me what this is all about."

So they did.

forty-one

Matthew approached the bedroom door. He turned back to Patsy. She nodded, urging him on. But he felt the heat of Olana's anger. He tapped so softly he hoped she wouldn't hear. Then he could go home. Try to get back in her good graces tomorrow.

"Come in."

Good, steady voice, he thought until he saw her swollen eyes. He approached the bed, kissed her cheek. "How was the opera?" he asked.

"Beautiful."

"Good. Did Madame Fremstad's aria break any of that fancy chandelier?"

"No."

"Well, that's good." Wasn't good. None of this was pointing toward good. "Did you all go to Coretta's after?"

"I didn't. I came back here, to wait for you."

"I left word, 'Lana. That I didn't know how long—"

"I wanted to wait."

"Well. It's late, isn't it? Maybe I should go home—"

"Sit down, Matthew."

"Sure. I'll just go and wash up—"

"Why?"

"Why?" He tried to laugh. "On account of—"

"Don't you dare lie to me, Matthew Hart! You don't want me to smell where you've been, what you've been doing!"

"Uh—yes," he admitted, remembering Annie's advice to tell her, tell her. He saw her eyes cloud with tears. " 'Lana. It ain't that often. Please, don't."

"How many?"

"How many?"

"Yes. How many have there been?"

"Here. In San Francisco, you mean?"

"Yes."

"Six."

"Six?"

"Yes. So you see, it's only now and then. And I don't go looking for it. They seek me out."

"Do they?" she whispered into her lap.

" 'Lana." He took her hand. It was cold. "I can't shut down a part of me because of what happened. I'm sorry if you don't like it, but I'm not going to stop. Gran's right. It helps with the nightmares. It's good for me."

"I hate her! I hate you!"

He was expecting some measure of understanding and got an ear-piercing wail. "Jesus, 'Lana, stop that! It's not like I set up shop!"

The back of her hand slammed across his jaw. One of the garnets on the ring that was his grandmother's cut his cheek, drew blood. "What in hell is the matter with you?" he demanded, grabbing her wrists before she could hit him again.

"Are they beautiful?" she asked in a rage-filled whisper.

"Of course. They're always beautiful."

"Tonight's? Was she beautiful?"

"It was a he."

"He?"

The strength went out of her arms. He released her. "Yes," he said softly. "Breech. Six pounds. They're poor people, 'Lana. Doctors in this damned city hear the name of their street and won't come. So they call on Annie and me—only when there's some trouble their own women are nervous about and—"

She brought her wrists to her face, inhaling the scent from where he'd held her. Then she grabbed his hands and breathed again, deeply. "Cloves! My God, cloves! Babies! You've been helping women have babies!"

"Ain't—that what we been talking about?" She still held his hands. ". . .'Lana?"

She brought his hands to her tear-stained face, and began sucking his fingers, her strong tongue gliding over the joints, circling the pads, flicking in and out, teasing the space between his fingers. By the time she placed his palm against the curve of her face, he had an aching need for her.

"Jesus, 'Lana," he whispered, "What are you doing now?"

Then she was straddling him, licking the blood from his cheek, whispering in his ear. "Babies. Coming into these hands, these beautiful hands." She placed them under her breasts, then ground her knee into his hip, the silk of her oriental robe singing. "You are for me," she whispered fervently, "I am for you."

Remnants of the birth exhilaration were mixing with his desire. "Sure, 'course we are, but—" Her able hands were at his clothes. "What happened, just now? What did you hit me for? 'Lana, stop that, I can't think."

"Don't think," she urged, then devoured his mouth.

Everywhere he touched her, the scent of cloves. Strong, mingling with her hyacinths. It reminded him of the night of Lavinia's birth—the cloves, and the fervor of her longing. Her breasts seemed the same as then, too. They were full, their areolas dark. She teased him with them now, playing erect nipples at his cheek, his bottom lip. Think? He could barely breathe as she placed his swollen need inside her wet caress. She rocked there above him, where he could see the glory of her body, the wonder of her shimmering hair. Rocking, rocking, before she collapsed onto his chest and into his arms.

He waited, patient, enjoying the feel of her, right to her toes stroking his calf. He led her hand down to feel that he was still hard. She shivered. Cold? Where were the covers? On the floor. He reached, turned, fell. Then they were both on the floor, laughing, entangled, starting all over again.

It wasn't until he was lying still in her arms that the realization hit. His shoulders began to shake. "Women? You thought other women were keeping me from you?" He followed the heat of her blush from her cheeks to where her waist flared out and rounded nicely beneath his palm.

"You're taking this very well," she whispered, contrite.

"No, I ain't. When I'm done laughing—"

She taunted his ear with her tongue. "You wouldn't chastise a woman who will be in need of your services?"

His hands stopped circling her abdomen. " 'Lana."

"In the fall. When your mother and Farrell return. And we—can go back to the farm, if you'd like, my darling."

He sat up.

"Matthew, say you're not angry."

"Angry?" He threw back his head and laughed. It had been so long since he'd done that. His thumb blotted a tear from the far corner of her eye. "Are you well?" he whispered.

She glanced at the rumpled covers around them. "Could any but a well woman feast on your love as shamelessly as I just did?" she asked at his ear. A slight coloring flared in his cheeks.

"I've done it!" she proclaimed. "Matthew Hart, I've made you blush!" She threw her arms about him, laughing.

He slid down in the anarchy of white damask, pulled the silk of her robe aside. He rested against the warmth of her full breasts.

"I should have known," he said.

"I didn't suspect myself. Again. Isn't it glorious?"

"It's soon. Not yet two years. Annie's going to have my head for not being more careful with you—"

"Oh, Matthew, it would be soon, if Lavinia were with us. Without her it's been an eternity."

His hand stroked her back the way it had during her labor. "Yes," he agreed.

"I know it's . . . complicated. But Basil and Sidney are ecstatic. It was quite touching really—"

"You told them? Before me?"

"Matthew, we thought you were turning away—"

"We? Who are we? You? Your husband? Sidney?"

"Yes."

"They followed me, didn't know what they were seeing. Suspected I had other women. Never thought to ask me."

"They thought of it, Matthew. But you are rather formidable to them, you know."

"I'm formidable to them?"

"It's foolish, I know, but—"

"Still you sought their advice."

"Matthew, they thought—"

"The child." His voice choked back twice, then sounded like someone was holding him underwater. "His people will come. Take her away. Away from me—"

"No. No they won't, love."

"They'll try."

"We won't let them."

"You think you can stop them? I'll be lucky if I get to be a doting uncle. Your husband's people—they're the fucking British Empire!"

"Matthew!"

"Goddamn it, woman! Why can't you let me have my own children?"

The silence hung dark and dead around them. He closed his eyes against the pain in hers and grasped a rail of her bed, shook it instead of her, but it didn't help. Olana pried his fingers loose from the cold brass, took him into her arms. Why did she do that? Why didn't she throw him out? He held on to her, smelling the sweetness of her changing breasts, soaking the silk of her robe with his ragged weeping.

"I'm sorry. 'Lana I'm so sorry."

"Hush now. It will be all right. Somehow it will be all right, for all of us."

Matthew didn't like it here, in the men's part of Olana's house. The Englishman peered over his shoulder. Basil Hamilton's lime and ginger scent mixed with what? Boredom? Fear? Helping Lord Hamilton to get his finances in order was just an excuse. What were Olana and Sidney up to? Matthew had never been alone with her husband, he'd avoided every opportunity. That's what Sidney and Olana wanted, the two of them to have it out. Because of the child who was coming, his and Olana's child, bearing this man's name. The pencil point broke.

"Damnation." Matthew swiveled the chair. Lord Hamilton was no longer behind him. He followed his lime and ginger to the closet's pocket doors, and pulled them open wider. "Jesus," Matthew breathed, looking inside. "It's half the room."

Basil Hamilton came toward him through the clutter, and deposited an arm load of clothes over his shoulder.

"I requested your help with my finances, not an initiation into your religious order."

"What?"

"Hair shirt penitential?"

Matthew threw the clothes on a chair and went back to the desk. "What in the hell are you talking about?" he muttered, sitting, pulling out his pocketknife and scraping at the errant pencil. Basil leaned over his chair.

"You'll never understand the fine art of extravagance. A priest—" he cocked an eyebrow, reconsidering. "Well, a druid priest, perhaps. That's what you are."

"You sound like Aunt Winnie."

"Aunt Winnie's like the fools in Shakespeare. Eminently sensible. And she's right. If it weren't for Olana, you'd still be living in trees and eating bark."

"You kill a tree, eating its bark."

Matthew felt the man's breath at his neck. "I'm teasing, Matt."

He didn't raise his head from the numbers. Numbers everywhere—on checks from abroad, record books, store accounts. "You're being ignorant, about the trees," he said, continuing to bury the bills under pencil shavings.

"But right about you. Of course, if you weren't a saint, I'd be dead, wouldn't I?"

"Dead?"

"You'd like me dead, wouldn't you?"

What game was this man playing now? Matthew closed the knife carefully, then pulled off his spectacles. "I can't figure these numbers and your nonsense at the same time," he said, standing. "Let's wait for Sidney."

But he didn't know which door led to Olana's part of the house. He searched among them.

"Yes, Sidney you can tolerate. He never turned against his nature, did he? Never played the part of a real man, a man like you! He never asked his 'sport' to marry him. That's what you hate about me, is it not?"

Matthew turned and did what he rarely accomplished with Olana's husband. He looked him straight in the eyes. "I don't hate you," he said. "But I want my child."

Basil Hamilton's stance eased. He smiled sadly. "Matt, listen. My mother dutifully presented my father with an heir—my brother, and a spare—me. My elder brother is in excellent health, has six ruddy, pink-cheeked children of both sexes. I am viewed as a miserable failure, insomuch as I could not even perform the simple task of marrying an American Rose rich enough to refurbish the tumbledown manor. My father doesn't care enough to write, never mind take any notice of progeny. Does that help?"

"A bit," Matthew admitted. "I'm sorry."

"Don't be, not for me!" Basil spun away, laughing. "I live, not in my past, but in San Francisco, where I can taste the glorious future! It's matchless! Except when I drive Sidney into debt, and Olana to distraction with stupid attempts to find your saintly feet muddied with clay."

"It was you alone then? You followed me to the birthings?"

"It would have been perfect, were it true. We would have taken care of Olana and the baby. We would have resumed being the way we were, only better. With a child. Goddamn you, why did you come back?"

The two men stared hard at each other.

"I got other work to do," Matthew finally said, turning. Wrong door. Another way into the damned closet. And Basil was yelling at his back.

"Where in bloody blue blazes are you going? Why don't you hit me?"

"I think you're hitting yourself hard enough for the both of us."

Basil Hamilton faltered, as if struck. Then he swept his hand in front of his face. Matthew approached, though he knew this man and Sidney did purposely what the men of the *Madeline* forced on him, and that had blighted his life forever. He swallowed hard. He didn't have to understand, isn't that what Sidney had said? But perhaps he did, if there was to be any peace in his convoluted family.

"Basil," he called quietly. "My father disowned me, too. When I was a boy."

"Whatever for?"

"Because I wouldn't fight Indians. Because I didn't resemble him. He called my mother a whore, he was so sure that I wasn't his. But I am. The darkness that you're afraid of, that comes from him. You don't have to be afraid. I won't ever hurt you."

Basil Hamilton took his shoulder, squeezed. Then his head leaned into his chest. Matthew felt the hot tears of Basil's relief penetrate his shirt. It was all right. It didn't hurt. Why hadn't they had this talk sooner? He patted the slight, silk-vested back awkwardly.

Basil released him, swiping at his eyes, laughing. "It's grown into quite a labyrinth, hasn't it?"

Matthew puzzled out the word. "The one with the bull in the center?"

"Yes, exactly!"

Did this man know anything about that bull? The one in his dreams? "Please stay," Basil said. He was again his old self, affable, polite. "I'll only talk dispersal of worldly goods, I promise."

"It's not so bad you have to do any dispersing. We just got to get you thinking numbers, and staying inside their limits. I had the same problem when I started out with Mr. Amadeo."

"Did you?"

"Sure. I was born in an army garrison, then lived with my gran who barters mostly, then in the wild. I could barely tell coins apart."

"Not so different from living inside a title in that respect!" Basil bounded back into the closet. "What should I do with these?" he called, holding up suit after suit of clothes. "Look," he urged, "hopelessly out of date! Help me spring clean before you unclutter my accounts."

Matthew knew less about current fashion than he did about numbers. This was ridiculous. Still, he yanked through the hangers. "Well, you could get 'Lana's things in their proper place, for a start." He pitched a dark blue, lavish velvet gown into Sidney's arms.

"This is not Olana's."

"Well, sure it is."

"Matt?"

He turned to see the second son of the twelfth duke of Spenser holding the gown against his chest. *"Regardez,"* he invited. The garment was cut precisely to his shoulders. Olana's weren't anywhere near the size.

"Jesus," Matthew muttered.

Basil pealed out his laughter. "Well, you were insistent! And this time wrong, for a rare and pleasant change."

He went back to his housecleaning, humming.

forty-two

Olana pressed her ticket stubs into her book on the bedside table. The date, April 17, 1906 stuck out as she turned down the lamp. Matthew was already asleep at her side.

Though Caruso's voice was even more heartbreaking than when she'd seen him perform in Rome, it was watching Matthew's face as he listened that gave Olana the most pleasure. He had somehow found a new serenity, she thought. She could feel him letting go of everything—his work, their jumbled life together, even his nightmares, as he listened, caught up in a ripping good story. It reminded her of their nightly readings of Mark Twain in his tree house.

And when they came home, ahead of the others who had gone on to celebrate Caruso's triumph at Delaney's, they'd checked the sleeping children together. Olana had watched him at his ritual—carefully memorizing where each was—Coretta's Andrew, Patsy's Hugh snuggled beside Possum. Possum was the only one who'd awakened enough to murmur, " 'Night, Daddy. You look like a fairy princess, 'Lana," before planting a dreamy kiss on their cheeks.

Now Olana lifted the covers and stretched out beside him. Matthew murmured into her shoulder, drawing her back closer against his chest. The shiver of excitement it produced quieted to a drowsy contentment. Olana's hands slipped inside her nightgown and touched the small bulge between her hips. This baby was showing faster than Lavinia had. Some of the opera patrons had even smiled knowingly at their box. Basil had taken her hand with what, a proprietary hold? No, not Basil, he'd promised never to hurt her. She couldn't be making the same mistake again. Surely Basil was a different mistake. But a mistake, Olana realized, suddenly weary. A mistake, the consequences of which another child would have to suffer. But not tonight. Tonight had been so close to perfect, and Olana wanted to continue to feel rich, full of families, no matter what forms those families took.

Later, Matthew's breathing became labored and punctuated with suffering. Olana felt him stumble from the bed. She followed him into the small adjoining sitting room, where his hands were shaking as he gripped the mantle. When she touched his back, he turned, looked somehow startled to see her, then traced her face frantically with his fingers. He was still out of breath when he spoke.

"I dreamed I fell."

"Fell?"

"Yes, through my life. I kept trying to wake, before the bad things happened between us, you know? I couldn't. I tried, but I couldn't."

"It's nice to have you back," she said softly. "Now. Right now."

"Is the city still here?"

"The city?"

"Yes."

"It's here."

"Look out the window. To be sure."

"Matthew—"

"Please."

She pulled aside the drapery, then the lace. "See?"

"Ah. Yes."

"Where would it go, darling?" she asked, returning from the window. But two drunken baritones were trying to sing tenor on the stairway, accompanied by Coretta's clear soprano and Serif's bass. Matthew smiled. "I think you have a few more house guests."

"We're becoming a regular salon."

"Good." He sighed. "That's good."

She pressed her hand to his chest. "And your heart beats steady again," she pronounced. "That's—"

He took her hand, kissed into the palm. "Easily remedied," he said. His tongue flicked a gliding path down her palm, then probed the pulse spot at her wrist. Her breaths came in short gasps as he nudged her nightgown off her shoulder, there before the sitting room's fire. "Easy now, Mama," he teased at her ear.

"I ain't your mama," she snarled back, her breasts rising, full and furious against his chest. "And there's nothing easy about loving you."

" 'Ain't?' Lord Almighty, Lady Hamilton, you'll be cussing next!"

He came down on her mouth before she could answer. He drew her closer, his thumbs massaging her hips, the rest of his fingers cupping her backside, drawing her against him. Behind them, the doors to her rooms swung open. Matthew groaned, burying his head in her shoulder.

"Seven, seven curtain calls!" Sidney announced.

"It was eight," Coretta corrected.

"Matt, Olana, settle this! Was it seven or—"

Olana viewed the segment of Caruso's opening night audience through the gaze of her own happiness as Matthew growled low. Only Sidney looked peaked.

"Can't you two at least turn your lights down before you start that! Why, if—"

Basil had him turned toward the door before he'd finished. "This is America, a free country," he chastised his lover. "Let's get Coretta and Serif a glass of champagne. Would you two like—" But Olana declined her husband's offer with a wave of her hand. A final "Ah, America" greeted her before Sidney closed the doors behind him.

Matthew Hart counted the tolling bells of Old St. Mary's. Yes, the tints of dawn were filtering in the window. Annie would be already about and in the kitchen, he surmised as he rose. He pulled on his pants, yanking the suspenders over his nightshirt. He intended to keep her company, there, a little while, downstairs. But when he returned to the bed to kiss Olana, she took hold of a suspender, held.

"Hey," he teased. "You're hell on my early morning routine."

"Is that right?"

Her voice was moist, dusky. She lifted the covers and the scent of hyacinths and peaches laid siege to his intentions. He climbed into bed beside her. She nuzzled close, gliding her leg along his.

" 'Lana. I have to go to work."

"Why?"

"I've got appointments. Clients."

"They'll understand."

"Mr. Amadeo won't. Not after sitting beside us at the opera last night and managing to get in on time himself. He's got a beautiful woman too, you know."

She traced his jawline. "Sidney will not be so hard on me."

He smiled. "You do handle Sidney well. You handled both carousing members of this family well last night."

Her skittering laughter felt good, but then came the "Oh, Matthew," and the tears. He would never get used to her tears. Or understanding their source. "What? What did I do?"

"You called them—Sidney and Basil—family."

"Well, what else are they?"

More tears. He attempted his stern voice once more. "Stop that now. We got a whole household lying about like—like artistic bohemians this morning. We've got to—"

"Join them?" she whispered at his ear. "Just a little longer?" Her fingers worked the buttons on the placket of his nightshirt deftly. She kissed the knot of stitches at the base of his throat. He surrendered, kissing her ripe mouth, crushing the glory of her hair in his hands.

It started then. With a rip, a buckling. Matthew closed his eyes and saw the trees first, the ancient redwoods north of the city, the ones he'd visited often, depended on, to help maintain his sanity. They were snapping like matchsticks. Falling. He heard deer, then coyote. From where? The closest place they roamed was Mount Tamalpais, wooded slopes close to the city. But not this close. Not this loud, panicked, in his ears.

Olana, against his heart, whispered. "Matthew. What is it?"

"Earthquake," he said. "Just an earthquake."

She laughed nervously. "What?"

The church bells of Old St. Mary's sounded, though it was only moments since they'd last tolled. They were not tolling, but clanging wildly, impossibly out of tune, but in a cacophonous waltz with the floor, the framed paintings and photographs on her walls, the furniture.

Olana was still in his arms. Or was he in hers? They were fighting each other, suddenly, fighting to protect each other's heads from the falling plaster.

forty-three

It stopped. Matthew looked down at his plaster-dusted hands, at Olana's hair gone the same gray except under where his fingers lifted. "Another's coming," he said. Though all the church bells of the city had joined Old St. Mary's in its mad tolling, she heard him.

"The doorway," she urged.

He pulled her from the bed, shouting down the stairs. "Gran! Patsy! Coretta! Get the babies in the doorways!" They had only gotten to the arch of her sitting room when it started again.

The undulating floor knocked him down first. He swept Olana beneath him, only giving her enough turning room to face him. The sitting room's chimney toppled, burying their dancing bed in bricks. Her wardrobe and dresser bounded through the bay windows. He heard them hit the street below.

Olana couldn't see, couldn't breathe except through the weave of his shirt. She felt pressure, incredible pressure, and released a small cry, just as the windows of her French doors blew out. Glass showered them, then flew out windows, whose panes were already gone from the first wave. Olana felt Matthew grunt and shake his head, as if bothered by a fly. He held her down lower as the tremor crescendoed to an impossible loudness, force. Then, it stopped. Everything was still, except something small inside her.

"Matthew," she whispered, cutting into the silence.

"Yes, love?"

"The baby's moving." She brought his hand inside her night-gown. "Here."

"That's good, darlin'." His hands left her childspace and glided over her form, checking for injuries. Olana saw a rivulet of blood trickling down from his scalp, pooling in the collar of his nightshirt. She reached, but he caught her wrist.

"Don't. The others, the children—"

"This first," she told him firmly.

"Best listen to her, Matt," Sidney cautioned, offering Olana his handkerchief.

Matthew Hart looked up to see him and Basil, still resplendent in their formal opera clothes gone gray. Olana threaded through his hair. Shards slid out until she found the wedged one. She doubled the thickness of the handkerchief and pulled. Matthew felt the deep red, clotting blood flow down the side of his face. He swayed between the two men holding his arms. Basil waved his opera pro-gram tersely.

"This is really too much. Now you've got a crown of thorns. Wasn't being a saint enough for you?"

Half Matthew's mustache quivered upward. "I'll gladly relin-quish my position," he said, before getting to his feet on the men's arms. From below, the moans and cries started.

Matthew bounded for the stairs, until he heard them creak and splinter. Olana gasped, the men called out his name. He stepped quickly to the side near the wall. "Stay behind me," he urged them quietly, reaching along the cracked wall for Olana's hand. She linked hers to Sidney's, and he linked to Basil. They passed rooms redec-orated by the earthquake into a jumble of fallen furniture, splin-tered glass, and crockery. But the beds were empty. Olana's guests had gotten to the doorways. In the first they saw Serif, still bent pro-tectively over Coretta and Andrew, who was happily climbing from Coretta's arms to his as she kissed the side of the giant's bald head. "We're fine. Keep going, we'll follow," she urged.

In the next doorway Patsy and Selby, still dazed, held little Hugh between them. Patsy's lower lip began to tremble when her eyes met Matthew's. "Possum was with Hugh. Right here . . ." She spread her arms around the room that was no longer there. Most of its floor was piled onto the downstairs entrance hallway, and that was in the basement's kitchen. There Matthew saw the small figure of his grandmother, standing beside the stove with a spatula in her hand.

"Gran?" he called, as if he were going to ask her where she put his fresh socks.

She looked up. "I'm all right," she said. "Find Possum."

He looked across the splintered gap in the floor, to where the front wall had been. Now the third-story balcony of the house across the street was there, its high ornamental tower still intact. Lying across the railing, in his pink robe over pink pajamas piped in maroon, was a man. He raised his balding head, crowned by a lump. Mr. Morgan, the music teacher. His grand piano had somehow flipped onto its back and was in Olana's sitting room below, its strings intersected by her gramophone's horn.

"Good morning all," he said, his voice as musical as ever. "Wesoma went inside to get my canary."

"Possum!" Matthew called. The rent in his voice was palpable, echoing in Olana's ears. She caught his hand, afraid he'd vault over the slanted, unsteady floor of debris. Possum appeared in Mr. Morgan's broken window frame, her white nightgown shimmering, a silver bird cage in her hand. "Look, Daddy!" she called out over the abyss, which was now hissing from leaking gas pipes.

"Good girl," he shouted back. "Stay there. Wait for us to get you."

"Get Mr. Morgan first. He's hurt."

Matthew looked up the stairway, his eyes smarting. Coretta smiled. "Another rescuer. She's your daughter, Matt. Gentlemen, ladies, shall we form a chain?"

"I will anchor," Serif informed them.

Before Olana realized what was happening, she found herself holding Hugh's hand while angling Coretta's Andrew unsteadily at her hip. She watched the human chain wind around the last of the room's flooring and connect to the tumbling balcony of Mr. Morgan's house. Possum put down the bird cage and helped her singing teacher to his feet. She gave his arm to her father and stepped back. Matthew passed the dazed man along the line. When Mr. Morgan reached Olana he bowed. "Good morning, Lady Hamilton. Quite a shaker this morning, was it not?"

"It was."

"May I assist you with your charges?"

"Yes, please."

The children went to him as if he were a favorite uncle with a teddy bear. Across the splintered and missing floorboards, Matthew had his daughter in his arms. She touched his blood-crusted face. "Daddy, you're all dirty," she chided.

The floor between them and Basil gave way.

"Get back!" Matthew shouted to his grandmother below. The bird cage slipped from the little girl's grip, and clanged onto an exposed pipe. Olana was sure Possum would follow, but Matthew's grip on her wrist held. He arched her behind him. She floated before her legs clamped around his back.

"Hold on to me, darlin'." Olana heard his whisper, and with it the knowledge he would not survive the loss of another child. She pressed her fist against her mouth when she saw his fingers' grip on the building's drainpipe. He inched his way along it until they reached the iron railing of Mr. Morgan's balcony.

"Here, Matt," Basil called out, holding the brass floor lamp, the one he'd brought to their marriage, the one Sidney teased him about, called "the funeral parlor lamp." Basil nudged Matthew's shoulder with its base. "Come on," he coaxed. "Trust me, Matt. I'm stronger than I look."

The skepticism in Matthew's eyes turned to hope. "I'm going to grab the lamp, Possum," he said. "Basil's got the other end, see? You think you might skitter across?"

"Then you'll come? And we'll find the bird?"

"Sure."

She loosened her grip on his neck, eased herself onto the ribbed brass bar. She looked back when only their fingers were still touching. "Like this, Daddy?"

"Perfect. Go on."

She reached Basil's outstretched hand. He passed her down the human chain, until she stood on solid flooring. Olana hugged the little girl close.

Another tremor. Matthew dropped his end of the lamp. Basil leapt on a new ledge that jutted out on the tilted building. Then all Olana heard was screaming, all she saw was a cloud of gray dust. She sheltered Matthew's child close against the one inside her. After an eternity of seconds, someone took her hand.

"Come." A voice. Matthew's voice. "Basil's fallen."

forty-four

The hall clock, stopped forever at 5:12 A.M., lay diagonally along a length of stairs.

In the kitchen, the dust still rose from Mr. Morgan's collapsed house. Matthew scanned the room the way he scanned the horizon of the Sierras. He stopped at the fallen-over stove, the spatula gleaming amid the dust. "Gran?" he whispered.

Nearby, her hand emerged, beaconing. Soon they were all flinging debris away. Annie Smithers reached her arm around her grandson's shoulder and spoke to her rescuers. "Careful. The boy's beneath me. I felt him breathing."

Matthew cradled her in his arms. They shared the same, winsomely slanted eyebrows, Olana realized, wondering why she'd never noticed it before. Olana took Possum's hand and followed him through the now byzantine passageway to the backlot garden, then through the narrow alley to the street.

There, Olana retrieved a quilted bedspread from her wardrobe and laid it over the cobblestones. Matthew set his grandmother down on it. Annie Smithers took his shaking hands while they were still probing the bones in her shoulders. "Stop fussing," she commanded. "Help them get Basil out."

"I can't do without you yet," Matthew breathed.

"Did Joe Fish heed you when you hauled him out of that tub?"

"He told you about—"

"Sure he told me. We had scant secrets by then left between us. I'll stay awhile, darling boy. But you got to stop shaking now. Plenty of work ahead."

"I love you, Gran," he whispered.

Mr. Morgan and the babies struggled through the crowd of wandering survivors and sat with them on the bedspread. Matthew planted a kiss on his grandmother's forehead, another on Olana's lips. He touched Possum's cheek before he disappeared behind the alley. Annie Smithers took Olana's hand. "The child?" she whispered.

"Moving."

"Good. That's good. Don't be frightened for Matthew. A touch of shock plaguing him, is all. He saw this day coming, you know."

"Yes."

"To know, and be powerless. What a curse his gift sometimes is."

Sidney's shout punctuated their quiet conversation. Olana stood, unsteady. Possum rested in Annie Smithers' embrace. That was strange, wasn't it? Why? Because Matthew's child hadn't touched her grandmother since the day Lavinia died, Olana remembered. Sidney called her again.

A stream of dust people appeared from behind the converged houses. Olana counted them, like lost jewels from a broken strand. Coretta and Patsy embraced their babies. The men gently placed Basil Hamilton on the street, hammocked in Olana's best white linen tablecloth.

"Go," Annie advised.

The circle opened to admit her. Basil's head was in Sidney's lap. Matthew knelt on one side of him, Serif on the other. Basil murmured in Sidney's ear. Sidney chatted back. It was as if they were up to one of their schemes, except for the tears that ran down Sidney's cheeks. Olana didn't think Basil could see the tears. She didn't think he could see anything.

Serif gave his place to her.

Her husband looked the way the rest of them did, except for how still he was lying. He coughed. There, another difference. Blood stained the front of his best cutaway opera formals.

Basil's hand found her face. "Olana. There you are," he breathed out. "And, Matt?"

"Here, Basil."

They didn't focus, but something devilish sparked her husband's eyes. "Now you won't have to kill me."

"Kill you?"

"As you did her first husband."

"I didn't kill him. My grandmother did."

"Ah—" Basil began to laugh a crushed, splintered version of his own laugh, until the fresh blood choked back that. But the bemused expression stayed on his face even in death.

"America," Sidney finished for him, closing the lids over his vacant eyes.

The five-story fortress that had been Agnews State Insane Asylum lay in ruins. Surviving patients were being tied to the small trees that somehow remained upright while the brick and steel lay all about them.

"Jesus of Nazareth is passing," yelled one. "I'm going to heaven in a chariot of fire—don't you hear the rumbling of the chariot wheels!" proclaimed another. Cal Carson sat up and looked over the small ridge. He smiled at people as demented as the new landscape after the earthquake. Why were the trees still standing? They could have quite a party if it weren't for the trees.

Cal bashed the dying attendant's head against the tree trunk, crushing bone. A last moan escaped the ruined face. No good. Cal was still entangled in his chains. Ezra rose from his work, ten feet away, his attendant dispatched with a single twist of the neck.

"Bloody murder!" came a shriek from a tree-bound woman, pointing up the hill, to them. Cal grabbed his brother's collar and pushed him down in the high spring grass. "Fuck her!" he spat out.

"Who?" Ezra asked, raising his head, "now?"

"Later," he promised.

"When?" his brother whined.

"Later. Get the key."

"Key?"

"In mine's pocket, dunderhead!"

The bigger man found the iron keys, unlocked his brother's chains and his own. They exchanged clothes with the dead men, then scraped away their beards and hair with the attendants' pocketknives.

Pleased, Cal sat back against the tree and surveyed the landscape behind them. They'd arrived at this place in the dark, in the rain, and had not been outside in all the months they were locked away in padded cells, restraint wings. On the single road that led to the asylum's isolated location, dust rose. The attendants stopped chasing their escaped charges and ran for the rescue team from San Jose. Fortuitous. Cal Carson stood.

"Well, brother dear, our way to an assignation with that wild-haired damsel is now clear. Though we will have to settle for vertical, rather than horizontal refreshment. After you," he said, with a mock sweep of his hand. Levity was lost on his brother, who was already running wildly down the hill.

When the woman saw them she screamed. But all of the madmen and women tied to the trees around her were screaming, too. Cal hoped Ezra wouldn't be long at it, as he was feeling the hot excitement, even while his brother fingered the madwoman's scraped and bloody arm as if she were a high-priced whore. Cal felt a hand at his shoulder.

"Attendant?"

He kicked his brother's shin before turning to the man.

"I'm Sheriff Ross."

Ezra turned. The woman shrieked louder. "I w-was trying to loosen her up—" he stammered.

"Your compassion for these poor souls is commendable. But you'll have to leave them bound. We've got the first batch of the worst injured ready for transport to San Jose. Can you drive the ambulance wagon?"

"We can, sir," Cal said.

"Good. Follow me."

They fell in step behind the officer. Cal's fingers itched.

"Sheriff?"

"Yes?"

"The road to San Jose will be full of escaped lunatics. Mighty violent. Oh, my brother and I could show you some scars!"

"Got but seven toes between us, sir!" Ezra tried to be helpful.

His brother shot him a murderous look, before he continued. "We'd want, if it came to it, of course, to protect the injured."

"I'll see that you're armed," Ross agreed.

"My brother and I thank you, sir."

"Murderers! Rapists! Murderers!" the woman bound to the tree shrieked.

Olana hooked the last of her light cape's closures within the privacy of the circle of women and girls all, caught, like her, in their nightgowns at the time of the earthquake. Only lark risers like

Matthew emerged even somewhat clothed. No matter. Now they were made decent by her wardrobe's crash to the street. She lifted the lid of the small chestnut box and drew out her brother's long-ago railroad car passenger version of her. She looked in the cracked mirror and smiled at her reflection. The clothes she wore almost matched the ones on the tiny doll, down to the peacock colors of the hat. She put the doll in the deep side pocket of her skirt and turned. "All finished, thank you," she said.

The women stepped back to reveal Matthew sitting on her vanity chair, his daughter on his knee, his grandmother blotting up the last of the crusted blood from his hair, his pale face. His plowman's nightshirt was now reined in by a maroon vest that he must have borrowed from Mr. Morgan's eccentric wardrobe. The single-breasted cutaway sack suit with its rounded lapels looked ten years out of fashion, and was too big. But it couldn't make him less handsome. Possum slipped off his lap. He stood slowly, taking her hand, looking at Olana as if he'd never seen her before.

Hoofbeats thundered in the debris-strewn street. The old black phaeton was drawn by a team of two fearless cab horses. Sidney Lunt, who had left wordlessly with Serif and the death wagon, had returned. He yanked two hastily clad men from the carriage, one short and bespeckled, the other lean and solemn. "Livermore and Wallace, clerk and reverend," Sidney announced.

The men looked at each other. The smaller one adjusted his spectacles. "I'm Wallace. This is the Reverend Livermore," he corrected.

Sidney frowned. "The papers," he instructed. "Hand them over. I'm on deadline."

"Papers?" Olana asked.

While the men searched, Sidney returned to the carriage and brought forth a huge bouquet of yellow roses and purple hyacinths. He approached, yanked a handful from his load. "Bride," he said, assigning them to Olana. He moved to Coretta. "Matron of Honor," he declared, shoving flowers into her hands. "Maid of Honor," he told Patsy, and "Best . . . Woman," honors went to Annie. "You get to give the bridegroom away. Flower girl," he said more softly, bending down and filling Possum's small arms with the remaining blossoms. Then he plucked single flowers for grooms-men Selby, Serif, and Mr. Morgan to pull through their buttonholes.

"What about the Best Man?" Matthew asked him quietly. Sidney emitted a quick shudder of a sigh. "He's . . . at another engagement. But I'm following his orders."

Olana touched his sleeve. "Sidney—"

He brushed her aside, scrutinized Matthew's suit. "You look like a damned organ-grinder," he pronounced. "Where's your watch?"

Matthew retrieved it from his vest pocket.

"Here's your wedding present. From Spense and me."

He handed over a gold chain that had belonged to Olana's husband. "Now you won't lose your watch. And you'll be on time for everything."

Matthew took the gift, then embraced the giver. Olana realized she'd never seen these men she loved best in the world do that, hug each other.

Word of the impromptu wedding of the peacock bride and her patchwork bridegroom had spread among the refugees of Stockton Street. They were closing in, whispering. Olana began to feel unbearably warm in her suit. Was this right? When Sidney reached for her, she backed away. He advanced. "You're not getting cold feet are you?"

"No. Warm. It's too warm."

He exploded. "I won't have it! Spense won't have it! This was all his idea, right down to where I might still find flowers! Are you going to refuse your dying husband's request?"

Olana ignored the heightened whispers. "My parents, Sidney. Aunt Winnie—"

"They were at your other weddings. Bring them some cake from this one. It's in the carriage."

"Cake?" She began a skittering giggle that she had to stop with her hand. He came closer, backing her further into the crowd. "Come on, sport. Wedding breakfast at your parents' house. Race you there. All right?"

"I don't even know if they're alive!" she almost screamed.

The sad-eyed reverend took her arm, searched her eyes. "Your generosity notwithstanding, Mr. Lunt, if this young woman is not up to it, I cannot possibly allow—"

"Up to it? Up to it? This is what she should have been up to two husbands ago, and she knows it!"

Olana felt Matthew's arms find her at last. She buried her head inside his coat. "Easy. Breathe easy, love," he advised softly. "They're alive," he whispered in her hair. "We would know it if they weren't."

Olana raised her head. "Do you think so, Matthew?"

"Sure. And it doesn't look like we'll be free to find them until Sidney has his wedding, so how about it?"

" 'How about it?' " his grandmother mocked his speech pattern behind him. "Looking to sweep her off her feet with your charm, are you?"

He cast her an irritated look, then was caught in his daughter's eyes, shining, expectant, above her bouquet. Other faces too, dozens of faces. "Uh—" he willed his voice to work. "Lady Hamilton. Will you do me the honor of becoming my legal wife in front of these here witnesses and magistrates before this city shakes itself into dust?"

Olana bowed her head so low he could only see the vibrant blue of the top of her hat. She felt the life inside her kick, and suddenly her mind cleared. "Oh," she answered the child's prompt, "yes."

After they'd pronounced their vows, Matthew felt a tug at his oversized coattail, then heard a small voice, his daughter's.

"Kiss her, Daddy."

"What?"

"Seals the deal," she informed him.

He looked to his grandmother. "Seal the deal," Annie Smithers told him in her brook-no-nonsense voice.

He raised Olana's face with his hand and discovered his grieving bride tear-stained. Suddenly her big hat was all the privacy he needed. He bent down and kissed her. He felt her reach around his neck, press him closer. Someone began singing. A piercing, breathtaking tenor.

> My love is like a red, red rose
> That's newly sprung in June.
> My love is like a melody
> That's sweetly played in tune.
> As fair art thou, my bonny lass
> So deep in love am I
> And I will love you still my dear
> Till all the seas gang dry.

It was Alisdair Dodge, bareheaded, with his camera. When he was finished, Matthew took Olana's hand and walked to him. She kissed his cheek.

"Why Alisdair, that was beautiful."

He grinned. "You think only the Welsh can sing?"

Matthew took the photographer's hand. "Alisdair. You're cold. You're so cold," he whispered.

"I was worried, about being here on time. To sing, to shoot a photograph—"Love in the Ruins" Mr. Lunt says to caption it, later, after the emergency editions. Later, when we're all laughing—"

"Take the photograph, double-quick. I've got a paper to get out!" Sidney interrupted. "Then get back up that hill, and keep shooting!"

"Take care of yourself, Alisdair," Matthew told him, before taking his place beside his bride, at the center of the glassplate image.

When the flashpot exploded, a cheer went up among the homeless of Stockton Street. The yellow bird rose up through Olana's house's ruins and headed west, toward the sea. Possum squeezed her father's hand. "He's free," she said.

Sidney gathered up the marriage papers hastily and handed them to Olana. "Here, you keep them safe. He'll be back down to his nightshirt before the morning's out." He nodded toward Matthew, who was putting his borrowed coat over an old man's trembling shoulders. Olana took the papers and put them beside her brother's gift in her deep pocket. She was ready.

"Come on," Sidney urged, "I'll get you up the hill to your father's house.

"We can't stop, Matt," he warned, as the carriage started up the hill, "I'm on deadline."

"Just slow down," he asked. Olana widened her stance behind him, holding onto his suspenders' braces as he hauled. By the time they reached her father's house, two wandering, shoeless children and a woman with a gash on her arm were added to the wedding party.

The mansion looked intact, there in the morning light. What struck Olana was the breeze blowing through the doorway, the open windows. No, she realized, not open, broken. Aunt Winnie was sweeping glass from broken solarium panes. She raised her head from her task as the coach drove up. "I knew if I looked after the greenery you'd come!" she called out. "Stop your crying you silly girl, we're fine, fine. Come in. Breakfast is on."

Matthew lifted the barefoot boy from Olana's lap and helped her from the coach. "Breakfast," she whispered.

"Imagine that?" he said. Sidney tapped his shoulder. "Send them my regrets. Got to shove off. Had to take your advice, Matt."

"Advice?"

"At the *Chronicle*. We've got no water, electricity, or gas. Yanked up the old hand-cranked machine out of the cellar. Serif's rigged a monkey wrench and flywheel to the press. We'll use our muscle to get out the morning edition of the story of the century."

"Watch your hyperboles," Matthew warned. "The century is young."

Sidney put the delicate buttercream confection of a wedding cake in Olana's hands and closed the coach door. Serif drove his team toward the *Gold Coast Chronicle* Building.

They turned, only once, before they entered James Whittaker's house, there on the top of Russian Hill. The morning's early light finally spilled over the rooftops, naked steel skeletons, and debris. Through it all, columns of white or black smoke rose from different parts of the city.

"Fires," Olana said.

Matthew's arm slipped around her waist. "Water mains are broke," he said. "Nothing will stop them."

"Couldn't you wait until I had some more of the nurse?"

"She was dead when you started," Cal explained again.

"Still pretty," Ezra contended. "And soft."

They sped faster now that they'd emptied their load of groaning injured on the side of the road.

"You're thinking, ain't you?" Ezra interrupted again.

"Yes."

"Of what?"

"Of the slim pickings around here. Of how this wagon deserves better, richer cargo now that we've ridded it of blaspheming loonies. I'm thinking of old scores. And where the real bounty will be."

"Where, Cal?"

"Why, San Francisco, brother mine."

forty-five

James Whittaker rose to his feet, leaning only lightly on his cane. Around him the babble of Italian, German, Irish, and Chinese neighbors silenced. He raised his glass, and spoke.

> He is half part of a blessed man,
> left to be finished by such as she;
> and she a fair divided excellence,
> whose fullness of perfection lies in him.

He watched with wonder as hushed, simultaneous translations finished. Everyone drank to his toast. He looked to the women at his side. "Was that all right, Dora? Winnie?"

"It was perfect," his wife assured him. His sister nodded her agreement.

He searched among the faces, the bandaged bodies, to find his daughter. She'd become a bride within the hour of being made a widow. Now she helped her new husband finish setting a woman's arm in a makeshift sling. Matthew's spectacles slid down his nose. Olana righted them, then held her champagne to his lips. She fed him a morsel of the wedding cake. Finished their joint task, she rested back in her husband's arms. He arched a wide, protective sweep of her middle. Good Lord, James Whittaker suddenly realized, she's carrying a child. He approached. Matthew stood, rolling his sleeves down.

"Is everyone comfortable, Matt?"

"Yes, sir." He pulled off his eyeglasses. "Mr. Whittaker, I think you should consider evacuation."

"What?"

"The fires. They've started already. There will be storms of them. Storms of fire."

"We've all had a terrible morning, Matt. But the house has withstood the worst. And we're close to the summit of second highest hill in the city. We'll be safe. We've become a refuge. These fires . . . the city will get them under control, son."

Matthew closed his eyes. "Maybe you're right," he said, though the firestorm raged there, behind his eyes. Olana hugged his arm. "I warned you there would be no moving Papa," she said.

"Go off to work, Matt," Mr. Whittaker advised.

"Work?"

"Yes. They will need you there, to assess damage, keep the bank open, prevent panic, that sort of thing."

Matthew looked around at all the need, and Olana. "We're safe. We'll be waiting for you," his father-in-law told him.

"Well. Maybe I can talk more sense into Mr. Amadeo," Matthew decided.

Olana held onto her father's arm. If she hadn't, she might have called after Matthew as he gave her that half-smile, before closing the gate. Annie had talked about the dazed look in his eyes. She'd called it shock. But didn't they all have it? Or was he seeing something else? Whatever it was, she wanted to be with him. Not safe. Her father patted her hand.

"Let him go, darling," he said. "Let him do something routine, normal. It will help settle him."

"Are you two crazy?" Matthew blared at the cashiers.

"Cra——zy?" Eltore, the one balancing the six-shooter, asked back.

"Give me that," Matthew said, putting out his hand and flinching only when the man did so, barrel first. "Eltore," he said more gently, "like this." Matthew pointed the weapon down, then placed it in his oversized vest's pocket. He sat on the stool, breathing deeply, trying to think. "Are your families safe?"

"Yes. And yours, Matthew?"

"We lost one."

"Who? Not your little girl?"

"No. One of my wife's people."

The cashiers patted his shoulder, looking puzzled. "Wife?" Titus asked.

"Olana. Lady Hamilton."

"Ah. Her lord . . ."

"Died. Yes. A fall. Helping me get my daughter."

"A good thing. He was doing a good thing."

"Yes. A good man."

They continued patting his shoulder as Matthew stared past them, at the three heavy canvas bags the two had been guarding when he walked in. "You brought our assets from the Bank of California's vault?"

"Same as every day," Titus explained. "We opened up at nine-twelve. A little late. No customers have come in. The women have not come in."

The women always knew best, Matthew thought suddenly. Olana didn't want him to leave her, leave her father's house. What was he doing here? "Well, without the women, we'd better close."

"Close?" Eltore didn't seem to understand the word any better than 'crazy.' "But, Matt, it is Wednesday."

Matthew flinched at the crash, then screams from the Chinatown refugees streaming past the storefront windows. He opened the door and fought his way through the running swarms to the middle of the street. It was strangely empty. And calm, like the eye of a hurricane. There'd been a collision between a merchant's and grocer's wagons. Crates of bamboo shoots, gaichoy, and dried sea slugs were still tumbling to the ground, gongs and trinkets were babbling in the hot gust of wind. Pinned under one wagon lay a big man in a gold embroidered tunic and greased hair. The dead merchant's crib girls were tied with silk cords that led from their wrists to iron rings on the brightly painted wagon. In their struggle to free themselves, their bonds were closing tighter. Their hands were swollen and purple. Their silk clothes were like bright, mad flags, their white painted faces, masks of terror. Around him, Matthew heard snatches of English among the panicked Chinese language. "Go back!" and, "Your brothers need you under the world!"

Matthew looked up the broad expanse of crushed stone and

brick, felled telegraph poles and bent back trolley tracks, to see the huge red bull of his nightmares. The sound the beast made pierced through all the others as a new machete entered his already bloodied side.

The bull stumbled, then raised his head. Their eyes met. Matthew widened his stance and stood, transfixed. He felt mesmerized by the strength and spirit of the animal, this bull caught with them in a labyrinth of destruction. Screams rent the air from the crib girls behind him. The bull swayed slightly, pawed the ground. Then he charged. Matthew's hands worked independently of his mind as they reached into his vest for the cashier's gun. It was only when he pointed it out in front of him that he had a fleeting hope that the weapon was loaded. He compressed the trigger. It was. The bull fell dead at his feet.

Matthew turned to the collided wagons. He put down the smoking gun and searched for his pocketknife. The girl he cut loose first fainted in his arms. He gave his knife to the one dressed in purple beside her. She freed the others, then all started bowing before him as he waved his hat in the unconscious girl's face.

"This little one needs water," he said. The woman in purple disappeared, but returned with a bowl she placed to the crib girl's lips. The girl drank, opened her eyes, smiled. Matthew gave her to another. They all began bowing again. He tried to show them how to rub the life back into their hands.

"There, good," he approved, when they followed his motions. "Best gather your things," he told their expectant faces. The one in purple translated. When he turned to battle his way toward the bank again, the small one tugged at his vest, then pulled her fine embroidered blouse down to reveal a primrose tattoo above her left breast.

"No," he said gently, taking her arm, leading her to where the one in purple was helping the others load makeshift packs for their backs. Matthew looked at their smeared, painted faces more carefully. They were children, underneath the paint, he realized sadly. They were all children.

"Master?" the girl in purple asked.

He glanced down at the fat merchant. "No. No more masters. Take care of each other now."

She nodded gently, and took the smaller girl under her arm.

Somehow Eltore and Titus had opened a pathway back to the bank for him. Mr. Amadeo stood in the doorway, shaking his head. A chain of hands worked against the crowd's flow to pull him inside.

His employer handed him the "closed" sign. Matthew put it in the window. Mr. Amadeo squeezed his shoulder as they watched the sea of humanity pass.

"Yes. The people leave. The bank will leave," he decided.

"The bank?"

The small man smiled. "We have no marble, no vault, no fancy chandelier. We have a movable bank, yes?"

"If we had wagons."

"Two wagons my brother, the grocer, will supply. Will that do?"

Matthew scanned the bank's chairs, desks, cabinets, and its three canvas bags of working asset currency. "Yes, sir," he said.

"Good. We must open again, Matthew. We must open where the people are." He glanced out the soot-laden window again. "Do you know where that will be?" he asked his employees.

Matthew saw the same disorientation he'd perpetually felt in this city mirrored in each of their faces. It was a comfort. He didn't care that it took an earthquake to accomplish.

"No? Well, first we find a place for our currency," Mr. Amadeo decided. From a distance, the men heard the dynamite squads setting off their first charges along California Street.

By late afternoon, the Bank of Naples was piled onto two wagons. Matthew looked back at emptied rooms that had given him his livelihood in this city. He felt unaccountably sad, even resistant. Behind a door of his office he found the new adding machine. He couldn't lift it alone. "Eltore! Mr. Amadeo!" he shouted, but they'd left.

Outside, the roar of fire, humanity, and explosions had grown louder. How was it affecting Olana, Possum, the baby? The thought made his heart race in panic.

"Matthew!" Mr. Amadeo called down from the driver's seat of the grocery wagon. "Come aboard!"

"The adding machine is still inside!"

"There's no more room."

"It cost three hundred and fifty dollars!"

Antonio Amadeo leaned down and tapped the side of his loan

officer's head. "We will have to depend on this adding machine for a little while."

"God help us," he muttered.

"Oh, he will, Matthew, he will!" His employer put out his hand and hoisted him up. "First, we go up Columbus Street, named for my countryman who loved America. He will guide us."

As they rode, Matthew saw the ferries running across the bay, their decks jammed with homeless. For how long would the ferries run? Mr. Amadeo took hold of his shoulder.

"Some go for Oakland. We must not. We must stay in the city."

Matthew sighed. "You sound like my father-in-law."

"Father—"

"Olana and I got married this morning, Mr. Amadeo."

"That's what Titus and Eltore were saying? It was her lord Englishman, the one of your people who died?"

"Yes."

"He was a gentleman, and I pray for his soul. But these are the Almighty's ways, Matthew, which your good Catholic daughter and I, we are trying to put into your heathen heart."

A fresh round of dynamiting. Then a shot rang over their heads.

"I said, halt!"

Mr. Amadeo's shaking hands dropped one of the reins, just as he was pulling in the other one. Matthew recovered it, and together they brought the frightened horses to a stand.

A dozen mounted federal troops surrounded the wagons. Their rifles were at the ready, bayonets fixed.

"Why didn't you halt when first instructed?" rapped out their leader.

Mr. Amadeo stood. "I am Antonio Amadeo—" he started.

"I didn't ask your name."

His second in command shoved his rifle butt into the banker's abdomen, sending him into Matthew's arms. "Shit," Matthew whispered out his bile of anger, then stood and faced the soldiers.

"We didn't hear you," he said evenly. An explosion that spooked most of the soldiers' mounts punctuated the statement.

"What are you carrying?" the commanding officer asked briskly.

"The Bank of Naples. Mr. Amadeo is the director. We three are his officers, Lieutenant."

One of the soldiers peered into the contents of the second

wagon. "Sure, I recognize this junk, sir! The dago bank! He pointed at Matthew. "This lunatic gave my sister a loan on the damned piano she uses to give lessons! She ain't even married!"

Matthew Hart smiled. "But the piano's paid for."

"It is?"

"Early—in eight months."

"Well, I'm damned."

"Here." The commanding officer shoved a printed paper at Matthew. When he slipped his hand into his vest pocket, Matthew heard the ram of a gun bolt. He froze. After the red bull, he didn't want to die for reaching for his spectacles. He showed them, watched the commanding officer. "Lower your weapon," the lieutenant finally told the rifleman. Matthew slowly pulled the wire rims out. His hands didn't shake. He willed himself not to give them that satisfaction. "Read it to them," the commander told him.

"There's a darkness curfew," Matthew explained quietly.

"In effect—" the officer looked, puzzled, into the black clouded sky, "uh—shortly. Follow it and the rest of the mayor's proclamation or be shot." The lieutenant drew up his reins, turning his mount. His second let his bayonet hover around Matthew's ear. "You're pale for a dago," he said.

The forces turned up Jackson Street.

Matthew growled low before he sat, opened his employer's vest and felt against the man's muscle walls. Mr. Amadeo lifted the paper from the seat beside him and read its proclamation.

"Authorized killing! Matthew, this is illegal!"

"Take a deep breath, Mr. Amadeo. In."

"Dictatorial!"

"And out."

"Unconstitutional!"

"Good."

"Mother of God! No! Not good, not here! Not in America!"

"We ain't in America tonight, sir. We're in Hell. And the army's in charge."

On Jackson Street, shouts were followed by three rifle shots. The banker resumed reading. "Three armies—'The Federal Troops, the members of the Regular Police Force, and Special Police Force.' We cannot reach my house before the black dark of night."

"Can we get these nags up Russian Hill?"

"Who is on Russian Hill?"

"It's where I left my family. Olana's father's house."

"You should be separated from your bride no longer," Mr. Amadeo decided. He turned to his officers in the second wagon. "The Bank of Naples is proud to stay in the city!"

Matthew sighed. "You'll get along real well with Mr. Whittaker, sir."

Olana felt so good pressed against him—clean, fresh, soft, with a lilac-colored ribbon wound through her braided hair. He kept holding her, letting James Whittaker trot off Mr. Amadeo for a tour of his house's defenses. "Have you eaten?" she asked him.

"Not since the wedding cake."

"Come inside. Mrs. Cole saved the last of the chicken for you."

He looked up at the sky. "No daylight. The day's done and there's been no daylight."

"It's because of the fires' smoke. Sidney delivered both editions of the *Chronicle*. It will explain. Come inside."

The entrance hall contained only a fraction of the refugees of the morning. "Where is everybody?" Matthew asked, feeling more like a dull child by the minute. Olana squeezed his hand.

"They've come and gone all day. Some went for the ferries, some to the Presidio, or Golden Gate Park. Some planned to camp out along Van Ness. Ours are in the kitchen, having a jolly time."

Matthew stopped inside the doorway to the back stairs. He saw the black cinders in her clean, fragrant hair. Where did they come from? From him? He kissed her forehead, leaving a smudge of black there. Yes, him.

Her smile quivered. "Matthew," she breathed. "We've had the newspapers. But also terrible stories. All day long. Of looters being shot, rats rampant, even of a red bull running loose from the stockyards, terrorizing. I—I can't stand to be separated from you any more. Where you go, I will have to go. I'm sorry!"

Her tears turned the grime on his shirt to sludge as he rocked her. "That's a good plan. I like that plan," he assured her.

In Mrs. Cole's kitchen, his grandmother was speaking to a roomful of survivors while Possum slept in her lap. "Not the Presidio.

I'm not going to be herded into any army barracks, and my Matthew ain't spending even a night under their rule again!"

He smiled sadly as he handed Annie Smithers the mayor's proclamation from his pocket. "Appears we already are, Gran."

She raised her head. "Look at you. You're not fit to partake of the last decent meal in San Francisco!"

Mrs. Cole blushed at his grandmother's compliment. They'd hit it off. He'd always known they would. Aunt Winnie came forward.

"Olana! Give him a bath."

"Upstairs," Dora instructed further, "in Leland's rooms. "Cold water, I'm afraid," she apologized to her new son-in-law.

"But—I'm starving!" he protested in the same tone he would have used with his own mother.

"We'll bring up supper on a tray. After you've eaten, and are feeling civilized, you may rejoin us," she proclaimed with formal, steely softness. An elderly Chinese man stepped between them.

"Bull slayer, you must bathe. To honor your elders, and to honor the spirit of the great creature." The small man's deep voice resounded off the brick hearth. It stunned them all to silence before he bowed politely. Matthew felt Olana take his arm. Her hands were as icy as the crib girls'.

"Matthew. It was true? There was a bull? And it was you?"

"He was all beaten down already," he tried to soothe her. "He was practically—"

The deep rumble of a voice from the hearth returned. "He was holding up a corner of the world! He would not allow himself to be killed by anyone unworthy of the task."

Matthew began rubbing Olana's hands. "I pulled a trigger. It doesn't take much sense to pull a trigger."

"You stole his spirit first," the Chinese man said, and smiled.

Matthew met his gaze. "Is that what I was doing? It felt like he was stealing mine."

"That is as it should be."

forty-six

The water was warmer than the mountain streams of the Sierras he'd bathed in, but Matthew groused about its chill, because it made Olana laugh, rub his back harder. She dug her fingers into his grimy scalp, but remembered to work around the morning's lacerations gently. Finally his teasing or filth or both must have overwhelmed her, because she threw the sponge at him, said "Soak!" and left the bathroom wiping her brow with the back of her hand.

Matthew wondered if he should go after her, but decided to obey, though there were tears in her eyes. They were the tears of the chocolate cake afternoon in St. Pitias, tears that were often threatening in those days they were waiting for Lavinia. If they could get through this dangerous crimson time, they would wait again, dream again. Olana would give birth to another child. A healing child.

He leaned back in the water, enjoying the pulsing silence. He closed his eyes. For only a moment he thought. But when he opened them she was back, her cheeks glowing as she stroked his forehead. The love he felt dug deeper into his being. The bathroom was warmed and scented by the candles she'd placed on every shelf in a lighted path back to the nursery's rooms. When he stood she placed a towel over his shoulders, but he preferred drying himself against her full white apron as he embraced her.

"You must eat," she told him between gasps. But it was her wondrous, changing shape that interested him now. He carried her to the bed.

Laid out on a table beside it, on cream-colored linen, was their wedding supper and the last decent meal in San Francisco. Matthew took a sprig of mint from the butter dish. He danced it against his bride's bottom lip. She bit into half, then pressed the rest to his mouth. He chewed slowly, pausing to kiss her temple, earlobe, neck, as his hands worked to free the ties of her apron, the mercifully few buttons of her simple day gown. She pulled the towel off him and began kneading his shoulders, urging with the vibrant tones of her full, rich voice.

When down to her last layer of fine cambric, Matthew drew her under the covers, taking a hyacinth blossom from Mrs. Cole's vase and coursed the flower along her bared side.

The heavy curtains were pulled against the red glow of fire. The explosions so continuous they sounded like a bombardment muffled and finally silenced under Olana's cries of pleasure at his ear. After her first peak, Matthew reached across her for a lily of the valley. He loved her until all the flowers had joined them under the covers.

Sleep was ambushing his empty stomach's protest. Olana nestled close. "Done, Mr. Hart," she whispered.

"Done?"

"We're consumated. I've got you now."

"You've had me since you pounded the evils of the world into one of my poor trees, Mrs. Hart."

He heard a soft knock. Olana soundlessly slipped back into her day gown before Matthew could figure out where he'd left his clothes. "At the bed's feet," she said as if he'd asked. As if they'd been consumated twenty years instead of twenty minutes. He reached for the long, starched and folded shirt, a leftover from another time, from his first stay in this room.

Olana opened the door. Matthew heard his grandmother's voice, uncharacteristically apologetic, then saw his daughter slip between the women's skirts and leap into the bed with him.

"Well, you had a good nap, Flibbity-gibbet," he said.

Possum touched the scar at his throat. "You came back," she cried, then buried her head in his chest. He cast a pained look toward his grandmother. She shrugged. "Seeing is believing," Annie said.

Possum lifted her head. "Did you find my mana?" she asked.

"Mana's in Ireland with Farrell," he told her gently.

"Did the sea swallow Ireland? Swallow them like it swallowed my mother?"

Matthew hesitated. "We'd best check the *Chronicle*," he decided. "Olana, do you have the latest edition?"

She put the four-sheet newspaper into his hands, as his grandmother found his spectacles. He settled back in the pillows with his daughter snug against him.

He looked up at the women. Annie Smithers' fine, worn hands were wound around his wife's waist. "Ah, here it is," he said, folding the paper to the story of the progress of the fire down Market Street. " 'We are happy to inform the citizens of San Francisco, and especially its children, that the rest of the world, including our own North and South American continents, Asia, Australia, Africa, and Europe, including that lovely green island known as Ireland, is safe from the calamity that has befallen us. Ireland and all its inhabitants are having themselves a fine spring day.' "

Possum tugged at his shirtsleeve. "What about the seals, Daddy?"

"Seals?"

"The ones on Seal Rock—down by the Cliff House."

"Oh yes, the seals. Ah, here it is . . . 'the boys and girls of San Francisco will also be heartened to know that the seals, whose antics they've delighted in along the city's shoreline, are safe. Being more intelligent than their human counterparts, they took themselves and their families to the open sea at the first sign of disturbance.' "

The little girl's eyes went suddenly sad. "I wish we'd gone with them," she said.

Annie Smithers' hold on Olana's waist tightened.

Matthew began searching through the newspaper again. "Hey, listen to this—'Though news of the earthquake dominates this edition, the *Gold Coast Chronicle* is pleased to announce that Miss Wesoma Hart of 435 Valencia Street now has a new mother to add to her collection of womenfolk including grandmothers, great-grandmother, godmothers, and fairy godmothers. At the ceremony Miss Hart was resplendent in a white nightgown trimmed in . . . ah, in . . .' "

He looked to the women for help and Olana mouthed "blue."

" 'In blue. She carried a lovely bouquet which set off her hair to new heights of beauty. The wedding party retired to the home of Wesoma's new set of grandparents, to eat a wedding cake of . . .' " Now he glanced at the top layer set out on the table. " 'Ivory roses and silver nonpareils.' "

He peered at his daughter above the rim of his spectacles. She was smiling.

"Is Alisdair's photograph of us in there, Daddy?"

Matthew searched through the sheets. "I'm afraid not, darlin'."

"I'll draw one and we can put it in the paper. I'll glue it right . . . there," she pointed.

"That's a good idea."

Olana sat beside them on the bed. Possum turned to her. "You didn't wear a white veil," she said.

"I wore my biggest hat."

"You looked pretty."

"Thank you. So did you."

"Will you take care of me now?"

"I'd like to help all your other mothers."

"Good. I like your house, Olana. It only shakes a little here."

Olana stroked the child's hair. "Would you have dinner with us?" she asked. "We were just starting."

Possum looked from Olana to her father, to the blossom-strewn sheets in that peculiar way that made Olana feel the child was older than both of them put together. She giggled. "Why are you eating flowers?" she asked. "There's chicken!"

Olana and Matthew stared at the two soot-covered men as they dug in the cold ashes of the servants' parlor hearth. On the sofa, beside Dora and Winnie Whittaker, three bags of gold and silver, still in their grapefruit crates, waited.

"Mr. Amadeo? Mr. Whittaker?"

His employer stopped his digging. He stood, and took hold of Matthew's shoulder. "As my senior bank officer, I charge you to remember where the liquid assets of the Bank of Naples are presently located. You will remember, even though it is your wedding night and your lovely bride stands at your side. Where, Matthew?"

"In the fireplace, sir?"

A grin lit the small man's face. "Very good! *Bellissimo!*"

"Stop teasing the boy," Dora Whittaker chastised, rising from the sofa.

"Can't you see he's falling asleep on his feet?" Aunt Winnie took up the cause.

"And he is not to join you mad chimney sweeps in your task," Dora insisted. "You look very nice, Matthew. Don't go near them."

Maybe he should have gone to bed, after his head fell into his piece of wedding cake, making his daughter laugh before she fed him the rest. Now he watched, astonished, as Olana's mother took up one of the heavy canvas sacks. "Here," she grunted, passing it to Winnie, who thumped it at the men's feet. They carefully buried it deep in the firebox.

"Your women are strong!" Mr. Amadeo proclaimed.

"They have been hauling me around for the better part of a year," James Whittaker said. Mrs. Cole entered the parlor with glasses of his prized champagne on a silver tray.

Mr. Amadeo took his. "Mr. Whittaker has provided our vault! His home becomes the Russian Hill branch of the Bank of Naples! We, the people will rebuild this city together!"

Matthew and Olana slept on Leland's bed, pushed into a doorway. Friends and family were all about. At Matthew's right side was Possum, while on Olana's right Coretta and Andrew dozed. Across their feet Annie Smithers was stretched out, snoring lightly. Under another arch, Olana saw her parents in the middle of a bed that contained Aunt Winnie and Mrs. Cole. Everyone, both loved ones and strangers, was within her sight. She didn't mind a whit.

She felt Matthew turn, encircle her waist as his daughter's leg crashed across his ribs. He winced. Olana giggled. She called Sidney, who was tossing nervously out beyond Annie Smithers.

"What is it, sport?" he asked.

"Can't you sleep?"

"I *was* sleeping."

Weeping too, she thought. At last. "Sidney?"

"Yes?"

"I think Basil would find our wedding night most amusing," she whispered.

On a hill of rubble in Chinatown, Alisdair Dodge perched. It was almost midnight, but he could see clearly enough to read the final edition of the *Gold Coast Chronicle* he held between his hands. Down along Stockton Street, a red wall of fire rose. Blasts of explosives rang out regularly. He read on, proud of the *Chronicle* for getting out two single sheet editions before the fire engulfed the building.

Alisdair had liked watching the faces of frantic, rumor-plagued people calm as they read the accurate account of the disaster. It was so accurate that the mayor had personally signed passes for his editor Sidney Lunt to distribute to his staff. Alisdair had his own safe in his vest pocket. He closed the newspaper, leaned his head on his arms.

He loved the streets of Chinatown, so different from the gray, worn concourses of his native Glasgow. He looked over the ruins, framing photographs in his mind's eye, out of habit. Even if he had any film left, use of his flashpots had been strictly forbidden as a fire hazard. Only the legalized arson and crazy dynamiting that was starting new fires all over the city was sanctioned.

Chinatown, deserted. Were the rumors that a giant red bull had caused the panic true? Did the population flee because of the ancient belief that the world was supported on the backs of four bulls, and one had gotten loose from the stockyards? Perhaps he could find the remains. Sidney would love the story. Olana could write it beautifully.

Olana and Matty, married at last, by executive order of her dying husband. That would never have happened among Presbyterian Glaswegians. He loved singing for them. His life had seemed perfect at that moment. Anything could happen, here on the wild western rim of America.

Alisdair crossed Columbus, turned onto Kearney. In the middle of that block something moved, something embedded in a mound of rubble. No, not rubble. Something alive, rippling with gray, black, brown, and red movement. An explosion in the distance lit up the night sky and Alisdair recognized the gleaming machete, and the rats swarming over the body of the bull. Rats, freed by opened sewer lines. Alisdair swayed back on his heels, sickened by the sight, by the prospect of another story—plague.

Wild, demented laughter cleared his head. Six men in National Guard uniforms lurched out of the shadows. They began bayonetting the rats, spearing two or three of them through their bellies with a single thrust. Alisdair slid behind the remains of a wall and watched. All of the men had gunny sacks. Once the quicker rats had dispersed, the guardsmen entered buildings, throwing out bronzes, brasses. Cramming their sacks and pockets with jewelry.

Alisdair pressed himself closer to the wall. He doubted his pass would do him any good if he were caught here, by these men. Across the brickface, someone had scrawled: "I hate the nigger cause he's a citizen, and I hate the yellow dog because he won't be one." Ugliness was here, too. In America. In the words. In these men's actions. The words increased his panic. It was all he could do to keep his legs from running. California Street. If he could reach California Street. The laughter came closer. He left the protection of the ruin, and began walking.

"Halt!"

He stopped, turned slowly. Two soldiers, their sacks dropped at their sides, their rifles pointed, faced him. "What are you doing here?" one of them demanded.

"I—have safe passage," he said, then reached inside his vest pocket. His fingers had barely touched the paper before the shot. He looked down below the second button of his vest and saw a gaping hole. He continued to pull the pass from his pocket. It was out before his knees buckled and the cobblestone street rose up to meet his face.

He was aware of overwhelming pain, so intense it distorted the gathering voices around him.

"Looter, sir."

"Not through the middle, you damn fool. Shoot them in the back. Shows they've been running away!"

Alisdair felt his whole body shake from the force of the second shot. But after it, there was no pain at all.

"Let's go. The fire's reaching Chinatown. The firemen are coming."

The footsteps faded. Alisdair was alone. Fire. Rats. He didn't want either one gnawing at him, even if he couldn't feel it. The pass fluttered between his fingers, white splattered with crimson blood. A large hand attached to a large man in a hospital orderly uniform, took it.

"Hey Cal!" he shouted, "What does this say?"

Another orderly, one who carried the left side of his body strangely, stood beside the first.

" 'Safe passage . . .' A pass! Signed by Mayor Schmitz himself. You've found a treasure, brother mine!"

"Here. I'll trade you for the long knife."

"Gather up your trinkets—we don't have to sneak about any longer. This is our passport to the richer realms of the city!"

Alisdair watched them go, sad that he couldn't hold on to the paper, sad that the men wouldn't be moving him away from the rats, the fire, even if he was dying. Another explosion lit up the midnight sky. He closed his eyes against the force of it. When he opened them again, the streets of Chinatown were alive again, more bright and beautiful than he'd ever seen them. People came out of their homes, stores. The red bull rose, glorious and strong and with laughing children on his back. No one was afraid as the bull romped among the vendors. The people's faces radiated joy, the joy Alisdair had only seen in quick flashes during parades and street fairs. The joy he'd been too much of a shy Scotsman to ever court. The crib girl, the one he'd taken a photograph of before she'd fallen to her death, now approached him, glittering in her beauty. She knelt down, lifted his head into her lap, and put something in his mouth. He closed his eyes in delight. It was Annie Smithers' peach pie.

Matthew Hart felt someone shake his left shoulder. He squinted into the darkness, saw a child standing beside the bed.

"Possum?" he whispered. "You need something, darlin'?" He propped himself on one elbow, squinting. The child pushed him down again.

"Matthew," he said, the impatience in his voice and coldness in his hands both familiar. "It's me."

"Leland?"

Someone stepped out of the shadows behind the child and put a hand on his shoulder. Matthew looked up, past the gaping red hole in the man's middle.

"Alisdair. Jesus, what did they do to you?"

"It doesn't matter now, Matty." He smiled. "But I'm wanting you to find my photographic film. Give it to Sidney."

"Where is it?"

"Lafayette Square. You'll pass there tomorrow."

"I will?"

"On your way to the park," the child said.

"What park?"

"Golden Gate. Tomorrow. Don't forget. The children are waiting, Matthew."

"What children?"

The boy glanced up at the man. "He's very curious, isn't he?"

They stepped back into the shadows together. Wait. Please. The words formed in Matthew's mind, but he couldn't push them past his lips. "Laney!" he called out.

"It's only the explosions," she promised, kissing his face, parting and reparting his hair with her fingers until his eyelids grew heavy again.

forty-seven

Matthew Hart walked under the sheltering leaves in her father's solarium. James Whittaker was already there.

"I've stolen your serenity place?" he said.

"I've stolen your daughter."

"Stolen?"

"We married without your permission yesterday. I ask your pardon for that, sir. It was the circumstances. I had to wrestle her down before she slipped away from me again."

James Whittaker smiled. "I think you might have that reversed."

Matthew sat beside his new father-in-law under the sassafras tree. "I'll work my life long to prove myself worthy of her," he promised.

"Matthew. Am I right in thinking Olana is with child?"

"Yes, sir."

"Can you accept the baby, Matt?"

"Accept?"

"As your own."

"It is my own."

"That is very generous of you to say, son, but—"

"It's not at all generous. Olana and I have been lovers for a long time."

"But, Basil—"

"Knew. Approved. He and I, we even became friends, by the end. Isn't that a wonder?"

"How—"

"Theirs was an unconsummated marriage, sir."

"Oh. Oh, I see."

Matthew shrugged. "Like you said, Mr. Whittaker. Olana shocks everyone. Even you."

"Especially me, Matt."

The rumble of the aftershock came, followed by the sickening sound of mechanical failure. The pump of the solarium's artesian well was broken.

"We'll fix it, shall we, son?" was his cheerful reaction.

"Uh, sure," Matthew agreed.

"I'll get tools."

Matthew felt like a child playing in the mud hole beside Olana's father, who never doubted they would succeed. "Matt, I think you and Olana's brother would have hit it off splendidly."

"Yes."

"He would have brooked no nonsense from either of you, though. He would have made you marry Olana years ago."

"I imagine so."

"Still, you found your own path to each other, didn't you? Maybe that will make you both stronger, for what's ahead. Matt, when I was locked inside myself, after the stroke, I remember reaching such a state of utter frustration that despair threatened. It was then I—now, you must promise not to laugh—"

"I won't laugh, sir."

"I thought my son came back. I thought he told me to be patient, because you were coming. As if the two of you were already old friends."

"Imagine that."

"I can imagine it, Matt. I can now."

The pump held together more on his father-in-law's optimism than workmanship. As they finished, a smoky dawn haze filtered through the trees of the solarium. Matthew had to obey his visions, his ghosts, just as this man did. With which of them would Olana stay? The thought of her between them pained him. "We'll fill all the bathtubs, every sink and basin," James said, "before you go."

"Go, sir?"

"Yes. I entrust my family to your care, Matt. So does Antonio. Will you find a good refuge for them all until we can join you?"

"Sure."

"Splendid. Antonio and I will concentrate on keeping the place soaked down."

"Mr. Whittaker, promise you'll leave if your hope for saving the house is gone."

There was a rustle of skirts in the solarium doorway. "We'll promise for him, because we'll be hauling him out!" Dora Whittaker said. Aunt Winnie put a cup of steaming coffee into Matthew's hands and peered down the hole.

"You'd better show me what you did to get that pump spewing again, forester," she said. "That rig-up doesn't look like it's going to hold past midday."

Matthew caught the scent of hyacinths through the dull gloom. He saw the tips of Olana's low-heeled lace up shoes. Her skirts folded over them as she bent down to give him her hand. Its third finger was circled in gold and garnets. She had her coat on, and his draped over her arm. "We're ready," she whispered in a steady voice that did not match her swollen eyes. She'd made her decision.

Sidney and Serif stood like sentinels at Olana's side. Her mother and Aunt Winnie performed the same function for her father, there in the doorway of the home she loved. Mr. Amadeo told Matthew possible places his family may have camped for the night, if he did not find them at home. Possum listened intently at her father's side. Everyone else was at the gate, waiting to join the early morning stream of refugees. Olana felt the strength of her parents' and aunt's last embrace. She was proud to come from such people, to be bearing a child who would carry their strength beside Matthew's gentle goodness.

Matthew shook Mr. Amadeo's hand and lifted his daughter high in his arms as they approached her father. Possum put her small palms on either side of his cheeks, the way she had on the days she visited him during his recovery. James Whittaker smiled slowly, consciously working to life both sides of his mouth together.

"How was that, little one?" he asked her.

"Perfect."

He took Matthew's shoulder. "Don't look so forlorn! Did you forget your Christmas vision? We have the champagne, if it comes to that."

Sidney cocked his head. "Champagne? That's right!"

Mr. Amadeo winced. "Is it not alcohol, gentlemen? Will it not feed the flames?"

"No," Matthew assured him. "The proof's not high enough." He looked sideways at Sidney and Serif. "St. Croix rum, now that's flammable." Olana watched her new husband's face break into a smile. "You'd sacrifice all that future happiness?" he asked her father.

"I have all the happiness I can hold." James Whittaker touched Possum's cheek fondly. "But I fully intend to romp with this grandchild and future ones. Here, in this house!"

When they reached Van Ness, they saw the field artillery weapons pointed from the far side of the avenue toward the houses opposite. Behind them, barricades of household goods, from trunks to beds to baby buggies were mounted against the enemy, fire. Matthew scanned the anxious faces of people who had gone a day and night without sleep. Some were numb with shock, some close to hysteria. He held Olana closer, smoothed the back of his daughter's small hand. He kept the wagons moving.

Along the barricades of Van Ness they heard screams that sounded like Mrs. Amadeo in childbirth, then men's shouts.

"Get out of there, you filthy dagos! You're blocking the way!"

"I wait! I wait for my husband!"

"Fifty dollars says he's boiled himself in his own tomato sauce!"

Matthew braked the wagon. "Selby, if you'll hold the reins?"

"Got them, Mr. Hart."

At the other wagon, Sidney and Serif slid down. "Go, Matt," Sidney instructed. He led their way through the circle. They found a small citadel of trunks, a sewing machine, mattresses, and three bird cages stuffed with silverware. Matthew recognized the bird cages.

"Mrs. Amadeo?" he called. A fork went flying by his ear and landed in Serif's massive arm. Serif grunted and pulled it out, grinning. "Mama, no!" Cara pleaded, "it's Matthew!"

A crack opened in the fortress. Children poured through, surrounding him. Two young women with delicate features, one carrying her pregnancy large and low, rushed to the wagons and their husbands, Eltore and Titus. Finally, Mrs. Amadeo stood before him, her squalling twins anchored to her hips.

She released her children to him. Then he helped her over the mound of mattresses. "My husband—"

"He sent us to find you, Ma'am. To get you to a safe place."

"Where is it safe, Matthew? Safe for the burning eyes, the deafened ears of my children?"

Possum appeared at her father's side. She squeezed the woman's hand. "Daddy will take us where it's cool and green," she promised.

Mrs. Amadeo's haunted eyes underwent a seachange. "Good," she said, kissing Matthew's cheek. "This I have prayed for. A green place. I have many sheets. Clean white sheets, so you and your women can help Josephina."

"Josephina?"

Matthew glanced at the pregnant woman on Eltore's arm. He saw a familiar look in her eyes. "Gran," he called. Annie Smithers' eyes were merry. "Easy, Matthew. Her first, and it looks to be early yet."

The men loaded sheets, blankets, mattresses, women, and children into the wagons. Mrs. Amadeo took charge of the bird cages and her frantic twins.

Even Sidney became disoriented as they rode through streets that held little more than charred rubble. They had used up most of their drinking water when he saw a patch of ground ahead.

"I—think that's Lafayette Park, Matt. There's a garden, or, there used to be a garden there, with a water supply, pumped up by a windmill."

Matthew sat up higher. "We'll stop, rest."

"The soldiers could confiscate the wagons. And Josephina—"

"Her pains are twenty minutes apart. We'll rest."

The men stayed with the wagons, Sidney's derringer and Eltore's six-shooter prominently displayed in their coats, while Matthew led the women and children through a square piled high with goods left by people burned out of their homes.

How could he find Alisdair's film in all this, he wondered, walking, scanning for the photographer's canvas bag. Nothing was familiar among all the abandoned possessions.

"Sit down, son," someone said. "You look spent."

The man was mostly bald, with a round, pleasant face. The soot everyone sported had set his face's lines deeper. But on him it looked different, because he had only laugh lines sprouting from his eyes. The man gestured toward a small ring of stones encircling a fire. Matthew took a place beside him and stared at the rows of delicate china cups mounted on saucers. Beside them plates piled high with crusts of buttered toast sat precariously among the ruin. The man put coffee into the Dresden china cup, then into Matthew's hands. "I was about to close up shop!"

"Shop?"

"Callahan's Coffee Shop and Musical Oasis—" he gestured to the abandoned upright piano. "Fursey Callahan, proprietor, and your own, your very own servant."

Matthew remembered Sidney's stories of price gouging, and backed away from the tantalizing smell of the bread and coffee. "I don't have any—"

"As much as you'd like for nothing," Fursey Callahan assured him, pressing the steaming cup into his hands. "Keep me company, there's a good lad." He gathered the remaining fine china cups, placing them gingerly in one of the two sacks he had strung across his chest. Even with the weight of his possessions, the elfin man seemed to Matthew as light as gossamer. And his coffee could revive the dead.

"Have you been here all night, Mr. Callahan?"

"Oh, aye. And it was great fun while it lasted. Look around you, son! Each stick of furniture, each carpet and painting shows what their owners prized most. Me, I was interested in food. Collected it, then the dishes, for my shop. Fed the folks all night, I did. But the rats, they're cheeky now, and big as tomcats. Time to move on. Eat the bread, your hands will get jittery from the coffee alone, Doctor."

"What?"

"Are you not a doctor then?"

"No, sir."

"But you use your hands in your work, do you?"

Matthew thought of shaking immigrants' hands, of holding Possum, of stroking Olana's hair, of the feel of new babies. "Yes," he said.

"You haven't had a care about the rest of your appearance, but your hands are looked after."

Matthew thought of Olana not letting him touch the splintered glass in his head. "That's my wife's doing," he said.

"Ah, a woman of true sensitivity, your wife! She knows what has value! Have more of the bread, son." He reached into one of his sacks. "I've got to travel light, so I can't keep my promise to the Scotsman," he said sadly, almost to himself.

Matthew's head jerked up. "What Scotsman?"

"A photographer fellow. Asked me to look after his stash. Said if he didn't come back, he'd send someone for it. I didn't want to be burdened, but the look in his eyes and our Celtic blood tie made me go all sentimental. He said the one who came for it would be easy to spot, seeing as he'd have a dozen or more women and children trailing after him. But there's been no one—"

"Here he is!" Cara Amadeo shouted.

Matthew felt Olana's arms around him first. She kissed his temple just as Possum jumped on his back. All the Amadeo children, hauling the twins, Hugh, and Andrew in a play wagon swarmed around him, grabbing the buttered toast from his plate.

"Oh, look. A piano!" Coretta shouted, and called the two women walking Josephina through her pains closer. She sat down and began playing "Home Ain't Nothing Like This" as they sang.

Matthew took the canvas bag of Alisdair's film from the sprite man's hand. "Would you like a ride to Golden Gate Park, Mr. Callahan?" he asked, convinced that even with his bread and crockery sacks, the man weighed nothing at all.

forty-eight

The shadows of the willow leaves danced gracefully on the roof of the makeshift tent. Even Josephina smiled at it, once her contraction eased. Olana wet the laboring woman's lips with a moist cloth. "Almost there," she whispered at her ear.

Matthew looked into Olana's shining eyes and found a haven. He turned to his grandmother. She was not beside him. A thin line of perspiration sprouted on his brow. "Where's Gran?" he whispered. Mrs. Amadeo touched his back.

"Called away," she answered.

"Away? Away where?"

Another contraction started. The young woman bellowed.

"Down," Olana reminded her, "send the push down."

Josephina looked between her legs. "A fish!" she screamed.

Matthew steadied her. "No," he explained quietly. "Your waters didn't break, remember? Keep pushing."

The head came into his hands, still inside the pod. Matthew tore at the membrane with his fingers. The water gushed forth, along with the rest of a purple baby. He put the child over his knee and rubbed her back.

"Come on, little girl," he coaxed. "Breathe." He put his smallest finger in her mouth, cleared it. The baby remained still. "Call her, Josephina," he heard his own steady voice urge, though his eyes were clouding with tears.

"Come," the exhausted young mother called in a high, heart-breaking voice. "Let me see you, my beautiful daughter."

He lifted the baby gently, his palm under her abdomen, and placed her between her mother's breasts. She hiccoughed.

"Alive!" Mrs. Amadeo shouted, blunting her cry with the back of her hand. The baby took in another breath, coughed, then howled indignantly at the laughter around her.

Once the afterbirth was delivered safely and he'd cut the cord, Mrs. Amadeo put her bundled new granddaughter in Matthew's arms. "Go, you and your bride. Take her out to visit with her father. Send in my Cara *mia*. Together we will make Josephina all beautiful, we'll make the basket a fine bed. Go, go."

Outside, the men were thumping Eltore's back, pouring red wine in his cup. When Matthew and Olana approached, he refused to take his new child into his arms. But he did rush toward the tent to see his wife, doubling back to smear Olana with a kiss and his thanks. Olana laughed, wiping her wine-stained cheek.

"You got it this time, did you?" Matthew teased. Olana took his arm and they walked the baby to a stand of locust trees. There they saw Annie Smithers, holding a pink flannel bundle. Matthew grinned. "Another birth," he said. As they met, he peered over his grandmother's shoulder.

"Boy," she said proudly.

"Girl," he retorted.

"Ten pounds," she counterattacked.

"Born in the sack."

"The mothers . . . ?" she tried to break their tie.

"Well."

"Well."

"Nice work, Gran," he finally conceded.

"Nice work, Matthew."

Olana laughed. "The end!" she pronounced.

"Oh no. There's plenty more," Annie informed them.

"More?"

"Three in active labor, seven fully dropped and ready to start. Turned away at the make-shift hospital—doctors say they're too busy with the injured and dying. Best make that tent bigger, they're all heading this way. You picked a fine spot, Matthew."

She turned and trudged in the direction she'd come.

Olana smiled. "It will certainly keep our minds off any aftershocks, or lack of comfort, or—"

He kissed her mouth, letting his birth exhilaration loose.

"Get that baby back to her mother!" Annie admonished loudly from the crest of the hill.

* * *

His grandmother leaned over them, her fists at her hips. "Rest," she demanded. "Both of you."

Matthew looked toward the young woman walking on her mother's arm. "But Mrs. Patterson . . . it's her first, Gran."

"You caught Mrs. Patterson's third boy two birthings ago, Matthew. That's Mrs. Peterson."

"Oh."

She wrapped them both in a blanket that smelled of cedar. Olana's eyelids were drooping, though the smile remained on her lips. Matthew snatched at Annie Smithers' skirts.

"Hey, Gran."

"What is it now, you rude boy?"

"You keeping count?"

She leaned over, drew the blanket to his shoulders. "I'd better. Ain't depending on any no-account banker."

"Then you know I'm still three up on you."

"Two. And we'll see how it tallies in the end."

"I believe you drugged me, just so you can catch up."

She gave out a snort of disgust. "Ungrateful apprentice," she muttered as she walked off toward the laboring woman.

Sleep ambushed Matthew Hart while he was still laughing.

The next he heard was Callahan's voice. "That does it. If the smell of my brew doesn't move him, he's departed this life." Matthew heard laughter and tried to pull his eyelids open. Then a woman screamed. He bolted up.

"Send it down, Ma'am, come on, baby's coming," he told Callahan, an assortment of wide-eyed children, nervous fathers, and sleeping dogs. Callahan's laughter continued as Matthew ran for the tent.

His eyes lingered on his wife's face as his grandmother spoke softly at his ear. "Mrs. Henley. Birthing a seven-month child, maybe five pounds. Short, fierce labor. Waters just broke and . . . we got a problem, Matthew."

The woman was not in one of the common positions for birth. She lay propped on her side, her eyes closed, moaning softly. Olana was on her knees behind her, holding a damp cloth between her legs. Matthew approached, lifted it to discover a tiny blue hand.

"Transverse," he breathed.

"I tried outside turning. Twice."

"Gran. This lady needs a doctor."

Annie let out an exasperated grunt. "Sent for. None's come." She took his face between her soft, tanned leather hands. "Darlin' boy," she whispered. "We will lose them both soon. I want you to try."

"All right, Gran," he said softly, trying to ease the burden she'd carried alone while he slept. He approached, knelt down on the mattress beside the laboring woman. "Evenin', Mrs. Henley. How's my wife treating you?"

A smile lit the woman's broad face as she opened her eyes. "She is an angel. I don't want to frighten her, her being this way . . ."

He glanced up at Olana. "Don't concern yourself on that account. She's braver than any three men, like the rest of you all." Mrs. Henley started to laugh, then grimaced as a contraction began. He put his face close to hers. "Blow it out, ma'am. Let it go."

Her jaw clenched. "I can't. I have to push."

He blew in her face. "Like this," he urged.

She blew back at him. He caught the scent of licorice root. "Good, good," he said as the contraction eased. She took his arm.

"I have six other children, Mr. Hart. All healthy," she said quietly. "They need me."

"Sure they do, ma'am. Keep thinking of that." While I'm putting you through almighty hell, he finished to himself. Olana's hand descended over the woman's brow and stroked it. Matthew leaned over and kissed his wife's knuckles.

"My," Mrs. Henley breathed there, under the kiss.

Matthew took her hand. "Do you give your other little ones horse rides, ma'am?" he asked.

"Not lately," she said.

Soft laughter.

"I want you to get up like that, on all fours, you know?"

"What?"

"We'll help," Annie told her, "and Matthew will keep you company while Olana and I make you decent."

"All right," she said uneasily.

Matthew shifted the pillows higher under the woman's head as Olana and Annie draped her lower half in sheets. Matthew rested his face beside hers on the pillow.

"Your baby's caught sideways, Mrs. Henley," he said. "Did Annie tell you?"

"Yes. She tried to turn it."

"I'm going to go inside you, ma'am. To dislodge the shoulder, so you can go on with your birthing."

She grasped his hands between her own, kneading them. "Good," she said, but her teeth were chattering.

"Gran!" he called. Annie drew a blanket up to the laboring woman's shoulders. Her chill passed. She inhaled between his hands.

"They smell like Christmas," she said.

He smiled. "That's the clove oil."

"And pine. Mr. Hart?"

"Ma'am?"

"Are we going to die?"

She had him. She had his hands, his eyes. Damn these women, he thought. These beautiful women. "Not if we three have a say in the matter," he finally offered. It was enough. She released his hands. "Good. To your work, then."

He left their patient in Olana's care while he rolled his sleeves high and scrubbed his arms with the dwindling piece of soap. He saw a boy standing in the tent opening, a steaming kettle of water in his hands. As Annie took it, the child peeked around her skirts.

"Hello, Mama," he whispered.

Mrs. Henley opened her eyes, smiled. "Hello, Pete," she returned his greeting as if he'd interrupted her hanging wash or putting bread in the oven. Matthew Hart pulled on his spectacles and held his arms over the basin.

"Pour," he instructed his grandmother.

"But Matthew—"

"Pour."

She put down the kettle. "Wait. You missed a spot."

"No I didn't."

"There, just under your elbow," Olana said.

Annie took up the brush and scrubbed around his elbows, then started his hands all over again.

"Gran," he chided her gently this time. "Pour."

When she did he gasped a string of blasphemies together so fast they were indecipherable. His skin turned red. The night air felt good as he shook off the excess water.

He approached. Annie and Olana nodded, their eyes calm. He touched the inside of the birthing woman's thigh. "I'm here, Mrs. Henley," he whispered. "Feel my fingers?"

"Yes," she breathed without opening her eyes, "warm."

He took up the tiny blue hand and felt a flicker of life. It sent a rush of hope through him for the tiny child. Olana felt it too. He saw a light in her eyes. He checked around the baby's hand for a chord. There was none. As he tucked the hand back inside the woman, his fingers probed deeper. Mrs. Henley's low, tormented groan ground into his ears.

Her womb was extended by six children before this small one. Matthew knew that would help his chances. He kept going. There. He felt the tiny buttocks. It fit easily in the palm of his hand. He stretched his fingers along the delicate spine and pushed. Mrs. Henley's groan became a long, sustained wail. Her baby was moving to its steady call. Annie and Olana encouraged, telling her to keep the cry open, telling her this torment would be over soon. He was causing it. He was hurting her, as he'd hurt other women over his lifetime. He'd never meant to, as he didn't mean to now. Still, her scream almost paralyzed him. It was his grandmother's hands on his shoulder that kept him sane, and moving. Matthew slipped his hand from the baby's torso down his legs. He hooked his fingers at the heels, and pulled. Small purple feet emerged with his hand. Mrs. Henley's cry sharpened. The feet began to curl, slip back.

"Down," Olana said.

"I can't!" she cried out. "He'll fall!"

"No he won't My Matthew's got him! Push!" Olana demanded.

Matthew heard them both groan together. A baby boy emerged slowly, to past his shoulders. Matthew slid his fingers along the upper arms, gently bringing each down across the chest and out. The baby's head rotated until it faced his mother's back. Matthew held the small body higher. Annie pressed on Mrs. Henley's abdomen with her next contraction. The boy's head slipped out, his wrinkled skin quickly matching the red of Matthew's arm.

Wise, almond eyes with paper-thin lids blinked in the room's dim light. The little mouth opened, gasped for air. Matthew held the legs higher. The baby gasped again. Kicked.

"A bold new son you have," Annie proclaimed as she and Olana helped Mrs. Henley to turn and lie back on the mattress. The mother's hands shook as she reached out for her child.

As he sat back and waited for the placenta to be born, Matthew realized that Annie's voice was not conciliatory, the way it generally was when she had little hope for an early child. She barked instructions to keep the little boy close against his mother's warmth, to be gentle with the delicate, easily bruised skin.

"So small," Mrs. Henley said.

Her son found, latched onto her nipple. He sucked vigorously. "You'll remedy that together," Matthew promised as the placenta came. He tied and cut the chord. When Annie Smithers examined the woman's perineum, her voice changed.

"Look," she whispered. "There's no tear."

"No? That's good. This poor lady's been through enough without—"

"Not even a small one."

His grandmother's eyes were as bright as he'd ever seen them. "It's her seventh child, Gran," he argued.

"Matthew, look. Look at how deep you were inside her."

He glanced up his right arm and saw blood and vernix smeared halfway to his elbow. He was glad they'd both scrubbed it, was glad for the hot water. When he looked at Annie Smithers again she was weeping.

"Hey Gran, what's the matter?"

"Nothing. You did well, Matthew. You did real well."

He took her in his arms. "Am I a journeyman at last?" he whispered into her fine silver hair.

Matthew stared hard at Sister Justina, trying not to think of his many obligations toward her and the sisters, the latest of which was blessed relief for his sleeping grandmother as they fanned out to offer assistance to the birthing families here in the park. Firm. He must remain firm, obeying the instinctual terror that her request provoked.

"No."

"Take our wagon," Mrs. Amadeo pleaded. "God will smile. Perhaps he will keep my husband safe. From the fire. Ah, Matthew, do this thing for the sisters. The babies will wait for your return."

"No," he said again.

"Now, Matthew," Sister Justina tried. "You know how close the Mission chapel is. It will only take an hour."

"Where are the priests?"

"Called away to administer Extreme Unction to the dying. The relics in the chapel are holy to us. As are the sacred hosts, the chalices, the patens, the ciborium. Gold, Matthew. So much gold, that is all thieves will see. We cannot trust anyone else to help us remove them."

Matthew thought of Possum's shining eyes during processions honoring the Blessed Sacrament that wound through their neighborhood. These women had welcomed his daughter into the parish, though she was of Yuork blood, and he a non-believer. And, much to her own embarrassment, this irritating woman had pushed and prodded him into finding Olana again. Still, the prospect of leaving the mothers and the babies gave him a clawing pain in his stomach, from the terror. He watched the two women in early labor reading to their children, their faces calm and serene between contractions. He walked to them.

"My grandmother is the best midwife in California. Wake her when you need her."

They nodded, smiling.

He reached Olana in three strides, the nuns still at his heels. "Want to take a ride, darlin'?" he asked.

Her cheeks flushed pink at his familiarity in front of the sisters. "Sure," she said.

When the wagon was ready, Possum buttoned up her father's shirt collar. "There's a storm coming, Daddy," she said.

Matthew looked into the soot filled sky. "I wish there were, little one," he said.

She pressed her lips to his unshaven cheek. "Not a rainstorm," she whispered close to his ear, "a storm of fire."

forty-nine

The red wall of flame rose high over the Mission District. Two days. The fire had been raging two days, started by broken gas pipes, by cooks frying ham and eggs on stoves connected to damaged chimneys, fed by the shifting winds, the close together frame buildings, the dynamiters and arsonists. Would it ever end? Olana slipped her hand in the crook of his arm. Matthew urged the horses on. He should have left her in the shade of the willow tree with his sleeping grandmother. He should have broken his promise not to leave her, rather than have her here.

On his other side, Sister Justina smiled at young Sister Ursula. "We're almost there, Matthew. Don't grind your teeth."

The ancient bell in the mission's tower began ringing with mad urgency. Sister Justina pursed her lips. "We're coming, Gertrude," she said. "Sometimes Gertrude takes her devotion to the Sacred Heart a bit too seriously," she confided.

Matthew lifted Olana down from the wagon. "It will be cooler inside," he promised. "And I'll find you water."

She touched his face. "I'm well, darling. Just don't leave me."

They followed the two sisters' heels down the cobblestone path to the sacristy. Sister Justina's annoyance echoed. "If they'd brought the sacred items through the courtyard for us to load instead of ringing that bell . . . oh, Jesus."

Matthew's head shot up at what sounded like a blasphemy from the nun's lips. Sister Justina stood inside, Sister Ursula in the sacristy's doorway. "Oh Jesus, Mary, and Joseph," Sister Justina finished her incantation.

Matthew recognized the scent that assaulted his nostrils. Blood. Not the blood of life that had sustained him through his toil over the hours of birthings. The blood of carnage. He took the young sister's arm and pulled her out of the doorway. Her eyes were glazed in shock, but he had to trust Olana to her care. He shook her.

"Sister! Would you take my wife to the courtyard for some air?"

She blinked. "Yes, yes of course." She reached for Olana's hand. Olana stepped forward. "Matthew, what is it?"

"I'll be right out. Go, darlin'."

"No. Matthew, please!"

He shut the door on her frightened face, but could not shake its image, even as he walked silently among the four downed nuns. He knelt beside each, felt for a pulse, shook his head. He watched Sister Justina drape each raped and cut-open body with a bloodsoaked veil or cast-off skirt. The old nun began a litany as they worked. She invoked saints, virgins, martyrs, confessors in a dizzying array that finally dropped him to his knees and clouded his eyes with tears. She halted, then pressed his head close against the crucifix at her heart. It cut into the wounds in his scalp.

He yanked the words through his constricted throat. "I'll do the births with you women. Not this. I don't have the strength for this."

"It's all right, son," Justina whispered. "Rest."

The bell above them pealed once more, feebly. "Gertrude," Sister Justina cried. "Matthew, Gertrude."

Matthew yanked in a steadying breath as he stood. He wiped his eyes with the backs of his hands as he ran to the bell tower.

Sister Gertrude swayed against the rope in her hands. When she saw them, her pale face broke into a smile. She pulled a gold chalice from the torn bodice of her habit and offered it to Matthew.

"Father?"

"Take it," Sister Justina whispered at his ear.

"No," he whispered, remembering his dreams.

"Take it."

He did, handed it to her, and caught the falling woman. Her skin was cold and clammy, her breathing shallow. But if he could find the bleeding. Stop it. Get help. He stumbled down the stairs, ran through the labyrinth of halls. Finally, outside to the street.

He searched for the Amadeo cart. Was it gone, or on the other side, at another entrance? He turned the corner. There was an ambulance wagon waiting there. He placed his burden in Sister Justina's arms. "Find the bleeding, press hard. Stop it," he instructed. "I'll get help."

"Matthew," she said gently. "She's dead."

"No." He backed away from them, and ran to the wagon.

"We're filled up, padre." The voice, thin, wheezing, familiar. From the driver's seat. "No room."

"Make room! She's the only one left!"

Matthew ran to the back of the wagon, threw open the doors. He could feel his own heartbeat as he stared at the chests, paintings, ornate chairs, jewelry. At the top of the pile were bloodied church fixtures, gold-encased relics, chalices.

"Oh God," he whispered, turning. Cal Carson blocked the dim sun. pointing a pistol between Matthew's eyes. "One step and I'll have Ezra break your woman's neck, Ranger."

Matthew stood, his fingers aching, watching his enemy. For damage. The sisters did not go to their deaths gently. One had torn at Cal's eyes. Tracks of bloody tears were crusting on his hollow, jaundiced cheeks.

Ezra Carson dragged Olana and Sister Ursula out from the shade of the wall. The nun was limp, her eyes closed. "Cal, I didn't break her, honest," Ezra said. "She just went all jelly jointed." Blood spurted from Olana's nose. "And his woman bites," Ezra complained, rubbing his inflamed ear against her hair.

"Hold them steady!" Cal barked, before he smiled slowly at Matthew. "Which shall we trade for you, Hart?" he asked.

"Both."

"Both? Do you hear him, brother? Thinks he's worth both. Maybe, at one time. When we had our sheep, or our mining equipment, or our toes. Before you crippled me with that hole in my side. Before we lost McPeal. Before Mr. Hopkins put us in a madhouse, all for stealing your woman's nightgown."

"Hopkins?"

"Also known as Moore, back when he was flinging young China girls out windows, and marrying troublesome heiresses. Yes. You were worth thousands to your woman's lovelorn husband then! Not now. But we've hit some of our own pay dirt at last! Why, we're so rich we'll kill you and your two ladies for the sheer pleasure of it."

When Olana kicked Ezra he dropped the nun. Matthew twisted

the wrist of the big man's distracted brother. Cal Carson fired two shots, one through the toeless part of his own shoe, another grazing Matthew's leg and embedding itself in the wagon's wheel. Finally the pistol hit the ground. Matthew kicked it in Sister Justina's direction.

Olana's scream changed into one of warning. He turned to detect the flash of something gleaming. Too late. It entered his side. The shovel was next, catching him square on the side of his face. Don't fall, the child inside him pleaded. Or was it Leland, looking for help for his sister? Matthew heard more erupting gunfire, before even that was extinguished in a cold darkness.

Cal Carson yanked at Olana's hair. Hard, though he was still having trouble controlling the frightened horses.

"That's not how I wanted it!" he raved. "I wanted it slow! I wanted him to watch us fuck you inside out first! That was too good, too easy, do you understand me?"

"Yes," she said, numbly understanding completely. Hadn't she been married to a man like this one? Empty streets glided by. She saw only Matthew. Still, so still, with the long knife rising up from his side.

"He saw what we did to the nuns," Ezra offered to his brother in consolation. "Must have caused him no end of misery."

"True. And no wonder I'm hungry. Let's celebrate, brother mine."

"But Cal, the fire—"

"We'll stay ahead of the firemen!" Cal Carson reached across Olana to shove his brother's massive shoulder. "I'll even let you have her first," he promised.

Matthew was thirsty. Thirsty like women get after childbirth, when they've given up so much fluid. He heard voices, saw hovering shapes. Giant loons, their wings black, white. A coat was folded under his head. He tried to speak, but his mouth wouldn't work. Then the little loon, the one who'd been so pale, Ursula, drizzled something along his lips.

"Holy water," she whispered.

His locked jaw loosened, opened. He drank. The hazy sisters cleared, and then swiftly, unmercifully, so did his mind.

"Olana?"

Justina leaned over him. "They took her."

"Alive?"

"Yes."

He sat up.

"Matthew, don't."

He tried to smile at their concern, but his face was stiff and unyielding. He lifted the red cloth from his side and found clean entrance and exit wounds. He raised his head. "Who pulled the knife out?"

The pale sister's quick blush gave her away.

"Good work," he said, stuffing the cloth harder against the wounds and buttoning his vest over it. He felt hands at his back, pulling the drawstrings hard.

"Go with God, Matthew Hart," Sister Justina said, releasing him.

The second-floor flat had been rocked soundly by the earthquake. Every framed picture lay smashed on the planked floor. An upright piano was overturned, sheet music scattered at Olana's feet. Only the figurines—a petite lady in a huge skirt and powdered wig, and her matching dancing partner in brocade coat and knee breeches were intact, still delicate, in blue and white porcelain. They perched in the glassless bay window. Perhaps the most vulnerable objects of the flat, in the most vulnerable spot, they had survived. Was this the final miracle in these days of miracles and nightmares?

Olana heard the Carson brothers guzzling food in the pantry. At first they had made her join them, pouring wine down her throat until she'd vomited, disgusting them. They'd hit her, making her nose bleed again, but not enough to send her into the merciful oblivion of unconsciousness. Tired, Cal tied her ankle to the sofa with a silk maniple from the chapel. Then they'd gone to the pantry revels.

When they came back, before they started hurting her again, would they unfasten her? Would she have the courage to go through the bay window so no one would have to find her the way Matthew found the nuns? Would she remember to be careful of the small, perfect, dancing partners as she jumped?

She closed her eyes and saw Matthew's fine, gentle hands. She leaned her aching head back, and thought she could feel him close, closer. Or was it their child who she felt hammering at her to stay alert, to survive?

She opened her eyes. There, on the sheet music to "The Blue Danube," a jagged piece of glass glinted. Olana slipped noiselessly from the sofa, watching, always watching the pantry doorway. Her hand reached the glass. She worked at the binding that held her ankle to the sofa leg, cutting until only threads remained. Then she allowed herself a small smile of triumph, for herself and her child. She put the glass into her pocket, beside her marriage papers. She had already dropped her brother's gift like a bread crumb in Hansel and Gretle as they hauled her up the stairs.

What had Matthew told her, long ago? The head or the heart. She would kill them if she could. If she could not, she would inflict as much damage as she could before they killed her.

The overladen ambulance wagon's ruts cut a deep path in the layers of cinders the encroaching fire had blown onto the streets. When Matthew's lame side and burning leg kept him from running, he settled for an addling gait. The deep ruts turned into an alleyway. Yes. The wagon was there.

He began working on instinct then, walking slowly, scanning the three-story frame houses. When he stopped, rested in a patch of shade, he saw Leland's miniature of Olana in a side entranceway. He raised his head and saw a glint of auburn hair through the house's second-story windows. He surveyed the roofs, cornices, and finials for a pathway up to her.

Was the fire approaching? Was that the strange chattering sound, like the demented cries of numberless monkeys coming down Sixteenth Street? Or was it Olana herself going mad, now that she'd lost him, lost everything in this city drowning in flames? No. There was the child. She had to keep her wits about her, as he would have, for their child.

A hand reached over the ledge. Olana knew the hand. The last threads holding her ankle broke and she helped her husband inside.

" 'Lana, you are . . .?"

"Yes. But oh, Matthew," she lifted her hand from his freshly bleeding side, "you're not."

"Gran will fix it, a few stitches."

He lifted the rope of tied-together bed linens from his back and fastened one end to the window frame. Olana threw out the length and it glided down the front of the house. Below, she saw the mattresses piled to ease their escape further. She placed the porcelain dancing couple in her pocket. "Ready," she whispered. Matthew kissed into her palm.

Cal Carson bounded from the pantry's swinging door, a loaf of bread in one hand, a dull green bottle in the other. "No!" he shouted pitching the bottle. It smashed into the window frame.

Ezra came through the door, complaining. "Hey, Cal, I thought you said I could have at her first—"

His brother smiled. "Apparently there's yet unfinished business with our persistent ranger before we take our pleasure."

Matthew kept Olana behind him as he turned to face the brothers. "Stay," he whispered, releasing her hand. He swayed, then staggered around the sofa.

Ezra laughed, signaling his brother closer. "What's the matter, Hart?" he asked. "Tough climb? You're not looking well, not at all well. Tell me. Are there two of us? Or four?"

Matthew passed his hand in front of his eyes, then fell to his knees. Olana screamed his name, but his whispered "stay" kept her rooted.

"Get her," Cal Carson instructed his brother, who grinned wide. "He can watch." As Olana groped for the splintered glass, Matthew sprang. The dense bulk of Ezra Carson went catapulting over her husband's shoulder and through the window frame, splintering the sash. They heard a dull thud on the street below, over the louder roaring sound.

Olana felt her wrist caught in a vise hold. Cal Carson yanked her over the sofa and flung her to the floor. "Filthy bitch!" he screamed. She tried to crawl, but had not gotten to her knees before he turned, then pinned her beneath his full weight. He took her neck between his hands and pounded her head against the scattered sheet music, the floor. Olana gripped the jagged glass and sliced a path from his eye down his neck. His hands finally released. Then his weight lifted off her. Matthew swung him into the wall, then out the window. The insane chattering had so intensified they didn't hear him hit the street.

Matthew eased the glass from her bleeding fingers, helped her to her feet. They stumbled to the windows together and looked down. The Carson brothers had landed on a mattress. Matthew and Olana watched, astonished, as the two men rolled to their feet. They laughed, dusting themselves off like circus entertainers.

"Jesus Christ, I can't kill them," Matthew said, defeated.

Then, the hot wind joined the approaching sound. Olana felt Matthew's grip on her tighten as they both struggled to inhale the blasting air through the terror of their own fear. A vent a few hundred yards down the street blew out a tongue of flame. The flame took on a life of its own. It advanced ahead of the roar of the main fire that was still blocks away. The darting blaze had its own sound, a popping and crackling. Like Chinatown on festival days, Olana thought. The Carsons saw it too, because they stopped laughing. They stood stock still, staring.

The crackling got louder, madder, even when Olana pressed the heels of her hands against her ears. Below them, the tongue of flame currented through the Carson brothers, transforming them into dancing balls of fire. Olana heard herself make a small, astonished sound. She felt Matthew tuck her head against his shirt. She closed her eyes. But he continued to look, Olana could tell somehow, from his rapidly beating heart. He needed to know that if he couldn't kill the men who'd plagued them for so many years, something could. There was no triumph, only exhausted finality left in his voice when he bent down and kissed her forehead.

"It's over," he said.

Olana raised her head, released her ears. The chattering was in the distance now. The flame bounded down another street. She looked at the still, smoldering black heaps lying side by side.

"Matthew," he breathed. "What was that?"

"I don't know, love. But we'd best go now. Go and find ourselves some green."

fifty

"Matthew, stay still!"

"Leave it alone! Where are my pants?"

"Sidney, pour," Annie Smithers instructed.

"Delighted."

Matthew knocked the bottle from Sidney Lunt's hand. "You're choking me, goddamn it!" he roared, cuffing his friend and sending a spray of champagne into his grandmother's face. She threw down her cloth.

"That's all," she announced.

Outside the tent, Olana sat between her parents. Her mother rubbed her back gently, her father held her undamaged hand. She felt a twinge of fear when Annie Smithers drew back the tent flap, stood with her hands fisted at her hips, and yelled her name. Olana leapt to her feet.

"Get in here," Annie demanded.

"What's happened?" she pleaded, the small scream in her voice.

The old woman's eyes softened. "Nothing's happened. I need you, is all."

When he saw her, Matthew bolted up as far as Sidney's hold across his shoulders would let him.

"Damnation! I told you not to let her in until you'd finished."

His grandmother raised one finger skyward. The gesture had hushed him since he was a boy. "And I decided not to honor your request," she proclaimed.

Matthew looked in Olana's frightened eyes and felt an avalanche of remorse. "Hello, darlin'," he said softly. "Come sit beside me?"

As his grandmother pierced his skin with her fired needle, his grip on Olana's hand tightened, and his teeth ground audibly.

"Breathe, Matthew," Annie Smithers instructed, without looking up from her work.

"Yes'm." He turned half his face into Olana's skirts. She cleared the damp hair back from his brow. "Sidney, read," she commanded.

"Read?"

"From your account of the saving of Russian Hill," she said.

"But it's still in first draft—"

"Read it!"

"Oh, oh, of course." He fumbled with the handwritten pages. "Listen, Matt. Between this and Alisdair's photographs, we're bound to be the definitive disaster edition! 'It was a victory fought for home ground,' " he began. " 'It was a brave, roistering fight fought by an Irish prizefighter and an Italian peasant, a Russian coat finisher and an American lumber baron. Its weapons were rugs, blankets, an artist's canvas, and a cellar full of the finest French champagne . . .' "

Matthew turned his face out again. "It worked?" he whispered.

"The whole block was saved," Olana told him.

"The whole block."

"Then we wasted the last drops of that champagne on you in one of your surly moods," Sidney added.

"Everyone's safe?"

"Yes, we're all together now," Olana assured him.

"If I may continue?" Sidney asked them pointedly.

"Sure, go ahead," Matthew granted, putting his wife's hands to his face and breathing in the clove oil scent.

Sidney Lunt finished his account of the rescue of Russian Hill simultaneously with Annie Smithers' sewing.

"There," she said, wiping her needle. "Fewer stitches than I had to put in Mrs. Millard after her eleven-pound girl, you great baby." But her eyes softened when she looked into her grandson's beaten face. She glanced away. "Clean him up," she instructed his attendants, "then put him to bed."

Matthew lifted his hand to his three-day growth of beard. "Jesus," he marveled at Annie Smithers' command, "I must look awful."

"You do," Olana let out all her remaining fears in a bubble of laughter. "You really do."

"Shave and a haircut?" Callahan popped up at the other side of the bed with all the necessary equipment.

It was early morning. Matthew could tell, there, where he lay on a salvaged iron bed under the great oak. He didn't need to look at Farrell's watch, chained to him now, by Basil's wedding present. He inhaled the same burnt air they'd been breathing for three days. No, the air was somehow different. It was charged with promise. Or perhaps it was delayed birth exhilaration he was feeling. Or the comfort of his family around him, safe.

Olana stirred. Matthew danced his right hand down her strong, beautiful back. She brought his left to her belly, where he felt a tiny ripple. "Hey, Possum," he called, easing his daughter over his bandaged side to feel the baby's movements with him. She yawned.

"He's hungry," she said.

Olana giggled. " 'He' is it?" Matthew asked.

Possum propped her elbows on his chest. "Yes, he. Gran says this one's a boy. But don't worry, you'll have more girls, too."

"Who told you that?" Olana asked.

"Sister Gertrude. In my dream last night. I'll get you and your baby some food, Olana."

They watched Possum's strong limbs carry her toward the small, careful campfires of the morning. Olana sighed. "I hope this child has dreams, too," she said. "It will be hard enough for him to keep up with you two."

Olana nestled under his arm and the sense of well-being washed over Matthew again. He reveled in the luxury of having his bride alone in bed for the first morning since their marriage. It almost didn't matter that they were under an open, soot-infested sky, with half the population of San Francisco awakening around them. He closed his eyes, and began to drift back to sleep. He was vaguely angry at himself for not waking, as there must have been a need—to check Olana's healing fingers, the babies, the mothers, to help his daughter find some food, once he uncovered those pants his grandmother was hiding from him.

The singing was like an echo at first. Solemn and joyful at the same time. In another language. Of another time. Latin. It reminded him of the friars singing at St. Pitias, except higher, and every so often accompanied by a tinkling cymbal, an oriental chime. He opened his eyes. The nuns of the Dolorosa Mission were on a nearby hill, singing matins, their brown robes commingling with the bright silks of the crib girls, the shine of their instruments. It sounded full, beautiful, as if there were not five missing voices, as if Basil and Alisdair were providing counterpoint. Matthew closed his eyes again, the tears escaping. He felt gentle hands at his brow.

"There now," Sister Justina soothed. "Only beauty today." She kissed his forehead. He smiled as the women finished their wondrous song. Then he propped himself on his elbows. Mrs. Amadeo was there, pushing him down again.

"Matthew," she whispered. "I sent you to the mission, gave you the wagon. It was a terrible thing. You are well?"

"Yes, ma'am. Say, Mrs. Amadeo," he tried taking advantage of her remorse, "have you seen my pants?"

"Pants?"

"Pantaloons?" he tried.

Her husband leaned over him. "I promise your grandmother I will not talk business. But you must get well. We have many new customers. Here, in the Golden Gate branch of the Bank of Naples."

"Clients?"

"Depositors! Other banks will be closed, maybe until November, they say. By then, there would be no city, no people here left to serve, I tell them. They don't listen." He shrugged. "So, we open here, now. With our assets, with the hidden-in-the-mattress money of our new depositors. It is a great city, Matthew, and a great country!"

"Yes, sir," he said, feeling tired. "Mr. Amadeo, I'd get up if you'll convince my grandmother to—"

Possum climbed onto the bed with him. "Look, Daddy," she said.

Around the bed, brimming platters appeared—food found, scrounged, cooked. Canned corned beef, beans and rice, steaming puddings, and campfire baked bread. Behind each platter were representatives of a family that now had a new member, or a smiling, sad-eyed cleric of Dolorosa Mission, or a client from the bank.

"My custard first," Mrs. Cole insisted.

"Please," he told his guests quietly. "Join us."

As they descended on the feast, new fathers brought their babies to him. He and his grandmother leaned over each tiny face, remembered and argued over the circumstances of each birth. Olana appeared with his grandmother's book, shaking her head and recording each new name. She was a more welcome sight than his pants.

The plumber beamed as he pronounced his new daughter April Francisco. Olana wrote a string of George, Peter, and Arthur, broken by two Louises, a Margaret, and Gladys, before Golden Gate, Karl, Deliverance, Oliver, Kee, Hubert, Sheila, Raoul, and Julia.

Annie leaned over Olana's work. "Seventeen," she tallied.

Annie grunted. "That's right. Eight each."

Matthew was enjoying the feel of Golden Gate Williams' fingers when the incongruity dawned on him. "Eight? That doesn't add up—"

Olana giggled. "I put the second Louise in parenthesis."

He raised his head. "What?"

His grandmother frowned. "She was already out and lying under a bush before I got to her mama. I only helped with the cord and afterbirth and all, so I won't claim her. Lucky you."

He smiled. "We had us a time, any way you add them up, Gran," he said.

"That we did," she agreed.

When she leaned over to touch his face, he snatched the striped trousers slung over her shoulder.

"Matthew Hart! I ain't finished mending. A bullet doesn't leave a nice tidy slice in the seam, you know!"

In the distance, a trumpet sounded just ahead of Sidney Lunt's breathless run to the bed. "They're out!" he announced. "Van Ness and the Mission District fires—out! The piers—all safe!"

A cheer rose up around them. Someone dragged the upright piano closer. Callahan began playing a waltz in ragtime. The bed emptied. Everyone was dancing. Annie Smithers eyed him pointedly. "Don't you dare," she intoned before setting Olana on guard beside him.

Matthew took his wife's face in his hands and kissed her. Then, with neither lightning nor thunder as a warning, it began to rain.

For a copy of the Eileen Charbonneau Newsletter please send your name and address to:

Eileen Charbonneau Newsletter
P.O. Box 20
Cold Spring, NY 10516-0020

EILEEN CHARBONNEAU has written for *The New York Times* and co-wrote *Endowment for the Planet,* an award-winning educational film narrated by Christopher Reeve. Her highly praised young adult novels are *The Ghosts of Stony Clove, In the Time of the Wolves,* and *Honor to the Hills.*

Eileen Charbonneau lives in the Hudson River Valley of New York State.